Devil's Eye

To Shannon —
With my sincere
regards.

al Ruhsenac

Also by the Author

Algis Ruksenas

Day of Shame

Is That You Laughing, Comrade?

Devil's Eye

A Novel

Al Ruksenas

Meridia Publishers

Printed in the United States of America

First edition 2010

ISBN 978-0-615-40498-1

Cover design by Peter Moffat
www.rooted-design.co.uk

Typesetting by wordzworth.com

Although some actual geographic and historical facts are mentioned, this is a work of fiction. Any similarity to actual persons, living or dead, is purely coincidental.

This book is produced by Meridia Publishers with the collaboration of Dynasty Effect, LLC. Inquiries should be addressed to Meridia Publishers, 29439 Sayle Dr. Willoughby Hills, Ohio 44092.

www.devilseyethebook.com

To my loved ones

Prologue

November, 1958

The lumbering helicopter seemed no larger than a dragonfly against the massive canyon walls as it wended its way towards the ancient monastery jutting out of the desert mountain in the remote wilderness of Egypt near the border of Sudan.

A new moon shone brightly in the clear, autumn sky turning the barren, reddish brown landscape into a cold crystal basrelief. In the distance, outlined starkly by the moonlight were the ramparts and watchtowers of a religious fortress. It blended so perfectly with the mountain from which it was carved that it seemed a natural part of it. The redoubt was totally isolated; inviolate amid the pockmarked, craggy stone formations of the Eastern Sahara.

The pilot looked intently towards the mountain as he edged his craft forward, trying to ignore the staccato sounds of the five-bladed rotor which echoed like cannon fire off the mountain walls. The brown and tan camouflage paint of the helicopter reflected by moonlight the same blueness as the jagged crags near which it maneuvered. No running lights betrayed its presence, but the sounds of the whirling blades seemed to echo from everywhere.

The co-pilot was peering into the darkness through his windshield and occasionally glanced at the pilot with a controlled nervousness that indicated he was not used to this type of night maneuvering between narrow canyon walls. The pilot, just as anxious, was relying solely on the light of the low-hanging moon and the stark outlines of the mountain against the sky to navigate towards the precipice on which perched this mysterious edifice.

Peering towards the fortress from the cargo area through port-holes at their backs were three men in khaki flight suits. They sat along a bench bolted lengthwise to the fuselage and strained their heads over their shoulders to see just how close they were to the menacing cliffs enveloping them. The man in the middle carried a pistol in a shoulder holster.

In one of the few utterances he had made since they left Aswan more than one hundred twenty miles to the northwest, General Anatoli Lysenko of the Soviet secret police—the dreaded NKVD—turned to his companion with the pistol and said loudly over the din of the engines: "Tell me comrade Colonel—are you superstitious?"

"No, sir," replied Nicholai Kuznetsov in a near shout. "But I am concerned that we are flying in an aircraft that is still experimental!" Although Colonel Kuznetsov was a bloodied veteran of SMERSH, the secret police's arm for sabotage and political murder, he had never shaken his innate fear of flying.

General Lysenko looked at him with a woeful smile, sensing that the Colonel had taken his question too casually.

Kuznetsov noticed the look. "No, comrade General. I am not su-perstitious. Why do you ask?"

General Lysenko didn't reply. He turned his head back to the porthole with the same woeful smile. He stared into the darkness of the canyon.

Nicholai Kuznetsov turned to his younger cohort, Major Yuri Rudenko to see if he had understood the General differently. Rudenko did not break his gaze from another porthole. He was staring fixedly at the dark outlines of the stone fortress beyond.

The monastery on the mountain was the only indication that hu-mans had ever wandered into this desolate wasteland, the domain of the scorpion, the viper, and the demons described in ancient writings. It had been built over a period of fifty years in the Twelfth Century to ward off those demons and to harbor a community of holy men who had consecrated their lives to be the living symbols of the forty days and forty nights during which the Redeemer had fasted in the wilderness before He was tempted by the Devil. The monks' own resistance over the centuries, however, was not as successful.

For generations stories had circulated in the bazaars of Cairo and Khartoum and whispered in the shadowy light of oasis campfires that the monastery was cursed. It had been built in defiance of early Church fathers and stood jutting out of the mountain for more than seven hundred years challenging the very laws of nature.

The priestly community which thrived there had over time lost the purpose of its existence. Some said it was the isolation of the Arabian Desert that drove men insane. Others claimed that sinister, supernatural forces had taken hold of the community. The monks had displeased their God by trying to emulate His feats in overcoming demonic temptation. Instead, they had succumbed to it. They took to brigandry, struggle for earthly power, debauchery, and Devil worship. They had become possessed.

From the darkness of that ancient edifice there now appeared a beam of pale, amber light that pierced the night sky. The helicopter tilted forward and flew straight for the beam. Moments later it was bathed in light, revealing the mottled pattern of tan and brown paint on the fuselage that was so faithful to the drab formations of the desert. Revealed in the beam was the silhouette of an Mi 6, a Soviet prototype helicopter that had been flown for the first time just the previous year. Although the craft had been designed for heavy cargo, the two engine cowlings mounted prominently in front of the main rotor shaft gave it the distinct appearance of some prehistoric flying reptile hunched in perpetual attack. Small wings protruding from the fuselage and slung with armament, a nose that resembled a shark and gangly tripod landing gear added to its primeval looks.

The Mi 6 had not been fully tested, but this mission demanded a long-range craft that could maneuver in mountainous terrain. It was the only helicopter in the meager, but growing air arsenal of the

Soviet Union capable of such maneuvering. A Deputy Minister in the Soviet secret police had requisitioned it over the futile and not too energetic protests of several generals in the air force.

The helicopter had been shipped specially to Aswan several weeks earlier from where it now flew. It had ostensibly left on an engineering survey along the Nile River in connection with the Aswan High Dam project being built by the Soviets at the request of Egypt's revolutionary government under Gamal Abdel Nasser. Instead of following the Nile, the helicopter had veered toward this remote mountain somewhere near the ancient ruins of Berenice as soon as night had taken over that late November day.

The giant helicopter was now enveloped in the beam of light and descended slowly toward its origin. As it neared the ground inside the monastery walls, the blades sent a massive swirl of sand raging all around it, as if protesting its landing. When the wheels touched the grit enshrouded courtyard the beam disappeared and only the sound of the rotor, lower pitched and slower as it decelerated, broke the eerie stillness of the night.

A hatch opened behind the cockpit revealing a dull red-lit interior. The three secret policemen filed towards the door led by General Lysenko whose portly figure belied an agile step. As soon as they alighted a group of hooded figures appeared from nowhere and surrounded them. They were dressed in the habits of monks and no one could mistake them for anything, but holy men, except that each carried a Kalashnikov rifle.

One of the hooded guards motioned for Kuznetsov's pistol, but the wary Colonel hesitated. General Lysenko gave him a wordless look that was a command and Kuznetsov slowly pulled the pistol from his shoulder holster and handed it to the robed figure.

The three Russians were then led through the darkness of the courtyard towards a heavy wooden door with wide metal braces. It was the main entrance to the abbey.

General Anatoli Lysenko threw an involuntary glance at a rubble strewn breach in the ramparts near the door. He was aware of the history of this place and had heard that thirty-two of the monks had leaped from the ramparts to their deaths early in the Twentieth Century. Accounts differed as to the exact year or why, but nomads of the region claimed the doomed monks' skeletons lay as they had fallen. No one had ever tried to retrieve them. Fear of the curse had kept the authorities—such that there were—from venturing any-where near the mountain stronghold. Though jaded by his own experience with violent death, General Lysenko nevertheless shud-dered upon spotting the gap in the wall, imagining what lay below it.

When the group approached the bulky door to the abbey, two more hooded guards opened it. Old, musty air emanated from the interior, It had the smell of ages—an unworldly smell that brought a chill to the spine.

The three Russian NKVD men, surrounded by their hooded reti-nue, marched down a cavernous hall flanked by their own shadows made grotesque by the dim light of oily torches. The hall ended at the face of a stone wall that appeared to be a part of the mountain itself. At its base was an uneven archway over a dark, gaping hole. Leading downward was a circular stairway laid from roughly hewn stones that were gouged deeply by a succession of feet that had traversed them for hundreds of years.

Two of the robed men lit torches while another motioned the three Russians toward the stairs.

Major Yuri Rudenko's palms were already clammy from sweat as he began the descent. He nervously rubbed them against his thighs as he ducked his wiry frame to avoid the ceiling of the cramped, narrow stairway. His long apprenticeship as a skillful executioner could not stifle the basic animal fear he sensed since he first caught a glimpse of this monastery in the moonlight

Even Colonel Kuznetsov, who stepped cautiously behind him, be-trayed a sense of apprehension. His mouth was so dry he felt he could not swallow and he kept glancing at his empty shoulder holster.

Kuznetsov was clearly uneasy whenever his special 9mm Makarov was not within easy reach. Kuznetsov's pistol was an extension of himself and he felt totally vulnerable without it.

Only General Lysenko, though awestruck by this netherworld, seemed outwardly assured. Lysenko, who was typically gray and somber and rarely displayed any kind of emotion, was a ranking member of SMERSH and a formidable presence in the principal administrative arm of the Soviet secret police, the NKVD. He alone knew the nature of their mission.

They filed silently down the gouged, circular stone steps eighty-five feet downward until they reached a cave-like antechamber with torches embedded in the walls. Illuminated by their flickering lights were old tapestries hung around the stone peripheries of this subterranean room. A shaft of light at the far end of the antechamber indicated the presence of yet another chamber beyond.

The colors of the tapestries were faded and the fabric was dusty and brittle, but the scenes were grotesquely vivid. A goat figure with dragon wings sat on a throne in one scene, surrounded by naked supplicants dancing in a circle. Another tapestry depicted a witch astride a wolf-like animal on her way to a sabbat. Next to it was a tattered representation of several men opening a sepulcher to steal a corpse for a midnight ceremony. On the opposite wall, with hands tied above his head there dangled a man being tortured by inquisitors. The light of the torches flickering on these tapestries, that moved slightly in air drafts generated from dark reaches beyond, gave the illusion that the man was actually dangling in front of the observer.

Each scene on a tapestry was an accurate reproduction of some illustration from an old book or manuscript about witchcraft and demonology. Each was a faithful rendition of medieval engravings and included works of some well-known masters.

No one spoke as the guards made a semi-circle around the three foreigners and waited. The Russian intruders' eyes darted furtively from scene to scene on the tapestries and then to each other for reassurance.

Momentarily, the shaft of light from the chamber beyond was disturbed by shadowy movement and there emerged from it two men in black hooded robes. One was young and gaunt with an angular face and goatee. The other was old with piercing, cat-like eyes and a long, narrow beard that trailed from his scowling face.

The Old One stared long and intently at the three secret policemen, studying each as if trying to read his mind. Then he spoke in a low and commanding tone:

"Tell me, comrades. Are you superstitious?"

Colonel Kuznetsov looked strangely at General Lysenko who had asked the same question in the helicopter. Now, it did not sound so innocent.

Major Rudenko stared warily at the old man whose face glared at him from the folds of the dark hood covering his head.

The Old One kept studying each of them intently—gazing as if in a trance—looking for a reaction.

"We have been sent here at the orders of Deputy Minister Vladimir Dekanazov of the Committee for State Security," General Lysenko declared bravely, trying to convince himself of his authority among these strange men who obviously displayed no fear of the dreaded NKVD. "We are to receive instructions from…"

"I am to give you instructions!" the Old One intoned. "Only in terms that are most vague. This is for the best, is it not? It is for your own safety and good," he declared with sarcasm. "Your Comrade Dekanazov, the one who sent you, wouldn't want to scare the *Devil* out of you, would he?" The Old One was so pleased with his remark that he broke into a loud and cacophonous laugh.

Just as suddenly he fell silent and stared at each of them again.

"Listen to me carefully! Very carefully! A most significant event has occurred. It has occurred in the United States of America. This event will change the course of history!"

He glared at the arrivals with slanted eyes ablaze, raised his hands triumphantly and shouted: "No! It will change the course of Destiny!"

"We had long hoped for this occurrence," the Old One now said calmly. "As had some very wise men in your own government. It is heartening to know my dear godless friends that you have colleagues in power who have not forgotten the lessons left them by one of our greatest students and devotees—a man whose singular influence had so decisive a role in the course of your own Revolution. Grigori Rasputin!"

The three secret policemen looked dumbfounded.

"Oh, yes. Yes, indeed," the Old One assured with relish. "Rasputin! The Mad Monk! Or so the uninitiated claim. Where might you suppose he gained his earthly powers? Eating your Russian bread offered by faithful peasants? Drinking your vodka with the czar? No, gentlemen. Rasputin has in his own time traversed these very grounds! He came away from here with a vision of a new world! The fruits of his labor still flourish in your country this very day!"

General Lysenko felt a bead of sweat course from the back of his neck down his spine. This information, he sensed, was not casually revealed unless it was meant to go no further. Anatoli Lysenko for the first time since they left Aswan became genuinely fearful for his own safety.

"The 'Mad Monk'—Rasputin—had a number of disciples," the Old One continued. "In fact some of your own kind, the czar's secret police— your predecessors—those who finally killed him—with the greatest difficulty as you know—became his strongest converts. They saw his super human powers! Your own Commissar Dekanazov is one of them. That is why he knows of this place. That is why he sent you."

The young goateed figure in the black hood stood motionless next to the Old One and stared fixedly at the three Russians while the master continued.

"Unimagined travail will be visited upon your greatest enemy— America! Her supremacy will wither in the face of her own self-doubt! Her nation will lose its perceived innocence and be the subject of derision! She will have great martyrs among her; after which will follow great confusion and uncertainty. Her leaders will hesitate. They will shrink and they will speak abominations. Those who appear strong will lead astray. They will be accused of weakness of the flesh. War will be called Peace and Peace will be called War. America will see the pronouncements of her highest ideals fall prey and be suspect of a disbelieving world. Evil will flourish in her shadow!"

The Old One fell silent, waiting to see if the full impact of his words were understood. His eyes flared and he continued.

"Your enemy will be called a war-monger and destroyer! Her good deeds will be perceived as wicked! Your own leaders in Moscow will, of course, be instrumental in propagating this among the peoples of the world."

He lowered his voice and said slowly and emphatically: "Then will come a most epochal event. Your own empire will fracture and your State will disappear!" The Old One let the words sink in. "But you need not despair, for this will divert your enemy for a time; a prelude to your own victory. When all this comes to pass—then will come the historical hour!"

Pointing his finger in majestic arrogance at the three, he lowered his voice again and said with assurance. "When all this comes to pass, then will occur the historical hour! Then will come the moment when you seize events and fulfill the most ambitious dream of which you ever dreamed—a red banner flying the length and breadth of this earth!"

The three Soviets stood frozen in beguilement and fear.

"Your enemy's achievements in science and the art of destruction will become the very means by which she will succumb to your power."

The Old One let his visitors savor his words.

"But hear me!" he declared. "You will have this only for a time. For the ultimate glory will be ours." He said this with longing and with unshakeable certainty. "Your own victory will be a prelude. It will serve to hasten the day when the entire world pays rightful

9

homage to our Prince—the Prince of the Netherworld!"

His cat eyes widened and his voice rose to a crescendo as he announced: "All this will come to pass because the people of America have at last—they have at long last been gifted with the visage of the Devil's Eye!"

The three Russians stood transfixed. To speak now was to risk mortal danger because the Old One's rolling eyes radiated: madness.

"You are to do but one thing," the Old One commanded. "You will infiltrate my young supplicant into the United States of America. You are practiced at these things. Even as we speak I know from your Commissar Dekanazov that you have well-positioned agents in the American system. You will use your established espionage networks and resources to get him there." The Old One looked at the secret policemen menacingly. "You are to assure that he remains undetected. You are to see that no harm comes to his person while he undertakes his great work.

"Another 'Rasputin'," thought Nikolai Kuznetsov apprehensively.

"Do you understand what I am saying?" the Old One asked with a hypnotic stare.

"We understand," General Lysenko replied immediately, fearful of causing the slightest aggravation in the wizardly figure before them.

"All the rest will be done by us," the Old One declared. "Your Commissar Dekanazov in Moscow has agreed to our little arrangement," he said with mocking emphasis on "little."

With a wave of his hand the Old One abruptly dismissed the entourage and started back to the connecting chamber from which he came. The three Soviets glanced furtively at each other and watched the young goateed figure slowly approach them. The hooded escort turned and started walking back to the stairway leading to the upper reaches of the abbey. The three secret policemen eagerly followed.

Just then three of the hooded men grabbed Major Yuri Rudenko from behind, pinning his hands and dragging him back toward the chamber where the Old One had disappeared.

"What is this? What are you doing? No! No!" Rudenko blurted with a quivering voice that suddenly released his pent up fear.

"Lysenko! Lysenko!" he pleaded. Major Rudenko dug his heels into the cavern floor, trying vainly to keep the hooded men from dragging him away. He squirmed futilely in the grip of his captors.

"Keep walking!" the goateed man commanded General Lysenko and Colonel Kuznetsov. "Do not look back!"

The two Russians fearfully obeyed.

They reached the stone stairs and scrambled upward, held back only by the unhurried pace of two of the guards ahead of them. Major Rudenko disappeared with his abductors into the chamber beyond. Moments later Lysenko and Kuznetsov heard an inhuman wail, high-pitched and reverberating with terror. It filled the cavern and chilled Lysenko and Kuznetsov to the bone. A low, incessant, hollow chant started by a number of voices was barely audible against the major's unworldly scream of fear and protest against impending death.

Suddenly Yuri Rudenko's voice broke into a muffled gargle. Then silence.

The chant became louder now, more incessant. More voices were joining in and the chamber beyond hummed with a repetitious ceremonial cadence: "*Elohim, Elohim, Eloah Va-Daath. Elohim, El Adonai, el Trabaoth, Shaddai. Tetragrammaton, Iod. El Elohim, Shaddai. Elohim, Elohim…*"

General Lysenko's thirty years of revolutionary struggles and even more deadly internecine intrigue which had molded him into a calloused, cold-blooded man could not quell the depth of terror coursing through his body, causing it to shake visibly. He missed a step as he clambered up the cramped stairwell, desperate to reach the outside.

Behind him the goateed man climbed solemnly with a wicked smile on his face.

Colonel Kuznetsov kept pace with Lysenko. The young major's scream was still resounding in him, sending shivers up and down his body. Kuznetsov tried to blot it from his mind and steel himself with a raging determination to get out of this cursed abbey alive. Colonel Kuznetsov, true to Soviet dictates, had never been a believer, but he could not shake the overpowering realization that if there was no God, there ought to be one now.

He climbed as fast as the retinue in front of him allowed, planting his feet hard on each stone, resolutely pushing away some unknown, but very real threat.

Some harrowing minutes later they emerged in the courtyard. Someone had already ordered the pilot to start the engines of the helicopter and the swirling blades were again shrouding the craft in blinding dust.

When Colonel Kuznetsov reached the hatch of the tadpole-belly of the helicopter, one of the hooded guardsmen thrust his pistol back into his shoulder holster and pointed him physically to the ladder. He scrambled up with lowered head against the sandy fury. General Lysenko was ahead of him, already disappearing through the hatch with the urgent tugging of the co-pilot. Next came the goateed man who wordlessly climbed aboard, entered the cargo area, and sat down on the bench opposite the two Russians.

The co-pilot was leaning out of the cockpit with one hand grasping the bulkhead, trying to see Major Rudenko emerge from the raging dust at the foot of the ladder.

"Close the hatch!" General Lysenko shouted.

The co-pilot turned with a puzzled look to the General, then eyed the new arrival with the goatee and hooded cassock.

"Close the hatch!" Lysenko commanded. "Get the devil out of here!"

General Lysenko sensed that as long as the goateed man was in the air with them, no sudden calamity could befall them. When they landed in Aswan, he assured himself, he would wash his hands of this strange sorcerer and let the Illegals Section do whatever they wanted with him.

The secret police general was visibly agitated.

"Come now, my General," the goateed man soothed with palatable cynicism, "you know that a pact like ours requires a seal of blood—a small token to assure our success."

Lysenko said nothing. He had to presume the sacrifice of Major Rudenko was approved by Commissar Dekanazov in the Kremlin. He looked at Colonel Kuznetsov, wondering how much more his subordinate may have been told. Colonel Kuznetsov's return challenging stare—so unusual in a subordinate and typically self-destructive during the Stalinist era—convinced him he was just as stunned.

Colonel Anatoli Kuznetsov's raging eyes were, in fact, demanding to know whether it could have been him, instead of Major Rudenko, who was sacrificed.

"It's no loss," General Lysenko felt compelled to murmur. "Rudenko was suborned by the American CIA," he lied.

The goateed man leaned back against the fuselage and listened to the rhythm of the toiling engines. He was pleased to see how handily his Teacher had sown fear and discord between the remaining secret policemen. The unholy monk knew his own task held great promise. His wicked smirk remained fixed in that satisfaction, obscured from view by his shadowy hood.

Urgently, the helicopter labored out of the dark recesses of the narrow canyon and headed westward toward the Nile in the moonbathed landscape of the open desert.

The Near Future

Chapter 1

Colonel Christopher Caine was leaning on the fender of a black limousine parked in the north oval of The White House. He gazed around the expansive grounds, drawing in the sweet smell of April and trying to locate an elusive mockingbird whose call was coming somewhere from the new growth of holly bushes lining the drive.

He spotted the bird darting in and out of the bushes toward the north portico. The charcoal bird swooped effortlessly around the cylindrical light that hung prominently above the entrance, then disappeared into another thicket of bushes along the white façade of the Executive Mansion.

A uniformed Secret Service officer standing at the entrance noticed it too and followed the flight of the bird with a leisurely gaze that indicated a momentary respite from the sameness of standing guard at the entrance to the President's residence. Colonel Caine's eyes met those of the officer. They nodded slightly, recognizing each other's presence.

Caine's ruggedly handsome features broke into a brief private smile. He was thinking of this peaceful interlude in an almost pastoral setting which surrounded the nerve center of the nation and to a great extent a large portion of the known world. Colonel Caine stood unchallenged in the driveway, but he knew that the Secret Service officer would confront him if he came onto the portico—his military uniform notwithstanding. Funny, he mused, just two generations earlier his great-great grandfather, a Cavalry officer in Robert E. Lee's headquarters command, was riding northward to win this place for the Confederacy.

Now, Colonel Caine stood here, an officer in the U.S. Army, a guardian of his nation and up to a point—the distance between himself and the Secret Service officer—a guest of the President of the United States. If the guard would even have an inkling that Colonel Caine was an officer in the ultra-secret Omega Group, there would be grounds for an investigation into a breach of national security. As it was, the Secret Service officer probably thought the Colonel was an overqualified driver for a pampered Pentagon general.

Caine's commanding officer, General William Bradley, had summoned him abruptly that morning to drive him to an emergency meeting at the White House. The General valued Caine immensely. His chief subordinate officer was a practiced expert at military strategy and tactics and a secretly decorated soldier of the new age of warfare.

He planned and led raids into the jungles of Columbia and Thailand to eliminate ranking chiefs of worldwide drug networks, incursions into Mexico to stem drug cartels brazenly battling the government, and coordinated secret missions into the lawless north of Pakistan to disrupt the resurgence of terrorist religious sects. Most recently Colonel Caine had coordinated clandestine operations in Africa. The dual purpose was to neutralize bands of renegade soldiers who were creating havoc in several countries which were trying to establish democracies for the first time in their histories, and to stop genocidal actions of certain African governments themselves.

Whenever United Nations peacekeepers were persuaded to enter world hotspots, their reluctance was eased when diplomatic leaks assured the likelihood that some clandestine commando organization had already been there to pave the way. No one knew its name, presuming "Delta Force" to be the highest level of specialized operations in the U.S. government.

But nothing worried western nations more than the persistent attempt by the old guard in the former Soviet Union to privatize nuclear weapons and use their possession as a coercive means to regain power. They were trying through familiar terrorist groups that had gained ascendancy after the U.S. was attacked by powerful religious blasphemers on September 11, 2001. The Omega Group was given extraordinary leeway to prevent that.

Colonel Caine had been waiting almost an hour, scrolling idly through the latest news on his smartphone when his eyes caught the outline of a military figure inside the glass door of the portico. The figure was blurred by reflections of outside images on the glass doors, including the darting mockingbird retracing its frenetic path along the Executive Mansion.

Caine scrolled quickly through an item, knowing his General would be out in a minute: "Rural Sheriff Investigates Animal Mutilations." The story had a familiar theme. Local residents in downstate Ohio had reported to authorities that someone was raising a ruckus on remote farmland in the middle of the night. Investigators had found little evidence of anything, except charred animal bone fragments and the remnants of what appeared to be a crude upside down cross. People suspected devil worship. The sheriff would not venture to speculate. "These kinds of things are blown out of proportion," the sheriff was quoted. "Just like flying saucers."

By now, General Bradley was coming toward the limousine. He was tall, barrel-chested and walked with a limp—a reminder of the second Iraqi war. Following General Bradley was the Secretary of Defense, Ronald Stack. They were accompanied by the Secretary of State, the National Security Adviser, the Chairman of the Joint Chiefs of Staff, and the Directors of the FBI and CIA.

All wore grim looks on their faces as they hurried to their limousines parked herd-like on the curved White House drive.

Colonel Caine had not remembered such a concentrated meeting of principals in the Omega Group since the time Middle East agents had been implicated in an attempt to sabotage Air Force One a year earlier during the President's summit trip to Europe. This was in apparent retaliation for the U.S. bombing of a terrorist headquarters in Sudan with the help of mercenary Arab adventurers. The plot was secretly foiled, but there followed a perceptible increase in aggressive fundamentalism throughout the Muslim world accompanied by increased acts of terrorist violence in western countries with even more vehement threats against the United States.

General Bradley approached the limousine. Colonel Caine stowed his phone, straightened his posture and opened a rear door for his commanding officer.

Bradley waved off the courtesy and gestured he would sit in front. This must be really serious Caine surmised. The General was muttering something as he climbed in.

Colonel Caine entered the driver's side and looked expectantly at General Bradley.

"Jeannie McConnell's missing."

"Jeannie McConnell? The Speaker's daughter?" Caine repeated in disbelief. He preferred to think she was spending time with some member of the diplomatic corps—obviously wanting to be discreet. He started the engine and slowly drove toward the White House gates.

Jeanette McConnell was a curvaceous blonde who floated freely in Washington and Hollywood social circles, not so much that she was the daughter of the Speaker of the House of Representatives, but because she was an uninhibited spirit who seemed a natural part of the social pulse of Washington and enjoyed the attention of the rich and powerful. She was linked intermittently with various high-profile men, younger and older, single and not so single.

"Her family's had no contact for over a week," General Bradley explained. "McConnell's checked her apartment, hangouts, friends. There's no sign of her. The Congresswoman says it's not like her."

"Are you sure it's…"

"I know what you're going to say, Chris. We all know about Jeannie and her lifestyle. I hope it ends up nothing. Normally, this would be a case for the Washington Police Department. We know there's been a couple of missing person incidents lately—women joggers. I still can't figure out why they run alone at odd hours in remote parks. Anyway, this does not fit the pattern. Jeannie's not a jogger."

"Something else then?" Caine urged. He looked ahead at two limousines in front of them heading toward the White House gates.

"This looks like a terrorist hit. A twist. No mass destruction, but hitting at the heart of our system. Up close and personal. Her mother's third in line for the Presidency. Maybe payback for Saddam Hussein's two sons who we iced before we arrested the old man."

"They were shooting at us. Heat of battle," Caine replied. "And that was a long time ago."

"Traditional blood feuds don't allow for such distinctions," Bradley countered.

"Yes, sir," Caine agreed. "But then, there've been a number of unsolved disappearances of young women in the Washington area over the past couple of years. None well-known, though."

"Damn, they should let you in on these meetings," General Bradley replied, "So I wouldn't have to keep repeating myself. The President received intel on this one. It's one of the Middle East terrorist groups."

"Al Qaida linked?"

"Who knows?" Bradley paused. "And who cares? They all spit the same bile. We're going to send you to find out."

"What's the lead?"

"Bob Coulson out of CIA," General Bradley replied. "He just reported to the President that a contact in Moscow knows that some fringe group pledging support for Al Qaida boasted that they have her."

"Who's, who and what's what out of Moscow is still a good guessing game." Colonel Caine noted. "Especially Intelligence."

"I know. But this information comes from Warlock," General

Bradley declared. "Coulson's been on the money with him as long as I can remember."

"Warlock again," Caine intoned with keen interest. "I'd sure give plenty to find out who he is."

"We all would, Chris. Bob Coulson's been in counterintelligence for years and he still doesn't know—even after the collapse of the Soviet Union. He just says that Warlock's been an unimpeachable source—a man deep inside the old KGB. An older officer. Very senior. He rose up the ranks very quickly when the secret police were still called NKVD."

"Late nineteen fifties," Caine asserted.

"That would be about right."

"That would make him pretty old."

"They're cannibals. If he survived that long in the Stalinist system, he's got to be genuine and know plenty—no matter how old he is."

"The Soviets groomed Arab factions for a generation," Caine said. "Even created some. I guess a former KGB commissar would have solid information about any groups in the region."

"We're betting on them now as friends," General Bradley asserted.

"Friends," Colonel Caine repeated in a tone inviting broad inter-pretation.

"I don't care how we get the information," Bradley replied. "The idea is to get Jeannie back."

"You'll have your orders by tomorrow night," he continued, "As soon as we finish the backdrop—contacts, rendezvous points. You're going with Garrison."

"Garrison? The two of us? To where, sir?"

"The two of you. You'll know by sometime tomorrow," Bradley informed.

"Meantime get what you can from the diplomatic corps."

"Diplomatic corps? All the people with immunity from our laws, sir? I thought Jeannie's socializing was discounted."

"It was." General Bradley glanced back toward the White House as Caine wended their limousine between security barriers surrounding the Executive Mansion. The limousine entourage separated. Caine, exited onto 15th Street and headed south toward the Tidal Basin.

"I didn't tell you that she was last seen leaving back there."

"The White House?"

"The White House. Jeannie was last seen leaving a State Dinner given last week in honor of Prince Faisal of Saudi Arabia. With Victor Sherwyck."

"Victor Sherwyck? That great philanthropist and confidant of Presidents?" Caine emphasized, mimicking the signature phrase associated with him in news accounts. "Do we arrest him?"

The General looked at Caine with mock sternness. He tolerated that kind of ironic humor from his aide. Their relationship was a bond of friendship. Actually, General Bradley seemed even fatherly with Colonel Caine after his own son, Jeremy, a Marine captain, had perished in a machine-gun attack by tribal gunmen in Africa during a U.S. led humanitarian mission in the mid 2000's.

"I don't have to say that the President is pushing us on this one. He wants Jeannie back. We can't let any terrorists know that we're still vulnerable; that they can get away with anything after nine-eleven—especially so close to the heartbeat of this government."

Caine nodded in agreement. He accelerated and sped the limousine in the general direction of the Pentagon on the opposite side of the Potomac as fast as Washington traffic would allow.

"What about Sherwyck, sir?" Caine ventured.

"No one's talked with him. It's an official investigation only since this morning. A very discreet one."

"How do we approach one of the President's best friends about a kidnapping—especially when he's been the last one to see her before she vanished? High level infidelity seems common nowadays...but high level foul play?"

"Chris. We're talking about terrorists here," General Bradley said emphatically. "No one's even suggesting anything about Sherwyck. They were guests at a White House State Dinner for chrissake!"

"The last person to see her is Victor Sherwyck and the next thing we hear is that terrorists are holding her," Caine declared.

"Something happened in-between," General Bradley retorted. "Talk to him. By all means. He should be very helpful. He's a bachelor, nothing to hide."

"He's an elusive snob."

"I know, Chris. That's why you'll have to do it in a social setting, among peers, non-directional. He can't think this is an interrogation."

Caine said nothing as he deftly switched lanes. General Bradley knew he agreed.

"In fact, there's a reception at the Smithsonian tonight. He's supposed to be there. You're probably invited yourself—being the southern aristocrat that you are. If not we'll arrange an invitation."

"Yes, sir," Caine remembered. He had planned on skipping that one.

"I know you'll be able to engage him in some cocktail talk. Ease information from him without—" General Bradley paused emphatically and then continued slowly, deliberately, "—without injuring his sensibilities. And for God's sake Chris, don't accuse him of anything! Sherwyck's been a close adviser to the last three Presidents. He's practically a national institution."

"Yes, sir." Colonel Caine gazed out his window at the Jefferson Memorial as they skirted the Tidal Basin toward the Potomac.

"Poor Jeannie," he thought. He remembered the few times, he himself, had spent with her; an uninhibited, beautiful young woman who thought the world was inhabited by people in tuxedos and evening gowns. It was Jeannie who was most vulnerable, he thought, and now Caine felt somehow better that he had never tried to seduce her.

As he drove his General across the George Mason Bridge a charcoal mockingbird sallied from the treetops lining the Tidal Basin and bounded along above them. When the car crossed the bridge, the bird veered off. It flew to the Lincoln Memorial then darted back along the

Reflecting Pool toward the Washington Monument and the Mall beyond, finally alighting on a ledge of the old red Castle of the Smithsonian Institution.

Chapter 2

"Damn it!" said the President as he entered the Oval Office and hurried to his desk. He was followed close behind by a small group of aides and advisers. He sat down heavily in his ornate leather chair.

"The conspiracy theorists are going to have a field day with this one. McConnell's been at my throat for most of my term. Legislative blackmail! She's a flaming ideologue! Now, I'll bet you half this country is going to think I had something to do with Jeannie's disappearance!"

The advisers arranged around his desk looked at him impassively. "All right. Half the *kooks* in this country," the President stated, as if in explanation.

"We understand, Mr. President," soothed George Brandon, his chief of staff. "It's just that it's sometimes hard to separate personal matters from affairs of state—especially in this age of the internet and tabloid newspapers. Everybody's an expert and anything goes."

"I know, George, I know," the President said with frustration. "Twenty or thirty years ago, this kind of reaction wouldn't have entered my mind—or yours. I'm afraid as a society, we've slipped down a few more notches. What is it in the last half century that we've lowered the threshold on everything we used to believe in?"

"Jeannie's disappearance could well be linked with affairs of state," added Paul McCallister, a senior adviser. "Unless we come by other information to the contrary, we have to presume that some terrorist group or network has raised the stakes on us. They're no longer going for numbers. They're going for well-known names in the heart of our system."

The President looked thoughtfully at McCallister then at each of the others. "Maybe so, gentlemen. Maybe so." He pondered a moment, knowing the last to see her was his close friend, Victor Sherwyck. "I know what we heard at the meeting, but do you think we might be overreacting? Maybe she is taking some extra time with someone—if you know what I mean."

"It's a terrorist operation," said Stanford Howard, the national security adviser. "The CIA's source has always been a good one. Warlock doesn't pop up often, but he's always been on the money."

"Who is this Warlock, anyway?" the President asked.

"It's an unusual setup, Mr. President," the national security adviser replied. Stanford Howard quickly looked at each of the men around him to assure himself that all had the level of security clearance to hear what he was about to say.

"Would you excuse us, please?" Howard said facing two of the aides.

The two dutifully left the room.

When the door to the Oval Office closed, Howard spoke. "Warlock presented himself to Senator Everret Dunne. Dunne was a junior member of the Foreign Relations Committee. He approached Dunne in Moscow during an exchange visit. Said he found religion. He's been feeding us information through Senator Dunne ever since."

"Found religion?"

"Yes, sir. Apparently he was turned by some life-changing experience with his cohorts in the secret police."

"He doesn't ask for anything in return?"

"No, Mr. President. He claims it's his duty to his fellow-man. For a stable world."

"Yeah, right!" the President mocked. "So, who the hell is he?"

The national security adviser glanced at each of the men present and spoke somberly. Senator Dunne says his name is Nicholai Kuznetsov. He was high level KGB."

"Senator Dunne says this, Senator Dunne says that," the President mimicked. "Is this for real? What does the CIA say? Is this old KGB? Warmed-over KGB, the Russian Organization for State Security? Russian mafia? What?"

"That's just it, Mr. President," Stanford Howard said hesitatingly. "The one condition Warlock gave was that no one else know anything about him—only Senator Dunne. Dunne is the conduit," the national security adviser explained. "Dunne passes the information to CIA through Bob Coulson, head of counterintelligence at Langley. And Warlock has been genuine each of the times he's given us information."

"Why isn't the CIA handling him?" the President asked. "This is very unusual."

"Yes, sir," Stanford Howard answered sheepishly. "Warlock insisted it be outside the CIA." The national security adviser paused, then continued cautiously—"He says we're infiltrated. He'd be exposed. So he deals with us only through Senator Dunne."

"Infiltrated?" the President asked sternly. "Again?"

"I'm certain, we're not, Mr. President," Howard assured. "Not anymore. We've taken extraordinary measures since the last time. But it's a common fear of any informant."

"More like paranoia," adviser McCallister added for emphasis.

There was an embarrassed silence. The President did not seem persuaded by the assurances.

"Why Senator Dunne?" the President asked with a skeptical look still on his face.

"It just worked out, I guess," the national security adviser replied. "The contact through Senator Dunne seemed to have been secure all these years, so Warlock trusted it. Now Dunne is Chairman of the Senate Intelligence Committee. Warlock couldn't have dreamed of a more high-placed sounding board."

"Or patsy," the President felt obligated to say. "How does Langley take all this?"

"They tolerate it, sir. As long as information is genuine. And it has been up to now."

"So, that's why we know terrorists grabbed Jeannie?"

"That's what we have to believe, Mr. President," Stanford Howard affirmed. "That's the only reliable information we have."

"That's the *only* information we have," the President corrected. "Did Everret give this guy his code name?"

"No, sir. Senator Dunne says Nicholai Kuznetsov coined it himself. Kuznetsov directed that that's how he should be identified. Warlock."

"And Dunne's met him?" the President reiterated.

"Yes," said the national security adviser. "He says the guy approached him in Moscow a long time ago, during an official visit. Now Senator Dunne is a valuable go-between for hard intelligence. We have to take it any way we can get it."

"Very well, gentlemen," the President declared. "It's an unusual step. Unusual, but I agree. As long as we get good intelligence—" the President let the sentence trail away.

Before the President could ask the obvious, Paul McCallister offered, "I saw the Senator two days ago. He told me Warlock sought him out in Moscow just as he was about to return from his fact-finding trip on our latest missile placement talks."

"That's when he told him about Jeannie?"

"As much as he knew, Mr. President."

"Shall we bring in Michelle McConnell?"

"No. As far as everyone knows this is a local police matter. I'll phone her and express my concern over her daughter. We can't let on that this is a matter of state. Not unless at some point we'll have to. I'll just tell her for now that we're closely monitoring the situation— unofficially."

"Yes, sir," several advisers replied in unison.

"Where's Victor Sherwyck?" the President asked abruptly.

"He's in town somewhere, sir," the chief of staff replied. "He's due at a reception at the Smithsonian this evening."

"Oh, yes, of course. Catch up with him. Put him on the schedule for a meeting—maybe lunch."

"Yes, sir," Brandon said perfunctorily.

"I want this whole thing wrapped fast," the President directed, knowing he had no real control over the outcome.

"If anyone can do this, sir, it will be the Omega Group," asserted Stanford Howard, the national security adviser.

"Show me, Stanford!" the President challenged as he stood up from his chair.

"Very well, Mr. President," George Brandon interjected. When his President betrayed irritation it was time for the chief of staff to remove the irritants. 'Stanford' instead of 'Stan' was a clue. Brandon stood up also, giving the cue to the others that the meeting was over.

When the advisers left the Oval Office, the President sat down again, turned in his leather swivel chair, gave a long sigh of frustration and stared out the window into the Rose Garden, spotting a large, charcoal mockingbird bobbing among the flowers.

Chapter 3

The young woman walked briskly through the main hall of the Library of Congress between curved wooden reading tables arranged under the dome along her way. They were occupied randomly by congressional aides doing research that would evolve into eloquent statements on the floors of the House and Senate, students, scholars and curious tourists testing whether they could really find a copy of every book published in the United States.

They paused, however, and couldn't help but notice, glance, or stare at the attractive young woman passing by. The black dress she wore outlined her shapely, soft body and the amber pendant around her neck swayed back and forth with the rhythm of her steps, made noticeably loud by her high heeled shoes. She smiled to herself, knowing that people don't normally dress up for a visit to the library. She strode purposefully toward an elevator at the far end of the hall hidden behind numerous stacks of reference books.

Laura Mitchell rode to the basement level, then wandered through stacks of literature until she came upon a small office overfilled with books in a corner of the building.

Hunched over his paper-strewn desk was an elderly gentleman, gray-haired, with distinguished features, but dressed in a well-worn, buttoned sweater that suggested he was more interested in things around him than on him. He was peering studiously at an old document.

"Uncle Jonas," Laura said in a sing-song fashion so as not to startle him.

He looked up immediately. "Laura, sweetheart! How nice to see you. Come in! Come in!" He stood up to hug her. "You look lovely. So dressed up. It's a young man, isn't it? " he declared with a sparkle in his eye.

"No, no, Uncle, nothing like that. I'm on my way to the Smithsonian. There's a reception at the Old Castle later. For new members of NATO."

"I see," he replied. "To better acquaint us with the cultures of our lesser known allies."

"There will even be a map," she said with a hint of irony.

"And what may I ask does a French History professor have to do with NATO?" he asked in a mock challenge.

"You should be pleased to know," she answered emphatically, "that Alvin Carruthers, the assistant curator, asked me to be a docent for the display from the Devil's Museum in Lithuania."

"Oh!" he conceded.

"He said some of the sponsors couldn't make it, so he asked me to fill in. Alvin knows how steeped I am in Old European folklore— thanks to you," Laura explained as she teasingly tweaked his cheek.

"The Devil's Museum," he said musingly.

"Yes. Which reminds me: How is your project coming along?"

"Fine. Just fine."

"You've been working on it a long time. You have more than five hundred pages. From what I've read, you could publish it right now."

"I'd trade most of those pages for a couple of missing pieces," he said somberly. "Factual pieces. Yes, I could publish it now—but it would be just another fantasy. I'm looking to do a history—so people will believe it. Maybe do something about it."

"I know, Uncle Jonas," she said solicitously. "I'm sure you'll get those pieces. Especially now that Russia's more open."

"Archivists, professors, bureaucrats. They opened all kinds of vaults, Laura. For gifts. For cash. For fresh air after a stifling, terror-filled century. What I need is in secret police files. Those that are even deeper and more inaccessible in the new, more open Russia."

Laura felt his frustration. She was laboring on a series of lectures herself in preparation for a book on the French Revolution, and material for her was boundless.

"Listen," he said tentatively. "When you're there—at the Smithsonian. Can you see who has more than a casual interest in that devil display? You know what I mean?"

"Uncle!" Laura replied with theatrical exasperation. "You and your conspiracy theories."

"You're right, you're right," he answered with resignation. "I'm grasping at straws."

"You shouldn't. Then you will drift into fantasy."

"I've got to get out of the library more," he said, anticipating what his niece was about to suggest. He shuffled idly through some papers on his desk.

She smiled then kissed his cheek. "I've got to run. Let's have dinner tomorrow. I'll treat."

"Okay. But it's on me. You pick the restaurant."

"I know just the place in Georgetown."

"And don't forget what I asked you!" he said as she disappeared through the door.

"I won't," her voice trailed back through the stacks of books surrounding his office.

Chapter 4

Thunderhead clouds, unannounced in the day's forecast, were looming over Washington as Colonel Caine sped his dark red Viper from Arlington back to the heart of the city. A slow, choking stream of traffic heading in the opposite direction signaled the end of the work day. Government functionaries and other bureaucrats were leaving the nation's capital for their homes in the burgeoning suburbs of Maryland and Virginia. Thousands of headlights pricked the April sky turned prematurely dark by the heavy rain-laden clouds.

He had driven his general back to the Pentagon and returned to his apartment in nearby Arlington to prepare for the reception at the Smithsonian. Caine was dressed in a light gray suit with subtle pinstripes instead of his military dress uniform. He did not want to appear too official in getting information from Victor Sherwyck. It also gave him an advantage to better conceal his .38 caliber pistol, a seven- round Sig Sauer P232 that he habitually carried as a back-up weapon.

The clouds released a violent torrent of rain just as he pulled up to the curb near the National Museum of Natural History on Constitution Avenue. He had planned a leisurely stroll across the Mall to the Old Castle, but now had to wait out the cloudburst.

He tuned his car radio to a news broadcast. It included an update on the item he had read that morning while waiting for General

Bradley at the White House—a rural sheriff in Ohio investigating animal mutilations and suspected devil worship. There were additional details of a similar discovery of animal mutilations near the Appalachian Trail in the Shenandoah Valley.

Authorities dismissed it as a cruel prank and found no connection to the discovery in Ohio.

"These things happen now and then," a park official stated. "They look like rituals for shock value. Malicious hoaxes. Unfortunately, there's a lot of sick minds around."

Caine wondered about these kinds of stories reported as oddities from various parts of the country. They appeared with periodic regularity. How many were undiscovered or unreported? The main concern seemed to be the loss of farmers' stock. No one ever suggested the perpetrators may be following a text of some standardized, bizarre ritual.

The heavy rain was dissipating. Caine turned off the radio and decided to make a dash across the Mall during the lull. He climbed nimbly out of his roadster and hurried toward the expansive stretch of greenery framed in the distance by the Capitol Building on his left and the obelisk of the Washington Monument on his right.

A striped alley cat—black and gray—crouched low in some bushes as he jogged along the sidewalk next to the museum building. The cat bobbed its head several times as Caine approached, crouched low and twitched its tail as if to pounce. The moment passed as Caine's hurried footsteps receded and the stray cat diverted its attention to other movement in the area.

The red sandstone mansion was an impressive Gothic Revival structure reaching into the past—seemingly out of place among the other official buildings whose light hues and linear designs set the Old Castle apart in the lineup along the Mall. It was the first building erected there and carried that distinction with ageless style.

As he neared the Castle, Caine noticed a derelict sprawled awkwardly under a budding elm tree. The man must have been sleeping off a bottle of cheap wine and at first glance might even have appeared dead. Satisfied by a quick glance that the man's unkempt face was not blue, Caine continued on his way. He was inured by the occasional sight of street people who for reasons of their own, or as a deliberate statement of their condition, frequented the areas around the White House, Capitol grounds and the Mall. Sprawled out as he had been, it was surprising to the Colonel that the derelict's clothes did not seem to be wet from the rain.

Moments after Caine passed him, the man stirred, seemingly oblivious to his surroundings, and as if driven by his own sense of time and place, shuffled off in his ragged clothes in the direction from which Colonel Caine had just come.

Chapter 5

Caine joined a small line of guests filing up the stairs of the brick canopy entryway. Others exited limousines that had backed up on Jefferson Drive in front of the building during the downpour. Standing at the door was a plain-faced doorman who seemed at first glance to be out of place in his red service jacket that was more than a size too big. The doorman looked indifferently at Caine's invitation and returned it upside down, motioning him inside.

He gave the same uninterested look to other guests; a look that appeared to say he would prefer to be somewhere else. In each case he returned invitations upside down. Most of the guests did not pay attention, while several gave the doorman a sideward glance at this apparent lack of grace.

"Some way to save a buck," Caine thought, presuming one of the maintenance crew was doubling as a greeter.

He passed the vestibule where the crypt of James Smithson stood eternal watch over the historical wealth he had presented to America. The English benefactor had been buried in Italy in 1829, but his remains were brought to the United States in 1903 by then Regent Alexander Graham Bell and interred in the vestibule. Caine nodded unconsciously in the direction of the crypt and wondered whether the man really would have wanted to become an artifact in his own museum. He couldn't help but think that Smithson was just like one of those human sacrifices ancient cultures placed in edifices of new buildings to appease the supernatural.

The vestibule opened into a cavernous hall with prominent deep brown pillars supporting a ceiling two stories above. Caine lingered near a pillar where several socialite friends of his family noticed and engaged him in conversation. All the while he was tuned to hear the voice or see the presence of Victor Sherwyck.

"Chris, my dear boy," said a distinguished looking woman. "We haven't seen you for such a long time. Samantha's been asking about you."

"Mrs. Davis. You look as charming as ever," he replied, adjusting the front of his jacket slightly to avoid exposing the holstered pistol at the small of his back.

"Oh, Chris, you're always so flattering. I only hear about you when your folks are visiting. That nasty Army keeps you away all the time," she said with mock indignation.

"I'll visit soon, Mrs. Davis," Caine replied with a polite smile. "I promise." He knew the lady from his childhood, but felt constrained lately by her efforts to pair him up with her youngest daughter, Samantha.

"You're such a fine young man. You ought to settle down," she continued with friendly and familiar concern.

Caine glanced at either side of him. He was growing a little embarrassed by her good-natured but ill-timed advice and took a little longer to gaze around the hall for Sherwyck.

"Mrs. Davis. Did you hear about Jeannie McConnell?"

"Why, yes, I did. Poor thing. She seems to be missing. Why I would never let our Samantha be so long out of sight, never mind living alone nowadays."

"I know, Mrs. Davis," he replied, realizing the question was futile. "I know. You take care of yourself, now."

"I want to see you at our home soon, y'hear?" She pressed his hand and smilingly turned to her circle of companions.

"Soon, Mrs. Davis. Give my best to your family—and to Samantha," he added as an afterthought.

The reception hall was filling, but Colonel Caine had not noticed Victor Sherwyck. He took a glass of champagne from one of the caterers mingling among the guests with serving plates of drinks and hors d oeuvres. This one was a woman with heavy makeup and hard looking eyes. She seemed preoccupied, not bothering to offer the champagne as she passed. Those with a taste for a glass either asked her for one or—as Caine had just done—deftly grabbed a glass as she jostled not too politely among small groups of the Washington notables positioning themselves to see or be seen in the reception hall.

Snippets of conversation included references to Jeannie McConnell, but few people knew even the sketchiest details: only that she had not been seen for more than a week.

"Crime is just so rampant..." said one woman he passed.

"Do you think she's a jogger?" asked another. "They never caught the attacker in the parks, did they?"

Caine took a hefty gulp from his champagne glass as he sauntered by, wishing it was bourbon, while his eyes kept scanning the hall for a glimpse of Victor Sherwyck. There was no sign of the well-placed financier and seemingly hereditary confidant of presidents. No one could miss his slim, even gaunt features that presented a commanding, aristocratic air and whose position and influence—no less his wit and cynical wisdom—magnetized people.

He expected to spot the man among the guests who were there to preview a cultural exhibit highlighting the historical and national character of states formerly submerged within the Soviet Union, but now members of the NATO alliance. Sherwyck would most likely be among some ambassadors or other dignitaries present.

Then he saw her; a tall, well-proportioned woman, speaking with several guests. With her was his friend, Alvin Carruthers, assistant curator of The Smithsonian. The woman was in quarter profile and even from a distance attracted Caine's interest.

The young woman shifted slightly and caught the Colonel's eye.

She looked at him for the briefest of moments then turned back to her circle of companions. There was something familiar about her. He worked his way in her direction, exchanging greetings and clipped comments with acquaintances.

As Caine approached, the woman stepped to a nearby exhibit, while Carruthers chatted with a silver-haired gentleman and his wife.

"Chris, how are you?" Carruthers invited as the Colonel neared. "We don't see you in Washington too much."

Caine joined them still looking in her direction, while the assistant curator introduced the couple. "Mr. and Mrs. Knowlton are two of our very generous benefactors, Chris. We pamper them as best we can."

Everyone smiled a jovial, social smile.

The Knowltons politely dismissed Carruther's comments, but were nonetheless pleased by his flattery in front of this urbane looking stranger with closely trimmed hair.

"We're firm believers in maintaining our national institutions," Knowlton said. "We're happy to be able to do so."

"A very noble gesture," Colonel Caine replied sincerely.

"The Nation's Attic!" the assistant curator intoned, repeating with pride the standard colloquial description of the Smithsonian Institution.

"Well, it certainly is and I'm glad," Knowlton said emphatically. "It's good to have a place where we can display everything we are as a nation. It's a symbol of ourselves and a real treasure for generations to come."

"As you can see, this particular exhibition is not quite *us*," the assistant curator said. "It's a special presentation from the nations of the former Soviet Union that have since joined NATO."

"A wonderful idea," Colonel Caine said politely.

"I don't think so," Mr. Knowlton replied authoritatively. "Why irritate the Russians at a time like this? Surrounding them with their former satellites as members of an organization that was specifically created to challenge the Soviet Union? Those new republics are chaotic, corrupt."

"That sounds a little arrogant, don't you think, Mr. Knowlton," Colonel Caine replied with a stiff smile. "They're no more corrupt—and I dare say a little less so—than Russia itself. Besides, it seems the new Russia is getting harder to distinguish from the old Russia."

"That's a very naïve sentiment, Mr....Mr...."

"Caine, Colonel Christopher Caine."

"A military man, no less," Knowlton spluttered, as his wife looked on indignantly. "Those people have no tradition of democracy. Look what happened in Iraq after all those years of our involvement. They were better off before, if you ask me. There was peace and stability. Just like in the former USSR."

"We had no tradition of democracy either, Mr. Knowlton," Caine replied firmly, but politely. "Many of our founding fathers were smugglers for profit and we weren't too enlightened either. Let's remember that Cotton Mather had a degree from Harvard University when he incited the hanging of innocent men and women in Salem. It seems our Anglo-Saxon tradition evolved from absolute rule of monarchs and a belief in witchcraft."

Knowlton was momentarily nonplussed while a startled look came over Mrs. Knowlton.

"You can't disallow democracy on the grounds that it's untested," Caine continued. "It was untested in every place it took root."

"So?" Knowlton managed to say.

"Gentlemen, gentlemen," Carruthers chimed in, but to no avail.

Knowlton, refined and distinguished in his black tie, took on an air like he had just been sullied. Colonel Caine had violated the etiquette of this reception, which was so outwardly defined by the dress and social demeanor of the guests.

Mrs. Knowlton looked sternly at the Colonel, as if he had dared penetrate some private domain. She wordlessly took her husband by the arm and briskly led him away.

"Damn it, Chris!" Carruthers fumed. "What's gotten into you? They're two of our major benefactors!"

"Seems the guy's a little too sensitive. So's his wife."

"They donated two million towards the redesign of the Hope Diamond Exhibit and the Gem Hall. You could have been a little more civil with them."

"Wasn't I?" Caine took a quick gulp of his champagne and wondered why the couple reacted so forcefully. "He seems too apologetic of dictatorships."

"He's an industrialist. He's used to giving orders. Companies are autocratic."

"And I suppose he thinks governments should be too," Caine concluded. "He forgets autocracies fail, just like rigid companies."

"I don't care what he thinks, Chris. That's probably a good couple of million dollars scratched off the donors list."

"Oh, don't worry, Al. I'm the one he's perturbed about. Not you. Not the Institution. I'm just passing through."

"They'll probably think I'm unfit because I'm a friend of yours. Not fit for their beloved Smithsonian. They have influence. They'll have me fired."

Caine smiled at this friend, enjoying his theatrical display of concern. "Don't worry, Al. It takes more than that to get you fired."

"I'm in a precarious business. A lot of my perceived talent and my position depends on rich patrons."

"You don't have to tell *me* about precarious," Caine retorted.

"Well…" his friend conceded.

"Look around, Al. This hall's full of millionaires looking for prestigious tax breaks."

"Yes, it is," Carruthers replied longingly. "Although that's not my department." He seemed assuaged and no longer upset with his friend.

"Have you seen Victor Sherwyck?" Caine asked.

"I know he has an invitation, but I haven't seen him. If you hadn't insulted the Knowltons," he said, resurrecting the moment, "maybe they could have told you something. They're good friends."

"I see," Caine replied. "But it's Sherwyck I want, not his friends."

"He's also a donor. Just don't insult him either. I have to be sure everybody's happy at these events."

"Well, make me happy, Al, and introduce me to the young lady."

"Ahh, yes, I figured," Carruthers answered slyly. "It's Laura, Laura Mitchell. Dr. Laura Mitchell."

"How about if you first apologized to the Knowltons?"

"For what?" Caine asked indignantly as he slowly and dramatically pulled back his jacket to reveal his pistol in a mock threat.

"All right, all right. I'll introduce you. But you're going to owe me one."

Chapter 6

She was facing away from them studying a mask in a display case featuring an assortment of statues—all of them devils.

"Laura, there's someone I'd like you to meet," Carruthers said.

She turned to them champagne glass in hand. Caine stood transfixed.

A recurring vision flashed before him. He was in the midst of a confrontation on a dusty road in the outskirts of Beirut. A single shot from somewhere had provoked a firefight between some armed men in a crowd and a military patrol, to which he had been attached as an adviser. Caine was running for cover when he almost stumbled over a young woman lying near a building. She was on her back. Her black dress was hiked up to her thighs. The fall had disarranged her dress and the neckline revealed a soft, full curve of an uncovered breast. Caine impulsively stretched out his hand to help her to her feet, but she stared blankly at the sky with her lips barely parted. Only then did he notice a small, but steady trickle of blood flowing down her temple and mingling with her long, black, unbridled hair. She was dead. A deep feeling of rage overtook him. He felt awkward for extending his hand to a dead woman and dreamed evermore she was reaching out to take his.

She extended her hand. "Hello."

Caine's heartbeat quickened. He was thunderstruck. It was as if the girl had risen from the dusty street, just as Caine had willed over and over in his obsessive dreams. The resemblance was uncanny and sent a shudder down his spine.

She was medium height, but her high heeled shoes made her seem taller, stately. Her long auburn hair seemed to glisten in the lights. The young woman's dress snugly caressed her body. Around her neck was a slim golden chain with a large amber pendant. Her eyes were large, round and green-blue. Her lips, though closed, suggested a sensuous mouth. They seemed to be curving into a modest smile.

"Hello," she repeated.

"Hello," he responded robot like, looking at her intently.

"I'm normally flattered," she said. "But you're staring."

"I'mmm... sorry," he replied hesitatingly.

"My, my!" Carruthers intoned. "Have I finally seen Samson undone? He's usually much more composed, Laura."

"Please, Al! You're embarrassing the poor man."

"Thank you," Caine responded.

"That's all right. I did say I was flattered," she replied with a disarming smile.

"It's a pleasure to meet you," he said slowly, regaining his demeanor.

"It's nice of you to visit the exhibition," she said sweetly.

"I noticed you admiring this mask."

"Not so much admiring as minding," she said, turning to the display. "I'm acting as an interpreter for this part of the exhibition."

"I see," he said. "And a lovely one at that."

"Are you being flattering again, or do I remind you of someone?" Laura queried.

"I'm just describing what I see."

She slowly took a sip of her champagne, smiled at Caine over the rim of her glass, and sauntered over to the other side of the display.

"What's that you were looking at?" he asked, pointing his own glass towards a mask.

"It's mid-nineteenth century. The style is quite primitive. It's carved from the bark of a tree and embellished with straw."

"I see," Caine said looking briefly towards her, then glancing back at the devil mask.

"It's reminiscent of some primitive cultures in Africa and New Guinea."

"You know a lot about devils," Caine toyed.

"It depends on who they are."

He looked playfully into her eyes and moved around the display case to be next to her. "And what about this one?" he asked. Her perfume now aroused his senses.

"This one?" She glanced at an intricate carving of an old man sitting on a tree stump smoking a pipe.

"It doesn't look like a devil at all." He peered intently at the light brown wooden figure, intrigued by his own question.

"Devils take on all kinds of disguises," she explained. "Often human beings. Otherwise, we'd avoid them, wouldn't we?"

Several passing guests lingered at the display to catch some of the woman's explanation about its unusual exponents. Caine periodically darted his eyes towards the guests for a possible glimpse of Victor Sherwyck.

"For all the detail and intricacies of this carving, you'll notice that this kindly old gentleman has no nostrils, even though he's smoking a pipe."

Some of the guests moved closer.

"People familiar with the folklore recognize that right away," she said.

"I'm sure they do," Caine replied as he studied other details of the statue. "I see that his feet take on animal form just as they disappear into his shoes."

"Yes. The kindly old gentleman has cloven hooves."

A lady onlooker curiously looked down at her husband's feet in champagne induced humor that brought polite laughter from those around her.

"Reminds me of 'Old Scratch' where I come from," Caine said.

"We don't hear much about him anymore."

"Nowadays it's more like grotesque science fiction monsters, aliens," Laura emphasized, as much to Caine as to the several guests eyeing the display. "But folklore is still very much alive in Europe— particularly Eastern Europe. This exhibit is just a small part of an entire museum in the city of Kaunas in Lithuania," Laura Mitchell continued, reverting to her role as docent of the display. "It's devoted entirely to devils from folklore."

"I think we've outgrown a lot of folklore here," Caine responded.

"It seems we have," she agreed. "And left behind some inherent wisdom with it."

A thoughtful moment ensued in which the assistant curator noticed them looking at each other expectantly, while some passersby drifted to other exhibits in the vast hall.

"All right, then," Alvin Carruthers intoned. He motioned to a passing server and scooped two more champagne glasses from his tray. He handed them to his friends who gave him their empty ones and turned to take one himself when the server lost his grip. A tray full of glasses clattered to the floor at their feet. There was a momentary hush around them as other guests stared at the result of the commotion. The server, a sullen looking dark-skinned man, muttered something to himself and walked away.

"Are you skimping on professional help for these fancy affairs, Al?" the Colonel asked, remembering a similar sullen man at the entrance. "Here!" He handed back the glass Carruthers had just given him. "You could use this right now more than I can."

Carruthers took a swift gulp. "We don't skimp, Chris. It's in their contract. The Union has insisted for years that their members be involved in all phases of maintenance and service around the buildings. It's like a little empire."

The assistant curator looked around the hall for another attendant. None was in the immediate vicinity.

"I'd love to get some real professionals to cater these events, but the Union keeps harping that we're taking work away from their people. And the Smithsonian Board doesn't like controversy. So we take the path of least resistance. It's really not worth the political fuss. And this kind of bungling doesn't happen too often."

"It could happen to anybody," Laura Mitchell offered in a charitable vein. "I've seen one of the fancier caterers in Washington stumble over the wife of the British Ambassador. Anybody can spill a tray."

"But not everyone has to act boorish," Caine replied with a friendly eye to Laura Mitchell.

"I agree," Carruthers interjected. "Our maintenance people are just not the types to interact with Washington society. They don't display the social graces. It takes special training and sensitivity," he explained in undisguised frustration.

"Our night crews should stick to taking care of the Smithsonian buildings. There's plenty of work and satisfaction for all of them. Those who end up catering events like tonight seem ill-at-ease. It's not the first time I've seen it. Outright unfriendly."

Carruthers glanced down at some shards too close to his burnished shoes, stepped back and continued.

"Chris is right, Laura. But their Union has a stranglehold and keeps insisting on total control not only of maintenance, but other services associated with our buildings. It's a long-standing contract. I remember Victor Sherwyck had a big hand in lobbying the Board of Regents for it. They know he's well connected, so the Board just leaves the labor contract alone."

"Well, I'm sure some of these workers would appreciate a change," Laura observed. "They really look like they'd rather be somewhere else."

"The theme for the evening," Caine muttered cryptically, thinking of the Presidential adviser he had planned to see. "Being somewhere else."

Carruthers had noticed the palpable attraction between the two and saw his opening.

"Speaking of being somewhere else, I promised Laura a ride back to her car at the Library of Congress. I have some things to attend to at another building. I wonder if...."

"I'll drive her back," Caine offered instantly. "If it's okay with you, Laura?"

"He's a good friend of mine, a military officer," Carruthers assured her.

"I'm fine, Al. I think I'm a good judge of character," she said pointedly with an inviting look at the Colonel. "I'll be happy to go back with you."

The assistant curator was satisfied with his unexpected but apparently well placed match and excused himself. "I must circulate," he declared. "The guests are waiting. Oh, and there are spilled trays to attend to. Now where did that wretched server disappear anyhow? "

Christopher Caine and Laura Mitchell looked on in bemusement.

As the assistant curator walked away Caine scanned the hall intently for Sherwyck.

"Well, first you stare at me like you've seen a ghost, now you look right past me, like I'm invisible."

"I'm sorry," he replied. "I could stare at you all night and forget to blink," he said centering his attention on Laura whose alluring figure was accentuated by the flow of the elegant black dress draping her body.

"I was hoping to have a few words with Victor Sherwyck who's supposed to be here. You know how it is—no Washington function is strictly social. They all have an ulterior motive: political advantage, entrée—" he paused—"intrigue."

"Always intrigue," Laura affirmed, taking another slow sip of her champagne. "So you're here on official business, then?"

"Not strictly. Especially, not now."

She accepted his flattery with a soft laugh. Their eyes fixed on each other for a longer moment.

"Intrigue, then?" She offered him her glass.

"Intrigue," he said and took a slow sip from it.

"Hmm," she intoned with interest.

"Tell me more about these devils." He slowly handed back her glass and pointed to a statue directly behind her in the display case. "What about that one?"

She turned around. "That? That's a very interesting one. It's one of my favorites. It's an imp. The pose first appeared in the late 19th Century. You can see by the hands both outstretched in a snubbing fashion in front of his nose, his tongue sticking out—he's an independent and even frivolous character. Not necessarily malevolent, but mischievous. A rogue. You never know what he might do."

"He seems quite predictable to me. All devils are."

"You know the type?" She looked at him with a coy smile.

Caine acknowledged the verbal play with a lifted eyebrow. "And what do you do when you meet one of these imps?"

"Oh, I just shoo them away." She hesitated, then said with emphasis: "Most of them are *imp-posters* anyway."

He contorted his face in a deliberately pained expression.

"I'm sorry. I couldn't resist that."

"You should have some suitable punishment." Caine motioned to a passing server with a tray of champagne.

"I'd like to, but I have to leave soon," Laura told him, expecting the offer of another glass. "Actually, I have to finish preparing for some lectures I'm giving."

"Old Folklore?"

"No, no," she replied laughingly. "I teach French History at George Washington University."

"What do French History and devil dolls have in common?"

"It's a long story. I'll tell you sometime," she said anticipating they would see each other again. "Meantime, I'll never get my lectures prepared."

"Improvise," Caine declared. "I can see that your intelligence is second only to your beauty."

"I know a line when I hear one."

"Can the truth ever be a line?" he retorted offering her another glass of champagne that he scooped from the tray of the passing server.

"I should say 'no'..."

"Don't say 'no', please," he asked earnestly.

"Well... I suppose..."

They sipped their champagne, eyes engaging each other in wordless conversation, then gazed around the reception hall. Most guests had circulated through the various displays and were huddled in larger or smaller groups socializing.

Some were leaving. Colonel Caine took in the festive scene with a searching eye for Victor Sherwyck.

"I don't think there will be much more traffic at this display," Laura ventured. "Would you mind if we left now?"

"Not at all," Caine replied, satisfied that Victor Sherwyck had not shown up.

They casually made their way towards the main door and passed within several feet of the Russian Ambassador's circle. Mr. and Mrs. Knowlton were engaged in animated conversation with the Ambassador when Mrs. Knowlton noticed Colonel Caine and Laura Mitchell walk by. She gave Caine a dismissing glance.

Nearby, Mrs. Davis looked disapprovingly at him in the company of the shapely woman with the black dress and vowed to herself that he would have to explain himself before he comes calling on her Samantha.

And eyeing Caine very intently was one of the members of the Russian entourage. He was distinguished looking, but slightly fleshy—the result of a perceptible weight gain during the first of a two-year assignment to the Russian Embassy as a consular officer. The man stroked back his full head of graying hair as he watched the Colonel and Laura Mitchell disappear through the main entrance of the Old Castle.

Chapter 7

Outside the Castle the long line of trees accenting the length of the Mall had become shadowy sentinels with a gathering wind hissing through the leaves in the growing darkness. The wind carried the smell of fresh earth after a rain.

Amid an exchange of small talk Laura and the Colonel did not notice how fast they found themselves on the narrow, tree-lined sidewalk along the west side of the Natural History Museum.

There were still signs of activity outside the Castle now farther across the Mall. Guests were leaving; some waiting for limousines, but this end was deserted in the darkness.

Caine's senses instinctively peaked and his eyes darted back and forth surveying the area around them.

It was then that they noticed several shadowy figures climb out of a dark panel van parked on Constitution Avenue ahead of them. The figures headed in their direction.

Laura looked with apprehension, grabbed Caine's hand, pressed it firmly in a gesture of growing alarm and quickened her pace.

She could feel the Colonel's body tense as he slowed back their pace and peered through the darkness to discern the figures who were perhaps twenty feet away from them.

"It's all right," he murmured firmly. He stopped and brought Laura around him—changing hands as if in a dance step—in case he decided to draw his pistol.

They were midway along the western side of the block-long museum building when three unkempt, but muscular men blocked the sidewalk before them. Two were black and the third was white. Just beyond them, along the wall of the building, slinked two more men, whose features he could not distinguish.

"Hey now! What's a nice couple like you doin' all alone out here?" taunted one of the black men.

"You're on our turf!" declared his white companion.

"Yeah!" emphasized the third.

Caine stared past them at the two figures along the building wall, making sure they did not disappear from his view.

"Hey! I'm talking to you," sneered the first man.

The three men glared at them menacingly.

Caine's eyes shifted to the man who was talking. He stared coldly into the man's eyes.

"Why don't you say somethin'?" the accoster taunted.

The Colonel said nothing. He knew their fixation with having him reply was distracting them.

Laura's heart was pounding violently with fear. She looked at Caine with eyes wide and mouth agape, describing in her look what he already knew.

Caine looked at her with such a deadly stare of determination that she shuddered.

"Hey now, man! Afraid to talk? No use playin' brave for your lady here. You're in the wrong place! This is our turf man! Our time!"

The three came closer and stood challengingly before them in an arc. Laura pressed against Caine, grasping his left arm with both of her hands.

"Now, that's a nice dress you have there lady," sneered the white man who was wearing baggy jeans and a dark zippered jacket over a blue sweatshirt. "I forgot to dress up for our date tonight."

As the assailant spoke he pulled a stiletto from his hip pocket and with a deft flick of a button flashed its long slender blade. He aimed the blade menacingly toward Laura then looked with a daring stare at Caine, reinforced by his two leering companions.

Caine's eyes narrowed and he leaned imperceptibly forward on his left foot.

"Now what would you do, man, if I cut that nice dress off your lady friend?"

"You'd be too dead to try," Caine spoke.

He struck with the speed of a lunging cobra. Caine pulled his hand from Laura's grasp with such force that she almost keeled over backwards. The thug with the stiletto shifted his weight backwards in stunned reaction. Before he knew what happened, Caine had moved in on him, grabbing the man's right wrist with his own right hand as he pivoted into the man with a backward embrace, his back pushing into the man's chest. In that same movement Caine rammed his left elbow into the man's midsection, while twisting the assailant's right wrist with such opposing force that the stiletto fell easily from his grasp. In the same motion Caine bucked his left foot upwards with deliberate force into the man's groin.

The Colonel then released his grip and took one step forward out of the man's empty embrace.

The assailant crumpled in agony to the ground.

Before the other two could react, Caine flipped back his jacket and deftly drew his pistol, pointing it squarely at the forehead of the man who had first confronted them. He saw the other men along the museum wall pull what appeared to be weapons of their own and crouch to a firing position. He cursed himself silently for not bringing his military issue Beretta, instead. It held 17 rounds, but would have been too obvious at the reception.

Caine grabbed Laura by the hand and pulled her several steps to one side so that the assailant, at whose head he was aiming the pistol, was now in the line of fire of the two other men crouched at the museum wall.

He gruffly shoved Laura downward, took a quick step backwards and fired seven shots in rapid succession past the ears of the thug in front of him.

The two figures by the museum wall crumpled like rag dolls.

The thug stood frozen after Caine's bullets whizzed past him. Then, with renewed bravado he taunted: "Bad shot, man! Bad for you!" He moved in on Caine with a cocked fist.

The other assailant undid a length of chain from his waist under his grimy sweater and began swinging it over his head and moving towards Caine.

The man Caine had disabled was still doubled up in pain on the ground.

"Ask your dead friends," Caine said to distract him. He grabbed another clip of bullets from his jacket pocket as he deftly released the empty clip from the grip of his pistol and in one continuous motion shoved the new clip in and chambered a round.

He aimed it at the arm of the man swinging the chain and fired one shot.

The assailant's hand, pierced by the bullet, dropped just enough to cause the chain he was swinging to complete its rotation onto the thug's own head. He crumpled with a short yelp of anguished pain, then lapsed into semi-consciousness.

The assailant in front of Caine froze again.

"Hey now, man! Don't shoot us! We don't have no guns, man!"

"Down!" Caine ordered. "On your back!"

"Hey man! You ain't gonna shoot us! We're just doin' like we're supposed to do!"

"Yeah, man!" added the thug who had pulled the stiletto. He labored back to his feet. "We're just doin' like we're supposed to."

"Shut up!" Caine barked, his body still throbbing with adrenalin. "Down and strip!"

The three assailants seemed puzzled, but momentarily relieved that Caine was not about to shoot them.

"Can't leave them here," Caine declared. He stared at the men lowering themselves to the ground. "They'll prey on someone else." Caine squatted near one of them, casually brandishing his pistol in their direction.

As they prostrated themselves, Laura ran up to the mugger whose stiletto she had instinctively picked up in the tumult. She grabbed his baggy jeans at the waist and cut them open. "Now what would *you* do, you creep, if I cut your balls off?" she seethed. He looked at her in horror. "Hey, man! Hey, man!" he called in Caine's direction.

Caine ignored him.

Laura ripped through the man's pant leg, grazing his inner thigh as she did so. She hesitated, then slowly straightened herself, while glaring into the thug's eyes. They were pleading. Laura continued to glare at the man, her feet set apart in a combative stance with the stiletto firmly in both hands pointed towards the attacker, her amber pendant dangling from her neck just above the stiletto's blade. She was breathing heavily as she stroked her tussled hair back with one hand.

"He's got a gun strapped to his thigh." she said matter-of-factly.

The man saw in her face a determination to lunge at him again, but Caine was instantaneously upon him, grabbing a Glock .357 caliber "pocket rocket" from a small holster.

"Thanks," he said and stepped away from the prostate man.

The Colonel wagged the powerful pistol at the lead assailant. "More reason now for you nice, honest folks to give all your clothes to charity."

Laura was still standing over the assailant.

"Are you about finished," Caine asked quietly.

She didn't respond.

Then slowly, calculatingly she backed off towards the Colonel, stiletto still in hand.

The three grudgingly removed their clothes, having to wriggle awkwardly on the ground to do so. The two injured thugs had to be helped by their companion. When they were stark naked Caine spoke pointing with his pistol: "Go up the middle of the street here while I call nine-one-one. I want to be sure the police recognize you. How shall I tell them you're dressed?" he asked facetiously.

The three reluctantly made their way into the street with their hands placed self-consciously on their groin areas. The man Laura cut was limping and adjusting his holster strap as a bandage for his bloody thigh, while the chain twirler walked dizzily in the middle bumping back and forth between his companions. They turned their heads to the museum to see the fate of their other companions who lay motionless against the wall.

As they approached Constitution Avenue they quickened their pace, the limp seeming to disappear from the man Laura slashed and the wounded man coming to his full senses from the effect of his own chain whipping around his head. They suddenly darted from the middle of the street to the tree lawn of 12th Street out of Caine's line of fire.

The van from which they originally had emerged, just as suddenly careened into a u-turn off Constitution Avenue, screeched up 12th Street, and stopped with a lurch as the three assailants leaped into its open side door and sped away towards Pennsylvania Avenue and into the heart of Washington.

Colonel Caine aimed his pistol in their direction. He squeezed off a round and heard a distant clunk of metal against metal. Caine turned with an assuring look of relief towards Laura Mitchell.

His gaze was met with a look of frightened concern.

"It's okay, they're gone," he said holstering his pistol.

"No, listen!" she exclaimed. "Did you hear that?" She turned her head towards the wall of the Natural History Museum. "Did you hear that?"

"Hear what?" His eyes followed her gaze to a window at an upper level of the building.

"It sounded like a scream! A woman's scream! Inside the building!"

"There's some feral cats roaming around here. It's spring. Are you sure you're okay?"

"Yes, I'm fine," she replied impatiently. "But I heard a scream in there! A long, piercing shriek! It ran the coldest chill down my spine!"

"Cats can make the craziest sounds," Caine asserted as they walked to the side of the building. "Their yowling sounds like human cries."

"Where do you see cats around here?" Laura retorted as she watched Caine draw his pistol again and approach the two men he shot.

He pointed it in their direction, but was certain they would do no more harm. Laura was close behind him as he stooped to examine the bodies.

"I know what I heard!" she persisted. "You should do something!"

"We'll do something," he assured, as he ran his hands through the sweaters and jeans of the two men lying in front of him. "We'll do something." He found no identifying papers as he had expected. Next to one of them, an Asian, lay an Uzi submachine pistol. Caine turned the other man onto his side. He appeared Middle Eastern. He, too, had an Uzi and had fallen onto it when three of Caine's bullets pierced his body.

"Lucky, they didn't get a chance to use these. They each could have sprayed us with sixty rounds. Mean weapons. Especially these automatics. Illegal, you know."

Caine's apparent flippancy was affecting her. "What about the scream? What are you going to do? What about these men? You shot them! Are you going to call the police?"

The Colonel realized he was totally preoccupied and ignoring her concerns. He got up and faced her. "I'm sorry. I didn't mean to put you through this."

She looked at him in a mixture of fear and relief and collapsed into his embrace, still clutching the stiletto.

They hurried to his car with the night breeze turning to a brisk wind that rustled the treetops in the Mall and swayed them back and forth in seeming mimicry of the assault that had just been thwarted.

In the roadster Caine grabbed his secure phone and raised the night duty officer at his Pentagon office. He asked the officer to relay a message about the two bodies to the Washington police. "I'll file a report." He signed off.

Caine looked with concern at Laura.

"If I'm going to keep seeing you, I'll have to take up karate," she said.

As the Viper's taillights receded in the darkness, a head peered from an upper window inside the Museum of Natural History. It looked intently through the pane at the scene of the commotion below. Even though the hallway beyond the window was dimly lit, the features of the derelict whom Caine had seen under the tree on his way to the reception were unmistakable. He glowered into the darkness outside, then disappeared into the depths of the building.

Chapter 8

Massive expanses of black-topped parking areas ringing the Pentagon were still void of cars that morning giving the vast complex the look of a fortress surrounded by a tar moat. Colonel Caine drove his dark red roadster into an area off I-395 and parked at an eastern entrance to the building.

Passing security, he hurried upstairs then along an infinite corridor towards the office of his commanding general on the fourth floor. It was in the third section of the five concentric pentagons making up the familiar headquarters of the Department of Defense. Due to the ultra-secret nature of the Omega Group, the office was deliberately located outside the prestigious "E ring" where the most senior officials had their offices.

As he passed the office adjoining his own, he heard the inevitable through an open door.

"Yo! Swamp Fox! The General's got our orders."

Caine looked in on his fellow-officer, Colonel Garrison Jones, one of the ranking field officers in the Omega Group. "Morning, Arie."

"It's the Middle East again," Jones said. He rose from his chair and approached Caine in the hallway. Jones, like Caine was athletically built and out of uniform that day. Still, his khaki slacks and matching safari shirt, complementing his dark complexion, gave him a crisp military bearing.

"Where to?" replied Caine.

"The old man will fill us in. I hear you were at the Smithsonian last night. Talking to mummies?"

"I may as well have," Caine replied as the two walked towards General Bradley's office.

"Didn't you catch Sherwyck?"

"There was no sign of him. But we got tangled up with some baddies outside."

"We? I thought I was your partner."

"Dr. Laura Mitchell."

"Here I am sittin' at my desk with paperwork up to here and you're mixin' it up somewhere with a strange woman?"

Caine did not reply to his friend's usual banter as they entered General Bradley's office. He was at his desk with a cup of coffee in his hand.

The General beckoned them to sit down on the studded leather sofa along a wall opposite his desk. He joined them and sat down in a matching armchair facing the couch.

"I hear there was some gunplay at the Smithsonian last night," the General said as he took a careful sip of his steaming coffee.

Jones looked over to Caine.

"Yes, sir," Caine replied. He recounted the details of the previous night's encounter; the three who fled and the two men he shot.

The faces of the two were fixed in Caine's mind. The Colonel remembered the Asian was frozen forever in a queer, hateful look that seemed triumphant even in death. The other, a man with Middle Eastern features—probably of Egyptian origin, Caine surmised—had a death look of simple surprise. Five of his seven shots had found their mark, he reported.

"It's unlikely it was a gang," Colonel Jones offered. "I don't know of any turf battles going on over the Mall or public monuments. It's out of the 'hood."

"These muggers were ethnically diverse. It's usually homogeneity that welds gangs together," Caine added. "Besides, they don't usually carry Israeli submachine guns."

"Our night watch got a call from the D.C. police," General Bradley interspersed. "They were on the scene within ten minutes after you patched through. They didn't find a thing. No bodies, no blood, no clothes."

"Impossible, sir!" Caine retorted. "The woman with me witnessed the whole thing. She got some licks in herself."

"Under your umbrella, I'm sure," General Bradley surmised. "I don't doubt you for a minute," he assured. The General took another slow sip of his coffee. "Actually, there is something. Chinks in the side of the Museum of Natural History and a couple of thirty-eight caliber cartridges in the grass. So, I know you shot at something. But that's for the Washington Police Department, there's no need for us to get off track here."

"Sir?"

"Chris, my boy," The general said paternalistically. "Under the circumstances a formal report would look a little empty. Why don't you just detail a memo for me—'Your Eyes Only'."

"If anything further develops, we can spend more time on it."

"The others must have returned for them. They picked up the bodies."

"That's unusual for street thugs," the General replied. "Especially when you routed them. Their only concern is to get away."

"They probably didn't want attention focused on the area," Colonel Jones offered.

"Let's file this away for now," the General reiterated. "Our attention is Jeannie McConnel. Not your average street muggings," he added with sarcasm.

General Bradley rose from the armchair and started back to his desk. "Our lead's in Beirut. That's where you're going. Things are dicey there again, so it'll have to be an insertion. Who knows who's in charge and we don't want you noticed. Rendezvous at Andrews at

Eighteen hundred. I called General Wittenfield for transport. Your orders will be waiting for you."

"Very well, sir," both officers responded and started to leave.

"By the way, General. What about Sherwyck?" Caine added.

"Talk to him upon return. If things pan out in Beirut, you may not even have to."

"Yes, sir."

In the hallway Colonel Jones turned to his friend. "You want me to find some appropriate get up for you? You know, something to help blend in at the bazaars, so you won't stand out as a former plantation owner lost in the desert?"

Caine responded with a broad smile. "Don't you forget your alligator shoes."

* * *

Colonel Caine drove back from the Pentagon along the George Washington Parkway towards Arlington. The sounds of the 600 horsepower rumbling engine, barely muffled for effect, and the sights of the contrasting fresh greenery around him absorbed his preoccupied mind. He glimpsed a portion of Georgetown across the Potomac as the treed canopy of the parkway parted near some grassy banks of the river and opened onto a vista of new condominiums rising on the other side.

His thoughts mellowed into an image of Laura Mitchell. He had offered to drive her to her townhouse in Georgetown. She asked if he could drop her off at her uncle's instead. She was all right, she said but would feel safer being with Uncle Jonas that night.

Colonel Caine sensed some continuing apprehension in her. At one point a sudden chill coursed through her body. He had turned on the Viper's heater.

He assured her it was a rare incident. She was a brave woman and he thanked her for helping him against the attackers. She insisted she had heard a woman's scream inside the building. He promised to check it out with their mutual friend Al Carruthers, as soon as possible.

When they reached her uncle's residence, she uttered a demure "thank you" and kissed his cheek. Their eyes locked for a moment and each knew they would see each other again. He waited until she was inside.

Caine felt an urge to cut across the Key Bridge to Georgetown, but figured he may not find her at her uncle's and he didn't know where she lived. He could easily find out, but there would be no time before reporting to Andrews Air Force Base. He contented himself with her smiling image, so familiar now after the harrowing incident that had welded their acquaintance.

Chapter 9

Ronald Stack, the Secretary of Defense, was riding in a limousine along Pennsylvania Avenue with the Director of the FBI. He had offered Richard Worthington a ride to their strategy session that day to coordinate plans for action on the Jeannie McConnell case and was taking him back to the Hoover Building.

"I still think this should be a police matter," the Secretary of Defense said, staring out the limousine's window. "We have much graver issues to handle in the Group."

Richard Worthington nodded slightly. He had heard the Secretary of Defense, but was preoccupied with another thought.

"Dick?" The Secretary asked turning to Worthington.

"I heard you, Ron. I was just thinking. If information from this Warlock contact is correct, we could really be in for high level blackmail. Imagine a family member of one of our highest officials being displayed on the internet with machetes at their throat. What would the President do? How would our people react? One of our roles in the Omega Group is successful negotiation in the most sensitive international hostage situations. This is way beyond local police work. We have criminals at war with governments. They don't have shock troops or tanks. They go for the underbelly. One by one. Things we treasure. People we treasure. What would we give up to get Jeannie back?"

"I don't know, Dick. What would we give up?" pondered the Secretary of Defense.

"I think that answers your question," the FBI Director replied. "We use our top resources to make sure we never face that kind of choice. The D.C. cops are good, but they have too many street shootings to deal with."

"You're right, Dick," Ronald Stack conceded with frustration. "I suppose my pitch to Congress for less vulnerable, higher altitude attack helicopters for the 'no man's land' mountains in Asia can wait," he recited with irony.

"We need to find her, Ron. That's all," the FBI Director said emphatically.

"Alive, I hope," the Secretary of Defense replied fervently.

Two blocks from FBI Headquarters their car stopped at a red light. Dust from a construction site was swirling around them at the intersection. Overhead a large crane had just hoisted a steel I-beam from a tractor trailer along the adjacent curb and was swinging it into place about four stories above them. Suddenly, for no apparent reason, the large eye bolt holding the hook that was attached to the braided steel cable holding the beam sheared in half with a bang and the half- ton beam came swooshing down as if propelled by a large, lazy slingshot.

It crashed at a perpendicular onto the roof of the limousine with a horrible grinding and popping sound, sending glass flying in all directions and freezing passersby into a momentary paralysis.

Seconds later there was disoriented movement in the limousine. FBI Director Worthington and two special agents gazed around in shocked bewilderment. The driver was hunched low, looking upward through the shattered space that had been the windshield, instinctively, but ineffectively, reaching for the revolver in his belt holster.

Ronald Stack, the Secretary of Defense, lay motionless, slumped backward where he sat. The force of the beam's collision had put an ugly V into the roof of the shiny black limousine. That part of the roof had collapsed onto Stack's head, snapping his neck and killing him instantly. The others were dazed, but barely scratched.

Secret Service and FBI agents were already swarming over the intersection, cordoned off by the Washington police, when General William Bradley learned of the accident. He quickly dispatched Colonel Garrison Jones to the scene. Jones presented his credentials and was let through the police lines. He approached the crumpled car with the steel beam embedded in it. The black limousine looked almost rakish with its crushed roof and carriage resting low over the tires, which were still inflated.

A crowd had filled the periphery of the intersection along the bright yellow tape barriers marking the restricted accident area.

Colonel Jones studied the car from bumper to bumper, trying to picture the positions of the men inside and imagining the beam whistling down on the car. It rested there, after the fact, almost jauntily, at a slight angle off parallel with the length of the limousine.

"They removed Secretary Stack a few minutes ago," a voice said from behind.

"How is he?" Jones asked.

"Not good, I'm afraid. He had no chance."

Colonel Jones turned around to see a well-groomed man in a crisp two piece suit talking to him. Jones recognized him as an FBI agent he had seen before.

"Colonel Garrison Jones," he said extending his hand.

"Jim Martin," he replied extending his. "Director Worthington and the three others were rushed to George Washington Hospital. They seemed okay."

"Very lucky," Jones said scrutinizing the wreck. "I can't see how no one else was killed or injured."

"Must have been some serious meeting," the agent speculated. "Two VIP's in the same limo."

"Aren't they all?" Jones said without sounding facetious.

"Looks like a freak accident," agent Martin speculated and turned his head upward. "We've got a couple of our men up there now.

You want to have a look?"

Colonel Jones followed the special agent into the skeleton of the new building.

They surveyed the scene from the fourth floor and joined in conversation with two workers in hard hats who were speaking with two other FBI men.

"We were liftin' this here beam, just like the others," a grimy, heavy-set construction worker was saying. "Dennis—that's the crane operator up there—he was liftin' it up this side here from the truck down there." The worker pointed out the action as he spoke. "Then he worked the beam around the corner, here, toward the front out there."

"He was liftin' nice and easy, like he always does," added the second worker, a younger man with a full beard. His tone seemed to be declaring that no blame can be placed on them.

"There was nothing unusual? No unusual sounds?" one of the investigators asked.

"No, nothin'," the younger worker declared with the other nodding agreement. "Suddenly, we just heard this ...Snap!"

"The cable holding the beam just snapped back like a whip," the heavy-set worker continued. "And then the beam just crashed down on top of the limo. That's it. There was nothin' anybody could do about it."

"Nobody up here was hurt?" Colonel Jones interjected.

"Naw," the worker assured. "But, I'll tell you, that snapping cable sure scared the living hell out of Dennis up there in his crane."

"Yeah!" the younger worker added exuberantly. "And it sure scared the living hell out of that bird that was sitting on the end of the beam."

Chapter 10

The President's advisers were seated in their customary places on several chairs and a settee waiting for him to enter with his signature phrase when confronted by a dilemma.

"Damn it!" he exclaimed entering. "If it's not one thing, it's another!"

"It always is, Mr. President," soothed his chief of staff, George Brandon with the usual clichéd, but very true response.

"He was just here on the McConnell matter," the President said.

"It was a tragic accident," affirmed Stanford Howard, the national security adviser. "A real freak accident."

"Ron was a good man. A real friend."

"Yes, sir," one of the aides replied.

"Why Stack, damn it? Poor Stack. You know how hard I had to fight to get him confirmed by Congress. With all the strategic changes going on today, our defense posture's one of the hottest issues going."

"Indeed, sir," said Paul McCallister, his senior adviser. "But we have excellent candidates to step in."

"Someone from your corporate world?" the President replied in frustration. "Ron was a good man, selfless. He'll be hard to replace. He was bright, dedicated, had a great grasp of history—that's rare nowadays. Helps keep us from stepping into strategic blunders all the time."

"Very true, sir," Brandon, the chief of staff, replied.

"They'll put any new appointee of mine through the ringer again," the President declared.

"This is all McConnell needs for another power play showdown in the Congress."

"The situation may be a little different now, Mr. President. What, with her daughter missing..." one of the aides offered.

"Speaker McConnell may be neutralized for now," the President said. "And I feel for her. But Everett Dunne, her counterpart on the Senate side, is just itching to grab back the White House."

"What about Philip Taylor, the Deputy Secretary?" Howard suggested. "He'd most likely get little flack."

"Anybody, but Taylor!" the President retorted. "He was foisted on me. Political expediency. It was a favor to Senator Dunne in exchange for letting some of my legislation go through. More effective caliber bullets for our troops in urban warfare. Remember?"

"I was meaning you could avoid a floor fight."

"I know what you mean, Stan. But any decision like that would mean I've capitulated to the Congress—to McConnell and Dunne. It's bad timing. The other party is the majority and they're already angling for the next election."

"Senator Dunne's own name has been floated for the presidency," Paul McCallister offered.

"Exactly! I can't boost him or his party by favoring his people and their policies."

"Yes, sir," an aide intoned.

"What about Ron? I need to call his family."

"We're arranging that, sir," replied the chief of staff. "Also, you were scheduled for the Country Music Command Performance tonight at Ford's Theater, but we're cancelling your presence in view of today's events."

"Of course," the President said in a preoccupied tone. "What about Michelle's daughter? What's new on that?"

"Everything is in play, sir," replied the national security adviser.

"It's too early to tell."

"What about Sherwyck? I need Victor in here. Did you set up that meeting? I want to pick his brain," the President declared.

"Or he pick yours," adviser Paul McCallister, the smooth, veteran Wall Street insider thought, but would not dare say.

Chapter 11

General Benjamin Starr was saddling his Appaloosa mare for his weekly ride along the lower reaches of the old Patowmack Canal. The Chairman of the Joint Chiefs of Staff kept his prized mount at the estate of a friend in the Virginia countryside south of Georgetown. General Starr was an expert horseman and had participated in more than one Olympics in his time, but as he rose in rank, he inevitably found that his military duties intervened with his consummate pastime.

His regular jaunt along wooded trails bordering the old historical canal was one of the few pleasures that he insisted upon. It invigorated his spirits and kept him physically fit, even though his robust appearance belied that. That morning, too, was dedicated first to his ride. The issue of the missing Speaker's daughter could wait until he returned later that afternoon. After all, there was only one real lead and it was being actively pursued. If any national catastrophe occurred that needed the personal attention of the Chairman of the Joint Chiefs, everyone knew where they could reach him.

"Damn overkill," he thought as he completed cinching the saddle on the restless mare. General Starr's saddlery was Western, while the gentry of the area would be found more typically in English tack and riding attire. His jeans, snakeskin cowboy boots and Stetson gave him an obvious Western air that reflected his individuality and confidence in his social and professional position. The General swung himself effortlessly into the saddle and with a nudge of his knees, signaled his mount out of the stable and onto a path leading along a road that eventually joined a trail leading into the National Park System.

His rhythmic and barely perceptible swaying back and forth in time with the Appaloosa's gait made them appear as one. The General figured that by the time the elite counter-terrorist group was fully mobilized for the mission, Jeannie would pop up somewhere and make everybody look foolish.

"We'll just do what we have to do, right girl?" he said spurring his horse and leaning forward to anticipate her response. The mount broke into a spirited gallop along the hardened dirt trail. Starr adjusted his Stetson more firmly on his forehead as the wind whistled in his ears.

He remembered the view of a predecessor, "Vinegar Joe" Stillwell—a personal hero, who coordinated efforts in the Burma Campaign against the Japanese in World War II. Horses were all "prance and fart" according to General Stillwell. Starr smiled musingly. "He didn't really know much about horses, did he girl?" he shouted at his galloping Appaloosa. "But he leaned over backwards for his men! Not afraid of his superiors! Eh, girl?" Not like some of his more recent colleagues, he thought. Generals advancing their careers and afraid to tell their Commander-in-Chief that he's up to his ears in horse shit. "Go, girl!"

General Starr gazed ahead along the trail to see if hikers were in his way. He saw nothing and heard only the rhythmic thundering of his mare's hooves on the ground. As they approached a gently curving bend, the General glanced quickly through trees on his left to see a glimpse of the trail ahead. He noticed a black flash dashing their way and heard a faint but distinct thundering along the ground.

"Another rider." General Starr lifted his head and reined his mount a little in case the other rider did not see them. As he did so, he noticed a shiny black stallion racing towards them out of the bend. It had a bridle and saddle, with stirrups flaying wildly on its sides as it thundered full speed towards them.

"A runaway!" the General blurted as his mare suddenly bolted to a stop and almost threw him over her neck. The Appaloosa neighed in fright and began to sidestep with the General pulling sharply on her reins and spurring her to respond. By then the black stallion was almost upon them. Its eyes were wide and showing white with nostrils flaring and ears pinned back in rage. The stallion slid to a sudden halt, kicking up dirt and pebbles in front of it. Just as suddenly it reared on its hind legs and flayed with its forelegs. The General's Appaloosa jumped sideways, lost its footing and stumbled in spite of General Starr's expert, but futile reaction.

Before he could clear his foot from his right stirrup the Appaloosa rolled onto her back as she screamed in fright and flayed her legs in the air to regain her equilibrium with the black stallion rearing up menacingly above her. By the time the mare's legs found firm footing she had rolled several times back and forth on her right side pinning and crushing General Starr beneath her full weight of 980 pounds.

As she rose in bleating panic, kicking the ground with her hind legs to regain her stance, she glanced her hoof on General Starr's forehead knocking off his Stetson, but the Chairman of the Joint Chiefs of Staff lay still and unconcerned. He was dead from the crushing weight of his favorite mare.

The intruding black stallion reared up several more times with raucous neighing as the Appaloosa tore back in full gallop along the trail. The stallion stood its ground, turned a full circle to survey its surroundings, sniffed around the inert body of General Starr, snorted several times, then galloped headlong from where it had come.

The terrified Appaloosa raced unerringly to its stable and darted for safety into its stall. The horse would be noticed only late that afternoon when a search for General Benjamin Starr, Chairman of the Joint Chiefs of Staff, would earnestly begin.

Chapter 12

A heavily laden C17ER Globemaster took off from Andrews Air Force Base late that evening bound for the American air base at Ramstein, Germany; headquarters of U.S. Air Forces in Europe. The giant cargo plane was carrying military supplies for the State of Israel in accordance with an ongoing treaty. This cargo held spare parts and electronic equipment for a fleet of F16 fighter jets that had been contracted several years earlier. Aboard, as the only passengers among a four-man crew, were Colonel Christopher Caine and Colonel Garrison Jones, the two American commandos dispatched by General Bradley to track source Warlock's lead on the terrorist abduction of Speaker McConnell's daughter.

Caine and Jones were settling in for the overnight flight, stowing their gear and making themselves comfortable on the sidewall seats attached to the fuselage. It was then that Caine noticed a bulky knapsack his fellow-officer was pushing under his feet.

"Something extra?" he asked.

"Oh, yeah!" Colonel Jones assured. "Something from the boys in the 'hood. The brass wants us to blend in with the crowd. But where we're goin's an armed camp."

"The brass wants no provocations," Caine said blankly.

"They'll get none from us," his friend responded. "But now, you do agree that nothin', but a satchel full of money, a small sidearm, and a happy smile are little comfort in no man's land?"

Caine peered at Jones with a look of resigned assent. "What've you got?"

Colonel Jones smiled at his fellow Colonel, satisfied that he was comfortable with the additional, but unauthorized equipment. He got up from his seat, pulled the backpack in front of Caine's feet, un-zipped it and leaned back with satisfaction onto one of the cargo crates lined end to end in the middle of the vast fuselage. Jones looked on as Colonel Caine peered inside. He pulled out two compact Uzi submachine pistols, and an MP5K and MP7A1—both armor piercing submachine pistols manufactured by the German firm HK for war and law enforcement.

"Where did you get these pieces?" Caine asked in an admiring tone.

"Two Beers," Jones replied.

"What? A cheap bet?"

"No, I got 'em from Two Beers."

"Someone's street code? A dealer?"

"No, that's his name. He's an Indian. Nez Perce."

"Okay, Arie," said Caine. "You're not going to leave me with that."

"You should come down to the 'hood more often."

"You should invite me more often."

"I got these from Two Beers. Not two or three blocks from Dupont Circle. "He's a 'go to' guy, kind of a *shaman*, a…"

"A gun dealer."

'Well, not in that sense," interjected Colonel Jones. "He buys guns from all kinds of sources, true, basically to get them off the streets. He's got great street 'cred."

"He's one of ours, I take it," Caine concluded, presuming he was undercover.

"He's on our side, if that's what you mean. He started off as a social activist for Native American rights; still is, actually. But he's spread into other areas. He grew up in Idaho, in typical Reservation squalor. He thought he'd do good there. He and some Indian Brothers applied for

social service funds from the State, as a needy minority. The State refused. Said: 'There aren't enough of you to be a minority'."

Colonel Caine nodded empathetically.

"Can you imagine that? 'There aren't enough of you to be a minority!' What the hell, then, *is* a minority?"

Caine nodded again with a raised eyebrow.

"Well, instead of turning militant, like some of the earlier Indian
activists, he moved to Washington. Closer to the seat of power, he
said. He moved into the 'hood and grew into a natural leader. Two
Beers has something about him. Some natural draw, even spiritual. A
lot of the folks who don't find satisfaction in the law or the church
pew find it through him."

"A friend of yours?"

"Very good friend."

"Well, then, I like this Two Beers already," Caine said. "How does
he pay for his 'collection'?"

"We sort of help him out."

"Omega's got a hand in this?"

"Not exactly. Not officially," Colonel Jones explained. "A lot of us
from around the area are interested in getting firepower off the
streets. Especially tracing where a lot of this military ordinance comes
from. Sometimes it leads to terrorist sources or drug cartels. That we
pass on to Omega. Regular hoodlums, we present to local police and
the ATF."

Caine nodded admiringly and looked again into the backpack. He
felt around and quickly recognized a hand grenade.

"There's four of them in there," Jones volunteered. "Two for you
and two for me. Just in case. And some C-four. You can never have
enough plastic explosive."

"Do you know something I don't know?" Colonel Caine said
dryly. "This is an inquiry trip. Not an invasion."

"As long as we're entering incognito, instead of a commercial flight
into Beirut International, I thought we might as well be prepared."

"I remember now why I wouldn't have anybody else as a team mate."

Colonel Jones smiled and sat back down next to Caine in the contoured seat.

"What about this Dr. Laura Mitchell?"

"She's a very interesting lady. A lovely lady."

"Tell her, when you see her," Jones prodded. "What I mean is the incident—the shoot-'em-up outside the Smithsonian. Any other details from her?"

"Not really. I'm afraid our relationship got off on a traumatic start."

"You said a couple of the dudes had Uzis. They were on perimeter. Three others accosted you. That doesn't seem like a usual mugging."

"I know."

"I'll check with some contacts in town."

"Your Indian friend might hear something."

"He might."

"Now that you bring it up, I do remember one of the scum muttering something when they were down," Caine reflected.

"So natural for a bully," Colonel Jones said dismissively.

"He blurted something like: 'We're doing what we're supposed to…'"

"Supposed to?" Jones asked with renewed interest. "Like—instructions from somebody?"

"I don't know. But they did seem organized, not random rovers. A van sped by and picked them up. I took a shot at it."

"Frustration? You know you could hit a passerby."

"I'd like to think I'm still a good shot."

"What about the two with the Uzis?"

"They were dead. Definitely."

"Well, like I said at the General's office. Someone felt the need to clear the area. No clues. No further investigation. More reason to think it's not a typical mugging."

"You know, Laura did mention she heard a scream coming out of the museum building," Caine offered.

"That would be extraordinary through those walls. Imagination, maybe? Especially after an adrenalin rush from a deadly ruckus."

"Maybe," Caine agreed. "It's more than an eventful week in Washington."

"Yeah, Jeannie McConnell, Secretary Stack..."

"Don't say: 'What next?' Arie. It's a cliché. Besides, something else *could* happen," Colonel Caine said wryly.

Each officer retreated into his own thoughts; their vital mission was just beginning. They stretched out in their seats and let the hum of the four gigantic turbofan engines lull them into needed sleep.

Chapter 13

The morning after the attack outside the museum, Laura Mitchell awoke with a start. The gaiety of the reception at the Old Castle was a blurred memory in a fitful night of dreams invaded by the vicious attack on her and her new acquaintance. She breathlessly blurted the story to her uncle over a hasty breakfast.

He listened absorbedly, eyes fixed on Laura's cereal bowl opposite him and nodding for emphasis, as if mentally piecing something together.

"I have to go to the museum."

"What do you plan to find?" Jonas Mitchell asked in a concerned tone.

"I don't know. Something. Anything," she replied urgently.

"Nervous energy isn't enough."

"What do you mean?" She arose from the kitchen table.

"Think first, Laura."

"I am. I'm calling Al Carruthers and having him meet me at the museum."

"And?"

"And. He's a curator. He knows his way around. I want him to show me what's in the east side of the building."

"Where you said you heard the scream?"

"Where I did hear the scream! Maybe Al knows something about the men the Colonel shot."

"Laura, please. This should be a police matter. At least wait until your new friend calls you or something."

"Don't worry, Uncle," she soothed coming up to him and kissing him on the cheek. "It's daytime. There's hundreds of tourists around. I'm just going to ask Alvin for a tour. I have to find out what I heard."

"You might even bump into your Colonel Caine?" he asked slyly.

"Uncle Jonas!" she said with her usual exasperation. "Besides, aren't you the one who wanted me to"—she mimicked for emphasis—"'see who takes more than a casual interest in the devil exhibit?'"

"That's something different," he said dismissively.

"Maybe it's not."

He hesitated. Her uncle knew he could not dissuade her. "Just call me, all right? I'll be at the Library."

"I will."

"Are you staying tonight?"

"Maybe. I'll see. I'll call you."

As soon as she left, Jonas cleared the table, gathered up his briefcase and deep in thought drove to the Library of Congress.

* * *

Alvin Carruthers stood at the grandiose colonnaded entrance of the neoclassic National Museum of Natural History. Large banners between the columns advertised exhibits and coming events. He spotted Laura hurrying up the terrace of wide stairs among gathering visitors waiting for the museum to open.

"That midnight blue outfit does wonders for you!" he exclaimed when she reached him breathing excitedly. "Lovely. But why the worried look on your face?"

"We were attacked here last night! A group of men!"

"Oh, my!" He raised his fingers to his lips, accentuating his reaction.

"You don't know?" she asked incredulously.

"Why no, I haven't heard a thing."

"It was right there around the corner." She pointed towards the side of the building. "Chris shot a couple of men."

"Oh?" he replied, still absorbing her words. "Well, I think he's done that before," he intoned slowly, regaining his composure. "But in a situation like this, he's the kind of man you want around."

"So I noticed."

"There's a lot of crime in Washington. But here? Outside the museum? This comes as a shock."

"Weren't the police here? Didn't they ask you anything? What did they say about the bodies?"

"I don't know, Laura. I'm sorry. I wish I knew more."

"You're a curator, aren't you? Aren't you supposed to know what's going on?"

"This is a vast organization, my dear. You know that," he said solicitously. "My office is way across the Mall in the Old Castle. If this happened last night, the news hasn't reached me yet. You know more than I do."

"I'm sorry, Al. I don't mean to press you," she replied, putting her hand on his shoulder. "I'm just sure after Chris fought off the muggers, I heard a woman shrieking inside the building."

He looked at her curiously.

"Through one of the windows on that side of the building." She pointed again towards the east wing.

"There *are* stray cats around. The first ones probably escaped from some haggard tourist families," he reasoned. "They rummage for leftovers from the cafeteria. And they yowl like heck in season."

"I know, I know," she said impatiently. "I heard that version last night."

"The main thing, Laura. Is that you're all right. I'll check with the police. Several jurisdictions overlap here, you know."

She hesitated, then asked offhandedly, "Did the Colonel call you this morning?"

"Why no, he didn't. I take it he didn't call you either."

She looked at him expectantly.

"Don't worry, dear. I know Chris. After such a dreadful night, I know he would have called. His work is very secretive, that much I know. I'm sure he'll get in touch with you as soon as he can."

Carruthers saw her face soften.

"Can you show me inside?"

"Sure. I can show you the exhibits. That's all there is, really."

They entered towards a large African bull elephant that was a signature display of the Rotunda. "Haven't you been here before?" he said as they walked.

"I have. But that's just it. I only saw exhibits," she explained. "Maybe you can show me what's behind them."

"If I can. Where do you want to start?" Carruthers swept his hand in a circle gesturing at exhibit halls radiating from the cavernous Rotunda, which was beginning to fill with visitors.

"How about that way?" she said pointing at the second floor atrium.

"The east wing. Minerology."

"Good," Laura replied, satisfied with her sense of orientation.

They rode an elevator to the second floor and walked towards the Gem Hall along an atrium with an open view of the Rotunda.

"This is one of eighteen exhibit halls in the museum," Carruthers explained as they entered a long hallway lined on both sides with glass cases. Subdued recessed lights shone on a vast array of gems and semi-precious stones. Visitors were entering behind them.

"Our gem and mineral collection is one of the most significant in the whole world." Carruthers said matter of factly. "We have fifteen thousand gems, and more than thirty-thousand meterorites in the collection."

Laura listened while noticing that the elaborate exhibit area had no windows to the outside.

They walked slowly along the displays as the curator dotingly pointed out particular exhibits. "We have the Bismarck Sapphire there. It's one of the world's largest at ninety-eight and a half carats. Then, The Napoleon Diamond Necklace given to his queen on the birth of their son. Together, that necklace has a total of two hundred seventy-five carats. The Hooker Emerald Brooch is a gorgeous piece at seventy-five carats," he said as he pointed. "It was from the belt buckle of a Turkish Sultan."

"You know this?"

"Of course," Carruthers sniffed.

Laura smiled. She was drawn into the dazzling, alluring displays and momentarily let her mind drift from her purpose by her friend's enthused elucidations, even though tag lines accompanied each exhibit.

"…the Smithsonian Canary Diamond, a beautiful amber hue radiating from a white diamond encrusted ring."

They turned a corner along the displays. "The hall is laid out in a rectangular. It guides the flow of visitors. We have several million people coming through here every year."

Laura figured they were now walking along an outside wall of the building. "Aren't there any windows around here?"

"They're at different levels. Some exhibits are between floors. This place is so cavernous, you can't count the number of floors by windows."

"I see," she replied thoughtfully.

"Over there," he continued, "is Napoleon's jeweled crown for Empress Marie Louise. Early eighteen-hundreds. It has nine-hundred fifty diamonds set in elaborate Persian turquoise. Next, the Star of Bombay—a stunning one hundred eighty-two carat sapphire from the actress Mary Pickford of early Hollywood. Then, of course, there is the Star of Asia Sapphire. It's the largest in the world at three hundred thirty carats."

"That's very interesting, Al. But you know, no matter how many carats other gems might have, diamonds still have some magic draw."

"Well. I guess that depends," Carruthers started.

"For example," Laura interposed. "What about there?" She pointed. "Those diamond earrings."

"Well. They are not the largest," Carruthers replied.

"But they're here on display."

"Yes. They're here on display," he said. "They are historically significant. They belonged to Marie Antoinette, the last, doomed Queen of France, consumed by the French Revolution. The story is that those earrings were taken from her when she was arrested. The royal family was trying to escape the revolutionary mob."

"Is that so?" Laura pondered as she peered at the tear dropped shapes lying on blue velvet and emanating dancing brilliance from within. "I'm doing some lectures on the French Revolution in my seminar."

"Then you can appreciate these," Carruthers said.

"Some researchers say the French Crown Jewels caused the bankruptcy of France and led to the French Revolution." Her gaze was still fixed on the earrings.

"That could well be," Carruthers replied. "You know, other jewels like rubies, sapphires, and emeralds were all the rage before cutters learned to bring out the brilliance in diamonds. That's why diamond adornments in earlier portraits of nobles look dark."

"I know," Laura replied. "The early cuts were minimal. They were called adamantine cuts—after a metal that didn't even exist."

Carruthers looked at her in admiration.

"It was a storied metal that was supposed to have mystical powers."

"I'm impressed."

"European royalty awoke to the brilliance of diamonds when cutters began to improve their methods. Kings started competing for diamonds and outdoing each other in about the Eighteenth Century."

"They did," Carruthers agreed. "And France lost, because the last French kings, particularly Louis the Sixteenth, raided the national treasury to buy and parade diamonds at the expense of his commoners and their well-being. That's why we have so much of the French Royal Collection in our displays. The revolutionaries appropriated the royal jewels and ended up selling them throughout Europe."

"And now they're here," Laura mused.

"And now they're here. Historical artifacts in 'the nation's attic'."

"But diamonds are still the queen of jewels. A girl's best friend."

"Yes, they are. And the few diamond cartels want to keep it that way. Actually just one, but I won't mention their name. They're big contributors to the museum, you know."

"Of course."

"Of course. They have the world monopoly. Diamonds are so plentiful they could be just another stone. But the cartel strictly controls their flow into the market. They own most of the diamond mines."

"So I heard," Laura said. "Actually, I'm writing a book on how diamonds came to be so prized among royalty—and how they shaped cataclysmic events. Louis the Sixteenth went into such a frenzy of buying for royal display—to mask his inadequacies—that he finally triggered the French Revolution, like you were saying."

"Will you autograph a copy for me?"

"I'll be delighted. As soon as I finish. You know, publish or perish."

"I know. But yours is a labor of love," he added. "It'll be good."

"Thanks. You're sweet. I could use the encouragement."

They had completed their stroll around the exhibit hall and found themselves in the atrium again, standing before a crowd of visitors filing into a smaller gallery centered in front of the u- shaped Gem Hall.

"And that, as you know, is the Hope Diamond Exhibit. It's probably the most famous diamond in the world. Not so much that it's the largest blue diamond known, but its history. The Gallery is named after Harry Winston, the jeweler who donated the Hope to the Smithsonian in Nineteen fifty-eight."

"Yes, I know," Laura said as she tried to gaze inside past the crowd of visitors. "Maybe you can show me after hours. It seems like such a rush of people."

"It always is."

"You have the key, don't you? You can come anytime."

"Well, yes, but it's a little more complicated. There's the security and alarms.

And there's also a little advertised fact about the Hope exhibit. It's in that tall rectangular enclosure of glass. It's three inches thick. The display is actually a specially designed safe. The diamond rests on an oval pedestal and the vault rotates every minute or so to give the viewers surrounding the display a good look. And you can see there are guards in the gallery."

"Okay, I'm with you so far," she said as she shifted the weight of her body, crossed her arms and leaned slightly to one side to get a better view past several people.

"Well," Carruthers continued in a softer voice and tilting his head towards hers, "After hours the display is lowered into a chamber under the floor. It disappears."

"Oh, I see." She tried visualizing the procedure. "So it's on a floor beneath us."

"Yes."

"And I presume that floor has windows."

"Yes. But the chamber is isolated'"

"Can we go there?"

"Well…no," he said.

"I mean the floor below us, not the chamber," Laura persisted.

"Oh, sure, we can do that, but it's just offices and work rooms. I know you couldn't have heard any screaming there. The only people around at night are security guards and the night shift cleaning crew."

He led the way to a stairwell. They descended a floor and came upon two pedestals with a red velvet rope blocking their way. A plaque stating "Restricted Area Employees Only" hung from the rope. The curator pushed a pedestal aside and continued along the marbled hall lined with several doors.

"What's past there?"

"Offices, work rooms, storage of artifacts not on display."

"Can we go through?"

"I would hesitate. You know there's a lot of construction going on. New exhibits, painting, remodeling. The union is very picky. Even if I try to open a door, they claim we're taking work away from them."

Laura smiled. "Oh, right! I've heard that before. It's a little empire over here."

"No, you should see them! The union people are very protective of their turf. I don't want any complaints filed."

"What about that big door there?" she asked pointing ahead. "It has no handle."

"That's the door leading to the chamber where the Hope Diamond is lowered after hours. It's right under the exhibit. Entrance is with a key card. Two, actually. Simultaneously."

"Oh, just like triggering a nuclear launch?" she said admiringly.

"What do you know about nuclear launches?"

"I saw it in the movies."

"Oh? Well the Hope *is* priceless, you know."

He turned to head back towards the stairway. "You know, the gem exhibit and particularly the Hope Diamond gallery were very special projects," the curator explained. "More than thirteen-million was poured into the Hope Diamond exhibit alone. Victor Sherwyck, the presidential adviser, was a major catalyst for the enhancements. He helped raise a lot of the money. You remember the Knowltons from last night? They donated a bundle. Sherwyck, also acted as an adviser to the board in the union contracts. This is a pet project of his."

They started up the stairs.

"The Hope Diamond is a magnet for tourists. In fact the east and west wings of the natural history museum were constructed in the early nineteen- sixties. I think it was to accommodate the increased visitations to the museum."

"For the Hope Diamond?" Laura ventured as they alighted the stairs.

"I'd like to think it was for a lot of interesting things," Carruthers said. "About a third of our new items on display were acquired after Nineteen fifty-eight. But I'm sure the diamond was a focal point. Construction of the wings started soon after we got it that year."

They reached the top of the stairs and drifted once more to the gallery displaying the Hope Diamond.

"The display seems such a draw," Laura observed.

"It is a dazzling diamond. The world's largest blue at forty-five and a half carats," Carruthers said in his expository tone. "The setting is surrounded by sixteen white diamonds, and it's suspended from a platinum chain that has another forty-six diamonds in it. The pendant is the same as when we received it."

"How is it blue?"

"There are traces of boron in it. That's what gives it the color. And interestingly enough, it radiates red phosphorescence under ultra violet light."

"And what gives it the curse?"

Carruthers broke into a mirthful laugh. "Come now!"

"But that's what draws the crowd, isn't it?" Laura asserted. "Look, it's in a gallery all by itself with people three deep waiting to see it up close."

"I must confess, Laura, that myth is a definite lure. But any bad luck to its owners was just coincidence."

"Marie Antoinette owned it once, and she lost her head."

"True," Carruthers agreed. "The Blue was part of the French Royal Treasury and the Queen may have worn it. But, as you said yourself, Royal hunger for diamonds in general helped precipitate the Revolution, not the blue diamond itself."

"How do you know?"

"Well," Carruthers smiled. "No one really knows."

"So, you like to let the mystery linger?"

Alvin Carruthers kept smiling.

"To bring in the crowds."

"Now, now, Laura. This is a museum, not a circus."

Laura smiled back.

"Anyway, I hope your concern is satisfied."

"I suppose," she replied tentatively.

"As long as I'm here, my dear, I'll ask around. Especially the shift supervisors. And I'll see what the police have to say about those men Chris shot."

"Thank you," she replied more assuredly. "I have to get back. I have a lecture this afternoon."

"I'll walk you to the elevator." He put his arm around her and escorted her down the hall. "You look lovely as ever," he said. "And don't worry; I'm sure everything is fine."

She smiled thanks.

When Laura entered the elevator, the curator blew her a kiss as the doors closed between them.

Inside stood a security guard who was repeatedly pushing a button, as if spurring the elevator to go faster. She stood next to him facing the door. Behind them was a man in workman's overalls.

"One please," she requested.

The guard looked at her with a blank stare, turned his head toward the panel and pushed the button.

She noticed the back of his neck. "I'm sorry, sir," she said spontaneously. "There's a blue smear on your neck. It might stain your collar."

The man quickly rubbed his left hand behind his ear, turned and glared at her. She looked back in sudden anxiety for support from the workman behind her. He was glaring too.

The door opened and Laura Mitchell hurried out.

Chapter 14

The huge, gray cargo carrier appeared out of a late morning mist in its final approach to Ramstein Air Base after an eight hour flight. Colonel Caine and Colonel Jones stayed aboard while the flight crew was rotated and the extended range Globemaster was replenished with nearly 36,000 gallons of fuel. Even though the plane was in the center of a major military air base, its 150,000 pounds of sophisticated and secret cargo was nevertheless closely guarded. Several hours later the four oversize turbofan engines lifted the Globemaster nimbly into the air for its final leg to Israel.

By mid-evening the two American officers were in the port city of Haifa in the sparsely furnished offices of General Itzhak Lovy of the Mossad — the Israeli intelligence and special operations service. Lovy operated out of a nondescript stucco building in the harbor area overlooking the Mediterranean Sea. Caine and Jones saw it as an obvious front; a convenient listening post in the midst of the port where the U.S. Sixth Fleet docked on a regular basis.

General Lovy paced back and forth in front of the two Americans and stroked his reddish curly hair with a lit cigarette between his fingers. His hawk-like, sun-sculptured face seemed locked in intensity. General Lovy was not sure of the exact nature of the American mission, because the abrupt and urgent request for assistance from Washington had not come through the usual channels. But his professional pride did not permit him to appear too curious.

Colonel Caine looked past the General through a large window and watched the brilliant sea reflecting golden, shimmering streamers from the setting sun. He glanced at his watch, then turned to Colonel Jones.

"We will be underway shortly, gentlemen," General Lovy said, reading Caine's glance at his fellow commando. After a thoughtful pause, General Lovy asked in spite of his apparent nonchalance: "Could it be that your mission is tied to the death of General Starr?"

Their quizzical look answered General Lovy's question.

"I'm sorry. I presumed you were aware," the Israeli intelligence officer said.

"General Benjamin Starr was found dead on a trail. It was late yesterday by your time."

"We were enroute here," Colonel Jones said evenly. "Minimal communications."

"Of course," General Lovy replied, less certain, now, of his conclusions about the nature of their mission.

"As we understand from our sources, General Starr's death has not been officially announced as of this time."—he paused—"There is an investigation underway. It appears there are some oddities involved."

The American officers looked at him expectantly, but said nothing.

"Yes. Witnesses in the area described a runaway horse with a strange hidebound saddle.

It terrified the General's mount, which fell and crushed him. No one knows where the horse came from and no one could locate it afterwards."

"Where did you hear this?" Caine asked.

"As I said, Colonel—our sources," General Lovy answered matter of factly.

"Odd, indeed," Colonel Caine muttered as he rose from his chair and walked to the window overlooking the Mediterranean. He stared outside for a minute that seemed longer in its silent intensity. Then he turned to the others in the room: "I suggest we get on with it."

By dusk they were aboard an Israeli patrol boat docked in the military area of Haifa's harbor. Its sleek gray lines were augmented and sometimes broken by the deck mounted machine guns, small cannon, torpedo tubes, and array of antennas and radar that jutted above the superstructure.

General Lovy filled them in on details of their rendezvous as the engines of the craft rumbled in readiness to depart. "Good luck!" he intoned. He firmly shook hands with the two commandos, hurried down the short gangway to the dock, turned and saluted them. Minutes later the patrol boat was lost from view and cutting its way northward through the swells of the Mediterranean towards Lebanon. Only the receding sound of the roaring engines betrayed the fact that it was out there somewhere in the embrace of the growing night.

Below decks the two operatives checked to make sure their gear was in order after it had been transferred into torpedo-like canisters for transportation under water. When they were finished they were escorted by a sailor into a cramped mess area amidships. Both accepted an offer of coffee and settled into leather cushioned bench seats surrounding a small table. Two steamy cups were brought before them.

"Is there anything else?" the seaman asked as his cue to leave.

"No, thanks," both replied.

When the sailor's footsteps had receded, Jones raised his head slightly after taking a cautious sip.

"That's a shame about General Starr."

"Two senior officials in two days," Caine said. "Freak accidents— if we take Lovy's word about Starr."

"No reason not to." Colonel Jones was ready to take another sip of his coffee, but set it back down. "Strange coincidence, though."

"What coincidence?"

"Well," General Lovy says a strange horse freaked out the Chairman's mount."

"So, he says," Caine responded fingering the rim of his cup.

"So, when that beam fell on Secretary Stack's limo, one of the workers made a comment about some bird perched on the end of it."

"Pecking away at the cable?" Caine said dismissively.

"No, no. That's just why I remember," Jones said, ignoring his partner's glibness. "It was an insignificant detail—but the worker noticed it—even in all the excitement."

"I could imagine the horse," Caine conceded. "But this bird business..."

"If the worker noticed it," Jones persisted, "it must have made some impression on him, even in the chaos of the moment."

Colonel Caine did not reply. He took a sip of his own coffee, then slowly lowered the cup. He stared vacantly into the mug cradled in his palms on the galley table. He swirled the cup and watched the dancing reflection of the overhead lamp in his coffee. It reminded him of the darting bird at the White House portico that had captured his attention two days earlier.

"Coincidence," he said idly.

"Hey man. Sorry!" Colonel Jones suddenly blurted. "We got serious work to do! That's why the old man, didn't inform us about Starr. Too much information dulls the senses." Controlled anxiety was beginning to show on his face.

"You are right, Colonel Jones!" Caine rose briskly from his bench with refocused determination.

"So, are you comin' in the ocean with me?"

"I am comin' in the ocean with you."

They checked their gear yet again, as time neared for them to depart the patrol boat. They would drift in the sea until the go-fast homed in on the transceiver attached to their raft. Colonel Jones fingered each item in the canisters as Colonel Caine read off a crumpled check list—clothes, money, documents. They each took extra care to see that the issued pistols and ammunition were intact. Then Jones removed the deadly contents of his backpack and divided them between the canisters.

"This makes me feel much better." He gingerly placed two of the submachine pistols, two grenades and the explosives into one of the canisters.

Caine smiled in tolerant acquiescence and packed his half of the additional weapons.

"Why two canisters?" the Captain of the Israeli patrol boat asked as he appeared with several crewmen. "Are they not too cumbersome for such a stealthy exercise?"

"Redundancy," both Americans offered in unison.

"Certainly," the Captain said. "I was not thinking."

"Gentlemen," he continued. "You will be disembarking soon. We will attach the containers with your supplies to a motorized skid that will float just below the surface on battery power. You can use it also to propel yourselves under water as you approach the shore. Stay in the raft unless you hear nearby vessels. You will recognize the sound of our cigarette boat, of course. Any other vessel, please presume is unfriendly"—the Captain paused for emphasis—"since we, ourselves, have no other craft in this area at this time. We have reached Lebanese waters. I suggest you move at your own pace on a bearing of zero-one-five degrees. This will take you towards shore. Your operatives will pick you up in a speed boat within an hour after we depart. For cover they will be acting as loud and carefree vacationers. This will help you also in location and identification."

The Captain paused. "Do you have any questions?"

"No questions," Colonel Caine replied.

"By the way, gentlemen. The Mediterranean is a well-tread sea. There are no creatures here that should cause you concern while you are in the water—or, at least we have never heard of any."

"Is this some kind of joke, Captain?" Jones declared.

"Merely reassurance, Colonel," the Captain replied with a prankish grin.

The officers were led to an area off the galley. They changed into wet suits and slipped on breathing tanks with a forty-five minute supply of compressed air.

Crewmen assisted them to the stern of the patrol boat where a ladder had been hung over the side. The raft and skid were already in the water, barely visible from the deck.

"We will be at this position for one half-hour at a time for the next two days," the Captain informed. "The speed boat will bring you back here. Good luck, gentlemen. You're going to Beirut at a particularly volatile time."

"You're always so encouraging, Captain," Colonel Jones said as he descended the ladder. "I hope your boat doesn't sink."

"For both our sakes," the Captain replied in the same vein of humor so prevalent among those operating in harm's way.

When they slipped into the raft, a crewman released the line that held it secure to the patrol boat and waved them good luck. Before they knew it the patrol boat had merged with the darkness and the night seemed to wrap tighter around them. The sound of the engines receded, then faded, replaced by the invisible, heavy rushing of ocean swells.

Caine clipped a lifeline onto his fellow-officer's utility belt and secured the other end to his own. "Just in case, Arie. So you don't get lost."

Jones didn't say anything, but busily looked at his compass, then peered through the darkness in a bearing toward shore.

"See anything?" Caine humored. He adjusted himself in the raft.

"We can't be that far from shore. The lights of Beirut ought to be somewhere along the horizon."

"Hold it!" Caine snapped. "Listen!"

Somewhere in the darkness a faint sound was fading in and out among the rushing of the sea.

"Is it our pickup?"

"I don't know. It's too faint."

"Do you hear any music, partying?"

"No. You?"

"Just engines fading in and out, but getting louder."

"Just engines," Caine affirmed.

"They're plying a grid pattern. Looking for something."

"That's not in the scenario."

"A Lebanese gunboat trailing the Israelis?" Colonel Jones ventured.

"They know their location. They wouldn't be zigzagging."

"Maybe it's time for a swim." Jones blew through his regulator to make sure his scuba tank was delivering air properly.

Caine blew through his own regulator in response then pulled his face mask into position. He grabbed the raft's leader line with one hand, leaned over the edge of the raft and flipped backwards into the water. Jones followed.

They held onto the leader line attached to the raft and quickly swam to the skid that was tethered behind it drifting slightly below the surface. Even though they wore wet suits, the initial plunge into the sea, coupled with the unknown, sent chills through their bodies. They turned full circle in the water to pinpoint where the engine sounds originated, but heard only repetitively louder and fainter revolutions.

"I don't hear any partying!" Caine rhythmically treaded with his fins and spat out the words with mouthfuls of water.

"A little reconnaissance!" Jones replied.

They quickly inserted their mouthpieces, turned on the skid's electric motor, released their leader line, and propelled themselves under water to a distance of thirty yards beyond their raft.

Within minutes a sleek silhouette appeared in outline against a faint contrast of the star lit horizon. Unerringly the craft pulled up next to their raft and several figures gathered at the gunwales.

Suddenly the two commandos felt the shock of an explosion. They cautiously broke the surface just in time to see their raft settle in shreds in the water and the wake of the blast coming their way. They instinctively dove to the submerged skid, and by practiced feel released the locking mechanism on their canisters. Caine pried his open against the pressure of the sea, groped for the nearest subma-chine pistol and before Jones could get a grip on his own, thrust it forward into his partners grasp. He groped again and felt the stock of an Uzi. Caine pulled it out and the canister clanked shut by the weight of the sea.

They broke surface again to get a bearing on the boat. Just then another explosion sent a shock wave through the water.

They signaled each other, submerged and hurried toward the boat. When they were within fifteen yards of the vessel they surfaced and tread water feverishly to be just high enough out of the water to aim their weapons in the direction of the large speedboat.

"Now!" Caine yelled with rage.

They opened fire and raked the boat back and forth with succes-sive bursts. Colonel Jones' armor piercing MP5K was especially deadly as its bullets tore through the gunwales and anything or anyone behind them.

They heard cries of shock and pain intermingled with foreign curses, followed by a splash in the sea. Then silence, except for the rumbling of the craft's engines.

Caine and Jones swam a wide circle around the boat holding their weapons just above the water. They approached the craft from the opposite side of where they had fired.

There was no sign of life.

Colonel Jones swam to the side of the boat while Caine indicated he would board from the stern. When they reached the craft, it seemed apparent they had shot whoever was on deck. Colonel Caine pulled himself onto the stern platform and leaned forward to investi-gate with his Uzi at the ready.

He saw two bloody bodies slumped on the port side of the cockpit along the bullet-riddled gunwales. They had been holding AK-47's. Several depth charges were strewn among the bodies. Another attacker must have fallen overboard, Caine reasoned by the earlier splash. He removed his fins, rolled into the cockpit from the short stern deck, and leaned over the starboard gunwale, motioning Jones aboard with his outstretched hand and holding the Uzi in the other, trained on the cabin in case someone came from below.

When Jones was aboard they removed their scuba gear and quickly checked the cramped cabin of the spartan, but powerful, forty foot speedboat, assuring themselves that everyone had been on deck, apparently to enjoy their handiwork.

"Well, it's a go-fast, all right—but the *wrong* go-fast!" Jones intoned, easing his weapon.

"Maybe it's the *right* go fast," Caine replied ominously. "Maybe we were set up."

The officers steadied themselves amid the two bodies crumpled in the rolling cockpit. The cruiser they neutralized bobbed idly in the swells. Their eyes fixed on each other with a look of chilling realization.

"We've got to keep going," Caine said determinedly.

"Yeah," Colonel Jones asserted. "Gotta' see if our contacts are waiting,"

"If they aren't ..."

"Someone around here set us up."

"If they are...."

"We were betrayed in Washington."

Chapter 15

The President was in his shirt sleeves at a desk in his study next to the Oval Office. He was leisurely scanning a number of wall-mounted television monitors tuned to twenty-four hour news broadcasts and political talk shows. Most were covering the death of his close friend and trusted Cabinet member, Ronald Stack, with emphasis on details of the freak accident that had claimed his life and updates on funeral arrangements.

Several commentators and political analysts were speculating on a replacement. More than one mentioned Philip Taylor, the Deputy Secretary of Defense. However, most agreed that his equivocal stand on space weaponry and new deployment of missiles in Europe was a major liability. One outspoken and popular commentator even ventured to say that Taylor's equivocation came from lack of knowledge and experience and that his current position as Deputy Secretary of Defense was a political sop for the President to maintain favor among a challenging Congressional leadership. He concluded that the good of the country in this particular international climate called for a strong, forceful replacement similar to Ronald Stack and that Philip Taylor, as a candidate, decent man that he was, would not serve the President or the country well at this critical juncture.

"I'll be damned if they're not right this time," the President muttered and reached for a cup of coffee from a silver serving tray on his desk. A large pot and several empty cups were on the tray.

He switched to some other stations with his free hand and caught one showing excerpts from the reception at the Smithsonian Institution for new members of NATO. He saw the Russian Ambassador posing with several prominent Washington socialites.

"Well, Igor, at least you showed up," the President thought. "Even though some of those new members stick in your throat. You might as well get used to it, because the list is going to grow."

A short clip showed a curator he didn't recognize pointing out an ethnographic display to some of the Smithsonian's board of trustees. The President smiled to himself, wondering why the ubiquitous Victor Sherwyck hadn't somehow managed to be in one of the shots. Items scrolled across the bottom of the screen: "Police search for leads in missing daughter of the Speaker of the House of Representatives....no indication whether foul play involved."

"It's foul play all right," the President muttered, entertaining the guilty thought that it would have been better if some local crime were involved over international terrorism. Less complication.

Several minutes later his secretary announced George Brandon, chief of staff.

"Send him in," the President replied while switching channels.

Brandon entered, nodding hello, pushed a chair to one side, so as not the block the President's view and sat down opposite him. He poured himself a cup of coffee from the pot on the desk and waited for a cue to speak.

"I see the funeral's to be at the Church of the Apostles," the President soon said. He muted the sound on the monitors.

"Yes, sir, I have the information. Services are to start at ten a.m."

George Brandon was at ease with his Chief Executive. He was in his forties, but looked older; the result of a dedicated and very active life in local and state politics that brought him to befriend the future President and eventually follow him into the White House as one of his most trusted advisers. He had the paunchy look of a man who spent most of his waking hours in and out of offices, totally consumed with his duties—which were, of course, formidable.

Those who ever had an occasion to deal with Brandon soon realized that his fleshy exterior hid a very quick and practical mind—not brilliant, but somehow tuned into the nuances of mainstream national thinking. He was deferential to his President without being sycophantic, protective, even loving, and for that reason was very demanding and oftentimes brusque with his own subordinates.

He held a note pad, but spoke from memory: "We had to change your schedule for Wednesday morning and cancel the afternoon appointments. The Pakistani foreign minister is set for Thursday at eleven; he's due at the funeral too. The meeting with Rudolf of the autoworkers' union is re-scheduled for Friday—we'll have an updated briefing for you by Thursday. The 4-H kids we left as is for Thursday at nine-thirty. It's a once-in-a-lifetime trip for them to Washington to see the President."

"Good, George. I'd hate to disappoint them. What about Victor?"

"Sherwyck? He should have been here by now," the chief of staff commented.

"Show him to the Cabinet Room when he arrives."

"Yes, sir."

"What about Michelle McConnell? Anything new on her daughter?"

"Nothing yet, sir. We should know something as soon as our operatives report from Beirut. General Bradley's informed us that his officers made contact with the Israeli Mossad and they transported them to the rendezvous site near Lebanese waters."

The President waited expectantly.

"And that's all we have so far, sir. The two officers should have made contact by now."

"Other developments?"

"No, sir. The terrorist angle is the only scenario we have. Nothing else pans out."

"That's all we've got?"

"That's all we've got."

"No one's taking credit for a kidnapping?"

"Not yet, sir."

"No announcements? No demands?"

"No, sir."

"That's a little strange, isn't it?"

"Well, sir, there's nothing predictable about these kinds of groups," Brandon attempted as an answer. "That's why our Omega operatives are following the only solid lead we have."

"That Warlock connection?"

"Yes, sir."

"What about Victor? Nothing from him? Wasn't he with her last?"

"So, we understand, Mr. President. No one's spoken with him."

"I will when he gets here. He's the only one I know who keeps the President waiting. If he wasn't a friend, I'd kick him you know where." The President was growing irritated.

"Yes, sir," the chief of staff concurred. "You and others in line behind you."

They both chuckled.

The intercom on the President's desk sounded with a mellow tone: "Mr. President. Mister McCallister is here. Shall I send him in?"

The President leaned towards his speaker phone. "Yes, Dottie, send him in."

"Mr. President," Paul McCallister acknowledged as he walked in. He strode to an armchair next to George Brandon's opposite the President.

"Coffee?" the President invited as he sat down.

"Thank you, sir."

McCallister looked fit and confident and had the bearing of a man who had achieved success in life and was recognized for it. His face still had the even tan of frequent winter visits to southern climates and his demeanor was authoritative. His New York brokerage firm was one of the top three in the nation and McCallister knew that his service in the White House would guarantee his position for as long as he wanted, even though he had to temporarily sacrifice salary, stock options, fringe benefits and other perquisites in the multi-millions of dollars.

Where Brandon had worked his way up with the President, McCallister had been called to service by him, because McCallister had an intricate private network of international contacts through his work with multi-national corporations. In fact, the President was confident—and for good reason—that McCallister's network rivaled that of the State Department itself.

"Mr. President," McCallister began. He adjusted his tie and suit jacket and leisurely poured himself a cup of coffee. "We did some preliminary investigation and have a list of potential replacements for Secretary Stack. Your apprehension about Philip Taylor, the Deputy Secretary, is well-founded."

"Is that your opinion, Paul? Or your favorite pundits?" the President retorted with a friendly laugh and pointed to the monitors.

"Well, sir, that's where the pundits get their information, isn't it? From us."

"It's a vicious circle," Brandon added jocularly. "Do we influence them or do they influence us?"

"Well, I'll tell you fella's," the President said more seriously. "More than once I've heard some news analyst give reasons for my actions that never entered my mind. But they sure sounded damn good—so I adopted their rationale."

The advisers looked at him with knowing approval.

"Tell me something the media hasn't said about Philip Taylor as the wrong choice."

"Well. Mr. President, not too much actually," McCallister started. "As you know, his public pronouncements prior to his present appointment would put you in a very awkward situation. If Taylor took over at Defense, the Russians would get mixed signals on our intentions. We're too far along on some real progress in arms control that would be good for our defensive posture and some real peace of mind; at least for a number of years to come. Taylor is definitely out."

McCallister turned his gaze to George Brandon, who nodded agreement, then turned his gaze back to the President.

"I know, Paul," the President declared. "That's what I was saying yesterday. So, let's get to the alternatives."

"We have four good possibilities," George Brandon said, looking towards McCallister.

"Former Senator Farris is probably the best choice," McCallister began.

"Let me decide that. Who else do you have?" the President interjected.

"Yes, sir," McCallister replied. "Besides James Farris, we have Evelyn Allport of the America Foundation. She's had a very good public profile over the last couple of years. Her strategic analyses are widely read. She was right on the money on the track that space weaponry would take. Very prophetic. I think she commands tremendous public trust."

"She's clean too," the chief of staff added.

"A rare quality, indeed," the President said with emphasis. "Nowadays that trait seems more valuable than talent."

"All four have very good backgrounds, Mr. President," George Brandon assured.

"They damn better," the President declared with growing intensity. "I want no more fiascos about Presidential appointments. It's as if the last couple of Administrations were jinxed or something. Scandals. Resignations. Financial frauds. High level crooks with tentacles reaching into the White House. I'll tell you again, gentlemen—" The President was now preaching. "There'll be none of that while I'm in the White House. I may not go down in history as the best President this nation has had, but I'll be damned if I'm ever accused of betraying the public trust."

Brandon and McCallister both shifted in their seats and looked at the President somberly.

"And no bimbos buzzing around members of my Administration."

"Certainly not, Mr. President," the chief of staff felt compelled to assure.

"It goes without saying, Mr. President." McCallister emphasized in a tone that suggested he was affronted at the very thought.

"I know, gentlemen, I know. I'm just re-emphasizing my convictions."

"Yes, sir," George Brandon continued. "William Cobb is another good choice. He's a retired general and his present position as U.S. Ambassador to the United Nations makes him a perfect blend of warrior and peacekeeper."

"That's a thought," the President replied and leaned back in his plush leather chair, as if some burden had just been lifted from him. "In fact, Cobb sounds very good. He's solid, intellectual, faithful to his uniform. But he was never a slave to the military mind. That's why I picked him for the United Nations. He's an excellent candidate, gentlemen." The President leaned forward again and rested his arms on his desk.

Both the chief of staff and senior presidential adviser smiled with satisfaction, pleased that they had screened at least one replacement for the Secretary of Defense who had immediately caught the President's interest.

"Who's the fourth?" the President asked. He arose from his chair and walked towards the window overlooking the Rose Garden.

"Gordon Thomas," McCallister and Brandon replied almost in unison as they rose from their own chairs and followed.

"Gordon Thomas. Yes. Possible. Thomas is a ranking member of the Senate Foreign Relations Committee. Jimmy Farris is a former Senator, good connections with military brass."

"They both have a good grasp of our defense needs," Paul McCallister offered.

"Certainly, Paul," the President replied. "I'd say they're a toss up. I guess the only advantage Thomas may have is that fatherly shock of white hair."

McCallister and Brandon both smiled at the President's remark.

The President unconsciously stroked his own snowy hair along his temple and thought to himself whether that wasn't the only visible reason why he, himself, was popular.

"Well, at least we all agree on Philip Taylor," the President said jovially. "He can't be the one, even though he would seem a natural choice as the next most senior official in the Defense Department."

"Would you like some other names, sir?" the chief of staff offered.

"No. I think any of these four are good choices. I'll let you know my decision. It's too bad we have to decide at all," the President said after a thoughtful pause. "Ron was an outstanding public servant. What a weird accident. It shouldn't have happened at all."

George Brandon and Paul McCallister nodded their heads in silent, solemn agreement.

The intercom sounded again. "Mr. President?"

"Yes, Dottie."

"Stanford Howard is here. He says he has some urgent news."

"Send him in." He turned to his chief of staff. "Some national security issue?"

"I don't know, Mr. President," Brandon replied. "It must be something new."

The national security adviser entered with a concerned look on his face. "Mr. President," Howard intoned as he walked towards the Chief Executive's desk, ignoring Brandon and McCallister. "General Starr of the Joint Chiefs is dead."

"What?" the President exclaimed.

Howard looked quickly to Brandon and McCallister.

"Apparently, something spooked his horse near the old Pawtomack Canal. We're still investigating."

"Investigating what?" the President demanded.

"Whether it was an accident or not."

"What the ff…?" the President caught his last word.

Chapter 16

Colonel Caine searched the two bodies lying in the cockpit of the bullet-riddled cruiser, while his fellow commando hauled in their tattered rubber raft. Colonel Jones ripped the transceiver from a special pocket inside the raft and threw it overboard.

"This one must be the chief," Caine said. "He's got a scrap of paper in his pocket. Coordinates scribbled on it."

"Our general location, no doubt," Jones replied as he took the wheel of the ocean going speedboat.

They heard splashing sounds to the port side and instinctively grabbed their weapons. Caine leaned over to see a body being jostled sporadically. "It's one of them. Something's chomping at him."

"Couldn't have happened to a nicer guy," Colonel Jones said coldly.

"What about his buddies?" Caine asked. "We should give them a decent burial at sea."

"It'll bring the sharks. Might keep them around here when we're in the water near shore."

"My thoughts exactly," Caine replied. He grabbed one of the bodies under the armpits, lifted it to the gunwale and shoved it overboard.

"Do you think they're devout militants?" Jones wondered.

"I don't see how 'assassin' and 'devout' go together," Caine grunted as he pushed the second body overboard.

Colonel Jones aimed the cruiser toward the Lebanese coast fifteen miles away, while Caine rigged the go fast with plastic explosives.

As dawn approached they were several miles off the escarpment rocks that jutted out from the northwest part of the city — a signature landmark of Beirut. Beyond them in lighted profile against the fading darkness stood the oceanfront buildings of the Raouche district along the Avenue du General DeGaulle.

"A brown Peugeot sedan's supposed to meet us at the escarpment overlooking Pigeon Rocks," Jones affirmed, as he cut the engines about one-half mile offshore.

"The ultimate test," Caine replied, heaving out the anchor. "Will they be waiting?" He opened the engine cowling in the rear and set a triggering device to detonate the explosives upon ignition.

The officers lowered their motorized skid into the water, put on their scuba gear and abandoned the cruiser. They signaled each other, adjusted their breathing devices, grabbed onto the skid and steered it just beneath the swells towards shore. Each surfaced several times to double check their bearings and within fifteen minutes the grinding of the skid on the bottom told them they were at the foot of the cliffs. They were at an overhang of the steep and jagged escarpment, out of view of several seaside patios and cafes overlooking the famous Pigeon Rocks.

Caine steered the skid north along the cliffs and into a secluded, narrow u-shaped grotto under an area of warehouses beyond the promenade overlooking Pigeon Rocks. They grounded the skid on the tiny strip of beach under the cliffs and quickly removed their scuba gear. Caine hurriedly emptied the canisters of their supplies, while Jones turned the underwater sled back towards the sea. He swam with it into deeper water then drove the skid into the bottom.

Back in the grotto, they quickly changed into the casual clothes provided and divided their deadly cargo into their back packs. Each thrust his military issue Beretta into his belt.

"How do I look?" Caine asked as he zipped up a maroon windbreaker over his pistol.

"Like an infiltrator dressed as a tourist," Jones replied. "What about the scuba gear?"

"Either way, we're not swimming. Let's bury it."

Caine looked along the steep cliffs and pointed to his left. "There's a path up that way." They climbed their way to the top and were soon on the boulevard in front of a large parking area and warehouse. They walked south along the boulevard and after a sharp hairpin turn found themselves in the area above Pigeon Rocks, joining light pedestrian traffic in the early morning hour. An old man on a donkey heavily laden with vegetables was riding nearby, while cars, trucks and a bus wended their way past him. The city was waking to a new day.

The two Americans approached the overlook, gazed at the ocean for a minute and spotted a speck offshore that was the cruiser they had rigged to explode. They looked back along the sidewalk, past several large buildings on the opposite side of the boulevard, towards their landing spot.

They focused on a sandy overlook where a brown Peugeot sedan was to meet them. Seeing nothing, they looked at each other and wordlessly concluded that their contacts must have been in on the plan to assassinate them.

"Looks like nobody's bothering to show up," Colonel Jones intoned. He turned his gaze back toward the sea and leaned on a railing.

Just as he said so, he saw a motorboat with four men aboard speeding through the swells in the direction of the cruiser. He tapped Caine who was still looking for the contact car.

"They're coming from the marina," Jones said.

"They're in a hurry," Caine observed. "A couple of 'em are sporting heavy weapons."

"Looking for their buddies."

The two Americans turned again towards their rendezvous spot when they noticed a dusty, orange Volvo station wagon driving in their direction. It passed them, made a u-turn on the divided boulevard, passed them again going in the opposite direction, then abruptly turned left onto the sandy overlook.

"Worth trying?" Jones asked.

"We have nothing else to do," Caine replied.

They walked cautiously towards the station wagon.

"Like expected, but it's not a Peugeot." Caine said as they hurried their step.

"It's not a man either," added Jones.

They approached the station wagon, one from each side.

"Pardon me, Miss," Jones asked in French from a respectable distance on the passenger side. "Can you tell us the way to the National Museum?"

The woman turned her head towards Jones. Long, raven black hair framed her beautiful olive features that appeared seasoned beyond her years.

"Please tell your friend to come around to your side," she replied in English. "You make me nervous."

Caine responded by slowly walking around the front of the car and stopping next to his partner.

"Can you tell us the way to the National Museum?" Jones repeated.

"Are you interested in the Mamluk Period?" she replied in a formal tone.

"No, the ancient idol from Byblos," Colonel Jones responded.

"The pre-historic one?"

"Paleolithic."

She eyed the two Americans sternly, throwing her glance from one to the other. "Get in. I'll drive you."

Caine and Jones nodded imperceptibly to each other, placed their backpacks onto the back seat and climbed into the station wagon.

She had to be their contact. She knew the countersigns and was overtly unaware that they were supposed to be dead. Otherwise she would not have bothered to meet them. The two Americans were increasingly certain that their betrayer had to be in Washington.

The woman started the car, spun the wheels a few feet in reverse, shifted to forward, made a sharp turn on the overlook, throwing up sand as she maneuvered, then darted back onto the boulevard heading south.

Just then a thunderous explosion resounded offshore. The woman jerked her head in the direction of the blast.

"Watch where you're driving," Colonel Jones said calmly from the back seat.

A knowing grin crossed her face.

Seabirds were suddenly in the air and people in the vicinity hurried to the overlook at Pigeon Rocks to see what happened. Passing cars pulled over to the sidewalk and people jumped out to stare offshore. In the distance was a large speedboat burning and settling into the water.

The woman weaved around several cars as she passed the promenade where passersby were gathering. A patrol boat and several other craft were already headed to the scene.

"Do you always advertise your arrival?" the woman probed as she maneuvered in traffic.

Neither officer answered.

She stared at Jones through the rear view mirror, her look presuming the two officers had something to do with it.

The woman drove another quarter mile southward then veered east from the oceanfront drive and onto the Boulevard Saeb-Salaam. They were headed into the center of Beirut towards the remnants of the battle line dividing Muslim west Beirut from Christian east Beirut along the Rue de Damas.

"We were expecting a man in a Peugeot," Jones eventually said looking at her through the rear view mirror.

"I am the man in the Peugeot," she replied coldly. "You arrived at a bad time. There was shelling here last night. There will probably be retaliation today. The man who was to pick you up was killed, unfortunately. The Peugeot was destroyed."

"I'm sorry," Jones said.

The woman showed no emotion. "We'll go as far as the Hippodrome then turn south at the green line and on to Colonel Hammad's headquarters."

"I see you still call it the green line, even after the war," Colonel Caine noted.

"It will always be so. It is peaceful for now. As you can see, the scars of the war remain on many buildings. The line of demarcation has shifted to the Old Airport Road—in Sunni and Shiite quarters. They are the most volatile at the moment."

"Too bad," Caine said.

"There is progress," the woman replied matter-of-factly. "Economic, cultural. Politics is the only uncertainty. The city is still a powder keg. Especially, after the assassinations."

"And Colonel Hammad is in the middle of it?" Caine asked.

"That is none of your business," she replied.

Her words were a reminder that the two Americans were not necessarily among friends. Colonel Jones straightened himself in the back seat and readjusted his Beretta in his belt.

"Why are you here to see him?"

"That's none of your business," Colonel Jones retorted.

She flashed her eyes at Jones through the rear view mirror, then stared ahead and drove on with a perceptible increase in speed.

Soon she pulled up to an intersection blockaded by sandbags and guarded by armed men dressed in casual civilian clothes. Decrepit stucco buildings lined the intersection and sand interspersed with litter covered the street. The woman said something to one of the guards behind a pile of sandbags and he motioned her through with a wave of his hand. Caine looked back at Jones who handed him his backpack.

After another half block the woman stopped the vehicle and climbed out. The two Americans followed her into an apartment building that looked condemned from the outside with soot stains and remnants of fires, shell holes, crumbling verandas, and broken windows.

They walked up two flights of stairs.

"I take it this is temporary," Colonel Caine said.

"Everything is temporary," she replied.

They approached several guards in a hallway. The woman cleared the officers through with a few words to the cautious men.

She pointed the Americans to a suite that looked like an explosive shell had hit it sometime recently. Pieces of wall and ceiling were lying about and broken furniture was arranged around what was left of the walls in the living room. A half dozen men were positioned throughout the apartment, each armed with pistols or AK-47 assault rifles. Two of them were in their very early teens.

A slim dark man with a trim mustache and goatee appeared in the remains of a glass doorway of the veranda. He was dressed in light gray slacks and a loose, print sportshirt. The only indication that he might be someone in authority was his wide military belt from which hung a holstered pistol. Caine noticed from the star on the butt that it was probably a Russian Tokarev. Two men in military fatigues armed with machine guns flanked him as he walked inside.

"Welcome, gentlemen," he said with exaggerated graciousness. "You are brave to come here. Perhaps even a little foolish, but that is your problem. Sit down, please."

The men sat down in the sofas and chairs lining the living room, while several guards positioned themselves around the room with weapons at the ready.

"An arduous journey such as yours requires routine supplies," he said eyeing the officers' bags. "So I can extend the courtesy of not searching you or confiscating your rucksacks," he said benevolently.

Colonel Caine nodded slightly in acknowledgment.

"I am Mustafa Ali Hammad."

"I'm Colonel Christopher Caine, U. S. Army on special assignment. This is Colonel Garrison Jones."

The militia leader scrutinized the two Americans. "I was told by our intermediaries that two American emissaries would come here with offers to finance our meager operations. Especially in this time of renewed violence. I take great risk in crossing lines of demarcation, currying favor with both sides." He paused and smiled. "No. Many sides. I curry favor with many sides. And each side is a potentially fatal risk: the Christians, the Muslims—Sunni and Shiite—the Druze, the Syrians, Israelis and Russians, the Americans, of course," he gestured in their direction. "Even the drug conduits from our Bekka Valley, although they are sometimes indistinguishable from the names I just mentioned. I am torn in all directions. My time is, therefore, very limited and very valuable. So I trust you will not disappoint me."

"Not for nothing," Colonel Jones retorted with a hint of indignation.

Hammad looked sternly at the Americans.

"We are seeking information on the whereabouts of a U.S. citizen," Caine interjected with deliberate vagueness. He paused for reaction, but noticed nothing. "We are told you may have information about this through your extensive networks," he flattered.

Hammad showed no sign of cognition. "Who is this person?"

"She is the daughter of the Speaker of our House of Representatives," Caine replied.

"Jeannette McConnell. We are told you can help us."

Hammad looked around at his men, then said with a dismissing smirk: "You want information about some woman? The daughter of a member of your Congress? How is that supposed to affect me? I am too busy with matters in my own humble surroundings to be concerned with such trifles."

"Our sources indicate that she may be in the Middle East," Colonel Jones said, ignoring Hammad's disclaimer.

"Miss McConnell disappeared more than a week ago," Colonel Caine continued. "From Washington. Certain intelligence sources tell us that she was abducted by"—he paused before saying "terrorists"—and said "operatives in this area."

"Are you suggesting?—" Hammad started.

"Not at all," Caine replied. "But we do know that nothing passes Mustafa Ali Hammad unnoticed in this region." He was hoping the flattery would tweak the militia leader's interest.

"We are authorized to pay handsomely for information," Jones interjected. "More than a king's ransom for Miss McConnell herself."

Hammad laughed. "A pity. I could use the money. I am benefactor to an entire people who depend on me. Unfortunately, you could offer me your entire treasury with no satisfaction."

Hammad turned to his men, then back to Caine and Jones: "Miss...Miss?"

"McConnell," Caine repeated.

Hammad turned back to his men and spoke in Arabic. They muttered shaking their heads.

"He's asking if they heard anything about a kidnapped American woman," Jones whispered to Caine.

"Whoever sent you was misinformed," the militia leader asserted. "A coup such as you describe would hardly have passed unnoticed in our circles. It is always unfortunate that my people are the handy scapegoat for problems you confront. You should look for your answers closer to home."

"Well, someone doesn't agree," Caine retorted. "Someone didn't want us to have this conversation. They tried to blow us out of the water last night." He looked for a clue in the militia leader's face.

"Forgive me if I am not moved," Hammad replied with sarcasm. "I have forgotten what it is to risk one's life. The rubble you see around you was an apartment last night. The men you see are what is left of fifteen who were with me here. Another shell might explode anytime. The fact that someone attacked you is of little interest to me."

"Your people were supposed to meet us with a go-fast," Colonel Jones declared.

"As you can see around you, we were delayed," Hammad said impatiently. "You may want to presume that this particular attack on our compound and your own episode may be connected—to upset our rendezvous. Or—" Hammad added with sarcastic emphasis: "So that your own operatives or Israeli intelligence can claim their usual 'mistaken identity'."

"Well, they weren't speaking English or Hebrew," Jones snapped.

"And just what were they speaking?"

"Strange words. They didn't sound Arabic," Jones continued. "One of them was jabbering something when we surprised them. 'Elo'..something, sounded like 'hello'."

"*Elohim, Elohim?*" Hammad intoned.

"Yes."

"Malek-taus!" Hammad declared.

"Malek-taus?" Colonel Caine repeated in a tone demanding explanation.

"Lucifer. The devil in remote places of Iraq," Mustafa Ali Hammad said with heightened interest. "And elsewhere."

Hammad rose from his tattered couch and walked towards the veranda. "There are people in this part of the world who worship the devil."

"I don't follow you," Caine answered.

"Of course not. I am talking about forces which you do not recognize exist. Forces that operate beyond the grasp of westerners. Beyond their infatuation with reason and technology."

"I think he means, we don't have *soul*," Colonel Jones said with a grin.

Hammad threw Jones a disdainful glance.

"One should look at this more seriously," he said. "There are evil forces in the desert. Forces that have caused turmoil throughout the ages. It is said that we are cursed to fight because of it; to destroy ourselves and our surroundings."

Hammad paused thoughtfully. "I—myself—am somewhat skeptical. Nevertheless, I do not venture into the desert at night."

He surveyed his gunmen around the room, seeing agreement in their wary eyes.

"Whoever tried to kill us last night was sure as hell evil enough," Colonel Caine declared. "But I doubt we can pull the devil into this one."

Mustafa Ali Hammad sighed and slowly shook his head. "You will never understand the forces about which I speak. You are too modern. However, I will thank you, nevertheless, for eliminating a formidable opponent of ours by your actions in the water."

One of the guards motioned him away from the veranda. Hammad continued as he returned to his couch. "Qaida operatives are trying to make incursions into Lebanon. Our government is tenuous enough to fall into any number of orbits. The latest fighting is to gain physical and political ascendancy in the various sectors of Beirut. Certain terrorists have taken on the cloak of that hapless Iraqi sect worshipping the devil. We are fighting them now. If you have eliminated any number of them, it is better for us."

"A cruiser exploded off the marina this morning," Caine said.

"We heard something," Hammad replied.

"You can add, maybe four more today, to whoever attacked us last night."

"It is written, then," Hammad replied with palpable relief. "The hydra is losing its heads. Now they have fewer agitators to lure supplicants."

Caine and his partner's concern was how such a deadly fringe group could know their top secret rendezvous point in the ocean.

Chapter 17

The President smiled to himself as he pictured Victor Sherwyck being escorted past the White House police, looking down his nose at them for deigning to check his credentials yet again, then striding into the White House along a familiar path, waving greetings to staffers like a lord surveying his domain.

The President rose from his chair, adjusted his tie, put on his suit jacket and strode out of his study to meet his friend and confidant. By the time the President walked into the Cabinet Room, Sherwyck was already there, being seated by a solicitous George Brandon who beckoned the President's guest to a chair along the center of the large, familiar conference table.

When he saw the President enter, Sherwyck immediately arose, a long welcoming smile crossing his angular face. His tall, thin frame, outlined by his tailored, dark pin-striped suit made him look commanding, even regal. Sherwyck was certainly beyond seventy. He had been around Washington since the time of President John F. Kennedy, but no one could really judge his true age. His face had a worldly appearance that gave no hint of time. The only noticeable suggestion of age was his shock of black hair streaked throughout with distinctive gray.

Sherwyck approached the doors of the Cabinet Room where the President had just entered and grandly stretched out his hands —

"Mr. President!" Sherwyck announced, slightly tilting his head.

"Victor!" the President responded and moved forward to greet his friend.

Sherwyck gripped the President's outstretched hand and shook it heartily. Then his face turned grave and he said solemnly: "I'm so sorry to hear about Ronald Stack. Such a senseless thing. Is there anything I can do?"

The President pulled his hand from Sherwyck's patronly grasp and continued into the room. He sat down at the end of the large conference table and motioned Sherwyck to the first chair on his right.

"Thanks, Victor. If anything, I'd like to bounce some names off you," the President replied as he settled into his chair. "Also, you know that the Chairman of the Joint Chiefs is dead."

"What?" Sherwyck said with a start. "I hadn't heard."

"Another freak accident. I don't know. It's being investigated. His horse rolled over him."

"That sounds so unfortunate," Sherwyck intoned. "What else could it be?"

"Well, it's a routine investigation. You know how it is about senior officials of the government. We have to check every angle."

"Yes, or course."

"Did you know him?" the President asked.

"Not as well as Ron. I met the General on a number of occasions."

"Well, it's too bad," the President declared. "This can't go on."

"I'm afraid, we can't control the fates, Mr. President."

"Don't say it with such anticipation, Victor," the President said teasingly. "We can't escape fate, but we don't need to go chasing after it."

Victor Sherwyck's response was an acknowledging stare.

"How was the Smithsonian? I tried to reach you."

"I'm sorry, sir," Sherwyck said in his deep, resonant tone. "Had I only known you wanted to see me," he continued solicitously, "I would have come immediately, of course. I found the most opportune time to catch Volotsyn, the Russian Ambassador—to follow up on issues of nuclear arms he had mentioned to you at the State Dinner the other day. I practically had to pull him away from some admiring socialites. You know this space weaponry business is a major hurdle in their thinking."

"I know," the President said absently. He wanted to broach the subject of the disappearance of Jeannie McConnell from that very State Dinner. He knew he had to do it in such a way as to avoid the inbred sense of superiority that Sherwyck would inevitably display— a sense of indispensability that Presidents before him had accepted— a sense of indispensability that had helped shape and control associations and friendships, including his own.

Sherwyck looked straight at the President, his eyes fixed on the Chief Executive's. They were dark and deep-set, but flared large and intense, hypnotic. The President almost flinched in response. Victor Sherwyck's commanding stare was at the same time demanding and reassuring. It was so penetrating as to suggest that he could see another's weaknesses and offer unspoken strength and guidance in return. It was, no doubt, a major reason why those entrusted with heavy burdens sought his counsel over the years.

The President looked away toward the door of the Cabinet Room, as if anxious why the steward had not arrived with brunch. He then turned back to Sherwyck, recomposed. He would ask about Jeannie later.

"I need to appoint a new Secretary of Defense soon, probably right after Ron's funeral. There are several good candidates under review."

"I'm sure any one of them would be excellent."

"Yes. But one of them has to be the best," the President emphasized. "Especially with those arms talks so close to a major breakthrough. We've been involved with this process since I took office. What? Three years ago, now? It's been such hell! Such minute scrutiny!"

"Ahh, but Mr. President, look where it has brought us. Look what it has done for the world. You have in your power the ability to guarantee that the world will never be destroyed by an act of nuclear war—or accidental blunder."

"You hope. That's why these talks can't fall apart," the President said urgently.

"There is absolutely no reason why they should," the President's friend replied and looked assuringly at him.

"Ron Stack had a knack with their negotiators. Even though he was tough, he had built up excellent rapport."

"It is not just one man on whom this process rests, sir."

"I know that. I know that, damn it!" The President rose and paced along the conference table. Then he turned to look at Sherwyck from a further vantage point. "I'm not sure how the Russians will read us with a new negotiator. They may retrench. We have to make sure we appoint the right person."

Sherwyck's eyes followed the President who returned to his chair and sat in thoughtful silence.

The chief of staff arrived accompanied by a steward who was rolling a chrome serving cart with brunch. George Brandon stood silently by while the steward efficiently laid out the china plates, linen napkins and silverware. He served each of them Eggs Benedict—the President first—with a choice of fruit juice and coffee, then stood back to see whether either would need something else. Brandon looked the President's way. A slight nod indicated everything was in order. Brandon, in turn, nodded to the steward who wheeled the cart out of the room, followed by the chief of staff who closed the door behind him.

The silence continued while the President and Victor Sherwyck sampled their food. After a tentative sampling, the President's guest spoke: "There is something else that burdens you. I've known you long enough to see."

"In my position everything's a burden, Victor."

"Certainly, Mr. President. But there is something else. Something besides the arms talks."

"Well, there is something." The President saw his opening. "It could put the arms talks on the back pages. It's potentially explosive. You know that Speaker McConnell's daughter has disappeared."

The President took a lingering sip of his coffee, studying his friend for reaction.

"I have heard. She hasn't been seen for some days. But is that real cause for concern? I also heard that she enjoys the company of the jet-setting *glitterati*."

The President was reassured by the answer. He sensed that Sherwyck's network did not include secret sources asserting abduction by terrorists.

"That's occurred to us, Victor. Her family's gotten calls in the past from Monaco, Tokyo, Paris. She's always called to say 'hello'—really to stay in touch with family."

"Of course," Sherwyck replied. "And this time she didn't."

"No, she didn't." The President sliced a generous serving from his plate and continued eating. It was as much to divert his attention from Sherwyck's penetrating stares as hunger.

"Well then, she either decided she's finally grown up, or..."

"Or something has happened to her," the President finished. "The reason I'm bringing this up—"

"Of course, Mr. President," Sherwyck interjected. "I understand. I was with her just so recently at the State Dinner here. What a charming young lady! I was her escort." Sherwyck anticipated the unasked question and continued: "In fact, Senator Dunne was with us when I dropped her off at home. I remember it was—"

"Please, Victor, don't embarrass me," the President interjected raising his hand. "You don't think for a minute that I—"

"No, no, Mr. President! Of course not! Of course not!"

The President pondered for a moment whether Senator Dunne could have inadvertently revealed to Sherwyck the Warlock connection; whether Sherwyck knew that Jeannie was the victim of terrorists. He dismissed the thought, rejecting the idea that the Chairman of the Senate Intelligence Committee would reveal top secret information to a friend, even as a boast over booze.

Any information to the public about a possible terrorist kidnapping would have to wait upon the return and debriefing of the Omega Group operatives from Beirut, the President thought.

"The reason I'm bringing it up, Victor, is the public uncertainty about Jeannie's disappearance. That's the problem. As you know, her mother opposes me in the Congress on the arms issue."

The President put down his silverware and looked seriously at Sherwyck.

"That could breed unspoken suspicion against the White House. Like as if we had something to do with it. The ultimate dirty trick to neutralize a political opponent. The Russians suddenly look clean and attractive and everybody leans to their position."

"Well, Mr. President, if I might say. Nobody can stop rumors or gossip, but we could still maintain the momentum of leadership by shifting our position, so the other side looks like they are catching up to our views. That way we still maintain the high ground in the battle of ideas and world opinion." Sherwyck now took a long, slow sip of his coffee, then looked at the President to see his reaction.

"We're doing everything possible to find her," the President said.

"I know," Mr. President. His friend tilted his head for emphasis. "And I have no doubt you will succeed."

The ring of confidence in Sherwyck's voice bolstered the President and reaffirmed his own belief that the Omega Group would find Jeannie.

"Meantime, the choice of a new Secretary of Defense who is right for this delicate stage of the arms limitation talks is critical," the presidential adviser said in a tone that made the obvious sound profound. "You have to neutralize Speaker McConnell's opposition on the arms issue. That way, Mr. President, you automatically eliminate any false rumors about even the remotest connection to Miss McConnell's disappearance."

"Victor! You know I can't look like I'm caving in to Speaker

McConnell and her Congressional supporters. Especially, when they have the glimmer of the White House in their eyes."

"Of course not, sir. But preemptive action with a lot of publicity creates momentum and people will forget what McConnell's position ever was."

The President pondered a moment.

"May I ask who you have in mind?"

The President reviewed the four names he and his advisers had discussed. "I also have some others in mind," he declared in case his confidant thought he was too limiting.

"You haven't reacted to the Philip Taylor issue?" Sherwyck's question was as careful as his sip of coffee.

"That's one I'm sure of, Victor. Philip Taylor's definitely not in consideration. Why?"

"You could make the wisest—the most canny move of all," Sherwyck said in a calculated, measured tone as he slowly lifted his face from his coffee cup and stared the President intently in the eyes.

The President stared back, suddenly uncomfortable over the familiar, patronizing look emanating from Sherwyck's deep, commanding countenance. "What do you mean, Victor?" The President looked toward one of the large windows in the Cabinet Room and then got up as if something caught his attention outside.

Sherwyck's stare followed the President. He waited until the Chief Executive turned again to face him from the window—from a farther, more comfortable distance.

"Mr. President!"

"Don't try to convince me otherwise, Victor. You of all people should know that Taylor would be a bad choice."

"But if you look at it this way, Mr. President," Sherwyck began. "The present posture of the Russians in world affairs—and on a tight rope in their own country—surrounded by militant states looking for nuclear weapons themselves—calls for a Secretary of Defense that would prove to be a brilliant strategist."

Sherwyck's tone was flattering. He smiled broadly. "Philip Taylor's position on space weaponry, open-minded as it is—would be just the kind of opening the Russians are looking for as a gesture of trust." He paused to let the thought sink into the pondering President. "Think of all the positive actions the Russians have taken in the recent past. We must get them to continue those actions by reciprocating with reductions of our own. If the news media harps that Taylor is ignorant or naïve about space weapons, that is immaterial. They have lost perspective in favor of rumors and titillation. They have turned open-mindedness into naiveté. Besides, Taylor is but one man. He is a mere spokesman in a grand scheme that will assure your place in history!"

The President's confidant opened his eyes wide. They enveloped with an all encompassing gaze that seemed in itself to promise a glorious destiny; inviting, lulling, assuring.

"Imagine, Mr. President, if a much more flexible Kremlin reduces its nuclear arms even further, because it sees flexibility and openness on our side. We will be that much more successful in keeping rogue or developing countries from seeking nuclear weapons. We will neutralize their common arguments that they have a right to nuclear arms, just because we do."

The President was listening carefully.

"And a cautious and even fearful world will support us wholeheartedly. But we and Russia must show the way. We must eliminate the argument that because we have nuclear arms, so can everybody else." Sherwyck stretched out his hand in a grand gesture. "And Mr. President, by choosing Philip Taylor, you not only eliminate loggerheads with Speaker McConnell on this issue, you squelch any whispered rumors about any connection with her daughter's disappearance, absurd as that is."

"But I'll look like I caved in to McConnell's view. This could hurt in the next election."

"Proceed like her view was yours all along. Her position will be left in the dust of your public relations offensive."

"I like it, Victor. I like it. I must say you are persuasive."

"Only when I speak the truth, Mr. President."

He looked thoughtfully at his friend and confidant, whose eyes were still fixed intently on the Chief Executive. The President returned to his chair and slowly sat down, measuring his sage adviser's argument.

"That's what I like about you, Victor. You're always so sure of everything. I am too, of course—in public. I'm expected to. But I have to admit I'm sometimes unsure in private. Aren't we all?"

"Not all of us, Mr. President."

The Chief Executive dismissed his friend's haughtiness. It was a tolerated trademark.

"What about the news media?"

"Even though much of the media editorialize that Taylor is not suitable, it will be those same editors who will smell blood when they know that they have, in fact, been the ones to sway you in making a critically wrong decision—in chiding you away from Taylor. It will have been their decision, not yours!" Sherwyck raised his voice for emphasis. "They will lose respect for you! How many times in the past have we seen this?"

The President nodded his head.

"Like it or not, sir," Sherwyck said softly after an interval, "the most important decision is the one which asserts your authority. Names and positions shift all the time. People forget what stand you took yesterday and don't care what stand you might take tomorrow. But they will remember determination or weakness. They will support strength, even if it is wrong and they will condemn weakness, even if it is right."

The President glanced back at Sherwyck. It was not so much his friend and adviser's words or logic that affected him. It was Sherwyck's demeanor, his fixed gaze, his commanding stare, his sense of assurance about the future. After several moments the President rose from his chair.

"Thank you for your time, Victor. I appreciate your views, as always."

Victor Sherwyck took his cue. He rose also and approached the President, extending his hand. "Thank you, Mr. President. Thank you for the wonderful brunch." He firmly shook the President's out-stretched hand and bowed his head slightly. "If there is anything more I can do, anytime." The formality of the surroundings belied their more familiar social relationship.

"I know, Victor, thank you. I appreciate it."

Sherwyck walked out of the Cabinet Room. His meal had been barely touched.

The President followed his friend part way until he saw him dis-appear past the door. He then turned to look out one of the imposing windows lining one side of the Cabinet Room. A large, black crow making a raucous noise in a branch of a tree near the window had caught his attention. No other birds were nearby, nor was there any evident reason for the crow's persistent cries.

"Now, there's something," the President murmured as he idly ob-served the bird's cackling. "First time I've seen a crow around the White House."

* * *

Meanwhile, Victor Sherwyck was returning past the guardhouse to his waiting limousine. One of the officers watched him pass then turned to his partner on watch inside the glassed checkpoint on Pennsylvania Avenue. "You know, Frank, there's something strange about that Sherwyck guy."

"Strange?" His partner's eyes were fixed on his computer screen where he was reviewing that day's schedule of appointments.

"Yeah, you ever notice that?"

"I've been here a long time, Steve." He made an entry into the com-puter. "I've seen a lot of people come through here from every corner of the world. 'Strange' is a relative term—you know what I mean?"

"I know what you mean, Frank. But there's just something about this guy." He watched Sherwyck climb into his limousine and the chauffer close the door behind him.

His fellow-officer studied the adjusted entries on the screen, then said in a preoccupied tone: "Your job's to guard the President's ass, not pick his friends."

As Sherwyck's limousine departed the White House grounds, the crow leapt with its flapping wings from the tree outside the Cabinet Room. It bounded along the roofline of the White House, ascended in a southerly direction towards the Washington Monument, then west along the reflecting pool above the Lincoln Memorial to the Potomac River, turning in a lazy loop southward along the river towards Sherwyck's estate near Alexandria, as if anticipating the route Sherwyck's limousine would take along the George Washington Memorial Parkway.

* * *

The President watched the large black bird for the few moments it was visible through the window, then returned to the Oval Office where he summoned his chief of staff and senior adviser. When they arrived he greeted them heartily: "Gentlemen! I've made my decision on the new Secretary of Defense. After giving it much considered thought and weighing all relevant factors, there can be only one choice—Philip Taylor!"

George Brandon and Paul McCallister looked dumbfounded at each other.

"It's settled, gentlemen. Have the Press Secretary prepare a statement for release after Ron's funeral."

When the two advisers left the Oval Office, Brandon reminded McCallister that the President had just met with Victor Sherwyck.

"It figures," McCallister intoned.

Chapter 18

Oleg Alekseev was the Second Secretary of the Russian Embassy in Washington, whose position was a thinly veiled cover for espionage. He was the ranking intelligence officer of the Federal Security Service, the successor to the KGB. As such, he was the first to receive news of the death of the American Secretary of Defense, Ronald Stack.

It was Alekseev's duty to analyze the situation and cable Moscow a rationale as to why the death occurred. Nothing in the Russian view was accidental. There had to be reasons behind everything — especially a case where a Cabinet officer in the American government, surrounded by security — dies in an accident. Something like that was hard to fathom. It was intrinsically suspicious, since accidents were a favored means of assassination in the former USSR.

Alekseev, dour looking in his ornate, wood-paneled office, seemed even more melancholic when he furrowed his brow, as an intelligence aide — a cultural attaché by title — described what happened at the Washington intersection when the steel beam fell on the Secretary's limousine.

"Hmm," was all he would say to indicate to the aide that he was listening. It gave him momentary mental distance to think of something else.

"What do you think, sir?" Yuri Menshikov ventured.

"Like we used to say," Alekseev eventually responded: "Whoever had to be eliminated—was eliminated."

He was trying to concentrate on rumors about the vanishing of the American Congresswoman's daughter. When Alekseev first heard of her disappearance, he had made a mental note of it, skeptical of its veracity. She was probably being extra discreet in some romantic, high level and most probably illicit liaison. Now, with these new developments, he thought twice.

His skepticism was heightened when he was informed that a day or two later the Chairman of the Joint Chiefs of Staff, U.S. General Benjamin Starr, was killed in a riding accident.

"Those horse trails are for rental nags," he thought. Alekseev knew the area. His spies had used it routinely as a dead drop for messages during the Soviet era. "No horse can gallop fast enough around there."

His inbred suspicions increased. He would have to see again the report on the American Secretary of Defense and the report on the missing Congresswoman's daughter. And he would have to find out more about the American General as soon as his sentinels reported.

But he did not trust his intelligence aide—the cultural attaché—to retrieve the reports for him. He would have to do it himself, unobtrusively. Alekseev did not want him or anyone else to make unnecessary and dangerous conclusions about the possible connection of certain events.

He did not know where his aide, Menshikov, stood in the ever changing corridors of power of the new Russian secret police. He smiled laconically. He did not know where he, himself, stood.

Oleg Alekseev only knew that he spent his career in the Soviet secret police with an obsession: an obsession on behalf of his wife, Natasha, who for decades was trying to find out what happened to her beloved older brother—Yuri Rudenko. Rudenko had disappeared on a secret mission somewhere in the Middle East when she was still a little girl. She had adored her older brother—little knowing who he was, but proud of his uniform and proud to see what apparent power he had over everyone around him. She matured in that elite circle of the Communist Party select—the *Nomenklatura*—and when she married Oleg Alekseev, whom she fell in love with at Moscow University, she urged that he join the KGB. He willingly did so, for he also knew where success in life lay in the Soviet Union.

Oleg Alekseev was a jaded man, but his love for his wife was real and stayed so over the years. His love for Natasha was the only constant in a tumultuous life of internal political intrigue. Her obsession over her brother, as it began to destroy her, became his obsession. He hoped by finding the answer to Rudenko's disappearance, he could save his beloved Natasha from creeping insanity.

In truth, there was little of real value that he saw in the system and in his career. He just knew that he was on top of a social pecking order and it was always others who were "enemies of the state." That was a major comfort to him over the years and a serious career accomplishment. Especially, when he saw many of his comrades putting each other in prison for various offenses, all capriciously defined.

They were all cannibals, indeed, but Alekseev prided himself in being a survivor, rising in the ranks—but carefully and not too ambitiously—for that itself could bring suspicion fueled by jealousy.

Another secret comfort Alekseev nurtured was his belief in God. He thought it could bring salvation in the godless system he served.

Natasha's words from years past perpetually haunted him. "Find out what happened to Yuri and I promise you, I'll believe in God too."

So it was, that the only true goal in his career, indeed, in his life, was to find out what happened to his brother-in-law, Major Yuri Rudenko. The only advantage that Oleg Alekseev had was that, he, himself, was in the KGB. He knew that if he made even the most innocent inquiries as a regular citizen of the Soviet Union, he would have been in Siberia long ago, most likely even dead.

His position allowed him to ferret out bits and pieces of information, but that quest, was itself strange and dangerous. Alekseev considered himself lucky to this day that the first time he inquired internally about Rudenko many years ago, he gave no indication of personal interest, but, as a junior officer, appeared to be relaying a request from a commissar. No one bothered or dared to ask who the commissar was. That innocent ploy saved his life, because any secret police colleagues who pursued any question linked to Rudenko's name or the nature of a particular mission into the Middle East—mysteriously disappeared. Naturally, any further inquiries suddenly ceased.

This never stopped Alekseev from his search for answers, it only intensified them. But it taught him to be redundantly sure that he was not connected to any of the initiatives. He also knew that his own sense of insularity could be illusory, especially since he was married to Rudenko's sister.

To this day he had not learned what happened to Major Yuri Rudenko and he never gave the slightest indication that he was interested. He did, however, gather over time fragments of information that there existed a fanatical faction within the inner circles of the KGB that was held in awe by all others. It had no titles and its members were found in all departments, adding to the fear that it was omnipresent and could reach everyone around it with sudden, silent efficiency that surpassed even the KGB organization's own reputation for ruthlessness.

Even as the Soviet system attempted reforms and abruptly collapsed, this nebulous inner circle within the KGB retained its fratricidal fanaticism. Rumors circulated and were embellished over the years that the circle was involved in some wild plan to take control of world powers in a very sudden and decisive way.

Rumors included the contention that the group was in league with some ancient devil cult; an odd observation in a system that was supposed to be atheistic, but a convenient folkloric metaphor to explain what was unexplainable.

Oleg Alekseev knew that there were certain factions left over from the old KGB that did not want to accept the reality of a new Russia, especially one groveling in the rubble of communism as it struggled for an elusive democracy.

"What would they do to turn back the clock?" he thought. "And how it heaven's name could they even think to accomplish it?"

Alekseev knew one thing for sure. After years of frustration he was resolved to seek answers outside the framework of his own government. He had picked Colonel Christopher Caine whom he had observed closely at a Smithsonian reception several nights earlier. The Colonel had displayed apparent interest in a devil exhibit from a Lithuanian museum. He might be receptive to what Alekseev might say, since it was quite incredulous for the average person to accept or comprehend.

He also knew that Colonel Caine was a member of some ultra-secret, extra- legal government action group called "Omega."

The Russian Embassy's eyes and ears had inexplicably lost track of Colonel Caine in the last several days, but it had maintained its surveillance of the young assistant professor who was with him at the Smithsonian's reception and had left in his company. Oleg Alekseev could not accept this as coincidence. She was of particular continuing interest to the Russian, because her uncle was one of the last covert combatants fighting the Soviet Union's occupation of Eastern Europe after World War II, had spent years of imprisonment in Siberia and now, in the United States, had become active again through his writings. As such he continued to be dangerous or useful, depending on the political winds. Since the uncle clearly idolized her, Alekseev saw the niece as a potential pawn in his quest.

She had to be followed.

Chapter 19

George Washington University was a short drive along Constitution Avenue from the National Museum of Natural History. The Campus was seven blocks west of the White House and just north of the U.S. Department of State in historic Foggy Bottom.

Laura Mitchell was formulating her lecture for that afternoon. She knew the material, but had to get the Smithsonian episode out of her mind—at least for now. She regretted the short time she had for preparation, arriving just in time to greet the students enrolled in her seminar.

The scowls of the two men in the museum elevator crossed her mind again and sent a visible shudder through her body.

"Are you all right, Dr. Mitchell?" a student next to her asked.

"Thanks, Abigail, I'm okay," she said softly.

Dr. Mitchell took her place among them in a rectangle of conference tables; her tailored pants suit the only indication that she was the professor among the twenty young men and women present.

"A funny thing happened on my way to class," she said as she settled in.

The students looked her way in anticipation.

She liked to present her material as an exploration, a common educational journey where she revealed facts and concepts and welcomed the students to arrive at sound conclusions based on readings she had assigned. She was not didactic—often theatrical—

and encouraged discussion and logical dissent, even if it meant modifying her own themes.

Therefore, she avoided PowerPoint presentations as too constraining and clichéd. Her well-heeled students were too sophisticated to follow along on a presentation in a darkened room reading from a screen instead of a book. That they can do on their own, she reasoned. As long as they were together, they would interact, if Dr. Laura Mitchell had anything to say about it. Her students (more likely their parents) were paying too much in tuition to accept mediocre presentations. And many of them would be following historical precedent of the prestigious university in the heart of Washington and go on to high level government and societal positions.

"I was at the Smithsonian this morning." She thought of recounting the episode of the two men in the elevator, maybe even the attack outside the museum the night before, thwarted by the new acquaintance she could not get out of her mind, but then thought better of it.

"I happened to see a pair of Marie Antoinette's diamond earrings," she said.

"Was she wearing them when they took off her head?" one of the men interjected to mixed laughter and groans from his classmates.

"Uhh, No, Mr. Powell, she wasn't. But, funny you should mention it. The story goes that they did let her hold her cherished Papillion to the end."

"Her dog?"

"Yes."

"They're a type of Spaniel," one of the women volunteered. "They were a favorite of the French Court. You know, the ones with the butterfly ears. My aunt shows them at the Westminster Dog Show."

"Very interesting, Amy," Dr. Mitchell replied. "Then you probably also know, there was another favorite breed at the French Court— the Pyrenean Mountain Dog."

"Yes," Amy Cabot replied. "The AKC calls it the Great Pyrenees here."

Some of the students looked around quizzically.

Amy noticed Dr. Mitchell's prodding gaze and continued. "It's a big, white sentry dog. It looks like a fluffy Labrador Retriever. They guarded flocks from wolves."

"Well," Dr. Mitchell intoned dramatically, "there was a particular dog around the Court at Versailles belonging to a country priest. The priest was Father Pierre Dumas, an itinerant monk. He was said to be a very charismatic and imposing figure. He was an occasional confessor to Queen Marie Antoinette. Father Dumas had a large, gray dog rumored at Court to be a cross between a Great Pyrenees and a wolf. The dog's name was 'Monsieur'. He was also rumored to be a familiar of the priest."

The looks on the faces of the students indicated surprise and keen interest.

"Whoa, that's a new one," blurted Corey Wynn, a divinity student.

"Marie Antoinette had many detractors and enemies," Dr. Mitchell replied. "Her reign is filled with intrigues and innuendos, much of them, unfortunately, fueled by her own behavior."

"What about this monk and his familiar?" the divinity student queried with skeptical interest. "A wizard or devil worshiper?"

"Apparently so, Corey. It's a good thing the Age of Enlightenment was taking hold in France and Europe generally at the time," Dr. Mitchell explained. "Otherwise, the likes of Father Dumas could well have been burned at the stake. The witchcraft hysteria was finally ebbing less than a hundred years before he came on the scene. But witchcraft in the late Eighteenth Century was still very prevalent."

"It still is today," another student announced.

Her classmates turned to her with bemused suspicion.

"I saw a program on public TV," she said defensively.

The peaked interest in the seminar class became palpable.

"What about this 'familiar' you mentioned?" asked another student.

"Corey. Would you like to explain?" Dr. Mitchell invited.

"A familiar is an attendant demon attached to a witch. They're like a servant. Familiars often took the shape of human beings, but typically they were animals: birds, cats, dogs, goats and the like. They're supposed to help bewitch enemies."

"The role of Father Dumas in the life of Marie Antoinette and the Court at Versailles prior to the French Revolution is vague and mysterious," Dr. Mitchell continued. "There is very little source material. And most that exists is in obscure writings and indirect references from letters related to other subjects."

"Why is that?" a student across from her asked, reflecting everyone's unspoken train of thought.

"For a number of reasons, Timothy, First, let's remember that the Catholic Church had overwhelming influence in France prior to the Revolution. That influence—including the power to tax, if you remember—is one of the causes of the Revolution itself. Second, the Church hierarchy identified with their noble peers, so there was underlying discrimination against rural clergy, even though they were in the same Church. A lowly country priest—a traveling monk—having influence at Court, was a major affront to church nobles. So they would try to downplay that kind of information. And this whole situation is exacerbated by the fact that Marie Antoinette for many years ostracized the Cardinal of France—the nobleman Louis de Rohan."

She looked around the seminar class, inviting explanation, since they had covered the influential relationship of the Church—the so called, First Estate—and the Monarchy.

Abigail Hitchcock, daughter of a network television producer, perfunctorily raised her hand and began: "Right. Louis Rene Eduoard de Rohan," she said proudly, remembering the full name, "came from a very noble lineage. But he was not liked at Court. He had been a diplomat to Austria. While there he criticized Marie's freewheeling lifestyle to the Austrian Queen, who happened to be Marie Antoinette's mother. This naturally enraged Marie."

"That's right, Abigail. So her ostracism was a monumental snub against Cardinal de Rohan, the highest clergyman of the Church in France, who was also known as a man about town—or about the Court, so to speak," the professor explained. "He wanted to become one of the King's ministers, like other officials of the Church already were—especially in financial affairs—but Marie Antoinette treated him as an outcast, because of his insulting criticisms to her mother. According to contemporary accounts, she didn't speak to the Cardinal for more than ten years."

"That's kind of a long time. It's very undiplomatic for a Queen." Tom Stuart, who was majoring in political science, ventured.

"True, Tom," Dr. Mitchell responded. "But it appears that her attitude was encouraged by Father Dumas. Unfortunately, it helped bring about her eventual downfall— the downfall of the Monarchy— and the bloody upheaval of the French Revolution."

"That sounds just like that weird monk Rasputin in the Court of Czar Nicholas and Alexandra just before the Russian Revolution in Nineteen- eighteen," Tom observed. "He was supposed to have had a lot of influence over events at the Russian Court leading to the Revolution. And no one really knows where he came from."

Laura Mitchell appeared preoccupied for a moment. "It is an eerie similarity, isn't it?" she finally said, "although more than a century apart. I'm glad you brought that up, Tom." She had been so absorbed in her research on revolutionary France, that she paid scant attention to the obvious parallel. She wondered if her uncle ever made any such connections in his conspiracy theories, but then concluded that the French monk was too obscure a figure to come to the attention of historians.

"How did this country priest manage to get into the Court at Versailles?" Abigail asked reflecting the obvious thoughts of the other students.

"No one really knows," Dr. Mitchell slowly replied. "But we do know that Marie Antoinette often said she longed for the simple life. You'll remember that she is depicted in several portraits dressed in muslin or peasant attire. That depiction itself caused animosity towards her as being improper for a queen. At some time she visited the countryside around Versailles and met Father Dumas, who evidently gained significant influence over her. She loved dogs and Monsieur, no doubt, drew her attention."

Dr. Mitchell related that a diary found by a member of the French Underground in a hidden vault exposed by a bombing during World War II, had belonged to one of Marie Antoinette's ladies in waiting. "It was kept in the family of one of the members of the Resistance. The diary has some telling passages."

She cast her eyes upward in thought, as if capturing the words. "I'm loosely quoting now—'the monk Dumas was capable of mysterious enchantment'—and—'his familiar named Monsieur kept everyone at bay when the priest was in the presence of the Queen.' A very typical entry is: 'Father Dumas once again imposed upon Her Royal Highness to change a decision advised by her ministers.' Or something close to that effect, since I'm going from memory."

The students were listening with rapt attention.

"Did you see the diary?"

"I did read parts of it. In fact I'm including it in some historical analysis on turning points in France's road to Revolution. You know, the research you're helping me with," she said with a sincere smile.

"I'm giving you full credit."

The students shared a friendly laugh.

Dr. Laura Mitchell glanced at the wall clock. "You know, I was going to cover something entirely different today, but Jimmy Powell's comment was a valid distraction."

Jimmy Powell smiled broadly, presuming her remark to be flirtatious.

"Marie Antoinette's diamonds are a fitting subject," she said. "And may, indeed, have contributed to her trip to the guillotine."

"Didn't she own the Hope Diamond?" Chelsea Smith asked.

"It was part of the Royal French Collection," Dr. Mitchell replied. "Actually, it was a larger version owned already by her husband's grandfather, Louis the Fifteenth, who presided over the virtual collapse of pre-revolutionary France. He had it set in his personalized design of the exalted Order of the Golden Fleece."

"Well, if France was collapsing around Louis the Fifteenth, couldn't it be because of the curse?" Miss Smith asked expectantly.

"It's a long-standing legend, Chelsea. It depends on if you believe in curses."

"We covered France's loss of India and Canada to the British in the Seven Years—slash—French and Indian War," offered one of the students.

"It was loss of empire to be sure," responded the professor, "but other countries lost empires also, didn't they?"

"Famine in France under Louis the Fifteenth," added another student. "Financial crisis."

"Again, same things have happened in other countries," she replied, enjoying the exchange as an educational exercise. "But we can't say it's because of a curse."

"Maybe this one had more of a focus," ventured Corey the divinity student. "Maybe it was meant to be cumulative."

"I'm not sure I follow you," replied Dr. Mitchell.

"The diamond was still in the collection of the French Monarchy when Louis the Sixteenth and Marie Antoinette took over and things got even worse, ending in the Revolution."

"Well, I guess you could interpret it that way," the professor replied after a thoughtful pause.

"And you did say that this Father Dumas was seen as some sort of witch or warlock who had influence at Court through Queen Marie Antoinette."

"It does seem to have some kind of crazy logic, doesn't it?" Dr. Mitchell replied.

"Maybe the French Monarchy was cursed because of the diamond?" ventured Chelsea Smith.

"Are we drifting into superstitions here? Or is this a history seminar?" the professor chided playfully.

"Don't some historians write that she got a raw deal?" asked Jerome Butler, a journalism student sitting to her right.

"They do, indeed," Dr. Mitchell replied as she shifted in her seat towards the student. "In part from a series of inflammatory pamphlets circulated from England by a conniving swindler, whose diamond caper helped trigger the French Revolution."

Dr. Mitchell paused, as much for dramatic effect, as to formulate her thoughts. Abigail Hitchcock, who was next to her, spontaneously offered her an unopened bottle of water.

"Thanks," she said accepting the gesture. "Now, this is not for credit," the professor announced jovially, as she twisted the cap and took a sip to the grinning of the other students.

"The Affair of the Diamond Necklace," she continued, "may have fatally sealed the animosity of the French people towards Marie Antoinette."

Dr. Mitchell took another sip of water and related that a woman calling herself Jeanne de Saint Remy de Valois weaseled her way into the Court at Versailles through a lover. She was the wife of a self-styled Count, Nicholas de la Motte. She was supposedly of noble birth, but her family had fallen on hard times. She longed to recapture the courtly life she felt she deserved.

Jeanne La Motte traded on her beauty and guile and eventually became the mistress of Cardinal de Rohan. The Cardinal believed that through her he could regain the Queen's favor, because Madame la Motte told the Cardinal that she, herself, was a lover of Marie Antoinette and would persuade the Queen to end his ostracism.

"The swindler hired a look-alike prostitute to pretend to be the Queen and rendezvous with the Cardinal in the moonlight at one of the gardens at Versailles. In a brief encounter the imposter declared through a veiled face that all was forgiven," Dr. Mitchell related.

"Cardinal de Rohan fell for the ruse, most probably because he was so desperate to get back in the good graces of the Queen and an appointment as minister—even prime minister. For Jeanne La Motte, the swindler, this was just the setup," Dr. Mitchell said conspiratorially.

Jeanne la Motte now told Cardinal de Rohan that Marie Antoinette was interested in having him procure for her the elaborate diamond necklace that her husband's grandfather—Louis the Fifteenth—had commissioned for his official mistress, Marie-Jeanette du Barry.

"Unfortunately, the King had died of smallpox and his mistress Madame du Barry was banished. Meanwhile, the jeweler was stuck with the most stunning creation of diamond jewelry and facing certain bankruptcy."

"It had cost one hundred million dollars in today's currency," Dr. Mitchell said.

"A hundred million dollars?" several students repeated in awe.

"A hundred million," Dr. Mitchell emphasized. "The necklace—the word does not do justice to the piece—was more like a cascade—it had nearly three thousand carats and was the most elaborate piece of jewelry ever created up to that time. All of European royalty was aware of it and the jeweler had even offered it for sale in the various Courts of Europe. There is an image on-line and in history books under various headings related to the French Revolution."

Laura remembered her conversation with Alvin Carruthers that morning at the museum. She repeated the details, smiling to herself at how conveniently it fit into her train of thought.

"Cutters were perfecting techniques of how to bring out the intrinsic brilliance of diamonds. Consequently diamonds became valued more than rubies and other gemstones."

The nobility now competed with each other for their possession, Dr. Mitchell explained. Commissioning the 3,000 carat necklace was a foolish act by Louis the Fifteenth to dampen his image as an ineffectual monarch. He spent lavishly to boost his image among his regal counterparts in other countries, even as France sank deeper into economic and political ruin.

As Laura remembered the exchange with Carruthers, she was in the museum again, the two glowering employees in the elevator, the deadly attack fended off by Christopher Caine. She visibly shook the thought away.

"Are you sure you're okay?" Abigail asked again.

"It's nothing, really. I just felt a chill going through me. I hope it's not a cold coming on." She would have to speak with Al again, she thought. "Where was I?"

"The swindler asking Cardinal de Rohan to get the necklace for Marie Antoinette," Abigail answered.

"Yes. Well, as it happens, the real Marie Antoinette had refused the necklace when her husband—Louis the Sixteenth—had actually offered to buy it for her much earlier. She is recorded as stating that the piece was much too expensive, and that the money would be better spent to buy a Man-of-War for the navy. Now, doesn't this go against the grain," she said with emphasis, "that Marie Antoinette was a frivolous spendthrift?"

Dr. Mitchell went on to relate that the swindler told Cardinal de Rohan that the Queen wanted him to secretly buy the necklace for her with la Motte as the go-between, because it would be unseemly to buy such extravagant jewelry at a time of financial crisis in France. La Motte showed the Cardinal a note with Marie Antoinette's forged signature indicating she wanted the necklace. The jeweler could then directly bill the Queen.

Cardinal de Rohan did procure the necklace and gave it to Jeanne la Motte to present to Marie Antoinette. Instead, the greedy schemer immediately had her husband break up the necklace into its component diamonds and abscond with them to England. They were eventually sold piece by piece and provided a comfortable life for the felonious social climber.

Meanwhile, Cardinal de Rohan was puzzled that Marie Antoinette kept ignoring him at Court and soon enough the Palace erupted in a fury when the jeweler presented her a bill for the necklace.

Polite, knowing laughter punctuated Dr. Mitchell's remark.

"Various high ranking nobles and church officials urgently appealed that the affair be settled quietly—either through the Palace itself or the Vatican. They argued that the Cardinal was duped, but was not guilty of any crime. And he was much admired by the people. They said a public trial would totally undermine the monarchy."

"Now here is the fateful turning point that likely sealed her doom: Marie Antoinette might have been persuaded to settle the affair quietly and not cause embarrassment to the Cardinal of France and the Church," the professor emphasized. "However, her confessor, the country cleric, Father Pierre Dumas, insisted that she not bend to the pleas of the nobility and the Church. He stressed that the fallacy of a lesbian affair with Jeanne la Motte and her honor as an innocent victim were at stake. Consequently, Marie Antoinette remained adamant that a public trial be held."

"The trial, conducted by the Parliament—the nobles of the Second Estate—was one of the most sensational in France and became a focal point in all of Europe," Dr. Mitchell continued. "The Cardinal was found innocent to the cheers of the people, while Marie Antoinette's reputation never recovered."

The professor looked to her students in the seminar room, but no questions or comments interrupted their absorbed attention.

She went on that most historians concluded that Marie Antoinette had nothing to do with the necklace affair, that Cardinal de Rohan was deceived, and that Jeanne la Motte and her husband were guilty of stupendous fraud and injury to the Crown. Still a majority of the French citizenry continued to believe that the Queen deliberately used the la Mottes to get at Cardinal de Rohan, whom Marie Antoinette publicly despised. The people also presumed the Queen must have been complicit in something, since the Cardinal was found innocent. Not only did Marie Antoinette's popularity keep sinking, but so did the role of the Monarchy itself."

"Jeanne la Motte was whipped, branded and jailed. She later escaped—most probably with inside help—and fled to England," Dr. Mitchell related. "There, living comfortably from sales of the disassembled necklace, she wrote her memoirs and continued publishing bitter, vindictive pamphlets against Marie Antoinette, which were enormously popular throughout Europe. Jeanne la Motte had become a poster child for the spirit of rebellion in France."

The professor took another sip of water, waiting for any reaction. The students kept listening, waiting.

"Maybe the events leading to the storming of the Bastille in Seventeen eighty-nine could have been avoided had Marie Antoinette agreed to settle the necklace affair quietly. The role of the monk Pierre Dumas in goading the Queen to have a public trial may be momentous. The legacy of the trial leads to the downfall and execution of Marie Antoinette and her husband, Louis the Sixteenth, in the fever of The French Revolution."

"Just like Grigori Rasputin," Tom Stuart repeated in a climactic tone.

"So, what happened to the monk?" Amy Cabot asked.

"After the trial he was never seen again," Dr. Mitchell replied. "The mysterious Father Dumas disappears from the historical record. But his dog Monsieur—his so-called familiar—was spotted running with a pack of wolves in the wooded forests south of Versailles during the Reign of Terror."

Dr. Mitchell paused, satisfied with the wide-eyed attention of the students.

"What happened to the Hope Diamond?" Chelsea Smith finally asked, breaking the reflective silence in the room.

"The jewels from the Royal Treasury were looted during the Revolution," Dr. Mitchell replied. "They were sold all over Europe. The so-called French Blue went through a number of hands and eventually reappeared as the Hope Diamond in the eighteen-thirties after Henry Hope, one of its later owners."

"I don't know the provenance, but many of the French Crown jewels eventually found their way into museums, including the

Smithsonian down the street. The Hope Diamond was donated there in Nineteen fifty-eight."

Some in class nodded their heads, indicating they had seen the exhibit.

"Next time we'll analyze what we missed today," Dr. Mitchell announced as the period ended. "The Third Estate—or the rest of France after the clergy and nobility—how the cries of 'Liberty, Equality, Fraternity' led to the Dictator Napoleon Bonaparte."

* * *

Following brief conversations with several students who had lingered after class, Laura Mitchell left Phillips Hall preoccupied with the recent menacing events outside the Museum of Natural History. Images of her walking tour with Alvin Carruthers, Marie Antoinette's diamond earrings, the Hope Diamond on its pedestal surrounded by onlookers two and three deep, and the penetrating scowls of the two men in the elevator raced through her mind faster than her hurried steps along H Street by the signature Kogan Plaza towards the parking lot on the next corner.

Following the assault outside the museum the previous night, she had become acutely aware of her surroundings. She glanced imperceptibly around her and noticed a young man in a suit jacket. He appeared out of place among the casually dressed students in the Plaza. His close cropped hair and prominent cheek bones suggested a Muscovite. She chided herself for being too paranoid, but wished impulsively that Christopher Caine could be with her.

She would take karate lessons for sure.

Chapter 20

The distinct sound of an incoming shell whistled through the midday sky in Beirut. Colonel Christopher Caine and Colonel Garrison Jones tensed in anticipation as the dull thud of an explosion emanated from the direction of a contested street two blocks away. Mustafa Ali Hammad's gunmen glanced around for scarce cover as sporadic machine gun fire followed the blast.

Hammad motioned to his men and bolted out of the building in what appeared to be a practiced routine. Caine and Jones followed them. They spilled into the street and dashed for available cover in doorways and behind rubble along the sidewalk. The two American commandos, together with Hammad and one of his men, ducked behind a portion of a wall collapsed from a previous battle.

"Our headquarters were pinpointed yesterday!" Hammad shouted. "It had been calm for some time! In the past two days, we have seen unusual action!"

Machine gun fire punctuated his words and several of his men returned fire in the general direction of the next street. Seconds later another shell screamed in their direction. This time the explosion was louder and the men could see dust and debris from the side of an apartment building across the block.

"Perhaps, someone is mad that you blew up their cruiser!" Hammad exclaimed with a sardonic look at Colonel Caine. "Maybe you killed some leader! They are scarce lately, praise Allah!"

"I'm glad we could help!" Caine replied in the same vein.

"You see, Colonel! We have enough to occupy us here! We have no need to invite the wrath of the United States over a kidnapping, let alone to host targets of our adversaries—like yourselves!"

"You do this pretty well without us!" Caine retorted.

"The shells are from the other side of the Old Airport Road!" Hammad shouted changing the subject. "The machine guns mean someone has crossed over. They're trying to establish a foothold on this side again! If we outflank them and leave, they will entrench themselves! We must either chase them back across the line or eliminate them!"

A third shell whistled above—much louder this time—and exploded in the side of the apartment they had just left. A shower of debris fell around them and dry dust obscured their sight of the street. They heaved between coughs searching for pure air.

An eerie silence followed the explosion, filled some moments later by the incessant barking of a dog which was soon joined by the nervous bark of another unseen dog.

Mustafa Ali Hammad motioned to several of his men to provide cover. As they sprayed the next block with automatic weapons fire, Hammad ran to the side of the next building along which was a narrow alley. It afforded a view of the street that ended at the "green line."

He looked back at Colonel Caine and Colonel Jones and pointed towards a narrow stretch of shrubbery that was a new "no man's land" between Sunni and Shiite quarters of the city. A hand signal from Hammad brought more covering fire and the two Americans rushed to join him. Colonel Caine unzipped his backpack and pulled out his machine pistol, while Jones did the same from his own backpack. They each then retrieved several grenades to the admiring look of the militia leader and pocketed them in their windbreakers. He checked his own Tokarev pistol in response.

"If we're going back towards the airport, we'll have to get past whoever's out there." Caine said loudly to Hammad.

"We are presuming it's someone upset, because you ruined their plans!" Hammad replied.

"Afraid of what we'd find?" Caine probed while looking down the alleyway.

"No, my Colonel! Afraid of what you would not find!" Hammad asserted. "Whoever did not want you to get this far! To find the truth! I assure you, there is no woman you seek around here!"

Colonel Caine nodded slightly to his partner, then to the militia commander.

"Who would you fight if we weren't here?" Jones asked.

"Whoever shoots at us! As I said, gentlemen, we are doomed to fight!"

Another burst of machine gun fire from an adjacent street punctuated their words.

"In that building!"

Hammad pointed to a four story structure that was ripped open on one side. It looked like a damaged doll house with an entire cross section open to view with furniture and appliances still in place and portraits hanging askance on walls. In front of the building facing each other were sections of a blue sofa set used for lounging and smoking darzheelies in quiet interludes on watch.

From somewhere inside machine gunners were firing at them sporadically.

"They are moving around!" Hammad declared. "It is difficult to locate them!"

"What do you do?" Jones inquired.

"We shoot back and forth! We move around until someone runs out of ammunition!"

"Do you advance?" Caine added.

"We don't have enough men! I told you. I lost eight good men in yesterday's rocket attack!"

"This reminds me of the setup in Kabul!" Jones shouted to Caine. "What do you think?"

Colonel Caine nodded with emphasis. "Signal your men to give us some cover!" he told Hammad in response. Caine looked back at Colonel Jones who nodded his head in approval.

Upon the militia leader's signal his men opened fire in the direction of the building. Caine and Jones sprinted to a section of cement block wall standing by itself in front of the building. It had been used as a makeshift planter for flowers and shrubbery. The covering fire ceased and Jones peered carefully around the wall towards the building. His attempt was met with a short burst of machine gun fire, but he had already pulled back.

Caine turned his body sideways towards the militia men arrayed behind them. The militaristic discipline of the casually dressed gunmen led by the slim, mustachioed commander in the bright sport shirt evoked a bemused grin from the Colonel. He raised his hand to Hammad who signaled his men for another burst of covering fire.

Caine and Jones spotted movement on the second story behind an overhanging floor from the level above. The sagging section looked like a massive envelope flap behind which a sniper could find perfect cover. As soon as Hammad's men had ceased their burst of covering fire, a volley of shots came from the second floor above them.

"Hit and run types?" Jones speculated.

"Likely. Their patterns of fire are too sporadic! Unfocused!"

"We should move in on 'em!" Jones declared. "Scare 'em off!"

"Give me some cover to that rubble of the floor beneath them."

Jones nodded. "I'm right behind you!"

"Now!"

Colonel Jones aimed his Uzi at the second floor and opened fire, while Colonel Caine made a crooked line dash to the building with his pack flapping wildly on his back. He stopped hard at a wall of a living room adjacent to the gaping hole of the apartment above him.

Observing Colonel Jones ready to spring, he aimed his Uzi around the wall and sprayed fire upward into the gaping apartment.

Jones dashed to join him. He grabbed a grenade from the pocket of his windbreaker, pulled the pin and nodded to Caine who again sprayed gunfire in the direction of the apartment above. Jones stepped quickly into the open and lobbed the grenade into the exposed apartment above him.

A momentary silence punctuated the action, broken only by the incessant barking of dogs and the ringing in their ears of their quickened heartbeats pumping adrenalin through their bodies. Suddenly, excited shouts filled the apartment above followed by the inevitable blast of Colonel Jones' grenade. Seconds later Caine and Jones glanced upward to see amid the heavy dust a man desperately scampering from among the rubble dangling out the building and clambering onto a veranda around the corner of the gutted floor facing the following street and away from the Americans. Close behind him was another man with a badly tattered polo shirt, ripped slacks and an ammunition belt falling from his shoulders as he fled.

Just as they disappeared numerous fragments of wall exploded from the side of the building from rounds fired by Hammad's men.

Colonel Caine waved in their direction. Everyone listened a moment for gunfire. Silence. He looked over his shoulder at Colonel Jones who was checking the side of the building where the men disappeared. He went to the blue sofa in front of the building and sat down unslinging his backpack with one hand and placing his Uzi next to him with the other. He stretched out his feet in momentary respite.

His partner was looking along the building toward the opposite street and the overgrown greenery beyond, his submachine pistol at the ready. The gunmen of Mustafa Ali Hammad emerged cautiously from cover and entered the building to check for casualties.

Satisfied that the attackers had returned to their side of "no man's land", Colonel Jones walked back over large pieces of stucco rubble and sat down on the other couch opposite Colonel Caine. Just as Jones was settling in two large dogs turned the corner of the building where

Jones had just been and bounded menacingly toward them. Caine spotted the black heavy set dogs charging them and his surprise alerted Jones.

"Behind you!" Caine yelled and grabbed the Beretta in his belt. He stood up and twirled behind the couch while Jones crouched lower in his sofa, grabbed his own pistol from under his windbreaker and turned toward the approaching threat.

Caine fired a shot over the dogs' heads to no avail. Jones rested his pistol on the back of his sofa and from a half-sitting position fired a shot into the closest animal, just as it was about to leap onto him with bared fangs. The bulky body went limp in the air, flew past Jones and came crashing onto the ground just past him in a dead 125 pound furry heap.

The other dog had leaped at Caine, but he deftly ducked behind the sofa and the dog landed past him. By the time the snarling beast could turn, Caine quickly dispatched it with two quick rounds from his pistol. Colonel Caine wrinkled his nose from the unfamiliar stench emanating from the dog.

"This is strange!" declared Mustafa Ali Hammad approaching them. "I don't remember dogs in these neighborhoods." He looked at the two hefty animals sprawled grotesquely on the ground. "This seems to be some mixed breed, unknown. Black with brown markings. Dogs in the streets are usually curs. As you know, much of Arab culture despises them."

"So these don't belong to anyone?" Colonel Caine asked.

"It is very doubtful."

"Maybe it's a new tactic of your—your opposition, whoever they are," Colonel Jones suggested.

"Why would they risk having dogs about? Success in street combat is in stealth and ambush." Hammad was pleased that he could still enlighten the obviously competent Americans. "Snipers could risk betrayal by an unwanted bark."

Jones wanted to retort that they had encountered fighting dogs with vocal chords removed, but let the militia commander have his moment.

Caine gave him a knowing nod.

Hammad called to his men. They filed slowly out of the ruptured building, peering cautiously around them. Several looked curiously at the two dogs lying near the sofas. The militia leader, with Caine and Jones, headed back to the sandbagged intersection where the two Americans had first entered Mustafa Ali Hammad's enclave.

"We owe you some debt of gratitude," Hammad said as they walked.

"You can get us to the airport," Colonel Caine replied.

"Certainly."

Jones caught the look of his fellow commando, anticipating his next words.

"Like I told you before, Arie. We should have flown in here in the first place."

"What? And miss the fun of getting here?" Jones replied.

The militia leader failed to see the humor of the situation.

"Our courier will drive you. You will have to forgive our lack of armed escort, but you see how we are preoccupied," Hammad said sarcastically. He paused thoughtfully, then added: "I hope, gentlemen, that the attack on us and your visit are strictly coincidental. I would hate to view you as a liability."

"That goes both ways," Colonel Caine replied coolly.

Hammad did not respond.

The dusty orange station wagon was parked alongside a sandbag barricade where the dark-haired woman who had brought them was chatting with several young armed guards. Their casual air suggested that the rocket attack and gunfight that had just transpired had never occurred.

"I am sorry that your foray is for nothing," the militia leader said. "But I think you would be better served to seek your answers at home."

"We'll see," Colonel Caine replied as he climbed into the back seat of the station wagon. He knew that his partner would want to sit by the fiery woman who had verbally dueled with him.

Colonel Jones bade farewell and climbed into the front seat, with a thankful glance at Caine. The woman had already slid behind the steering wheel.

"Give my regards to your General Bradley," Hammad said with a knowing grin as he waved off the travelers.

The Volvo spun its wheels in the dirt covered street, then peeled off towards the Rue de Damas. The young woman careened around a corner and turned south along the main street that used to be the border between the main rival factions contesting dominance over Beirut and Lebanon in the previous civil war. Battle damaged buildings still marked their route very distinctly.

Just as the woman was about to turn into an intersection towards the Avenue de L'Aeroport, a light brown Peugot screeched out of a small side street ahead of them intending to block the station wagon, while a battered gray Mercedes pulled in front of them from a parked position along the broad avenue.

The two Americans—reacting instinctively—grabbed their remaining grenades from their windbreakers, rolled down the windows, and pulled the grenade pins. Their wordless actions gave the driver the very clear impression that they had experienced this before.

"Don't slow down!" Jones ordered. "Pull up between them!"

"We'll smash into them!" she exclaimed.

"Make it their problem!" he affirmed.

She drove the Volvo straight ahead to the surprise of the armed occupants of the Peugeot who had expected her to slow down. The driver quickly reversed to avoid being broadsided, then lurched forward with a sharp left turn to meet the station wagon side by side. The driver of the Mercedes trying to cut her off suddenly realized that the station wagon would smash into his side. He veered back to his right. His armed companions looked at him and shouted something.

The three vehicles were now speeding abreast no more than two feet from each other with the Volvo in between. The attackers trained their machine guns through open windows on the woman and two Americans, but couldn't fire for fear of hitting their henchmen on either side of the station wagon.

Caine pitched his grenade into the Peugeot. Jones threw his into the Mercedes.

"Go! Go! Go!" each of the officers shouted.

Both cars veered violently away with their occupants yelling wildly inside. The doors flew open and several of the men from the Peugeot and Mercedes dived out, just as explosions ripped the cars one after the other.

As the bedlam ensued traffic in both directions stopped and effectively cordoned off the block-long battle scene. Bystanders had ducked for cover in doorways and behind parked cars, as if they were used to such interruptions.

By the time the surviving gunmen could gather their wits, the dark haired woman had veered around several stopped cars and sped away with a wicked smile on her face.

They reached Beirut Rafik Hariri International Airport—named after the assassinated former Prime Minister—without further incident. The airport had been a target in its time for competing militias and even bombings by the Israeli Air Force during armed struggles in the first decade of the 2000's. The United States Embassy still bypassed the coastal airport after arrangements it had made with the Lebanese government to fly helicopters directly to its Embassy compound in the Awkar area of northern Beirut.

So, no one paid much attention to the white Sea King helicopter with U.S. Navy markings and a sash of red paint at its tail rotor when it swooped in from the ocean. It landed at one of the private operator sites away from the main terminal. The Volvo's occupants were waiting, standing alongside the station wagon.

"How will you return?" Colonel Jones asked with genuine concern, turning his head to the woman. "This orange wagon is a moving target."

"I will wait for Mustafa," she replied. "He is my cousin."

Colonel Caine picked up the backpacks they had placed on the hood and passed them to his partner with a gesture.

Colonel Jones, in turn, handed them to the woman. Inside were the armor piercing machine pistols and the Uzis.

"Give him these," Jones said. "With our compliments."

"And thanks for his information," Colonel Caine added.

"But he did not tell you anything."

"I think he did," Caine asserted. "Until we meet again."

Caine started towards the helicopter with the blades still whirling. Colonel Jones hesitated and turned towards the woman. They looked probingly into each other's eyes.

"My name is Aida."

Chapter 21

The Sea King rose, tilted nose down and instead of heading in the direction of the U.S. Embassy, sped back out to sea. A fuselage painted green and a slower, steadier maneuver would have identified it to observers as the same type used by the American President as Marine One.

The two commandos were settled in their jump seats, silently watching the receding coastline of Lebanon. Colonel Caine eventually turned to his companion.

"I see you'll be looking for a way back to Beirut."

Colonel Jones turned to him with a knowing smile. "I think, maybe so."

They both knew any such effort would be difficult. Their membership in the Omega Group forbade private travel to any potential hot spots in the world that could compromise their person or reservoir of top secret information.

Once over international waters about 150 miles southeast of Beirut, they spotted the looming deck of the aircraft carrier U.S.S. Dwight D. Eisenhower. It was heading west across the Mediterranean with several escort warships after a courtesy visit to the military base at Haifa, Israel.

The white helicopter looked stark against the carrier's gray superstructure near which it landed. Colonel Caine and Colonel Jones hurriedly climbed out and were escorted inside the "island" painted with a large, white numeral 69. An elevator lifted them four levels to the bridge. Upon entering they saluted the Captain who welcomed them aboard, then turned to salute a grim-faced General William Bradley, their commanding officer. He had flown from the United States for a debriefing aboard the "Ike" after he learned the two commandos had been ambushed midpoint in their mission while waiting for the nighttime pickup in the Mediterranean.

The exit from Beirut by helicopter was a contingency in the event of any interruption in their original plan. The isolation of the aircraft carrier assured secrecy and eliminated the presence of virtually all parties involved in the background and planning of the original mission. General Bradley had arranged to arrive unannounced and alone. All he had with him was his battered, leather briefcase—a sentimental attachment from his early career.

The Captain asked his Executive Officer to escort the three men to a ready room off the bridge. Here amid an array of the most advanced electronic and communications equipment, General Bradley opened his briefcase and spread onto a large glass tabletop several manila folders that looked quaintly out of place amid the sophisticated electronics.

The two commandos looked expectantly at the folders.

"So, why don't you go first?" General Bradley said instead.

Colonel Caine and Colonel Jones looked at each other.

"We were set up!" Caine declared indignantly. "Someone tried to blow us out of the water!"

"Couldn't we start a little more neutrally?" General Bradley responded defensively. "A chance encounter with pirates or smugglers?"

"No, sir," Caine retorted. "They knew we were coming."

"They were plying a definite search pattern," Colonel Jones explained. "There's no question, it was a deliberate attack."

"It could only mean someone knew our orders."

"The Lebanese contacts set a trap?"

"Negative, sir," Caine asserted. "They met us, as planned. There was some confusion. They were targeted too. Things had been relatively quiet until we arrived."

"The setup is somewhere between Washington and Tel Aviv," Colonel Jones concluded. "A piece of paper on one of the bodies had our rendezvous coordinates written on it."

"They were definitely looking for us," Colonel Caine emphasized.

General Bradley listened thoughtfully.

"There's no chance it was on the Lebanese side?"

"No, sir. They took fire to bring us in and they took fire to get us out. I don't think they were play acting for our benefit," Colonel Caine explained.

"So, who wouldn't want you to make the rendezvous? Someone who knew what you would find?"

"No, sir. We don't think so," Colonel Jones continued. "Someone who knew what we *wouldn't* find. Someone who didn't want us to know that Warlock's lead was a bad one."

"If Hammad was in on it, he could have just lied to us. Led us on further," Caine reasoned.

"We promised a fortune for information on Jeannie," Colonel Jones said. "He could have played us along, but didn't."

"If Warlock's lead was false, we'd find out sooner or later anyhow," General Bradley countered.

"Maybe someone's playing for time," Caine said. "An obvious diversion."

"What does time have to do with ransom for Jeannie?" General Bradley continued.

"It gives the kidnappers more time to cover their tracks," Colonel Jones interspersed.

"Or they may have more than ransom on their minds," Caine offered.

General Bradley heaved a loud sigh from his barrel chest. "I want a full report. Cover all possible angles. 'Your Eyes Only'." He leaned heavily over the glass topped table, head lowered in thought. "For now, don't speak of this to any other member of the Group," he muttered with lowered chin, staring at the manila folders lying on the table.

"We should still talk with Sherwyck," Colonel Caine declared.

"Yes," General Bradley replied absent mindedly.

"There's something else," he finally said. The General fingered the manila folders.

"General Starr of the Joint Chiefs is dead."

"We heard, sir. General Lovy of the Mossad informed us," Colonel Caine emphasized.

"A riding accident," Colonel Jones added.

"So it appears," General Bradley replied. "There was no need to distract you when you took off for Ramstein. Details were too sketchy. It's a weird accident. But you know how it is when several freaky events happen at once. You start to wonder."

"How's that, sir?" Colonel Jones asked.

"Well, Jeannie McConnell, the freak accident killing Secretary Stack, now this thing with General Starr." Their commanding officer flipped open the manila folders.

Inside were black and white photographs of General Benjamin Starr's accident scene.

"We took a lot of pictures at the site. Actually, more than necessary. We couldn't keep the area cordoned off too long. We were afraid people will start speculating about the accident. Getting suspicious. Starting rumors. Accidents should be cut and dried affairs. This one doesn't seem so," General Bradley explained.

"I didn't want to transmit these anywhere, so I brought them personally. I don't want any hackers or leakers making hay with this." General Bradley caught himself, not intending to create a pun from a horse ride turned fatal.

"Here's the scene," Bradley said as he spread a dozen photos on the table top. "What do you make of it?"

The two Colonels looked at their commanding officer, then peered at the photographs. The pictures showed the prone body of General Starr from several angles; pictures of hoof marks around the body and along the trail; close-ups of hoof marks in the dirt taken at different angles; shots of the trail in one direction and another; and a leaf strewn channel along the park trail that was the remnant of a waterway for canal boats originally conceived by George Washington, himself.

As the officers handled each photograph in turn, General Bradley talked. "Several people saw a horse galloping along the trail. We couldn't place it. We checked every estate in the area with horses—and we're still looking—but no black stallion."

"Could have been someone with a trailer," Caine surmised. He was bent over looking intently at a close-up shot of hoofmarks in the dirt.

"Good point," General Bradley replied.

"What did witnesses say about this horse, sir? General Lovy made it sound kind of odd when he dropped the news on us in Haifa."

General Bradley straightened himself from the table and stretched. His had been a long journey from Washington to the aircraft carrier. "I know this guy. He's always trying to make it sound like he's on top of everything. The Mossad, you know. He has to maintain its: 'We know everything you Americans don't know' attitude."

Caine and Jones smiled. "How did he learn about General Starr so quick?" Colonel Jones wondered.

"I don't know. Spying among friends, I suppose," General Bradley replied lightly. "I certainly didn't tell him."

"Somebody who's not our friend betrayed our rendezvous in Beirut," Colonel Caine reiterated. "It could be the same pipeline."

"I'm backtracking every planning and operational step relating to your assignment," General Bradley assured. "As far as I'm concerned, it only confirms the terrorist scenario for Jeannie's disappearance. If she was just shacking up with somebody, there would be no need for anybody to try to neutralize you. You two were obviously on to something. I'd say it just goes to show that source Warlock was right in pointing us to Beirut."

Colonel Caine wanted to agree with his General's reasoning, but something held him back. He was more preoccupied with the obvious implication of a traitor somewhere in their network; or at least a major breach in security. Caine preferred to suspect a traitor. A real patriot would not take advantage of a breach in security.

"Well, we have everything, but a picture of the horse," Colonel Jones said with fatigued humor.

"There were supposed to be some strange trappings on this horse—a weird saddle, or something?" Colonel Caine recalled the Mossad general's words. "But no rider?"

"That's true, Chris," General Bradley confirmed. "The witnesses who saw the animal—and there weren't too many of them—all said it had some kind of stretched hide or hairy saddle. It was supposed to be 'pointy', whatever that means. Something like out of a sword and sorcery story. I don't know. You ever see a saddle like that anywhere?"

"I can't say that I have," Colonel Caine replied.

"Maybe in a 'Dracula' movie?" Colonel Jones offered.

"That's where it belongs, as far as I'm concerned," General Bradley retorted in frustration.

A naval officer entered the room. "Excuse me, Gentleman." He paused. "The Captain requests your company for dinner at Nineteen-thirty hours. That's in two hours time. We have some service khakis available for the two Colonels. An officer will be on call to escort you when you're ready."

"Thank you, Lieutenant," General Bradley replied turning to him. "Tell the Captain we welcome his invitation."

"Very well, sir." The lieutenant saluted and left.

The three army passengers glanced appreciatively at each other.

"It could have been just a regular saddle, maybe Western, maybe

Mexican style," Colonel Caine offered as they continued their speculation. "You know how witnesses are in excited moments. Especially if they just caught a glimpse of what happened."

"The witnesses weren't all in one place," their General replied. "They all referred to a strange saddle."

"Was somebody ever riding this horse?" Colonel Jones wondered.

General Bradley shook his head. "That's the part that stumps me. It's the most obvious question, but there's no answer. Obviously, someone had to saddle the damn thing! But nobody was riding it and we still can't find the horse—let alone the rider. All the stables in the area are accounted for."

"A trailer?" Caine repeated.

"There were some people along the main road," his general replied. "Somebody would have seen a truck or trailer."

"It could have been parked farther along somewhere," Colonel Jones joined in.

"I want you to look closely at these photographs," General Bradley instructed. "The horse scenario is still being investigated." He picked several photos from the group and glided them on the table towards Caine and Jones.

"A runaway horse spooked the General's mare. That's the working theory. So take a real close look at these."

Colonel Caine scrutinized one of the photographs. General Benjamin Starr was lying sideways on the ground. Around him were a series of hoof prints. Some were whole, some were partial. Several were deeper than others. Some had extensions in the dirt, indicating motion.

Colonel Jones scrutinized another photo. It depicted hoof prints going in either direction on the trail. Another photo was of hoof prints going back and forth in another part of the trail.

"The set showing prints going back and forth in this part of the trail are from the General's mare," General Bradley pointed out. "Horseshoes."

"That's the direction from his stable," Colonel Jones reasoned.

"And this set from the other direction of the trail, has to be the runaway mount," Colonel Caine added.

"That's how we figure it," General Bradley replied.

"What have we here?" Colonel Caine asked staring at his photograph with some amazement.

Jones looked over quickly. "A hoof print. Why?"

"Is it the angle of the light? The camera? Time of day?" Caine looked closer with heightened interest.

"Is that a split in the middle, or am I hallucinating?"

"Well, I'll be damned," Jones intoned slowly. He looked at the photo from several angles to be sure he was not seeing a shadow or reflection.

"A split hoof," General Bradley confirmed.

"A cloven hoof," Colonel Caine repeated as if in reflection.

"A runaway bull?" Jones offered.

"That's the only explanation we could muster," General Bradley declared. "But there are no bulls in the estates nearby."

"With a saddle, no less," Colonel Jones dismissed with a smile.

"It has to be some kind of fluke," was all the General could conclude. "Witnesses saw a horse. A black stallion."

"If there was a saddle on this animal," Colonel Jones reasoned, "and it was whisked away in a trailer, or something, and if no one is coming forward"—he paused following his own logic— "I'd say it indicates intent."

"You mean no accident," General Bradley suggested.

Christopher Caine did not respond. He was deep in thought, piecing together disparate incidents and conversations.

"You know, Hammad did imply that our attackers were some kind of cultists," Caine reminded. "Based on some mutterings we heard when we surprised them in the water. Devil worshippers, he said."

A speculative silence woven with fatigue overtook the officers staring at the photographs on the glass tabletop. Finally, General Bradley broke the spell induced by the subdued, but consistent hum of the aircraft carrier making headway in the Mediterranean.

"Some scientific skepticism as we proceed, all right, gentlemen?"

Then, as he gathered the photos and returned them to his briefcase, the General added, "Let's get back to our immediate concern—the ambush in the ocean—unless you see some connection here."

Chapter 22

"Well?" Jonas Mitchell asked his niece when he saw her approaching his book strewn office in the basement of the Library of Congress.

"Al walked me around the museum, but he doesn't know anything," Laura replied. She sat down in a chair along a bookcase.

"At least not yet. He's going to find out if there were reports about anything unusual that night—like I don't already know. It's kind of creepy, though. These two workers gave me some mean looks in an elevator when I was leaving. Someone should really do a personnel review there."

"They should," her uncle replied seriously. "After everything you told me about that attack outside the museum?" He paused and looked at her seriously. "I think I finally have the missing piece in my research."

Laura looked back with some skepticism, but her expression invited further comment.

"Maybe it was right in front of me all the time." He grabbed a visitor's guide to Washington from among books and papers on his desk. His unerring reach indicated he had used it very recently. Inside the pages was an onion skin sheet of paper with a hastily drawn pentagram.

"What's that?" She got up from her chair and went to her uncle's side, peering at the figure over his shoulder.

"It's the ubiquitous sign for devil worship. The five pointed star inside a circle."

"I know that!" she said impatiently, "but what does it have to do with anything?"

"Patterns," he replied. He positioned the figure of the pentagram on a tourist map of the Washington Mall. "I'm looking for patterns."

Laura watched him adjust the transparent sheet to center the pentagram on a small square indicating the National Museum of Natural History.

"Okay," she said slowly, inviting further explanation.

"It's obvious," he declared. "Depending on how you position this thing, one point of the star extends to the U.S. Capitol, another point to the White House, another one toward the tidal basin and by extension to the George Washington Parkway —"

"Where they found General Starr."

"Exactly," he declared almost triumphantly.

"And one point extends north past the intersection where the construction beam fell on Secretary Stack's limousine."

He turned his head up towards her.

Laura was staring fixedly at the map with the pentagram overlay. "This can't be!" she declared. "It's just too obvious! It's crazy! Nobody would believe it!"

"Do you believe it?" her uncle asked in a subdued tone.

She kept staring, reluctant to answer.

"There should be some sentinels or attendants along the axes of the star," Jonas Mitchell explained. "When they have their rituals, they have candles lined up along the axes. A pentagram of this size, encompassing Washington, should have human devotees along the axes."

"And how are you going to prove that?"

"Walk the star."

"Walk the star? And look for who?"

"Someone displaying signs of the black arts."

"I don't know, Uncle Jonas. I don't know," she said solicitously.

"Facts are facts and myth is myth. But when you mix the two...."

"Let's just stay with the facts," he affirmed with authority. "You were accosted outside the museum."

"A street mugging."

"You heard a scream inside."

"A yowling cat."

"Are you playing devil's advocate for me, now?"

"No, Uncle," Laura replied somberly. "I'm trying hard to think of some reason why your conclusion shouldn't be true. It's too incredulous!" She paused, battling with her own sense of logic.

"And what's at the center of this pentagram?" she asked, knowing what the answer would be.

Chapter 23

The President was hosting a contingent of decorated Boy Scouts in the Rose Garden with the White House Press Corps attentively looking on. Coincidentally, members of the Omega Group were gathering unnoticed next door in the Eisenhower Executive Office Building. If reporters had not been trying to intersperse some critical questions during the photo session with the scouts, they might have noticed that something unusual was happening in the huge, ornate building next to the White House, given the variety of high ranking officials entering into it.

Stanford Howard, the national security adviser; Senator Everett Dunne, chairman of the Senate Intelligence Committee; FBI Director, Richard Worthington; Robert Coulson, head of counter-intelligence at the CIA; and several ranking military officers, including General William Bradley; and Undersecretary of Defense, Philip Taylor, the President's choice to replace Ronald Stack, were filing into the historic Treaty Room.

They entered a vast hall covered by grandiose murals depicting events in American history. Members of the Omega Group typically met in varying places to avoid regularity and unnecessary attention. Vice President, Louis Mansfield, was already there, having arrived through an underground tunnel from the West Wing of the White House. They greeted each other and seated themselves around a massive conference table for their first briefing since the crisis meeting at the White House days earlier. Two blue leather chairs stood conspicuously empty at the long rectangular table—one for the Secretary of Defense and the other for the Chairman of the Joint Chiefs of Staff.

Vice President Mansfield took the principal chair at the middle of the table. Across from him was Senator Dunne whose smooth round face, rimless glasses, curly light hair sprinkled with gray, and robust body, gave him a cherubic air. Next to the Vice President was Philip Taylor, the Undersecretary of Defense. He was slim, with chiseled features and pale, drawn skin.

Taylor looked silently around him, assessing what the others might be thinking. Unofficial word was already circulating that he would be succeeding Ronald Stack as Secretary of Defense. His cool confidence challenged any lingering doubt among those present that the President had categorically excluded him from consideration to become Secretary of Defense—until the Chief Executive had brunch with Victor Sherwyck.

"Gentlemen," intoned the Vice President. "There are several major operations we have to discuss." His voice was somber. "But first, I want to acknowledge with profound sadness the untimely deaths of two of our members—Ronald Stack and General Benjamin Starr."

The men around the conference table lowered their heads as he spoke.

"I know, as you do, that both Ron and Ben would want us to carry on as if they were here. It would be the greatest tribute to their memory and work of the Omega Group."

"Hear, hear," several voices murmured in agreement around the table.

"A moment of silent reflection in their memory," Vice President Mansfield said.

After a hushed interval, the Vice President invited Stanford Howard, the national security adviser, seated diagonally across from him, to conduct the proceedings.

"Thank you, Mr. Vice President." Stanford Howard glanced around the table. "As you all know, our first and most pressing item is the McConnell case. What developments do we have?"

The presidential adviser looked around those assembled and caught the eyes of Richard Worthington of the FBI. Worthington took it as a cue and began his report.

Meanwhile, General Bradley glanced purposefully around the table, assessing each face before him.

Worthington was reporting that the FBI had alerted all its field offices and was pursuing possible leads or connections with other cases under investigation.

"We've placed particular emphasis on communities with ties to the Middle East," Director Worthington said. "So far, we've come up with nothing. But it's also very early in the investigation."

"I urge we continue the Middle East angle," Senator Dunne said. "We have to follow up on our best lead to date."

General Bradley saw his opening: "Two of our operatives were dispatched to Beirut. But, I'm afraid I have bad news."

"That's a real shame," Senator Dunne replied immediately. "I'm sure our man, Hammad, would have given them valuable information. He's been a go-between for us in the past—a lot of Arab-Israeli stuff. Very useful. Very reliable. Too bad."

General Bradley looked coldly at Senator Dunne across the table.

"Why do you presume they didn't meet him, Senator?"

Senator Dunne's pale round face flushed red. "What do you mean, General? What are you saying? I'm not presuming anything!"

"Our operatives *did* meet Mustafa Ali Hammad, Senator. Why would you think they didn't?"

"This is outrageous!" sputtered the Senator. "I said no such thing! What are you trying to imply? "

"I'm not implying anything, Senator. Our operatives did meet Hammad. Even though they encountered some—shall we say—obstacles on the way. Hammad professed absolutely no knowledge about Jeannette McConnell. He was surprised by our queries, let alone indifferent to our monetary inducements."

"Well, he's unreliable," Senator Dunne retorted. "He plays all sides. He's lying."

"I thought you just said Hammad is 'our man', a reliable source," the Vice President chided.

Senator Dunne stared back at the Vice President, his face still flushed.

"I think everyone learns the 'flip-flop' when they join the Senate," Stanford Howard said jokingly, trying to curb the rising tension in the room.

A burst of laughter rewarded him.

"So, what *is* the 'bad news', General?" the national security adviser continued, looking at Bradley seated across from him near the Vice President.

"That's what I wanted to tell you," Bradley replied innocently. "Our operatives met with Mustafa Ali Hammad and were satisfied to learn that he had no knowledge of Miss McConnell's disappearance, nor is she anywhere in his orbit of knowledge or influence."

"Well, he's playing a double game!" Senator Dunne declared, regaining his composure.

General Bradley figured it was time to lay out the scenario he concluded with Colonels Caine and Jones enroute home aboard the "Ike".

"Gentlemen, if you will," he began. "It was in Warlock's interest to have us get a lead on Jeannie from our contact in Beirut. But, at the same time, someone did not want us to find out what Hammad would tell us. Why? Because Warlock's lead is a false one."

"Preposterous!" Senator Dunne blurted. "He's been right by us all these years!"

"Maybe, he's been setting us up all these years for a big fall." General Bradley ventured.

He knew he was on thin ground, but confident in the conclusions drawn by his trusted charges, Colonels Caine and Jones.

"This does get in the realm of unfettered speculation," Stanford Howard replied. "How do you come to such conclusions?"

"Our operatives were attacked at the pickup point in the Mediterranean," General Bradley announced. "They were not supposed to get to Beirut."

"Very few people knew they were going," the FBI Director offered.

"Very few," General Bradley reiterated and looked around the room.

"When they succeeded in repulsing the attack, they did meet the Beirut contacts, as planned. If the attack was hatched in Beirut, the contacts would not have bothered to show up. So they knew nothing about it."

"Someone did not want them to meet Hammad," ventured Robert Coulson, the counter-intelligence chief of the CIA.

"That's our premise," General Bradley replied. "And when they did meet him, Hammad's compound was attacked."

"Someone didn't want Hammad to tell them anything," Coulson followed.

"That's right," said General Bradley. "Or not come out alive to talk about it."

The men in the room were listening attentively. Only Undersecretary Taylor was rolling his eyes demonstratively, while Senator Dunne shifted in his chair.

"Now why would that be?" Philip Taylor asked incredulously.

"Because Hammad's information would flush out Warlock as a false lead," General Bradley declared.

"After all these years! Suddenly, Warlock's a false lead! Absurd!" Senator Dunne retorted.

"We're just piecing together the facts," General Bradley said.

"Well, how about this for a fact," Senator Dunne said boldly, regaining his ground. "Your operatives could have stumbled onto some maritime brigands in the ocean and the attack on Hammad is business as usual among rivals in Beirut." He punctuated his statement by demonstratively stroking back his curly hair.

"We don't think so," General Bradley said coolly. "There are factors that spell deliberation, not happenstance." He purposefully kept back details of their coordinates his commandos found on an attacker's body.

"I think your scenario is too far-fetched," Senator Dunne replied.

"And I think—as the Shakespearean cliché goes—'thou protests too much'," General Bradley challenged. "Why were you so quick to presume they didn't meet Hammad?"

"I presumed no such thing!" Senator Dunne retorted and removed his glasses for emphasis.

"Gentlemen! Please! This is an important meeting, not a duel," Stanford Howard interjected. "We understand your frustration and concern for you men, General. We know they dodge bullets to do their work. We deeply respect and appreciate it. And we understand your loyalty to a long-standing source, Senator. It takes many years of nurturing and finessing. We're all supposed to be on the same side here."

"We're *supposed* to be," General Bradley said forcefully, aiming it at the traitor he believed to be among them.

Chapter 24

"We're too far afield here," said Vice President Mansfield. "I see a lot of speculation so far—not that that's bad. But we've got to get a firm grip on something."

Members of the Omega Group seated in the Treaty Room nodded in agreement, some of them murmuring to each other and shifting in their chairs.

"Our source Warlock claims it's Middle Eastern terrorists who have Jeannie. Given the turmoil over there, and our identified sympathies with the Israelis, it's a very plausible scenario—even without Warlock as a factor," the Vice President reasoned. "We can presume that the attack on General Bradley's operatives only strengthen that kind of conclusion."

General Bradley felt stung by the Vice President's summary, but he said nothing.

"The only factual results of the past couple of days are the losses of two of our good friends and colleagues—Ron Stack and Ben Starr," Stanford Howard, the national security adviser added. "We are investigating the circumstances."

"You don't say that their deaths are tied into this?" FBI Director Worthington asked in frustration.

"Of course not! If you're talking of conspiracies, they're not even in the line of succession to the Presidency," Howard added for emphasis.

Polite laughs accented his comment.

"No, they're not in line of succession to the Presidency—" General Bradley said, regaining his bearing. He paused, then added with authoritative cadence—"As a matter of fact, they *are* in the Chain of Nuclear Command."

"Now, wait a minute! Wait a minute! What is this?" the national security adviser asked keenly. "The Chain of Nuclear Command?"

"Yes," General Bradley affirmed. "Ron Stack, the Secretary of Defense and Ben Starr, the Chairman of the Joint Chiefs, were in the Chain of Nuclear Command."

"A sad coincidence, I hope," ventured Robert Coulson of the CIA.

"Wait a minute! Wait a minute!" Stanford Howard repeated with urgency. "The Secretary of Defense and the Chairman of the Joint Chiefs of Staff are in the Chain of Nuclear Command. It's not the standard line of succession to the Presidency—President, Vice President, Speaker of the House—Jeannie's mother, as a matter of fact—President Pro-Tempore of the Senate, Secretary of State and so on. Right?"

"Right," several voices replied.

"The Chain of Nuclear Command is the President, Vice President, Secretary of Defense, Under Secretary of Defense, and Chairman of the Joint Chiefs of Staff," Senator Dunne recited quickly to regain his place in the proceedings.

"You mean, there's only the President and Vice-President between you and the nuclear button?" Stanford Howard asked Philip Taylor jokingly who was seated across from him next to the Vice President.

Taylor stared wordlessly at the national security adviser.

"What would you do if the President and Vice President were gone, Phil?" added Coulson of the CIA.

"Anything he wants," FBI Director Worthington answered, drawn into the black humor.

Some tentative laughter resonated around the conference table.

Philip Taylor maintained a dour expression. He did not seem

moved by the jocularity of his colleagues.

"Well, gentlemen," Stanford Howard concluded with sarcasm, "The only thing we seem to know for sure in our search for Jeannie McConnell, is that Philip Taylor, our untested colleague here, is two heartbeats away from controlling the fate of the world with the nuclear button."

The laughter this time was subdued and nervous.

The Vice President sat stoically, not at all amused.

Chapter 25

General Bradley paced back and forth in his Pentagon office and recounted the meeting to Colonels Christopher Caine and Garrison Jones.

"I should have given him more rope," he declared. "He jumped at my statement about 'bad news', but I called him out too quickly."

"You think he's our man, General?" Colonel Caine asked.

"I'm sure of it. He was just able to squirm out with some plausible scenario. I should have strung him along a little more—let him slip on something more. More specific knowledge of the ambush."

General Bradley stopped at his desk and sat down. "The Vice President picked up on his rationalization of your encounter," he said in frustration "Predictable—no conspiracy given the political climate over there. I should have given Dunne more rope."

"Understandable, sir," Colonel Jones said. "You have to be careful in how you approach a senior senator about a matter like this. Or anyone at the meeting for that matter."

"I'm quite aware of that, thank you, Colonel," General Bradley curtly replied.

"He knows you're on to him, sir," Colonel Caine offered. "I'm sure he'll stay nervous and slip up somewhere."

"Look where we're going, gentleman. Are we crazy or something? Suspecting a senior U.S. Senator of treachery? A name thrown around for the presidency? Are we digging ourselves a big and unnecessary hole?"

"Senator Dunne and the Warlock leads are inseparable," Caine replied. "So if Warlock's information is false, it has to be Dunne, since he's the conduit."

"We haven't considered that Warlock may just have been wrong this time," Colonel Jones stated for argument's sake. "Someone giving him ratty information. After all, he's been reliable for many years."

The three officers sat silently for awhile, pondering the possibility.

"I don't think so," Colonel Caine finally said. "We were targeted deliberately. Someone was protecting Warlock's lead and didn't want us to hear Hammad's disclaimer. If it was just a bad lead, it would have been an innocent dead end. We've had plenty of those in the past. No one tried to kill us over bad leads before."

"This was deliberate false information," Colonel Jones reaffirmed.

"I have no doubt," Colonel Caine replied.

"Why?" General Bradley asked.

"Like we discussed before, General. To buy time."

"For what?"

"I don't know, sir," Caine replied. "But I can't help, but think that there's got to be some connection here. Everything's happening at once. Two fatalities of high level officials. Curious details surrounding them. They're in the Chain of Nuclear Command. Someone trying to stifle the fact that the Middle East connection on Jeannie is bogus. The shooting outside the museum with peculiarities we discussed. Something's going on."

I'd like to agree," General Bradley said. "But it's nothing definitive for the Omega Group. Too much *abra cadabra*."

"A real dead end for a career," Colonel Caine said, noticing his general's stern return look. "No offense, sir."

"None taken."

General Bradley sat thoughtfully for a moment. "You know, when Dunne kept vouching for Warlock, he did slip out a tidbit some of us weren't privy to. Top Secret information."

"What's that, sir?"

"Warlock's identity. He's Colonel Nicholai Kuznetsov. Old time KGB."

"Heavy. Dunne must have been feeling the heat," Colonel Jones observed.

"Colonel Nicholai Kuznetsov," Caine repeated. "Interesting."

"Needless to say. That information goes no further."

"We understand, sir," Jones affirmed.

"Arie. I need you to look deeper into these accidents. In light of everything, I've still got to urge some new approaches for the Group."

"Yes, sir."

"Chris. Go see Sherwyck. Jeannie's still out there somewhere."

"Maybe Sherwyck, sir." Caine said in response. "Maybe he's the one buying time. He was with her last."

"Don't say that out loud, Chris They'll have you a Private in some Arctic assignment in no time."

Colonel Caine nodded slightly in reluctant assent.

"I'll make nice with Senator Dunne," General Bradley declared. "Maybe I can tease some more information from him—or apologize. In any event, I want to keep him off balance."

Caine looked over to his fellow officer. Both rose slowly from their chairs to see if General Bradley would say anything more. Their General seemed preoccupied. He raised his hand in a half salute, half wave of dismissal.

"Can someone get me a cup of coffee?" he said past them.

The two Colonels uttered "thank you, sir" and left.

* * *

"What do you think?" Colonel Jones asked his partner as they left the Pentagon Building.

"I don't know, Arie. There's something nagging about that museum. I shot two men and it's as if they didn't exist. I need to find out more. Besides, I promised the professor, I'd check it out."

"Pro-fes-sor," Colonel Jones stretched teasingly. "Check *her* out, maybe?"

Caine eyed his friend with a raised eyebrow. "Then I'll drive out to Sherwyck's estate."

"Don't you need an invitation?"

"Not if I'm investigating a matter of national urgency."

"Don't forget what the General said."

"No political correctness in cases like this, Arie."

"I agree. Just watch your back."

They walked to the parking area at the northern wing of the building looking for their vehicles in the expansive acreage.

"I'll look up Two Beers. Things always filter up from the streets."

"Stay in close touch. Especially if you run into trouble."

"Aren't you the one shooting up Washington?"

Colonel Caine looked at his friend seriously. "Somebody around here tried to sink us in the ocean! Remember?"

Jones looked at him. Caine knew he did not need reminding.

The roar of his Viper's engine demanded his attention as he drove out of the Pentagon complex onto Washington Boulevard winding his way southward around Arlington National Cemetery. He wondered for an instant if he might prematurely find himself on some hallowed lot inside.

Caine shifted into third gear and shook the thought from his mind. He could have left it in second, but the higher pitch of the engine would be too distracting for other motorists. The dark red roadster—meant more for the racetrack than the street—was a form of relaxation in the secret, often deadly world of his profession.

He smiled roguishly at the thought of Laura Mitchell. He could envision a more normal existence in the stimulating company of the lovely, vivacious professor, so different from the staid, ritualized mannerisms of the genteel Davis'. They seemed trapped in their own traditions and behaved as if on cue. He liked them, to be sure, but could not see continuing those traditions with their Samantha. He barely knew Laura, but she mesmerized him.

As Caine entered the cloverleaf for the Columbia Pike toward Arlington Village, he began to take note of traffic. After a third look in his rearview mirror, he noticed a dark blue sedan was keeping an equal distance behind him. He deliberately accelerated and the sedan kept pace. He slowed down and the car did not pass him. Being followed was not a new phenomenon for him. He often drove to places in a deliberately roundabout way to test or shake off tails. Working his roadster through the gears added to a devious pleasure in traffic because it quickly weaned out whoever might be deliberately behind him.

Colonel Caine presumed it could be one of the intelligence arms of a foreign embassy posing under some other title. He matter-of-factly presumed that other powers had at least an inkling of his membership in a secretive operations group. Caine credited his own operational successes and longevity on the basic presumption that there was no such thing as a well-kept secret.

Now he even had reason to believe that someone in his own government wished him ill. He was resolved to ferret out the source one way or another.

Caine downshifted, gunned the engine and lurched his Viper forward. He quickly accelerated, changed lanes, shifted back into higher gear and saw the blue sedan recede farther and farther in his mirror behind a line of traffic moving normally along the city boulevard.

"Inter-agency nonsense or inept foreign agents," he thought as he glimpsed the sedan turning off the Pike into a side street. "It could be someone from the brass," he thought smiling to himself. "Maybe the General's decided to see if we're all there," he reflected more seriously. After all, he and Colonel Jones had reported some strange scenarios and added curious asides involving birds, dogs, and cloven hoofed animals in their search for Jeannie McConnell.

Christopher Caine drove quickly to his townhouse, taking several customary detours along the way. Arriving there he carefully hung up his uniform and took a long, hot shower to ease his battle ready muscles. He put on a favored old, green bathrobe, poured himself a generous measure of fine bourbon and stretched leisurely in his leather lounger for a meditative rest.

After some minutes he turned on the television and found a British made travelogue about Niagara Falls. The interviewer was questioning an old man by an inlet in the Niagara Gorge where the water formed a quiet pool in contrast to the foaming rapids beyond.

"And how many bodies is it that you find here?" asked the interviewer off-camera.

"About fifty-eight a year," the man replied. "The river always brings 'em in to the inlet. So we get a pole and drag 'em in. If they're too far out to hook, we get a boat."

"Most of the bodies float into here then, do they?"

"Yeah," the old man replied. "The bodies do. Other junk, if it's heavier, floats right by."

"Other junk?" thought Caine. The fellow must have forgotten the nature of his undertaking—grown callous, indifferent. He wondered about his own targets. Many of them were quite formidable, not like these poor wretches who—for whatever reason—ended up in the river. His targets would just as soon have killed him if they had the chance. No, there was no room for complacency.

He took a sip of his bourbon and idly changed channels.

His telephone rang.

"Chris?" asked a soft woman's voice.

"Yes." He knew instantly who it was.

"It's Laura. Al Carruthers gave me your number. I hope you don't mind."

"I'm glad he did," he said readily and rose from his lounger. "In fact, I was getting ready to find you myself."

"Can you come over? It's about the museum."

"I hope that's not all," Caine said spontaneously.

"Well..." she started.

"I'm on my way."

She recited her address. "I'll be waiting."

He finished his bourbon and hastily dressed in casual slacks, a blue sport shirt and a gray sports jacket. At the small of his back in a belt holster he clipped his Sig Sauer .38 pistol.

Now he felt fully dressed and left for Georgetown.

Chapter 26

Upon arrival at her townhouse he stepped briskly from his Viper and hurried up a terraced walkway to the brick colonial with a light blue door. The mellow light of the evening sun bathed the entrance in a tranquil glow.

He rang the bell and took a step backward.

She opened the door cautiously and sighed in relief.

"Chris! I'm glad you're here!" she blurted impulsively.

"Are you all right?"

"I am now. Thanks."

Laura beckoned him inside. She was dressed in designer jeans and wore a low cut pastel blouse that accentuated her generous curves. She was barefoot. A hint of perfume reminded him of their meeting at the Smithsonian reception.

"Please, make yourself comfortable." She motioned him to a couch in the living room. "You want to take off your jacket? You're making me feel underdressed."

"Sure." He removed his jacket and gave it to her. "Just be careful," he added as he deftly unclipped his holster and stuck it into a pocket.

"I guess you want it close by," she said without flinching. "I'll just drape it over this chair."

"I want to thank you, again, for saving me from those men," she said earnestly and returned to the sofa.

"I'm happy to do it, and thank you too. If it wasn't for you I might have missed the gun on one of them."

She sat down beside him, curling one leg under the other so she could face him. Her look was serious.

"I went to the Smithsonian the day after. Al didn't know anything about that attack on us."

"It was erased real quick, that's for sure. It might take Al or anyone else some time to know what the circumstances are."

"He did say he would try to find out. He showed me around. Especially the second floor in the gem area—where the scream came from."

Colonel Caine listened dutifully.

"You told me you would check into it."

"I am, Laura. The only thing is that this is a police matter. We have to go through the local authorities. I'm an army officer. I can't involve myself directly. It's theoretically against the Constitution."

"Theoretically," she emphasized.

"My work is outside the borders of the United States."

"Theoretically," she said again and shifted her body slightly forward.

"Theoretically," he said looking her in the eyes, hoping she would understand his drift and not ask him something that would force him to lie. "I'll see what more I can find out—unofficially, of course."

"The point is," she continued. "There's something going on over there. You know, the Hope Diamond has a gallery all to itself."

"It's immensely popular," Caine replied leaning slightly towards her. He could sense her anxiety.

"It's cursed, you know," she said warily.

"Everyone knows that. That's why it's so popular."

"Exactly! There's so much popular myth about it, that people end up discounting it, dismissing it with a smile."

Caine leaned back into the sofa.

"Can I get you a cup of coffee or something?" she offered, trying to figure how best not to sound like a crackpot.

"What's the something?" he replied lightly.

"Well, I have some of my uncle's brew here," she said easing herself out of the sofa. She leaned her torso towards Caine so she could free her curled leg. Her ample breasts burgeoned against her blouse and sent a sudden rush through Caine. He watched her walk with an unconsciously provocative gait across the room to a small bar near the kitchen.

She stretched downward in profile and pulled a dark amber crystal decanter from a shelf. She noticed Caine observing her. A tingling shudder went through her body. She lifted the decanter up to the light. Her nipples hardened and she felt self conscious that they might be outlined through her blouse.

She glanced at the Colonel and felt an uncontrollable attraction to him. He seemed agile and aware, like a leopard that had just made a kill, serene and at rest in a pose that belied the deadly capability she had seen so brutally used just nights before. What could trigger him now? What were the limits of his civility and charm? Laura felt uneasy, because she was not in total control of her own senses and that in itself made her body tingle with nervous delight.

In spite of her self-consciousness, Laura artfully returned to the couch with the decanter in one hand and two cordial glasses held casually by their stems in the other.

His eyes remained fixed on her as she eased herself back onto the sofa, extending to Caine her hand with the glasses. He took one and held it upright.

"This comes from an old medieval recipe." She poured some of the rich looking liquid into his glass, then poured a measure for herself. "Here's to you and everything you did. I'm deeply grateful."

"And I'm grateful we met." He clinked glasses with her and took a slow, exploratory sip.

The flavor of honey and various spices awakened his taste buds, then the strength of the brew announced itself through a simmering sensation deep in his mouth that grew to a pleasant burn that followed a path down his throat. "Whew!" he said with an involuntary shudder. "This stuff is strong!"

She smiled a knowing smile as she carefully sipped her own.

"But, it is good, I must say," he continued.

He finished the glass with his next, more liberal swallow and she poured him another measure.

"What is it?"

"It's from an ancient recipe handed down through generations," she explained, finishing her own drink and pouring one more. "A honey-based liqueur that's very popular in parts of Eastern Europe. It's said to be a wizard's elixir, a powerful potion to lure your enemies and overpower them."

"And today?"

"Today, it's just a special, homemade liqueur."

"All the flavor and none of the venom." Caine noted.

"Well, yes and no," Laura replied. "There are stories that circulate in some of the countries, especially those in the former soviet empire. Strange stories of sorcery and politics. Especially now, with all the changes going on over there. The confusion. How we're ripe for some kind of influence from there."

She caught herself and looked for his reaction.

He took a slow sip of his drink.

"What if?" she leaned towards him again. "What if someone was actually working the curse of the diamond? You know what I mean? Like those voodoo rituals. A sorceress or wizard does incantations, sticks pins in dolls and the person who the doll represents goes into convulsions or dies or something."

Caine took another sip of his liqueur.

"You think I'm a little too bizarre, don't you?" she declared.

"Not at all." He took another sip of his glass.

"Some of my students reminded me of parallels when I was lecturing on Marie Antoinette. The Hope Diamond was part of her royal collection. An obscure country cleric—one Pierre Dumas—was written to have extraordinary power over her—and helped pave the way for the French Revolution. Rumor was that he was some kind of wizard. Nobody knows where he came from. One of the students compared him to Grigori Rasputin—the influential 'mad monk' of the Czarist court before the Russian Revolution. Nobody really knows where he came from either. I hadn't thought of that kind of connection before."

Colonel Caine was gazing at her, saying nothing.

"What do you think?" she probed.

"I'm listening."

"So there's two separate periods of western history— revolutionary periods changing all of society—with mysterious, self-appointed persons manipulating events." She spoke fluidly, as if lecturing. "At the center of one of them is the blue stone that later is known as the Hope Diamond. That same diamond is displayed as a unique attraction— like on an altar—at the Smithsonian's Museum of Natural History. It's lowered into an isolated chamber every night."

"That's only if sensors detect a disturbance. For security," Caine interjected.

"You know this?"

"Al told me."

"I asked if he could show me the exhibit after hours and he said it was lowered out of sight every night."

"Maybe after hours was just inconvenient for him. All the security issues."

"Or something's going on after hours," she declared. "When I was leaving after Al's tour, two men in the elevator—workers, a guard and a painter or something—gave me the creepiest feeling."

"What do you mean?"

"I thought I was being polite and told one of them he had a paint smear, a blue dab, on the side of his neck. I didn't want him to soil his shirt. The two looked at me like they could kill."

He tilted his head in curious interest.

"Luckily, the door opened. I mingled with people and hurried off to class."

"I'll have to talk with Alvin about that."

Laura poured two more measures of the honey liqueur.

"You have to meet my uncle. He's been doing this research on old folk tales and grand conspiracies—witchcraft and demonology. He has a lot of historical information and is looking for some missing link to tie everything together."

"What kind of missing link?" His mind resisted, but his instincts fed on Laura's words.

"When I told him how we were attacked outside the museum the other night and I heard a scream inside, he went back to his papers." She looked the Colonel directly into his eyes.

"He drew a pentagram over a map of Washington. The center was over the museum—over the Hope Diamond—those accidents with the officials –the Defense Secretary and the Chairman of the Joint Chiefs—they extend along the axes of the pentagram."

"That could be coincidental," he felt obliged to counter.

"I'll grant you that," she replied. "I didn't want to believe it either. We're educated people, right? We're not superstitious. "

"No," he replied thoughtfully. "We're not superstitious."

"The only way to see if this is for real is to see what's along the axes. My uncle says the proof of the pentagram would be some believers along its axes exhibiting signs of the black arts."

"It's a very intriguing scenario, Laura. But why the Hope Diamond? Its owners were supposed to be cursed. Now, it's in a museum."

"Exactly! It's a national treasure! Imagine! Millions of people standing before it every year! What if they're absorbing the aura of its power? They probably don't have the slightest inkling that *they* are the owners! It was donated to the people of the United States in Nineteen fifty-eight!"

"And now it rests in the 'nation's attic'," Colonel Caine said pensively.

"So, *we* are the owners," Laura emphasized.

"We are the owners," he mused.

He raised his glass towards her. "Are you sure it's not this talking?"

"Of course not!" she said huffily. "Why do you suppose we were attacked outside the museum that night? When you cornered those freaky goons, they said they were doing 'what they were supposed to.' Remember?"

Caine nodded thoughtfully. "Keep this brew handy," he intoned slowly. "We may need it for the original purpose it was intended."

With a quick flip, he finished the rest of the glass. His face became a mask screening his thoughts which churned the events of the past several days and sorted them into a strange, but increasingly compelling picture.

Laura lowered her eyes to her glass. She took a slow sip of her liqueur.

"You probably think I imagine too much."

"No. Not at all," he replied with a preoccupied look still on his face.

She leaned back into the sofa and smiled at him. "There are some forces that just can't be explained."

"Like love and desire?"

"Like evil."

"That too," he acknowledged a little crestfallen. "I prefer to deal with forces that are known," he said rebounding. "They're easier to explain—and control."

He placed his arm along the back of the sofa.

"What would you do with forces you can't explain?" she asked.

"I'd see where they lead me," he said emphasizing his words.

Laura's serious tone disappeared into a knowing smile. "Are we talking about the same thing?"

"I certainly hope so."

She turned her head towards him.

He leaned slowly in her direction, his arm moving from the backrest to her shoulders. He pulled her closer and gazing into her eyes he gently, but deliberately moved his mouth towards hers. Her lips parted slightly and she began to close her eyes. He pressed his lips onto hers and felt her respond. She felt his tongue in her mouth.

Laura stirred, at first tense, unsure, then abandoning the testing and reserve of their short acquaintance. She put her arms around his neck, drew herself fully onto him and thrust her own tongue onto his.

Laura moaned slightly as she felt him press his body along hers and draw her even closer, as if trying to enclose her into his own body and being. She felt moist and alive, her nerves tingling, her heart pounding. Parting her thighs slightly, she rubbed against him and embraced him harder, her mouth now moving excitedly on his—inviting, wet, eager.

Chris breathed heavily into her mouth, kissing her repeatedly, passionately, then roamed his lips and tongue toward her neck until he felt her ear. Laura stirred again and in increasingly bolder, circular motions on his body, brought her hands to his pelvic area where she stroked his thighs and the hardness in his loins.

His mouth ranged to her shoulders. He kissed them then licked the beginnings of her breast, moving his head lower until his tongue felt the edge of her demi bra. He pulled it down gently until his tongue felt the hardness of her right nipple, kissing her breast as he did. He put his lips again on the nipple, kissed it wetly and held his mouth on it, while circling his tongue on the peak. She cringed with delight and put her own mouth onto his ear, sticking her tongue deeply into it.

With rhythmic movements of his hands he ranged over her body, stroked her belly and put his hand several times between her thighs. He could feel the warm moisture of her excitement.

Chris gazed at her and saw an ecstatic peaceful gleam in her eyes and a glisten on her parted lips. He undid two buttons of her blouse, then cupped her right breast with his hand, stroking it rhythmically around the nipples.

She leaned her weight onto him, unbuttoned his shirt and put her hand on his chest in stroking motions toward his left nipple. She felt part of a scar that extended upward toward his shoulder.

He began to undo her jeans and she loosened his belt while they kissed with abandon.

Suddenly they heard a loud scrape across the length of the back door.

"What's that?" she exclaimed breathlessly. He felt a shudder go through her body.

"It's okay," he murmured. He rose slowly, reluctantly and stalked cautiously to the door, listening and looking back towards his jacket draped over the dining room chair. Another scrape resonated through the door. The sound was familiar. He cracked open the door.

Standing squarely on the landing facing him from several feet away was a snarling dog. It looked black in the dark, broad in the shoulders and hefty, but he couldn't place the breed. The two dogs attacking him and his partner during the gunfight in Beirut flashed across his mind.

He stared at it a moment, wanting to shoot it right there for the interruption, then with a dismissing frown, closed the door and returned to Laura.

"It's nothing." He sat back down, conscious of apprehension she must feel from her ordeal outside the Smithsonian. He put his arm around her. She huddled next to him.

"What is it?"

"It's all right," Caine soothed. "Your dog's just jealous. I wouldn't worry too much with a pet like that around."

"I don't have a dog!' she blurted.

Chapter 27

Caine leaped from the sofa, grabbed his holster from his jacket, drew his pistol and returned to the door. He opened it cautiously and peered outside. The dog was gone. He opened the door wider and scanned the small, fenced yard, aiming his pistol into the darkness.

All he could see were the lights of neighboring houses and sounds of traffic on Wisconsin Avenue beyond.

He locked the door and returned, slowly holstering his pistol, this time leaving it on the dining room table.

Caine sat down and put a comforting arm around her.

"What dog?" she insisted frightfully. "How did it get in the yard?"

"Just a stray wandering the neighborhood," he ventured to reassure her.

"They don't allow strays around here."

"Maybe it's lost or hungry. It's all right, really." Colonel Caine tried to sound as reassuring as he could. But the same question nagged him too.

"Why would it want to get in here?" she persisted.

"It's gone now, don't worry." He looked into her eyes for response.

They were wide with apprehension.

He noticed she had adjusted her bra, but her blouse was still unbuttoned.

How about one more of your wizard's elixir?" he asked, trying to divert her concern.

She smiled weakly, unconvinced. Slowly, she reached for the decanter at the end table and poured each of them another measure of the liqueur. Her languid, automatic motions betrayed thoughts that were suddenly elsewhere. She remembered talk of familiars in her lecture. Monsieur. The diamond. Her uncle's pentagram. She sipped her drink, even as she handed the Colonel his glass. A sudden chill shook her.

"Are you sure you're all right?" Caine asked feeling her shudder in his cradled arm.

"What?...Yes..Of course...I'm fine," she replied as if startled out of a trance. "You know, after everything that's happened, you get jumpy."

She got up and sauntered into the middle of the room, composing herself. "I hope you're hungry. I have a couple of steaks in the refrigerator."

"I'm hungry, all right."

"Are we talking about the same thing again?" she asked with a knowing smile.

"I sure hope so," he repeated. He joined her and raised his glass. "Here's to you."

"And to you," she replied pensively.

"And to whatever forces brought us together."

She grimaced. "Please! I'm not sure I want to drink to whatever forces brought us together. I want to forget that!"

"What I meant is the forces right now."

"That, I'll accept."

They clinked their glasses. He intertwined his arm around hers and they sipped the amber brew.

He put his other arm around her waist and pulled her towards him. They shared a lingering kiss.

"What's that scar you have?" she asked catching her breathe.

194

He looked down his open shirt. "That's the last earthly mark of a drug crazed Somalian brigand who tried to split my head open last year with a samurai sword."

"I see you've used that phrase before," she teased. "It's well polished. I hope it wasn't used on too many other women."

"Oh, no!" he replied fervently. "I am an officer and a gentleman."

"I'll put on the steaks," Laura retorted to break the suggestive gaze they were giving each other.

"Let me help with something."

"It's okay. I don't like to put guests to work."

"I hope you don't have too many," he countered.

She put her hand demonstratively on her hip and with a furrowed eyebrow said: "Would you be jealous?"

"Wildly so."

"Good," she answered with self satisfaction and motioned him to a tall swivel chair at a counter facing her open kitchen.

"How do you like your steaks?" She busied herself preparing two cuts of filet mignon.

"Medium rare." He leaned on the counter and watched ardently her graceful movements around the stove. "I'm sorry I didn't think to bring some wine."

"It's all right, Chris. I was ambiguous in my invitation."

She bent slightly to check the oven. Caine stared at the proportioned shape of her back outlined invitingly by her contoured jeans. He wondered if their foreplay was just a spontaneous expression released by tension and drink or a threshold of deeper attraction.

"I do have a bottle around here somewhere..." she started and turned to him.

"I did tell you how lovely you look, didn't I?" he said.

"Actually, not in so many words. Thank you. But I do remember how you stared at me when we met."

She joined Caine on a chair next to him and swiveled so her knee gently touched his thigh. "Remind me about the steaks. I'll get involved and burn them to a crisp."

He poured them another measure of the amber drink. "Your uncle sure knows how to make this stuff."

"He's a real dear. I first thought he was getting a little eccentric in his perennial conspiracy research. But now everything seems suddenly plausible, real."

She eased herself off the chair and returned to the kitchen to finish preparations. "What's your preference? We could eat at the counter or the dining room table."

"How about here? It seems like less trouble."

"Fine," she replied. "Could you grab that bottle of wine on the bar? I think I have a Merlot there somewhere."

Caine drifted to the bar area and found the bottle with several glasses hanging in a rack. He returned and uncorked the bottle at the counter, slowly pouring each of them half a glass.

"Conspiracy is a pretty universal theme," Caine ventured. "And a slippery subject. It's tough to get your hands around it."

"I know." She passed a serving to Caine and put her plate next to his. Then she returned to the chair beside him.

"But this is deeper," she said as she sampled the steak. "What I want to tell you fits into Uncle Jonas' theories."

She paused for the Colonel's reaction, taking a slow sip of her wine.

He said nothing. He had just bit into a piece of steak.

"How is it?"

"It's outstanding. Thank you," he said between bites.

"Actually, Uncle Jonas' theories are not unheard of. Like I said, there's similar talk in various circles—mainly countries of the former USSR." She took another bite of her steak and then a sip of her wine. "But no one raises such questions here."

"Why would that be?" He cut another piece of his filet mignon.

"It fits too nicely into the 'babushka' stereotypes. Romantic, unrealistic people steeped in mysticism and superstition. People longing

196

for a strong leader. People who can't rule themselves."

Caine sensed the bitterness in her tone.

"I don't think the people are like that," he declared. "I think the tyrants who ruled them fed that kind of stereotype to justify their oppression."

"In fact, my uncle did start looking into secret cabals after he spent time in Siberia with a secret police cellmate—a "Chekist" who came under suspicion. He probably didn't kiss Stalin's ass enough."

She looked at Caine probingly. "The former secret policeman eventually told him things, crazy things. He felt betrayed by his superiors. This was his revenge."

"What kind of things?"

"Uncle Jonas can tell you himself. You have to meet him."

"I'm looking forward. He seems like a very interesting guy."

"I didn't want to believe a lot of those theories. They were too much in the grand conspiracy category. Too far-fetched. Then when he drew that pentagram, I was jolted." She finished her meal and drank the rest of her wine.

"Don't rush," she said easing herself from the chair and taking her empty plate into the kitchen.

Caine noticed that he had been eating slowly, just then realizing that he was absorbed by Laura's train of thought. He took a few more bites and was finished.

"Thanks. It was delicious."

"I'm glad. I'll bet you haven't had a real meal in the last couple of days," she ventured, recalling Al Carruther's words about his frequent, unscheduled assignments.

He hesitated with an answer, since his whereabouts were top secret. "Well, I don't always eat on a regular schedule, if that's what you mean." He did remember, however, the sumptuous meal with the Captain aboard the aircraft carrier Dwight D. Eisenhower enroute home from Beirut, envisioning himself then exactly as he was this night with Laura Mitchell.

"You want to relax on the couch? It's more comfortable."

"You sure, I can't help with anything?" he answered as he started for the other room.

"No, no. I'll just put everything in the sink."

"There's more to all this than meets the eye," she said as she finished clearing the counter and preparing the dishes for washing.

"What you say is very intriguing," Caine said returning to the sofa. "But at this point, it's conjecture. What can you do with that kind of information?"

"There's not much you *can* do, I guess," she replied. Laura poured two more measures of the honey liqueur. "It happens to be what my uncle's researching. If it fits into the real world—it fits. If it doesn't—it doesn't. That's half the problem with this world. People ignore things they can't understand. Or they're afraid to believe the unconventional. They let things happen."

She gave him a calculated look from behind the counter. "I have to find out what's going on at that museum."

He sensed she might try something that could prove dangerous.

"I'd go in the daytime," she continued, anticipating his reaction. "And, besides, our friend Al Carruthers is there."

"Just don't go alone."

"Now you sound like my uncle."

"Tell me more about this pentagram business."

Laura sauntered over to him with a drink in each hand. She hovered over him, kneeling with one bare foot on the sofa, and straddling him with the other. Handing him a glass of liqueur, she began to sip her own. He held his glass in one hand and wrapped the other around the back of her thigh, looking up at her with concerned desire.

"I'll show you in the morning."

Chapter 28

Caine woke up to the smell of bacon and eggs wafting from the kitchen. He forgot the last time he had felt such comforting domesticity. Meals were usually perfunctory, seldom finished, and often overlain with danger.

He arose slowly, put on his trousers and looked around curiously. He glanced into the kitchen and saw Laura busying herself making breakfast wearing nothing but his blue shirt.

He smiled. "Do you always get up this early?"

"Usually much earlier. It's already nine o'clock."

Caine nodded sheepishly.

He joined her in the kitchen and embraced her from behind, kissing the side of her neck.

She flexed her shoulders in response.

"We'll have breakfast, then we can walk the star."

"Walk the star?" he asked still embracing her.

"Yes. I told you I'd show you the pentagram today. You have time?"

"I'll make time."

He began to unbutton his shirt, as if he was wearing it. "You know," Caine murmured, "your body is a roadmap of beauty."

"And yours is a roadmap of violence." She quickly turned in his embrace, as if trying to catch her words, then wrapping her arms around his bare torso she gave him a lingering kiss.

"I mean..." she muttered with her lips still on his.

"I know." He pressed his lips more fully on hers, stifling unnecessary explanations.

"Do you want breakfast to burn?" she murmured between passionate kisses in a roaming, blissful embrace.

"I won't blame you," he muttered stroking her body beneath his shirt.

* * *

An hour later they were strolling along Wisconsin Avenue several streets from Laura's townhouse. Gray pinstriped slacks snugly contouring her hips, a tan leather suit jacket and a dark blouse elicited a commanding, confident air. She looked up and down the busy street. Laura thought she saw a figure in a suit jacket lingering about a block away.

"Did you ever think you were being followed?"

"All the time," he replied lightly.

"No, I mean, really," she persisted.

"Really."

"You see that man down the block? I think he's following us."

"Possibly. But is he following you or me?"

"You're making fun of me."

"No, Laura, I'm not," he replied seriously. "Why do you think I drive a race car?"

He smiled at her reassuringly. "We're just out for a stroll. He'll probably be confused by what we're doing."

"Maybe you're right," she said and turned theatrically to the southeast. She stretched out her hand.

"Okay, as you know," she said pointing her finger, as a tourist might. "Wisconsin Avenue ends at M Street, then jogs to Pennsylvania Avenue and on to the White House and beyond. Farther down is the Mall with the various monuments and the Smithsonian Institution—

particularly the Natural History Museum."

"Okay," he answered expectantly.

"That's one leg of a pentagram, if you center it on the Museum of Natural History."

Laura turned, pointing animatedly in a southwesterly direction. "Okay. The George Washington Parkway –down that way—is within the pentagram's axis going southwest, past the Tidal Basin, the Jefferson Memorial and beyond. That's where General Starr's accident happened. And then, going northeast"— she turned again as she pointed—"with the museum as the center—Secretary Stack's car was crushed by that falling construction beam. That was somewhere in a line towards Union Station."

Caine listened with focused curiosity.

"Then, we turn northwest up along Wisconsin and we have Cathedral Heights."

"And?"

"And that's where Secretary Stack's funeral is going to be."

His eyes narrowed, an eyebrow raised quizzically.

"Half of Washington will be there," she declared. "If my uncle is right..."

"You don't have to say it," he interjected. "Nothing should happen. What about this 'walking the star'?"

"Practitioners nurturing the purpose of the pentagram. They keep its energy active."

"Can you find me one?"

"I hope so."

They walked along Wisconsin Avenue heading towards Cathedral Heights. Pedestrian traffic seemed routine, but vehicular traffic was growing perceptibly in the direction they walked with noticeable numbers of limousines.

At an intersection not far from the Naval Observatory they came upon a street vendor who had two card tables lined up along the curb. Arrayed on a black velvet tablecloth were various trinkets and favors. Standing next to the tables along the curb were gaudily painted plaster cobras poised to strike and several snarling plaster tigers. They were meant to be ashtrays. A dark skinned man in a flowing white robe and fez stood sullen watch over the tables. He ignored Laura when she glanced at the wares and fingered several metal pendants with various symbols.

"Look at these. How intricate they are," she exclaimed to Caine.

"Interesting," he replied, not wanting to offend the eccentric vendor, who he concluded had absolutely no sense of artistic taste.

"How much are these?"

"They are not for sale," the man said coldly.

"What do you mean they're not for sale?" Laura challenged. "Isn't everything here for sale?"

"Take this," the vendor replied impatiently as he pointed to a tinny set of earrings.

Laura gave Colonel Caine an emphatic stare, then addressed the vendor again.

"But I wanted that pendant with the interesting design."

"Someone has bought it," the vendor snapped.

"What about this other one?" she persisted.

"That too!" The man grabbed a small wooden elephant and thrust it towards Laura. "Here! Buy this! A nice souvenir."

"Well, I never....!" Laura feigned when Caine interrupted.

"You won't sell her this nice pendant?" He fingered the silvery symbol soldered into a square. Actually, it looked quite mundane and artless to him.

The man stared at him wordlessly.

"Even though you have a dozen more just like it?"

"It's a free country," the man replied belligerently.

"It's not nice to turn away customers. Bad for business," Caine said sarcastically with emphasis on *business*. The man's face froze into a sullen, challenging sneer. "I do what I have to do."

Similar words played in Caine's memory.

Laura tugged at his arm and led him quickly away. They turned at the nearby corner.

"He's one of them!" she declared breathlessly. "Those pendants he wouldn't sell are symbols in necromancy!"

"Necromancy?"

"The black arts. Divination to call up the devil. Through a dead body."

"I've heard of it, but—"

Caine turned back around the corner. The vendor was gone. Only the card tables with the black velvet tablecloth stood empty on the curb. Next to them a brown and black dog was sniffing at one of the plaster cobras.

"Uncle Jonas is right! Different vendors around Washington have those pendants! I remember seeing them. All of them are different— different symbols—and none are for sale! I'll bet we find more and I'll bet they're on the axes uncle talks about!"

Caine nodded assent, but thought, "Then what?" He eyed the dog, which was now sitting next to a plaster tiger. He suspected it might be the one at Laura's door the night before. It wasn't worth provoking on a busy sidewalk.

"First, I want to meet your uncle."

Before she could say, "He's at the Library of Congress," they were already hurrying towards his roadster.

"We can catch a late breakfast on the way," he offered.

She tapped his arm in playful reproach.

Chapter 29

Within twenty minutes they were driving along 17th Street N.W. past the White House grounds and around the Ellipse to Connecticut Avenue. Laura kept her eyes peeled for anyone she thought might look like a devotee of the occult. She noticed nothing among a number of people along the way, particularly those lingering in the vicinity of the Ellipse and Lafayette Park.

The Colonel sped along Connecticut Avenue to 2nd Street and turning south approached a guarded entrance booth for one of several parking areas around the Library of Congress. He showed the attendant special identification and was waved through.

"Good morning, Professor Mitchell," the attendant said smiling to Laura.

Caine glanced at her with a bemused smile. "I guess you're pretty regular around here?"

"Oh, yes," she replied matter-of-factly.

Inside Caine displayed his special identification again, the guard recognizing that he could carry a weapon into the building. "Good morning, Laura," the guard said as he gestured them past the security desk.

She led him to her uncle's basement office tucked beyond shelves out of the way and rarely used. The door was open to add visual space to the cramped, but cozy quarters.

"Uncle Jonas!"

Jonas Mitchell had already heard footsteps and was at the door. He eyed Caine as he hugged his niece. "And you must be the handsome young officer she spoke about."

"Uncle Jonas," she chided.

"At my age, I have to take shortcuts. I can't be as presumptuous about time as you can. Besides, I haven't seen such a sparkle in your eyes for a long while."

"Uncle Jonas!"

He hustled to his desk and opened a bottom drawer. "This is an occasion. You're the only man she's ever brought down here. It's Mr. Caine, isn't it? Christopher Caine?"

"Yes, it is. I'm very pleased to meet you. Your niece has told me a lot about you."

"Well, I hope she hasn't exposed me as a paranoid crackpot," he said as he pulled a bottle of bourbon from the drawer.

"No," the Colonel said slowly viewing the bottle with a hint of a smile. "Quite the contrary."

Jonas Mitchell placed the bottle unerringly on a rare uncluttered spot on his desk, then felt around the drawer and pulled out three crystal shot glasses.

"Uncle Jonas. What are you doing?"

"Nothing, Laura. Nothing. This calls for a celebration." He poured three measures.

"First and foremost, I want to thank you for the other night—the night you held off those hoodlums at the museum. I can't imagine what would have happened otherwise."

"Thank you, sir, but I did it for both of us."

"Nevertheless," Mitchell replied and raised his glass in a toast.

"Uncle!" Laura started.

"I believe it's not polite to turn down a toast in one's honor." The Colonel picked up the glass and looked at her.

She shrugged her shoulders, satisfied that Caine did not appear affected by her uncle's forwardness. They both looked at her expectantly.

"Oh, I guess. Just this one." She picked up the remaining glass. "Just because you're toasting Chris."

The two men downed their bourbon in a gulp while Laura took a tentative sip, then downed the rest. She grimaced.

"You're absolutely scandalous!" she declared. "In the Library of Congress, no less!" Her voice betrayed solicitous affection for her uncle.

"We came here to tell you we found one!" she declared.

"Found what?" he asked absentmindedly.

"The sentinels along the axis! The occultists!"

"Of course. Of course! I knew you would!"

"Yes. And Chris wants to know more."

The elderly man picked up the bottle again and slowly poured two more measures of bourbon, his thoughts seemingly elsewhere.

"Well," he started as he sat down at his desk. "Laura's probably told you that I've been doing research of many years—obsessing is more the word—about the influence of folk stories and legends in real life."

"She has mentioned it."

"To what extent they may have roots in actual events. What credence they have in technological societies compared with more traditional ones."

He leaned forward and picked up his glass.

"It's about witchcraft and demonology," Laura declared.

"I'm sure it's pervasive in primitive lands," Caine agreed. "But I think modern society has outgrown that."

"That it has," Jonas Mitchell said. "But there are curious historical parallels. Curious connections that have always intrigued me."

"You mean the so-called 'collective subconscious'," Caine offered.

"No. It's not quite *collective subconscious*," the elderly gentleman said with a tone that was turning reflective and serious. "Being lately of an academic background, I'm almost afraid to say it—because it would seem unscholarly. However, it seems from years of research through obscure sources, that it's turning out to be not so much *subconscious*, as—"

"Conspiratorial!" Laura interjected.

He raised his glass to the Colonel, hesitated with a glance to his niece just long enough to indicate agreement and drained it.

Caine looked at him and raised his own glass in return. He tipped it slowly to his lips, as if taking in the man's words with each sip.

"To steady the other leg," Mitchell said. "It's an old Eastern European tradition."

"But with vodka," Caine replied with a smile.

"I know. When in Rome.... I have taken to drinking the predominant blend in Washington circles. It gives me more the appearance of an insider."

Caine smiled knowingly at his observation.

"Chris is in the military, Uncle Jonas. Don't get him drunk, because he may be called to go halfway around the world at any time." A hint of resentment shaded her voice over that possibility.

"I was in the army once. A partisan army. I went straight from my studies in university to the forest."

"I presume this was in the Baltic area?"

"Yes, it was. Not too many people know of that guerilla war against the Soviets who had occupied our country. The OSS—which became the CIA—and British Intelligence were helping us. The notorious Kim Philby was our liaison in British Intelligence—MI-6. As you know he was a high ranking British traitor. He betrayed us to the NKVD from the very start. Still—we held off the Soviets for ten years."

"How did you end up here?" Colonel Caine asked with professional curiosity.

"I was captured in an ambush and sent to Siberia to die. But I fooled them. The tundra could not do me in. I was lucky. I met a

Russian there in one of the prison camps. He was an NKVD man whom I befriended—or he befriended me. It doesn't matter."

Laura's eyes glistened as she heard her uncle once more recount his ordeals.

"It was he who turned me towards folklore and old legends. Heaven knows we had time to get involved in esoteric subjects. Looking back now, I think that's what kept me alive."

"That's strange," Caine interjected. "I wouldn't give those old NKVD goons much in the way of abstract intelligence."

"It wasn't that," Jonas Mitchell replied. "He spoke of daily events, eerie events and old stories from life. Unnatural things. Things he heard in the Lubyanka Prison in Moscow. Secret police whispers in the halls."

Mitchell looked Caine in the eyes. "You know why I remember it all? Because it was so strange coming from a person who doesn't believe in God." He paused for emphasis: "But it seemed obvious he believed in the Devil."

"He spoke of an ancient cult located somewhere in the Middle East," Mitchell continued. "A cult of cursed monks who had fallen prey to evil. Their goal through the ages was to turn the world to the worship of Beelzebub, the Prince of Darkness. Throughout history they had sent agents into the world to influence events in their favor—directly and indirectly—until one time the whole world would be in their power. Some small, diabolical circle inside the secret police had apparently become a part of that cult. Supposedly, that mysterious monk, Grigori Rasputin, somehow figured into the genesis of that inner cabal."

"It sounds like the ultimate conspiracy," Caine offered. "The Devil Theory of History."

"Yes, it does. And I'm glad you said it, not me," Jonas Mitchell emphasized.

"Because that's the problem. Few people take it seriously— perhaps too few. Most people dismiss it with a laugh. There is no way to get a handle on it," Mitchell said in frustration.

"What if you don't believe in the Devil?" Caine probed. "Or God for that matter?"

"It doesn't matter," Mitchell asserted, as if expecting the obvious question. "People can do evil acts in the name of the Devil, or even in the name of God—like many religious fanatics do. The results are real. People are hurt. People die. It's just as if there was a Devil—whether you believe in one or not. Just like people who believe in God—they do good, as if there is a God—whether there is one or not."

"Of course," Caine agreed.

"So, on earth, as we grope for the truth, we have to make sure that the people on God's side win."

Caine nodded assent.

"And throughout history there have been elaborate rituals by believers to evoke the power of good, as well as the power of evil."

"And you're searching for such rituals."

"Yes. Rituals. Traits. Outward signs. Historical coincidences that have a predictable pattern. Pentagrams. Things done upside down or in reverse. Grotesque ceremonies. Sacrifices. Familiars—cats, dogs, birds. Any animal really. Objects that emanate power."

Caine furrowed an eyebrow. Jonas Mitchell's descriptions were sounding eerily familiar to him.

"Laura tells me you theorize there's a pentagram centered over the Museum of Natural History at the Smithsonian."

"There's an object there that emanates power."

"Yes. Supposedly."

"And I don't think that attack upon you and Laura at the museum was incidental. They were protecting something."

Jonas Mitchell looked at his niece, then at Colonel Caine. "Laura said you were going to investigate that incident."

"We are. I can't do it directly as a military man, but we are cooperating with the local authorities. We're still waiting for results of the investigation."

"Thank you," the uncle replied. "I know you'll find something that may answer a lot of questions for all of us."

"I certainly hope so," Caine replied sincerely.

"I think I could have learned more from my Chekist prison mate," Mitchell continued. "He died after several years. I think he lost his will to live. It was his own punishment for his own past. He was bitter. The Soviets were always the last to realize that they were supporters of a system that fed on its own."

Jonas Mitchell looked at Colonel Caine as he lifted the bottle of bourbon and made ready to pour. Caine's slight nod signaled acquiescence.

Caine fingered his newly filled glass and waited for the old man to continue.

"After Stalin died in Nineteen fifty-three—a lot of us prefer to say 'croaked'—many of us who survived in the tundra were released. I returned to Lithuania. The secret police still harassed me, because I had been a partisan fighter. I found work on the side with the help of the underground. I delved in folklore and ancient customs: the typical non-political curricula. By then the NKVD had become the KGB. I really thought that eventually they would do me in—a drunken fall into a river, perhaps a slip from a second-story window, a delivery truck ramming a friend's Moskvitch. My friends and colleagues were dying in like fashion."

Colonel Caine took a small sip of his bourbon and studied the drawn, but dignified face of Laura's uncle. She sat quietly looking at him. She had heard him relate his ordeals many times, but listened once more with loving affection and bitter emotion—as if she could recapture some piece of his life story and avenge it.

"You are wondering, of course, how under such circumstances I found my way out of the country—to America."

Caine nodded slightly.

"It was the self-interest of your own intelligence services. As soon as they found out that Kim Philby in England was a traitor, they tried to get every piece of information they could. Leads to other networks. Likely contacts in America. Other traitors. After all, he had been groomed to become chief of MI-6 itself. "

Mitchell shook his head in dismay, while Caine sympathetically looked on.

"As soon as Philby was unmasked, I think the CIA took a personal interest in getting me out. They needed information from anyone who had contact with Philby. I had been high in the ranks of the partisan movement that he had betrayed to the Soviets, so the CIA naturally thought I might be of some value in ferreting out his network. A missing link, a name, a phrase, a rendezvous, a piece of the puzzle that might undo his network. I received a visa to go to an academic conference in East Germany. From there Uncle Sam smuggled me across the Berlin Wall."

He stopped for a moment, adding with amusement. "It's funny to think that after all that, the Wall is no longer there."

"The counter-intelligence officers here were very good to me. They helped me get this position at the Library of Congress. I've been here many, many years. I even wrote a couple of books on folklore. Meanwhile, I assisted the CIA in developing tactics and strategies around guerilla warfare."

He looked at Caine with a knowing eye.

"Guerilla warfare—unconventional warfare—the new name of war."

Colonel Caine, the new age warrior, showed no reaction.

"Of course, Mitchell, is not my real name. It's anglicized. For protection. Mine and my family's."

"Of course."

"Finally, I think I found—actually stumbled upon—a key element of my research. Something that ties together disparate facts and events occurring over time. Actually, Laura triggered it when she told me about one of her lectures. It was in front of me all the time. "

"Your pentagram over the museum?"

"Yes. There has to be some kind of cabal, some central, powerful group manipulating events to their ends."

"How would we stop it? You, yourself, said this would be dismissed as outlandish quackery."

"I know. That's the problem. That's the best cover for their activity. It's relegated to supermarket tabloids next to invasions from Mars."

"Well, Mr. Mitchell, I'll see at least what more we can find out about that attack by the museum. I took it very personally and I'm sorry Laura had to go through it."

"Thank you, Colonel...Chris."

"If it leads to something, I'll let you know what I can."

"I've got to see more of that museum," Laura declared. "Behind those 'Personnel Only' signs."

Colonel Caine glanced at her warily, then stood up to leave. He shook hands firmly with Jonas Mitchell. Laura hugged her uncle and they left the distinguished old man among his books.

Chapter 30

The funeral of the Secretary of Defense was held at the Church of the Apostles in Cathedral Heights north of Georgetown. The gothic structure was a jewel of the Episcopal Church in the United States. The faithful had spared no effort in building this edifice as a symbol of their unity following years of theological struggle over the application of their faith in socially controversial issues. They had overcome issues of women ministers and homosexual clergy. The Church of the Apostles was built to withstand any storm; real or abstract. It was a testament to their faith in God and in themselves.

Twelve immense marble columns along the interior length of the main aisle supported the arched ceiling of this vast cathedral visible from Embassy Row less than a mile away. At the top of each column was an ornate bracket upon which stood an exquisitely carved life statue of each of the apostles, from which the name of the church derived.

Camera crews from local and national televisions stations were filming unobtrusively as family and dignitaries filled the pews to the cavernous sound of the pipe organ playing requiem music.

Mourners included dignitaries from virtually every country with which the United States had diplomatic relations. Both the President and Vice President were attending, but protocol and the Secret Service required that everyone be in their places before the President and Vice President arrived.

When the pews were occupied Vice President Louis Mansfield entered and was ushered up the main aisle to the left of the bier and was seated in the third pew next to Victor Sherwyck. The gaunt, goateed presidential adviser was sitting near one of the twelve marble columns. He and the Vice President nodded somberly to each other.

Finally, came the President escorting Mrs. Stack and her three children. They filed into the first pew to the right side of the bier.

The funeral service was begun with favorite hymns of Ronald Stack sung by his daughter's high school choir. The President occasionally leaned towards Mrs. Stack and whispered supportive words to her and her children.

After appropriate readings from the Gospel, the Reverend Milton Rand, a long-time friend and confidant of the Stack family and beloved evangelist of the nation, delivered a poignant eulogy.

"No words are adequate enough to express what we feel here this day," the fatherly, silver-haired Reverend intoned. "Ronald Stack was an exceptional individual. A devoted husband and father. A source of strength and guidance to his family. And a source of strength and guidance to his nation. He was a public servant of the highest order who was called upon by his President to serve his country—his fellow-citizens. Ronald Stack did so unfailingly. He left our midst unexpectedly in the performance of that duty."

The Reverend paused in reflection.

"Our Savior tells us in the Good Book, that there is no greater love than that of a man who gives his life for his friend."

Reverend Rand glanced at the President while saying so and the President nodded slightly in acknowledgment.

"There can be no greater sacrifice," Reverend Rand continued. "For that sacrifice and for the monumental legacy of his work we honor Ronald Stack in memoriam today. And in doing so, we must strive to continue his vision."

The Reverend's words resounded in the expansive alcoves of the cathedral. Family members and friends quietly sighed or dabbed at tears. The President listened stoically, remembering his friend and what a truly effective and insightful Secretary of Defense he had been. The President began to realize just how much he had relied upon Ronald Stack and how much he would miss him.

As the Reverend's assuring words drifted over each succeeding pew where ambassadors and dignitaries and others less personally connected to the Secretary of Defense were seated, the depth of grief diminished from personally felt loss to more affected, but nevertheless sincere demeanors of sorrow.

Everyone in attendance, even representatives of countries manifesting less than friendly relations with the United States, seemed outwardly united in this hour of grief and shared acknowledgment of their common individual destinies.

Only one person in the church, presidential adviser Victor Sherwyck, who was next to the Vice President in the third pew, felt somewhat uneasy.

Sherwyck's eyes periodically darted upwards into the higher reaches of the cathedral where murals depicting heavenly scenes competed with brilliant stained glass windows for the viewer's prayerful attention. But Sherwyck was not here to pray. He never felt comfortable in church. In fact, a church was the only place in which he felt actual fear.

At some point in the service, when one of several doors to the cathedral had been opened to facilitate security surveillance, a charcoal gray mockingbird swooped inside and bounded toward the ceiling where Victor Sherwyck had cast his surreptitious glances. The bird extended its feet reminiscent of a raptor and awkwardly grasped a frame supporting one of the stained glass mosaics. It vigorously flapped its wings while trying vainly to gain purchase, then flew to one of the statues atop the marble columns. It alighted on the statue's head.

A number of people saw the bird fly into the church, including General William Bradley who was seated in the middle of the cathedral. No one paid the bird any obvious attention. To appear too curious would upset the decorum of the somber ceremony and reveal a mind too easily distracted by trivial anomalies. Birds in malls, old arcades, airport terminals and even large, cavernous churches were not an unusual sight. A trail of bread crumbs would probably lure this poor navigator out, thought General Bradley.

Victor Sherwyck was thinking something vastly different. When the mockingbird alighted on the statue above them, he went into deep concentration. *"Elohim, Elohim, Eloah Va-Dath,"* he silently and fervently conjured in his mind. *"Elohim. El Adonai, El Tzabaoth, Shaddai, Tetragrammaton. Iod. El Elohim, Shaddai."*

The bird on the statue cocked its head one way, then another.

Below, Sherwyck's eyes narrowed. He stared intently ahead and repeated, but this time softly aloud. *"Elohim, Elohim, Eloah Va-Dath..."*

Vice President Mansfield turned to him.

"How's that again, Victor?"

Sherwyck did not respond. He intoned just a little bit louder and turned his head to the Vice President so no others around them could hear. He repeated more intently in challenge to the prayers Reverend Rand was reading from the pulpit. *"Elohim, Elohim, Eloah Va-Dath,"* Sherwyck picked up the cadence, but at a barely audible pitch. *"Elohim, El Adonai. El Tzabaoth, Shaddai. Tetragrammaton. Iod. El Elohim, Shaddai."*

The Vice President kept staring at the mumbling Victor Sherwyck. He turned to the pew behind him to see if anyone else was hearing this gibberish. Everyone's eyes seemed fixed on Reverend Rand at the pulpit. Vice President Mansfield turned his head towards a side aisle where a Secret Service agent was sitting. The agent instinctively returned his gaze and noticed the quizzical look on the Vice President's face.

Before either could communicate, the marble bracket supporting the statue failed, causing it to teeter forward and fall below at a diagonal. The statue's feet hit the cathedral floor, shattering. In microseconds the rest of the saint's sculpted likeness brushed past

Victor Sherwyck, splintered the backrest of the pew in front of him, and as the rest of the statue shattered, it clipped Vice President Louis Mansfield's head just enough to kill him.

In the moments it took for everyone to realize what had happened, Victor Sherwyck sat triumphantly amid the rubble, gloating that even in this house of God, this place he feared, the prayers of all those assembled were too perfunctory to overcome the challenge of his Prince. His cause, he concluded with a satisfying smirk, was still much greater.

While Secret Service agents formed a cordon around their now dead charge, Sherwyck glanced quickly at the shattered statue before he, himself, was shunted away with other dignitaries. It was John, The Evangelist, whose sheared marble face stared serenely from the rubble on the cathedral floor.

"How fitting," Sherwyck muttered cynically, daring anyone to hear him in the confusion. "The author of the Apocalypse."

The President's detail several pews ahead was already spiriting the Chief Executive away past Reverend Rand at the pulpit and through the sacristy of the Cathedral to his waiting motorcade.

Other security services were hurrying their own dignitaries out of the cathedral even as Reverend Rand raised his arms and pleaded above the din. "In God's name. Please! Everyone stay calm! There's been a terrible accident! Please!" The Reverend was not sure himself of what exactly had happened.

Due to the uncertainty of why the statue fell and that eleven more were perched above, the funeral service was stopped. It would either have to be delayed or continue as a private family service in one of the smaller alcoves in the church. Family and close friends huddled around the Reverend and urged him to continue at a side altar. A larger memorial would have to be rescheduled at a later date.

Chapter 31

"It's the Vice President, sir! A falling statue hit his head! We don't know of other casualties! Most of it landed in the aisle!"

George Brandon, the White House chief of staff, was nervously repeating incoming information as the Presidential motorcade rushed from the Cathedral southward on Wisconsin Avenue.

"Is he dead or alive?" the President demanded.

"I'm afraid it was a fatal injury, sir," Brandon replied, trying to soften the finality of the question.

"The Vice President? Good God! I don't believe it!"

Buildings along the sidewalk seemed a blur as the limousine sped behind its wailing escort. "Where are we going?"

"Andrews!" a secret service agent replied from his jump seat. "It's safer on Air Force One, Mr. President! Until we get a handle on this!"

"No! Return to the White House! We can't act like it's some national catastrophe. It was an accident. We don't want panic, like we're under attack, or something. We need calm. It was an accident—wasn't it?"

"It looks like it, sir. But we can't take any chances."

"I know, I know. Return to the White House. We can hold off an army there."

"Yes, sir."

"Prepare statements. Condolences to Lou's family. And the Stacks for the tragic interruption of Ron's funeral. Assurances that everything is stable under the Constitution. And we're investigating an unusual and tragic accident."

The President paused for a thoughtful, long moment. His five vehicle entourage sped along the cityscape with the White House grounds looming in the near distance.

"Why do I keep repeating that we're investigating an unusual and tragic accident? This is the third time now! The Secretary of Defense, the Chairman of the Joint Chiefs of Staff, and now the Vice President of the United States! No one will believe it! And, frankly, I don't blame them!"

"That's all we can say right now, Mr. President," George Brandon explained. "I don't think we want to give official rein to wild speculation. I'm sure a lot of people will spin conspiracies around this, but we can't give them fuel for their fire."

"These can't be coincidences!" the President declared. "I don't care how random and accidental they seem!"

"We are investigating, sir," Brandon assured. "The Omega Group is on top of it."

"Find out every detail, every word, every sound involved in these...these *incidents*! I don't believe they're random anymore! And all this on top of Jeannie McConnell vanishing!"

"There's no logical way to tie these together, Mr. President."

"Try something illogical!"

Brandon was not sure if the President was serious or venting his frustration with cynical humor.

No more was said as the motorcade sped onto the White House grounds and snaked into an underground garage.

His senior advisers were already gathered when the President appeared at the Oval Office.

"So, what in the hell is going on?" the President declared to no one in particular. He plopped into his leather chair and leaned back, waiting for any kind of answer.

"It's another freak accident," Stanford Howard, the national security adviser ventured.

"You can't have too many freak accidents!" the President scoffed. "That's why they call them 'freak'. They're unusual and—I daresay—rare. We've got too many senior officials in our government suddenly dying from 'freak accidents'."

"We'll have an explanation, sir," Paul McCallister offered. "The Omega Group is investigating everything."

"Well then, explain to me this: How is it that House Speaker McConnell is suddenly next in line for the Presidency and her daughter just happens to be missing?"

"It's an unusual coincidence, sir," was all that McCallister could muster, reflecting the bewilderment of the other advisers in the room.

"Does that mean I'm the final target for the terrorists who will then blackmail the next President with her daughter? Challenge her maternal instincts?"

"It is a curious scenario," Stanford Howard posited. "It's just as curious as the other one. Only it's not as funny as when we joked about it with the Vice President."

"What do you mean?"

"At our last meeting we told him he was the only one between you and Philip Taylor in the chain of nuclear command."

"What?" The Presidents stood up and started pacing the room.

"All the accidents that occurred involved men in the chain of nuclear command," Howard explained. "Ron Stack, the Secretary of Defense—Benjamin Starr, the Chairman of the Joint Chiefs of Staff—and now the Vice President."

The President stopped pacing and turned to Howard.

"In case of some calamity—heaven forbid—should something happen to you, Philip Taylor would have control over the nuclear button."

The President stared at Howard. "I never wanted Taylor in that position!"

His advisers said nothing.

He knew they agreed with him, but remembered that his friend Victor Sherwyck had persuaded him otherwise. Victor Sherwyck, who had last seen Jeannie McConnell before she disappeared. A vague unease came over the President.

"Cancel my public appearances before I get choked by some damn 'welcome' sign!" he scoffed. "And find out what the hell is going on around here!"

Chapter 32

"Caine?" General Bradley's voice sounded urgent over his secure line.

"Yes, sir." The Colonel had just dropped off Laura Mitchell for her afternoon seminar.

"There's been a freak accident at the Cathedral. I'm afraid this time it's the Vice President."

Caine felt adrenalin surge through his body, and Laura's words through his mind. The Cathedral was on the axis she described.

"Where are you?"

"I'm leaving the campus of GW, sir."

"Taking courses, again, huh?" General Bradley said with dark humor. "Looking for a more placid lifestyle?"

"If only I could, sir."

"I'm on my way from the Cathedral. Meet me at the Army and Navy Club. It's close for both of us. I already called Colonel Jones."

Caine acknowledged and sped to Farragut Square, the location of the exclusive membership facility catering to military personnel and distinguished civilians.

He parked his roadster and made a cell phone call. Laura Mitchell answered from her seminar class.

"Am I interrupting?"

"Yes, but it's important. I know why you're calling. We just heard about the Vice President. Poor soul." She didn't mind that her students were hearing her conversation.

"I was afraid something would happen at the Cathedral," Laura said. "My uncle's theory is proving right."

"I'm on assignment," Caine replied without acknowledging. "But I need to see you."

"Can you come tomorrow to my seminar?" she asked expectantly. "It's about omens, no less. How Napoleon lost his empire."

"That sounds like what I need to hear." Caine replied. "I'm thinking about you."

"I'm thinking about you too," she said more softly so her students wouldn't hear.

Professor Mitchell ended the call, put her phone on the seminar table and looked to her students. "I'm sorry. Where were we?"

The students wanted to know more about her uncle's theories.

* * *

Caine hurried to the second floor main dining room. General Bradley and Colonel Jones had arrived ahead of him and were settling into a far corner table overlooking the Square. The twenty-foot ceiling framed by rich wood coving, chandelier lights, wood paneled walls, an ornate clock at the far end of the hall attached to a wall size marble mantle and traditional furniture gave it an unmistakably formal air. The Colonel could not enter until an attendant gave him a tie that did not quite match his blue shirt and gray sports jacket. No one thought to ask if he was armed.

He knotted the tie reluctantly as he approached his fellow-officers, both of whom were dressed in the uniform of the day.

"Details are sparse," General Bradley said as Colonel Caine sat down opposite him and nodded to Colonel Jones.

"It looks like one of the statues let loose from its perch on top of a column. Vice President Mansfield was right under it."

As he was talking a waiter approached. "We're sorry gentlemen. Due to the latest news about the Vice President, the governing board has requested that we close today out of respect. He was a member here."

The officers looked at him with an understanding demeanor.

"We weren't going to dine," General Bradley replied. "We need a few minutes for some urgent business."

"Certainly, gentlemen. A few minutes." The waiter continued on to some nearby tables.

"It's just as well," the general said. "I don't want someone to overhear what I'm about to tell you."

Caine and Jones pulled their chairs closer to the table and leaned forward.

"Another odd thing happened during the service," General Bradley said in a hushed tone. "A bird flew into the Cathedral. It flew around like it was lost. At first I thought it was no big deal. Then it landed on the statue."

General Bradley looked at each of them. "Shall I go on?" he asked expectantly.

"The statue came loose from its pedestal and fell." Colonel Jones finished.

"Now the obvious explanation," General Bradley went on, "is that the base was degrading and the weight of the bird was all that was necessary for it to finally give way."

"Or it was just a simple coincidence," Colonel Jones offered.

"But we're reluctant to buy into it, right, sir?" Colonel Caine anticipated.

"Reluctant," the General agreed. "I'm thinking of those weird little anomalies surrounding the other incidents you told me about. Birds, the dogs that attacked you in that firefight in Beirut, and those unusual hoof prints around General Starr's body. Cloven hooves. We still haven't figured that out."

"Familiars," Caine said blankly.

He related to the officers his conversations with Laura Mitchell— her students drawing parallels with Grigori Rasputin in revolutionary

224

Russia and Father Pierre Dumas in revolutionary France, the dog at her door, meeting her uncle Jonas—his ordeals in the Gulag, the mysterious cabal within the Soviet secret police and Mitchell's pentagram scenario.

"That pentagram, at least coincidentally, seems to tie in with the locations and details surrounding the accidents. It's unusual that they occurred in such a quick sequence and involved officials directly linked with the succession of power in our government."

"What details?" his general asked.

"Like you said, sir. The bird on the statue, the cloven hooves around General Starr."

"And the bird on the girder that let loose on Secretary Stack's car," added Colonel Jones.

"All resulting in Speaker McConnell ascending to Chief Executive if anything now happened to the President," Colonel Caine said.

"And it's her daughter we're looking for," General Bradley stressed.

"She'd be ripe for blackmail!" Bradley said loudly, then quickly looked around as if to catch his words. The dining hall was empty, except for an attendant waiting patiently by the entrance.

"That's why it *is* terrorists who have her," General Bradley declared. "Hammad in Beirut was misleading you."

"With due respect, sir, I don't agree," Colonel Caine responded. "Arie and I were attacked in the ocean, so we wouldn't make our rendezvous with Hammad. I think somebody—somebody here—was stalling for time. You, yourself, suspect Senator Dunne somehow betrayed our mission."

"Mustafa Ali Hammad was helpful, willingly or not," Colonel Caine emphasized.

Garrison Jones, his fellow commando at the scene, slowly nodded his head in agreement.

"We were trying to figure out who the attackers were and mentioned some gibberish the bogies were humming in their boat when they tried to sink us," Caine said.

"Hammad immediately linked it to some devil- loving cult from the desert," Colonel Jones affirmed.

"Too many incidental and unrelated factors seem to point in a certain direction," Caine said.

General Bradley nodded his head slowly, as if coming to a mental agreement with Caine's explanation.

"Now, maybe, Senator Dunne's bad, but I don't think that he would see any future in tying in with terrorist networks. They're dust- eating criminal vagabonds. They'll never have a state to rule. The world won't stand for it."

"Civilized world," Colonel Jones emphasized.

"So, who would he tie in with?" General Bradley asked with redirected interest.

"Traditional adversaries, sir. The Chinese. They *are* communists. The Russians, a lot of their leaders still act like communists. They're actively working for world hegemony—directly or indirectly. They could offer a traitor better conditions than living in a cave."

"It's a lot of conjecture, Chris. And a lot of pushing of the proverbial envelope," General Bradley said, but did not negate his subordinate's reasoning.

"There's no way we can prove anything. We need something solid to grab onto."

"You remember, sir," Colonel Caine said deferentially, "that the Russians used to have a special political arm in the Soviet Army under Colonel General Dmitri Volkogonov."

This elicited a bemused smile from Colonel Jones, marveling at how his fellow officer recalled such details and wondering if General Bradley did remember.

"Their purpose was to wage psychological warfare against the United States. This was in the nineteen-seventies and eighties. For that purpose they delved into parapsychology and mysticism."

"Looking back on it, it seems kind of bizarre," Colonel Jones ventured.

"Yes. But obviously some high level commissars in their government thought it was worth the undertaking," Caine replied. "It ties in with Jonas Mitchell's story of a cabal within the KGB trying to work some sorcery to take us over."

"So, there's got to be some connecting link here?" Colonel Jones followed.

General Bradley was listening, not sure whether to entertain this kind of reasoning. He remembered the CIA experimenting with mind-altering drugs during that same period, but in his view this was different.

"We'll be a laughing stock if we start chasing ghosts and goblins," he postured. "Do you want to go to the Omega Group or the President and tell him that we're following a sorcery lead? How's that for a career killer?"

"True sir. But the effects of certain events are real," Caine emphasized. "We have dead people to prove it. And Jeannie McConnell is missing. Their collective absence has put us in a very vulnerable position. And if any of our conjecture is even remotely close, the President is in potential danger."

"Speaker of the House, McConnell, moving into the Presidency is susceptible to coercion with her daughter missing," Colonel Jones recited. "And Philip Taylor—Sherwyck's protégé—simultaneously inherits the nuclear button."

"A double whammy!" General Bradley declared.

"And one prominent link stares us in the face," Caine continued.

"Victor Sherwyck," General Bradley said slowly.

He turned to the entrance of the dining hall and motioned for the attendant.

"What was the Vice President's favorite drink here?"

"A vodka gimlet, sir."

"Not bourbon?"

"No, sir. He was from New York."

"Of course. Give us three, then," General Bradley said and noticed the hesitation in the man. "—in his memory."

"In his memory, sir. Yes, sir."

As the waiter left for the bar, the General assuaged his subordinates. "The place is closed, gentlemen. So, we're not officially drinking."

They understood.

"I know there are some odd things in play here," the General continued, "but it doesn't mean that they aren't what they seem—freak accidents."

After setting what he believed was a necessary common sense benchmark, he continued: "Having said that, I should note that Sherwyck was sitting next to Vice President Mansfield at the Cathedral. Someone said he was muttering something just before the statute fell. Sound familiar?"

Caine and Jones were anticipating.

"But no one could make out what it was."

"It does sound familiar," Colonel Jones agreed. Then mimicked softly, "Do dee do do—do dee do do."

"Right, Arie!" the General said scornfully. "That's all we got—the twilight zone."

The waiter came back with their drinks. "Complimentary, gentlemen. In memory of the Vice President."

"Thanks," General Bradley replied, sounding more solicitous. "We'll be leaving soon."

He raised his glass and declared more reverently: "To Vice President Louis Mansfield."

"Hear, hear." both Colonels responded. They took a sip.

They repeated the salute to Defense Secretary, Ronald Stack and Chairman of the Joint Chiefs of Staff, General Benjamin Starr.

"And a promise to Jeannie McConnell," Colonel Caine added.

Putting his empty glass on the table, General Bradley asked, "Does anyone know where he came from?"

"It was before my time," Colonel Caine responded.

"No one ever asked, as far as I know," Colonel Jones added. "I'm not sure anybody knows."

"Over time he just moved into the power elite of Washington," General Bradley stated. "He has an estate not far from Mount Vernon. Influential, rich—and therefore appealing to presidents. A succession of them. "

"And no one knows where he came from?" Colonel Jones repeated.

"How did he amass his fortune?" Colonel Caine wondered.

"No one ever looked the gift horse in the mouth," General Bradley replied. "By the way, Chris, you probably haven't seen him yet."

"Haven't had the chance, sir."

"Do it now."

"Socially?"

"Act official!"

Chapter 33

The late afternoon sun was already casting a golden hue over the lush April landscape as Colonel Caine sped along the George Washington Memorial Parkway towards Mount Vernon. He apologized silently to himself for his aggressive manners as he weaved his roadster among southbound motorists who were driving more leisurely down the scenic boulevard along the Potomac River.

At the grounds of George Washington's iconic Mount Vernon Estate the Mount Vernon Highway branched off sharply northwards surrounded by expansive wooded tracts of land. Caine followed the Highway and saw the entrances to several estates in the pristine surroundings buffering Mount Vernon from urban neighborhoods farther north. Their location announced power and privilege.

Caine approached a long driveway that looked more like a street and cruised slowly towards a colonnaded, white Georgian mansion evoking a vague mimicry of George Washington's own Mount Vernon. Arabian horses grazed on several acres of luxuriant lawns on either side of him. Farther to the right of the mansion was a long building housing the stables and built in the same Georgian style.

Scanning the baronial splendor, his eyes caught the rear section of a dusty green van parked behind the far end of the stables. He was fixated on dark vans ever since the attack outside the museum and this one seemed out of place in the manicured environment of the property.

Caine kept peering towards the stables where he heard the spirited neighing of a horse. Instead of pulling up to the broad stairs extending the length of the mansion, he veered down a paved drive to the stables.

"Wait! Stop! Not that way!" a man shouted from the veranda.

Caine ignored the command and halted near the van at the end of the long building. He hurriedly climbed out, looked around and instinctively adjusted the holster at his belt in case he needed to draw his pistol. He approached the van, looking intently at its rear door and the metal around it. Closely scrutinizing the back of the van, he suddenly felt an adrenalin rush when he spotted the unmistakable hole of a bullet. Caine smiled in grim satisfaction as he circled his finger around the small puncture of naked metal where velocity and heat had flecked away the paint.

He was certain it was the van he marked with a well-placed shot the night of the attack outside the museum.

A groom came out of the stable and approached him.

"Are you one of the new initiates?"

"Uhh, yes, I am," the Colonel replied. "What is that neighing in the barn? Aren't all the horses outside grazing?"

Caine looked past the groom's shoulder and saw a man hurrying towards them from the mansion.

"Oh, that's Blaze. Mr. Sherwyck's favorite. He's different. Only Mr. Sherwyck can handle him."

"I appreciate good horseflesh. Can I see him?"

Before the groom could answer, the man from the mansion—who appeared to Caine like a butler—was upon them and confronted the Colonel.

"Who are you? What are you doing here?"

The groom seemed puzzled and backed away into the stable upon the butler's commanding stare.

"I'm Colonel Christopher Caine," he replied casually. "I'm here to see Mr. Sherwyck."

The man looked at the Colonel curiously, knowingly.

Caine misread the look. "I know. I'm not in uniform."

"You won't find him in the barn!" the man said reproachfully.

Something about the man was evocatively familiar, but Caine could not place him. Given the setting and the contrasting situations, the Colonel did not recognize him as the derelict he had seen under the tree in the Mall that rainy evening on his way to the Smithsonian reception.

"Well, if he's not in the barn, where can I find him?" Caine rejoined with growing irritation at the man's continued challenging stare.

"Mr. Sherwyck is not present," the butler finally said. "He has not returned." The butler avoided saying 'cathedral'. "There was an accident, you know," he said coldly.

"I know. When do you expect him?"

"Mr. Sherwyck is an extremely busy man. He has strict rules. No visitors, unless invited," he said ignoring the question.

"Oh, I'm not a visitor," Caine replied, and relished the uncertainty that flashed across the man's face.

"You have to leave! I'll inform him you were here," the butler said, as if to mollify the Colonel.

Caine studied the butler's face, then purposely walked to the stable door and peered inside.

"Leave here, before I call the authorities!"

"I *am* the authorities, my friend," Caine said with self satisfaction while observing a paddock midway in the stable. Visible to him was the head and neck of a shiny black stallion snorting inside his enclosure with the groom standing a respectable distance away.

Caine turned and slowly walked back toward his Viper. "That horse wouldn't have split hooves, would it?" he asked as he climbed in. He turned the ignition, looked penetratingly at the butler, gunned the engine and fish tailed the roadster towards the entrance of the estate, leaving a circle of tire marks in front of the scowling man.

* * *

Victor Sherwyck opened the front door of his mansion and stepped onto the veranda just as Caine's car was turning into the highway. He was still dressed in the dark suit he wore earlier in the day at the funeral for the Secretary of Defense. He stared at the front entrance where fumes from the Viper's exhaust were dissipating into the air. He could still hear the changing pitch of the engine. Sherwyck knew that Caine was on to something. He could tell by the determined shift of each gear.

His attendant returned from the stables.

"Did he see Blaze?"

"Only from a distance, sire."

Sherwyck's face turned sullen. He descended the stairs and walked towards a wooded area behind the mansion. A sudden rush of wind stirred the trees from the usual stillness of the hour that quietly transforms late afternoon into evening. He looked up at the rustling leaves and the sky beyond. Approaching night was the favorite time for Victor Sherwyck—especially with the promise of a full moon.

His eyes narrowed. "With the death of the Vice President, we are close to success. Colonel Caine and his ilk will not get in our way."

* * *

In a remote park near a small town in northern Arkansas eight teenagers gathered around an evening fire, recounting horror movies they had seen and thinking up scary ghost stories. Several of the young men produced cans of beer and two bottles of cheap whiskey. They passed around the pilfered treasure, laughing, joking and leering at one another with each swallow of the intoxicants.

"Hey!" said Jimmy Gruber as the stories began to evaporate. "We covered the witchcraft trials in Salem in our social studies class. Weird!"

"Salem—just like here!" Jessica Smith chimed in.

"Yeah! We're in Salem too. Are you a witch, Jessica?"

Everyone guffawed.

"No, but I can bewitch you pretty quick!"

Hearty laughter resounded around the fire, followed by chants of "Bewitch! Bewitch! Bewitch!"

Jessica stood up and postured in front of Jimmy. She swiveled her hips in her tight jeans and slowly pulled up her University of Arkansas sweat shirt to reveal ample unbridled breasts.

Jimmy gaped while the others laughed or smirked. Several girls were tempted to impress by doing the same, but hesitated.

Jessica quickly pulled down her sweat shirt and sat back cross-legged in front of the fire with her friend Gerri Lindquist giggling beside her.

"Hey! Did she bewitch you?" another of the young men asked to the accompaniment of more laughter.

Jimmy saw further opportunity.

"The Puritans were anal, man. They couldn't have fun so they faked it."

"How did they fake it?" someone asked while Jimmy took a swig of whiskey from the circulating bottle.

"They made groping official," Jimmy said tipsily to the amusement of his friends. "Sex was taboo, so they made it official."

"What do you mean, 'made it official'?" Tiffany Hauser asked after a gulp of beer.

"They felt up young girls who said they were possessed by demons. It was part of the exorcism."

"Come, on!"

"They told us in class," Jimmy announced.

"Pervert teacher!" Frank Wallace declared while throwing a new log on the fire.

The friends laughed heartily.

"Sure," Jimmy continued. "What a setup. The young ministers felt up the girls to chase away demons and the girls loved it. That's why they were so hot to say they were possessed. They accused a bunch of people of being witches."

"So the Puritans kept feeling up the girls to chase away the demons?" Ted Schwartz said suggestively.

"Yup."

"And the girls kept accusing people?" Stephanie Wilson asked.

"Yup."

"And you said you didn't like social studies," Tiffany exclaimed.

The resultant laughter fueled by their drink was infectious.

"Hey, I'm possessed," declared Susie Jackson in a sultry voice.

"Oh, yeah?" the young men chimed.

"Yeah! What about it?" she said and leaned backwards from a sitting position onto the ground.

Encouraging whoops, yelps and laughter arose from the group.

Frank Wallace, who was hoping to get better acquainted with Susie, crawled up to her on hands and knees. He leaned back on his haunches, placed his hands on Susie's stomach and began to massage, working his way upward toward her breasts. As he did so, her sweat shirt rose above her midriff.

"Oh, oh!" two girls on either side of the pair chimed, as others took swigs of their drinks.

Frank looked lustily at Susie, who returned his gaze.

"If you're going higher, you better chant something," Jessica Smith urged to more laughter from their friends.

Everyone looked with desirous interest as Frank stroked Susie's torso, fondling her breasts with his hands under her sweat shirt then roaming down between her slightly spreading legs.

Soon the crackling fire was the only sound as the high school classmates sipped their drinks and watched the suggestive mock ritual.

Jimmy Gruber hovered above Susie and Frank. He dangled a whiskey bottle loosely in his hand and grandly recited: "Come forth, you spirit from the dark—*abracadabra*—*hocus pocus*—I call you Satan from the fire! Come and fulfill our desire—*Elohim, Elohim!* I conjure him!"

"Hey, stupid!" Stephanie chided. "You're supposed to chase out a demon! Not call one!"

Abruptly, Susie rolled away from Frank and stood up adjusting her sweatshirt and dusting off her jeans. Frank looked around, startled.

No one laughed. They huddled in the wooded darkness around the light of the dwindling fire, listening for unfamiliar sounds around them.

"Should we put another log on the fire?" Jimmy asked.

"Why don't we just get outta' here!" someone answered.

* * *

At his estate not far from Mount Vernon, Victor Sherwyck felt a subtle tingling of energy course through his body. He smirked in self satisfaction.

* * *

Sarah Maddington, an attractive red head, closed her antique shop at nine in the evening and hurried out of the tourist mall off scenic highway 50 in West Virginia not far from Parkersburg on the Ohio border.

She was the High Priestess of a witches' coven that met every month by the light of the full moon in a secluded mountain glen outside of town. She was quivering with anticipation, because one of her "sisters", a beautiful co-ed at a nearby college, had found an initiate—a handsome young man who had become infatuated with her. Maddington gathered the necessary paraphernalia from her home and hurried to the gathering spot.

The co-ed, Rebecca Shaw, was already there with Rick Masters, the young man studying the occult as part of a theology curriculum. Others of the coven soon arrived in several cars and a pickup truck with a camper top. Seven comely young women dressed in flowery long skirts and colorfully printed blouses eventually gathered around a flat, worn granite outcrop in the glen.

Next to it was a fire pit readied for use with a pyramid of wood. They chatted amiably, introducing themselves to Rick. He noticed that some had local accents and several did not. They were presumably students or residents from elsewhere, maybe assigned to the Social Security Administration, which had an extensive, but unheralded fiscal operation in nearby Parkersburg.

Thirteen members would be an ideal number for the circle, but the practitioners were cautious and extremely careful in their screening of new believers. Meanwhile, they were thrilled to have this handsome, dark-haired specimen of a man as their ceremonial Priest. Trusting and enamored as he was with the attractive and smart Rebecca, he had, nevertheless, earlier had some boilermakers to calm his anxiety.

"Wait by this stone, now," Rebecca said with a sweet Appalachian drawl as she and the other women went to the vehicles parked nearby.

Soon they returned, each wearing a long, gray, silk robe. Several of them carried woven baskets , and one was holding a black velvet robe draped over her extended arm. From the split at the front, it was obvious from an occasional flash of thigh and curve of a breast, that they wore nothing underneath. A warm anticipatory glow came over Masters.

The women formed a circle around the stone and fire pit when Rick noticed that Rebecca was leading a black Billy Goat on a leash. She led the goat onto the broad stone and indicated that Rick should hold the leash. The young witches then strode in formation around the stone and began to hum. One stepped out and lit the fire. Another produced a long pipe, lit it from glowing kindle and took a deep drag before approaching Rick. She offered it to him with outstretched hands that widened the opening of her robe. He took a deep drag while staring at her voluptuous upper body and immediately felt lightheaded. She indicated he take another drag and then returned to the circle.

Flames from the fire soon leaped upward, lighting the glen and warming the air around them.

"Air and fire!" the witches chanted. "Air and fire, fulfill our desire! Air and fire fulfill our desire! Water and earth give us new birth! Water and earth, give us new birth!"

They repeated the chant as they walked in the circle, passing the pipe to the sister behind and chanting until they seemed in a trance. Then the High Priestess left the circle and approached Rick Masters. She undulated in front of him, her robe occasionally revealing her sinuous body. She methodically began to undress him while humming in time with her chanting sisters. He did not resist and felt no embarrassment as his body reacted to the alluring movements before him.

Rebecca came forward and draped the black velvet gown over him. She eased each hand into a sleeve and swayed back and forth in front of him too.

"Horned god of yore, become this vessel we implore!" the High Priestess chanted.

"Horned god of yore, become this vessel we implore!" the witches droned.

As they did so, each walked in a practiced gait back and forth around the restless Billy Goat, retrieving dried flower petals from pockets in their robes and scattering them in their tracks, until an obvious figure of a pentagram appeared.

"Horned god of yore, become this vessel we implore!" the High Priestess repeated. "Horned god of yore, become this vessel we implore. Hear our call for unity!"

"Manifest your dual identity!" the others chanted.

After several more incantations the Billy Goat bleated.

"Tis true! Tis true! The god is in you!" Sarah Maddington intoned. "You've heard our call! We're your maidens, all!"

She began to stroke Rick Masters over his body. Two blondes approached with a sultry gait and held his arms outstretched, making him look like a living cross.

One by one the women slipped out of their robes and placed them together on the ground at Rick's feet. The High Priestess let her gown slip from her body while the two holding his arms, pulled the black gown from Rick. They urged him down onto the robes. He was woozy and happily complied.

After erotic stroking that fired common excitement, the group was in an orgiastic revelry laughing, gyrating, and engaging in lascivious acts with abandon. Several of the nubile witches were just as interested in each other as they were in their newly initiated Priest. Writhing bodies mingled and intertwined looking ghostly pale under the light of the full moon.

No one noticed the fire was dwindling until one or another of the young women's energy was spent or they felt climactic satisfaction and lay sprawled on the ground. One of the witches, a long-haired brunette, crawled over to the embers and tossed more logs on the fire. Soon the flames were alive again, throwing shadows of the witches and their Priest on the overhanging canopy of trees in the glen, appearing as a simmering cauldron under the beam of the full moon.

One by one, the members of the coven moved closer to the fire. The pale contours of their bodies disappeared, looking more alluring in the light. Each member draped a robe upon another and the two blondes draped the black velvet robe upon Rick. They arrayed themselves in a circle around the fire.

Sarah Maddington now opened one of the baskets. From it she took soybean meal, and murmuring incantations, presented it to the goat resting on the granite outcrop.

Masters was glad he met Rebecca on campus. He truly liked her, her lilting accent, self-assurance and wit. And she offered some real field work in his major. These were free spirited women who worshipped nature. Can't be anything wrong with that, he rationalized. He looked in a happy daze at the striking young women around him. "We don't cackle," he recalled Rebecca saying. This must be a coven of white witches and not the other kind—the demon worshippers. "It's better to mix it up with these beautiful hotties," he thought, "then to have to kiss the ass of that goat and swear allegiance to the devil."

Rick Masters determined he was one lucky scholar.

The High Priestess returned and ceremonially opened the other baskets. Inside each was food and intoxicating drink.

"Our energy is one with you!" she intoned kneeling on her haunches. "Air and fire. Water and earth," she said more softly and bowed. "We thank you for your sustenance."

Then raising her head towards the sky she proclaimed loudly: "Our gift to you is our spent desire! May it drive the energy of Gaia, Mother Earth!"

"May it drive the energy of Gaia, Mother Earth!" the others said with finality.

The coven now relaxed in convivial, ordinary conversation, a midnight picnic. Some kept their robes draped casually over their shoulders, others stuck their hands through the sleeves as the night grew cooler and the fire waned.

Rick Masters munched on a chicken wing, his black velvet robe draped over his shoulders. He tilted his bottle in salute, took a swig of beer and smiled at Rebecca near him.

This small town in West Virginia would not be so boring after all.

"Where did you get that—" he hesitated lest he offend someone— "where did you get Pan for the ceremony?"

"He's from our farm," Rebecca replied. "My folks have a shop at the mall. The tourists love goat milk fudge."

* * *

At about the time the High Priestess was summoning the horned god of yore, Victor Sherwyck was swirling a snifter of Brandy in front of a fire at his mansion near Mount Vernon.

He felt a surge of rejuvenating energy as he took a liberal sip.

Chapter 34

E. Theodore Rawlins was walking his two bulldogs, Cisco and Juanita, along a densely wooded foot trail in Rock Creek Park several miles northwest of the National Mall. The Park meandered for more than twelve miles along Rock Creek between 16th Street and Connecticut Avenue to the border of Maryland.

Rock Creek Park and other parks circling Washington were a legacy of the Civil War when nearly 90 forts were built in a ring around the capital to protect it from Confederate attack. Now the old fortifications were part of vast urban woodland—much of it isolated and quite rugged—encompassing thousands of acres in and around Washington managed by the National Park Service.

Rawlins was a retired professor from Georgetown University's Public Policy Institute. He specialized in International Security and was an occasional consultant to the government on homeland security issues. Actually, he had been eased out as a scaremonger because of his persistence—even to an annoying degree—that Washington was very vulnerable to attack from the public attractions known as the Circle of Forts. The wooded preserves were a perfect hideout or a staging area for terrorists bent on doing harm in the heart of Washington. Rawlins had occasionally said so publicly and was perceived by various colleagues in the prestigious university as somewhat paranoid and a negative influence on tourism.

He had received anonymous death threats that his government sources suggested might be of foreign origin related to his security consultancy. They urged he retire with full pay and benefits and stay in touch. Rawlins remembered the old adage: "If you want a friend in Washington, get a dog." He did so, on both counts.

He bought the dogs for companionship and protection. Cisco, the white male, and fawn colored Juanita—both looking like overgrown pit bulls—were eager for their daily off-leash exercise in the hilly woods they loved to explore.

Rawlins was mindful of the fact that the remains of two sensationalized crime victims were found in the vicinity some years earlier. The skeletal remains of a female government employee were found in a wooded ravine more than a year after she disappeared. And the body of a young Washington administrator was found in the Creek in the same general vicinity. Both victims had lived several blocks from each other in Washington. A suspect was eventually named and jailed—but on an unrelated charge, because the investigation was lacking firm evidence.

The prematurely retired professor had no compunction about walking the trails in the early morning hours. Fixated on his security threat theory, he envisioned himself as a private patrol. He was accompanied by two fierce looking dogs, and he had his cell phone with quick dial numbers to several government agencies. His ultimate comfort, however, was the Smith & Wesson .38 Special he carried ever since federal law permitted concealed weapons in national parks.

Cisco and Juanita were following their noses along a treed embankment while Rawlins ambled along the parallel trail. Farther ahead of him was Military Road, which bisected Rock Creek Park and united east and west portions of Washington across the rugged parkland. Some morning traffic could be heard on the road, unseen through trees, but obvious by the drone of tires on pavement where no other urban sounds interrupted.

Suddenly Juanita's fur bristled and she uttered a low growl. Cisco perked his head up and sniffed the air in her direction. Rawlins looked their way and slowly put his hand into the pocket of his windbreaker, grasping the handle of his revolver. The two large bulldogs disappeared over the embankment. Rawlins, who was in his mid fifties, scurried up the gentle slope and looked through thick underbrush toward a fallen tree trunk that bridged a small ravine. Through the brush he glimpsed flashes of white and tan busily circling a small mound under the tree trunk, whining and sniffing frantically.

Instinctively, the retired consultant on national security drew his revolver and looked around him. He shuddered involuntarily, suspecting what he might find. He pushed aside some bushes with his revolver in hand and made his way towards his dogs. Rawlins stooped under the tree trunk. He noticed jutting from the earthen mound what looked like polyester legging from a jogging suit. The dirt around it was fresh and recently turned.

"Why am I not surprised?" he said aloud in a plaintive voice.

Cisco and Juanita pawed at the mound and snagged the crook of an arm.

Rawlins was already on his cell phone dialing a programmed number while he stood next to the fallen tree trunk, his dogs sniffing, growling and whining at the ground near his feet.

* * *

Within an hour the area was cordoned off with yellow tape. A half dozen patrol cars with a laboratory and coroner's van were parked along Ross Drive south of the Military Road interchange. Several scenic roads branched off towards populated areas of Washington. Park rangers, together with Washington Metropolitan police officers, were huddled around the fallen tree trunk. Among them was Colonel Garrison Jones, whose number Rawlins had called. He had arrived in a civilian suit so as not to draw undue attention, and was there to ascertain whether the victim could be the missing Jeannie McConnell.

Forensic technicians had carefully removed dirt to reveal the face of a female who had been placed on her back with her arms crossed over her chest. When the pawing dogs snagged her arm they had pulled back an unzipped jacket that revealed part of a pattern of blue markings on her upper body.

Several men and a woman probed gingerly with medical gloves to uncover more of the face and torso from the dirt. One of them stood over the corpse and took pictures from various angles.

"Another sad story, Todd," Colonel Jones uttered looking towards Rawlins who was calming his dogs after leashing them. "Thanks for calling it in."

"It's the least I could do," Rawlins said patting the heads of Juanita and Cisco in turn.

"Thanks for taking walks in the park," Jones emphasized.

"Like I said, Arie, it's the least I can do."

They both turned their attention to the investigators who were carefully digging around the body as if on an ancient archeological find.

"From the looks of things, she hasn't been here too long," one of them said.

"There's some strange markings on her torso," the woman technician added. "Some incisions too."

"Not like others we found," her colleague replied.

"Well, the others were skeletal, so we'll never know."

"True," the first technician remembered. "So it's still likely there could be some connection."

"That'll take some serious investigation."

Colonel Jones hovered over the forensic specialists. "Those markings don't seem random," he ventured. "It looks like blue grease paint. Almost a design."

"Maybe so," a technician muttered, a little irritated at being second guessed by this stranger with credentials. "We'll know after a complete forensic analysis."

"Any idea who she might be?" Colonel Jones asked impulsively.

"No. You?" the technician replied coldly.

"No. Poor thing." Colonel Jones didn't feel right to tell him he was relieved the victim was not Jeannie McConnell.

He stepped back towards Rawlins who was a few feet up the ravine. The Colonel patted the dogs, thinking of the two burly ones lunging at him and Colonel Caine during the firefight in Beirut. "Thanks for the call."

"I wish I didn't have to make it."

"I know."

They bade good-bye as a police officer cautiously approached Rawlins, wary of the two bulldogs. Colonel Jones nodded to the officer, pushed aside some brush and made his way back towards official vehicles lined up along the isolated park road.

Chapter 35

The two operatives of the Omega Group were already in General William Bradley's Pentagon office in the pre-dawn hours, when Colonel Jones received the urgent call from the retired professor.

The looks of General Bradley and Colonel Caine posed the same question as they listened: Could the victim be Jeannie McConnell?

"Head out there," Bradley ordered when Jones hung up. "Make sure of an ID. This could change the tone of the whole investigation."

He rose from his leather armchair and went to his desk, instructing an aide through the intercom. "Call the park rangers and metro police. Colonel Jones will give you details. He's just leaving."

Bradley returned to the armchair opposite Colonel Caine, who was sitting on the studded leather sofa along the office wall. Between them was a glass coffee table with sweet rolls and coffee as fuel for the debriefing the General had been conducting.

"Well, Chris, if your speculation about Sherwyck is anywhere near correct, then that victim in the park can no way be Jeannie McConnell."

"I agree, sir."

"Too bad, though, whoever she is. It's not the first body found in that reserve."

A thoughtful silence ensued. Both officers drank their coffee and sampled the continental breakfast.

"You think there's any connection?" General Bradley eventually asked.

"When there's a deadly pattern, I always do, sir. Only innocent things can be coincidences. Evil is typically repetitive, even cumulative."

General Bradley nodded slightly.

"So, you think that bullet hole you found in the van at Sherwyck's has some connection to something."

"It's the van that picked up the thugs who attacked us outside the museum that night."

"Because you marked it with a bullet? For identification?"

"The only option, sir. It was speeding away in the dark."

"You did the right thing under the circumstances, but do you have any idea how many vans around Washington could have bullet holes in them? Look at any dented street sign in parts of town, or along the highways."

"True, sir. But things tie in here. There's something going on. Who'd have an armed gang outside the museum at night? In fact, it reminds me that the waiters at the official reception that night were out of place. Carruthers tells me it's a union contract provision: only their members attend to the museum at night. Sherwyck shepherded that contract as a museum trustee. Something ties in with that whole diamond business."

"When people talk about the curse of the Hope Diamond, they do it with a smile, Chris. Like I said before, I don't think you'd want to present a fairy tale at a strategy session of the Omega Group."

"Circumstantial evidence suggests it might not be a fairy tale," Colonel Caine said unshakably. "What's scary, General, is that Laura Mitchell, the woman demonstrating her uncle's pentagram theory for me, predicted something was likely to happen at the Cathedral during Stack's funeral."

"I'll grant you that, Chris, but we can't act unless we have something air tight. Something that practically hits us in the face."

Caine sat back cradling his cup of coffee and prepared himself again to hear caution.

"This is not some neighborhood roust of a burglar. We're talking about accusations against a renowned national icon. And let me remind you," the General emphasized, "you haven't even seen Sherwyck, let alone speak with him. You're tying together a series of tragic accidents and implying conspiracy. The only thing right now that even remotely connects them are some coincidences. And not logically related at that. We're speculating here about esoteric theories. The occult."

General Bradley took a deep breath. "You know, even my suspicion of Senator Dunne as the leak that got you attacked in the Mediterranean was smoothed over by the Vice President—God rest his soul—during our Omega Group meeting. A plausible coincidence, he said, given all the violence going on over there."

Colonel Caine raised an eyebrow as he slowly took another sip of his coffee. The General no longer implied treachery by Senator Dunne, but used the defensible, even innocent word "leak."

"And the black stallion in Sherwyck's barn? General Starr?"

"Don't get me wrong, Chris. I'm with you on this. We can draw a very connected picture. But is it actionable? I'm hearing bizarre theories. Who do we accuse? Of what? And how? That some tragic accidents happened? That there were some animals nearby? That some cabal is working black magic with their gibberish?"

General Bradley leaned back in his armchair, frustrated at his own words.

"If the various accidents were evil acts, Chris. In your own words. How do we connect them? How are they cumulative? Where's the evil hand guiding them?"

"Well, sir. There is one clincher that could hit us in the face. But I hope to heaven it doesn't happen."

"I know, Chris. I know. Your theory would be proven if some accident befell the President."

"Right, sir," Caine emphasized. "If our speculation is correct. That's where all these events are leading. Like we discussed at the

Army and Navy Club."

"Michelle McConnell assumes the Presidency and she's automatically ripe for blackmail by whoever has her daughter."

"Right, sir. And Philip Taylor simultaneously has authority over the nuclear button."

"But there's nothing against Taylor," General Bradley noted.

"True, sir. Except that the President was dead set against him to take Ron Stack's place as Secretary of Defense."

"As far as we know that's just political gamesmanship," General Bradley countered. "One party versus the other in the perpetual race for the White House. Taylor has a reputation as a professional bureaucrat."

"The only thing that's against him right now, is that Sherwyck insisted upon his appointment when Defense Secretary Stack died."

"That's just it, Chris, you and I are holding that connection against him. No one else is. He's an upstanding public servant who's been in the government who knows how many years."

"All that aside, sir," Caine said to shift emphasis. "We have the potential of Michelle McConnell suddenly becoming President of the United States. Her daughter is missing and presumed kidnapped. I think the Middle East lead was a stall for time. The attack on Arie and me in the ocean was meant for us not to reach our contact. Why? Because our contact, Hammad, would tell us that terrorists had nothing to do with Jeannie's disappearance. When they couldn't kill us in the ocean, they attacked Hammad too. And it all looks like just another day of factional fighting in the Middle East."

General Bradley shifted his weight onto his elbow on the arm rest. His eyes fixed on his operative as he listened.

"I think that the ultimate blackmail scenario is being worked on by someone right now!" Caine asserted.

"You're suggesting somehow by means of that legend? The curse of the Hope Diamond?"

Colonel Caine leaned back in the sofa looking resolutely at the

General across from him. He didn't answer.

"You know how far we can go with this, don't you?" Bradley continued.

"Obviously, sir. We couldn't present this to the Omega Group."

"Obviously! Can you imagine the public reaction if word ever leaked out that high level government officials were dabbling in the occult? Entertaining sorcery as the cause of a major crisis?"

Colonel Caine lowered his eyes and focused on a glazed donut on the coffee table. His face took on a distant look.

"Although, General, someone in the Omega Group knows exactly what we're talking about," he added cryptically.

A voice on the intercom announced that Colonel Jones had returned.

"Send him right in," General Bradley answered without hesitation.

Colonel Jones hurried into the office announcing, "It's not her!" even before he sat down in another armchair around the coffee table.

When he settled into where he had been an hour earlier, he looked to General Bradley and his fellow commando. "From her clothes, it appears like another jogger. They'll be doing further analysis. The lucky thing is, the body was hidden there recently. Todd Rawlin's dogs discovered her while roaming their usual haunts."

"Good old, Rawlins," General Bradley interjected. "We should bring him in for another seminar. He deserves some appreciation after the rotten deal he got at the university."

"True, sir," Colonel Jones said. "You can never be too eccentric."

"Too bad he found a body," Bradley lamented with morbid humor. "Maybe someday his dogs will spot a camped-out terrorist shitting in the woods."

The three grinned at the visual image.

"Victims in the past were too far gone," Colonel Jones continued.

Bradley and Caine nodded concurrence.

"They had just enough from the bones to prove foul play. This poor thing was only there for days—no one's sure exactly how many—there were strange blue markings on her torso."

"Blue markings?" Caine suddenly lurched forward on the sofa.

"From the part I saw, it looked like some kind of design."

"Draw it, before you forget!" Caine urged as he stood up.

"With your permission, sir." Colonel Jones left his armchair and went to the General's desk. He grabbed a legal pad and an ink pen from a commemorative stand. The General and Colonel Caine were already hovering over him when he started to trace a shield-like design with an X through the middle.

"That's the part I saw," Jones noted.

"What the hell is that?" General Bradley asked for all three.

"I don't know, but it sure looks purposeful," Colonel Jones replied. "Why else trace it on a body?"

"I might have a witness," Caine declared.

"What are you saying, Chris?" General Bradley inquired.

"Two workers gave Laura threatening looks in an elevator."

"And?"

"She told one of them he had a blue streak on his neck. Might smear his collar."

General Bradley and Colonel Jones stared at Caine expectantly.

"Didn't you tell me she heard a women screaming inside the museum?" Colonel Jones added.

"I'm beginning to think she was right!"

"When? The night you were attacked?" General Bradley pressed.

Colonel Caine nodded.

The three officers peered with grim curiosity at the design Jones had drawn.

"There's someone who could help us with this," Caine said tearing the illustrated sheet off the pad."

"Sir?" He looked to the General.

"Carry on!"

Colonel Caine saluted and hurried out of the office.

Chapter 36

Laura Mitchell was discussing with her students the impact of Napoleon Bonaparte on early 19th Century Europe. She smiled to herself when she heard the loud rumble of a car's engine outside a window of her seminar room. She recognized it as Colonel Caine's roadster. The rumble faded in and out several times.

"Can't find a parking space," she thought, then after a mirthful pause, continued.

"Napoleon's decision to invade Russia in Eighteen- twelve was a momentous event in his reign as Emperor. It ultimately cost France her dominant role in the world."

Everyone in class heard the engine again. This time a loud roar, then silence. Professor Mitchell was tempted to go over to the window, but did not want to disrupt the discussion.

"Napoleon's advisers and generals had cautioned him not to invade Russia, but his sense of infallibility prevailed," she said firmly to refocus everyone's attention.

"Why did he insist?" asked one of the students.

"He announced that Czar Alexander would sue for peace within six weeks," Dr. Mitchell replied.

"Napoleon was self-assured and always invited candid remarks from his close advisers. They kept urging that he not invade Russia, but he didn't listen. He always had some logical reply and would often tweak an adviser's cheek in fatherly reproach."

She paused for affect, then declared. "But there is one sign that Napoleon should have heeded, given the beliefs of the time."

"What's that?" asked Corey Wynn, the divinity student.

"An omen!" Dr. Mitchell replied.

Just then Colonel Caine peered into the seminar room and caught a glimpse of the professor who stood out in her cream colored skirt and jacket, accented by her ornamental gold chain with the signature amber pendant. Several students looked up to see the military man standing in the doorway.

Without interrupting her trend of thought, Dr. Mitchell continued.

"Napoleon's army was arrayed along the Nemunas River in Lithuania, ready to cross into Russia. It's June, Eighteen-twelve."

Caine stepped back and leaned casually against a wall near the door, so he wouldn't divert attention, but could still hear the lecture.

"There's an ironic parallel here," she pointed out. "Adolf Hitler attacked Russia more than a century later on the same night in late June. Critics predicted failure for the Nazis, based on Napoleon's disastrous invasion of Russia more than a hundred years earlier."

"But Napoleon didn't have any lessons to go by, when he tried," Tony Powell interjected as a punch line.

"Oh, but he did, Mr. Powell. He did." Dr. Mitchell said emphatically. "When Napoleon invaded Russia the warnings of calamity were much more simple, even mystic. In those times people were more prone to superstition and believed in omens."

Having urged more information in the previous lecture about her uncle's theories, the students were listening eagerly. Colonel Caine in the hallway unconsciously leaned closer to the doorway.

"The night before the invasion, Napoleon made a moonlight reconnaissance along the banks of the river to choose the best place to cross his troops. As he galloped through a wheat field, a startled hare ran between the legs of his stallion and made it swerve. Emperor Napoleon Bonaparte fell off his horse."

"I would say, that's a sign," commented the divinity student.

"What's interesting, Corey," replied Dr. Mitchell, "is that this appears to be the only recorded time in the reign of Napoleon Bonaparte—as Emperor—that he fell off a horse."

"Who recorded it?" asked Amy.

"One of his generals in a memoir. He was a close adviser and Master of Horse. Armand de Caulaincourt."

"Did anybody else see him fall off?"

"Oh, yes. Other generals and officers. In fact, Caulaincourt writes that Napolean's fall struck him as a bad omen. Other generals thought so too. One of them grabbed Caulaincourt's hand and said: 'We should do better than to cross the Nemunas. That fall is a bad sign'."

"I could see where strategic reasons would cancel the invasion," offered Tony Powell. "But omens? They were all educated upper crust, weren't they?"

"That's a good point," replied Dr. Mitchell. "But I have a quote from the memoirs indicating that many of Napoleon's officers did believe the fall was a bad omen."

She glanced at notes in front her and read: "Some of the headquarters staff observed that the Romans, who believed in portents, would not have undertaken the crossing of the Nemunas, writes the general. It appears that Napoleon's officers agreed. Napoleon himself is described as cheerful and confident before the fall, but serious and preoccupied after."

"What about that hare? Could that have been someone's familiar?" Corey Wynn asked.

Dr. Mitchell grinned. "I don't know, Corey. No one's ever been linked to the hare," she added satirically.

"What about that monk, Pierre Dumas? Was he around at the time?"

"No one knows. By the time of the Revolution, he was gone from the historical record. But that doesn't mean he wasn't around. Besides, his supposed familiar was a wolf dog."

"Familiars are supposed to be able to change shapes," Corey reminded.

"True," Dr. Mitchell said more seriously. "True. If you're into that kind of thing."

"Are you into that kind of thing, Dr. Mitchell," asked Abigail Hitchcock. "You sure talk a lot about it lately."

The professor grinned sheepishly. "You're right. I have talked about it a lot, haven't I?"

Colonel Caine, listening in the hallway, smiled in acknowledgment.

"So why did he go ahead and invade Russia?" asked Amy Cabot. "It cost him his rule."

"Hubris," Dr. Mitchell intoned. "Classic hubris. Haughtiness, arrogance, a sense of invincibility."

She thought of the recent events occurring around them and her uncle's pentagram centered on the Museum of Natural History. "What Napoleon should have had—" she emphasized, and said more loudly for Colonel Caine's benefit in the hallway—"is a little more taste of superstition. He crossed the Nemunas River and went on to monumental disaster in Russia. That hare apparently was trying to tell him something."

"It seems there's always some signs before major disasters," Tom Stuart, the political science major observed.

"I can't argue with that," Dr. Mitchell replied.

"What do you think about those accidents with the Secretary of Defense and Chairman of the Joint Chiefs?" he followed. "And now the Vice President?"

"Well," she replied slowly. "If we follow the trend of thought we've just had, it could be something predictive."

"Some kind of conspiracy?" Tom ventured.

"This sounds like it would be a great movie," Abigail Hitchcock, the television producer's daughter, said enthusiastically.

"Maybe," Dr. Mitchell replied. "Yet another lesson for our own time. But, again, this is a history seminar on the French Revolution. We could explore more esoteric subjects over coffee in the student union sometime. "

The looks of her students indicated interest. She glanced at the clock on the back wall. "There are fifteen minutes left. If it's all right with you, let's stop here for today. Next week we'll discuss how the rest of Europe reacted to the invasion and to Napoleon."

"Waterloo, Waterloo," a sing song voice responded as the students gathered their material and filed out. Several lingered around the seminar tables, chatting with classmates.

Colonel Caine stepped in.

"Omens, omens," she said cheerfully in greeting, but her smile disappeared when she noticed his somber demeanor.

"Can you come with me? It's important," he said.

"I can imagine." She gathered her notes and a laptop computer, put them into a beige briefcase and followed him out of the room.

"I'll see you next week," she said turning to the several students still in the room. They were smiling at her and the officer.

He took her hand and wordlessly led her out of Phillips Hall. Outside, the earlier roar of an engine became clear. Caine's Viper was parked illegally on the curb in front of her building with a flashing blue light on the dashboard. "This must be something," she thought as they approached the vehicle.

As he rumbled in low gear along H Street through the busy campus grounds, he turned to her and finally spoke.

"They found a body in Rock Creek Park."

Laura looked puzzled.

"It had blue markings on it."

She gasped.

"A woman?" she asked catching her breath.

"Yes."

A visible shudder coursed through her body.

"Where are we going?" she asked nervously.

"To see your uncle. Tell me again about those two men in the elevator."

Chapter 37

Senator Everett Dunne was walking along the imposing modern sculpture dominating the nine story atrium of the Hart Senate Office Building. He had just recessed a hearing of the Senate Intelligence Committee and was hurrying to the private Capitol Subway that would take him to the U.S. Capitol Building for a floor debate on nuclear arms limitation. His plans changed when he met a colleague turning a corner along the sculpture.

"Did you hear? They found a woman's body in Rock Creek Park."

Senator Dunne listened with familiar interest.

"It was in the same area where they found the bones of that missing secretary. Remember? The case that ruined Senator Rowan? His affair with her? But they couldn't pin anything on him?"

Senator Dunne's round, boyish face turned red and his heart quickened.

"No. I haven't."

"I'll betcha' some of the good ol' boys around here are hoping their mistresses are safe in beds," he added slyly. "Are you heading to the Chambers? I'll come with you."

"Uhh, thanks, but I've got to make a stop," Dunne quickly answered. "I'll be there." The Senator changed direction in the airy marbled hallway and hurried to the covetous first level of the three-tiered underground garage. His dark blue sedan was parked in a privileged spot near the main entrance to Constitution Avenue.

His screeching exit seemed uncharacteristic to several Senate staffers passing by. Soon he was speeding south on the George Washington Parkway towards the estate of Victor Sherwyck.

Sherwyck was walking his stallion from the stable to the lawns in front of his mansion when Dunne drove onto the grounds. He parked midway along the drive to intercept them.

The Senator climbed out in haste and approached Sherwyck, whose black jersey and slacks matched the color of his shimmering horse. Blaze snorted and pulled on his lead trying to rear up on his hind legs. He reared slightly — the red bell boots on his hooves flashing in a blur — then landed restlessly and stomped on all fours as Sherwyck shortened the lead and calmed him with a soothing stroke on the neck.

"What are you doing here?" Sherwyck snapped.

"What am I doing here?" Dunne replied indignantly. "I'm a ranking United States Senator! Isn't that enough?"

Sherwyck gazed at him with a pathetic grin.

"They weren't supposed to find her so fast!" the Senator blurted and nervously stroked back his curly hair. "What about the grease paint? They'll find us out!" He stepped back and forth trying to gauge a safe distance from the restless stallion.

"You are still too timid," Sherwyck said coolly as he continued stroking the horse's neck. "You cannot be afraid. You have to feel assured."

"Assured?" Dunne nervously adjusted his wire rimmed glasses. "How can I be assured when there's suspicion all around? That General accused me at the OG meeting of setting up the two commandos in the ocean. Now this!"

"What came of the meeting, Senator?"

"Well, nothing."

"Nothing!" Sherwyck asserted.

"Nothing so far," Dunne pressed.

"We have sent them on wild goose chases after their favorite targets—terrorists," Sherwyck said with authority. "They are obsessed with them. You need not worry."

"What about the girl? They weren't supposed to find her with all those symbols on her! The others weren't discovered for a long time, for God's sake!"

"For God's sake?" Sherwyck haughtily raised his head. "For *God's* sake, you say? Is your commitment faltering? Are you not praying *our* way? Do I need to worry about you?"

"No! No, of course not! It's just an expression."

"Expressions are telling, my Senator. Very telling."

Dunne was flustered as he watched the gaunt, composed figure eyeing him sternly and stroking the neck of his agitated steed.

"Our moment is here. There is no need for fear of exposure." Victor Sherwyck spoke out as if preaching: "Our strength lies in our roots! The fantastical world of superstition and disbelief!"

His voice rose. "That has gone on for ages! That is why we succeed! Reasoned minds cannot begin to grasp our task or our works! Those who try are ridiculed! Any discovery will be too late! We will have accomplished our purpose! The final stroke is imminent!" he announced climactically.

Victor Sherwyck stared coldly and penetratingly into the Senator's eyes.

"Are you up to it?"

"Of course, I'm up to it!" Senator Dunne declared with renewed composure.

"Then follow our long established agreement and do not falter! It is your presence here and your anxiety that puts you at risk."

"Me at risk? Me at risk? What about you?"

"I am above risk!" Sherwyck declared

"Well, I'm a United States Senator!" Dunne repeated and proudly arched his back.

"An obsequious one, I expect."

"Of course, of course," the Senator affirmed. "But what about Taylor?"

Sherwyck responded slowly, as if calculating whether to enlighten Senator Dunne how deeply the presumptive Secretary of Defense was involved in their cabal.

"Taylor has acted in the Ritual, my dear Senator. You have not. Your supreme test is looming, together with our final stroke. The unmatched sacrifice for the highest prize!"

Dunne stared expectantly.

"The President!"

Sherwyck sounded cryptic again, but Senator Dunne was used to such utterances.

"You will have to be firm!" Sherwyck announced. "Unwavering!"

"Then! Then, you too will be above risk!"

The assurance from this commanding figure controlling the powerful stallion with the red hoof coverings stepping in place next to him was enough for Dunne to hear.

"I am firm!" Senator Dunne mustered in response. "I never exposed you!" he declared bravely to regain some psychological equilibrium in front of this magnetic personage.

Sherwyck responded with a piercing stare and loosened his grip on Blaze's lead. The stallion reared on his hind legs and two-stepped closer ready to alight his forelegs on the Senator's head. Dunne reeled back and Sherwyck tightened the lead as the forelegs hit the ground. The stallion snorted with lowered head and pinned back ears.

"You will never try to betray me!" Sherwyck commanded.

"No, no never!" Senator Dunne exclaimed fervently.

He knelt on one knee and made ready to kiss Victor Sherwyck's outstretched hand.

The Sorcerer peered down on his supplicant with a wicked sneer.

Chapter 38

Colonel Caine and Laura Mitchell hurried into the Library of Congress and headed for her uncle's basement office. Approaching it, they saw through the open doorway a tall bookcase from the back wall toppled onto his desk.

"Uncle Jonas?" Laura called excitedly and both ran into the office.

Her uncle lay splayed on his back along his desk. Two books were on his chest and several others were arrayed next to him. A chair lay overturned nearby. Colonel Caine quickly noticed a small trickle of blood from Jonas Mitchell's mouth. He grabbed his cell phone and immediately dialed 911, but could not get a signal.

He raced out of the office and charged up a spiral staircase near the room leading to upper levels. He bounded up to the next level filled with more stacked books and encountered a young man looking down the narrow walkway.

"Quick! Have the desk call Emergency! There's an injured man down here!"

"Yes, sir," the young man—by all looks a student—instantly replied to the commanding figure in front of him. "I thought I heard a noise here somewhere."

"Hurry! Basement office!"

The young man squeezed past the Colonel and scurried up the spiral staircase.

Caine rushed back to the office where Laura was cradling her uncle's head.

"Careful, Laura! Careful!" he said firmly, but soothingly. "We don't know how bad he's hurt. Don't move him."

"It's.. all right, Christopher," moaned the old man. "No... pain....just..tired."

"Don't talk. Lie still," Caine knelt on one knee beside him. He looked concernedly at Laura. He didn't want to say that her uncle probably had internal injuries.

"Injury.. inside," Jonas Mitchell said. "Don't.. know…"

"You'll be all right," Caine soothed.

"Yes, Uncle," Laura repeated tearfully cradling his head. "You'll be all right."

"Getting…book," he wheezed. "…Chair...Cat..into ..room…"

Laura and the Colonel glanced at each other. Their looks signaled the same thought.

"Some..thing.. happ...happened…fell," Jonas Mitchell struggled to say.

"It doesn't matter. Help is coming," Caine assured. "You'll be all right."

"Maybe..yes…maybe no."

"Don't talk. Rest," Laura repeated.

Mitchell persisted with labored breath. "Laura, dear. You.. finish…manusc…my work."

"How, Uncle, how?' she asked desperately.

"Chris…topher will…help. I know. Good…man. The star…the center…the…star."

Caine could hear the faint sounds of sirens outside. He felt silent relief, but hoped it was not too late for Laura's uncle.

"They're coming, Uncle Jonas! They're coming!" Laura said.

"…Laura, my.. sweet. Brothers…of the forest…waiting. I.. out..lived them.. outlived the Gulag... lived…to tell the.. story. You..have ..wonderful friend." He gasped.

"Not so fast, Uncle. Not so fast," Caine intoned. "You're not going anywhere just yet."

"We...shall...see." Jonas wheezed and lost consciousness.

Laura was quietly sobbing, kneeling with her uncle's head in her lap and Caine's hand on her shoulder when three paramedics arrived. They quickly took over. Caine held her in his embrace comforting her and answering occasional questions from the paramedics. They administered oxygen and placed probes on the old man's body for remote reads at the trauma center of George Washington University Hospital.

They were instructed to get him there immediately. "Is someone coming along?" one of the paramedics inquired.

Laura gazed into Caine's eyes and he nodded assurance.

"The marks?" she whispered anxiously. "The meaning?"

"We'll find out. Who did them is more important."

The paramedics carefully shifted Jonas Mitchell to a stretcher, raised the accordion frame and wheeled him slowly towards the elevator with Laura walking alongside. She glanced back at the Colonel. He gave her an assuring smile.

Caine viewed the disarray around him and stared imaginatively at the toppled bookcase. It had to have been a strange accident, he pondered. There was no way it could fall over by the old man pulling a book from a shelf. The chair had solid footing, no casters. What might cause him to grab the bookcase and make it top heavy? Jonas' labored remark that a cat came into the room was nagging at him. Unlikely in the basement of the Library of Congress. A semi-conscious hallucination? But then, the other incidents?

He perused the top of Jonas Mitchell's desk and fingered the manuscript on which the old partisan and scholar was laboring. The Colonel flipped the pages with curious interest. Interspersed among paragraphs were occasional hand drawn symbols. The pentagram inside a circle was illustrated in several places with variations inside the star. His eyes widened, when he came upon a familiar design.

"That's it!" he murmured half aloud. He was looking at the complete representation of the partial design Colonel Jones had drawn from the markings he saw on the body in the park.

It illustrated a paragraph about Black Magic. The shield was there with the X through it, as Jones had drawn. The lines of the shield then continued at the bottom and reversed with a flourish as if a base for the shield with barbed endings. Under the shield was a V with barbed peaks. Under the illustration were the Latin words: *Grimorium Verum*.

He read around the illustration and learned the symbol represented the defining instructions for Black Magic rituals.

"Coincidences, like hell!" he declared aloud.

Caine gathered up Jonas Mitchell's manuscript and hurried back to the main hall of the hallowed Library. A librarian was leaning low and calling under one of the semi circular reading tables to the amusement of patrons seated nearby.

"Here, kitty, kitty! Here kitty, kitty!" echoed in the arched chamber. "How did that damn cat get in here anyway?" she exclaimed with uncharacteristic frustration.

A large black and gray striped alley cat scooted from under a table to the entrance, stood momentarily with its tail twitching in anticipation, and darted outside as another patron opened the door to enter.

"Like hell!" Caine murmured coldly, quickening his step and following the cat out the door. He looked left and right along the esplanade, but saw nothing. A splendid view of the Capitol before him was suddenly marred by his realization that what it represented was vulnerable to threats abstract and inexplicable.

He put Mitchell's manuscript on the concrete balustrade in front of him, pulled out his cell phone and dialed General Bradley.

"Anything new?" the General responded.

"The markings on the body deal with Black Magic," Colonel Caine said flatly.

"Okay. We can tell that to the police, if they haven't figured it out already. Kooks usually concoct a reason for killing people."

"We have to focus on the museum. The blue grease paint is a direct connection."

There was a momentary silence. Caine imagined his general leaving his desk and pacing back and forth in his office, irritated and frustrated.

"Our assignment is Jeannie McConnell," Bradley continued. "The body wasn't her, so let's get back to our priority number one."

"There's some connection, General."

"What?"

"The Hope Diamond."

"We talked about this, Colonel." The General shifted from the familiar to the formal. "Imagine the headline. This is not a direction we can take. You've become obsessed with this *mumbo jumbo*! I was beginning to believe it myself! We have a good portion of the Omega Group investigating Jeannie's disappearance and you're the only one going off on a tangent."

Caine felt deflated as he looked languidly at the Capitol Building taking on a luster of gold in the afternoon sun. He knew that any discussion now about Jonas Mitchell's accident, his manuscript, the cat in the library would frustrate General Bradley even more.

He imagined his General by now had aggravated his war wound with his pacing and was limping back to his desk.

"Chris," the General said more evenly. "Let's get back on track here."

"Yes, sir," was all he could muster. But he was determined to pursue what for him was no longer a theory or fantasy.

Chapter 39

As Colonel Caine sped towards George Washington University Hospital in the waning light over Washington, the sun was hovering in late afternoon over the Golden Gate Bridge on the West Coast.

Much had changed in the Haight-Ashbury District of San Francisco since the late 1960's when youthful hippies saturated the area with a peaceful, placid drift through life in drug induced euphoria. As the fever of the times subsided and the area became gentrified, some wishing to maintain that self-indulgence and new converts joining in it, needed a defensible rationale for their licentiousness. Anton Dupre provided it with the Temple of Satan.

The Temple was in a non-descript storefront along Haight Street, mostly ignored by passersby who equated it with any number of unusual attention seeking fads and trends peculiar to the city.

Members of the Temple of Satan were waiting for the sun to disappear over the Pacific so they could gather for their morbid rites. Often, when spectacular layers of clouds, saturated with dark purple and pink, veiled its descent, Dupre would discourse that their Master felt particular favor as supplicants entered into the domain of night.

The vapid looks of a group of men and women entering the Temple indicated each was susceptible to cult-like manipulations in which Dupre excelled. Now and again a number of the curious had joined following local publicity about the Temple of Satan. They soon drifted away when they realized Dupre did not form his sect as a publicity stunt, but actually believed in deviant powers.

"We follow the Left Hand Path," he had declared to a skeptical reporter. "We don't actually worship Satan. We merely see him as a symbol of carnal values. We revere natural forces, forces that no one can control."

"But the so-called Left Hand Path is practice of the black arts," the reporter countered. "Black Magic. Isn't that evoking evil powers?"

Anton Dupre smiled and replied, "No. You must really understand what we do to understand it."

That seemed enough for the reporter, who wrote Dupre off as a crackpot.

Believers had gathered in the front area of the storefront. Its glass façade was blacked out with a one-way tint and the interior was outlined with black draperies adorning the walls. Black velvet robes with red piping were neatly hanging in rows along one wall. Members draped the robes over their shoulders and began the ritual by lighting several large pipes filled with marijuana and passing them ceremoniously among themselves. This would prepare them to enter the next room — the Temple.

Half a dozen sconces with long black candles lit the periphery of the Temple. The sconces were thin black metal worked into the shape of elongated goat face silhouettes. Along the walls were red painted credenzas with macabre plaster skulls and gargoyles. Interspersed among them were handwritten scrolls, mimicking medieval script. In the middle of each credenza was an incense burner evoking a subtle smell of sulfur, and around each was arrayed a number of silver tinted metal chalices.

In the middle of the Temple room was a conference table wrapped in black padded felt. On it lay a voluptuous nude woman with long blonde hair draped casually over her breasts. She seemed oblivious to her surroundings. Between her slightly spread thighs was a large decanter filled with a dark elixir. At the head of the conference table, now an altar, was Anton Dupre, ready to start the ceremony. His robe was similar, but had a high collar distinguishing him from the other supplicants. His robe accentuated his long, black hair tied in a pony-tail. Dupre had exaggerated his eye brows with makeup—an upward sweep reminiscent of horns—while a slim goatee accented his chin. Elaborately groomed sideburns curved like a ram's horn on the sides of his face. Black shirt and slacks, with patent leather shoes and contrasting red socks completed his vestments.

Their celebration centered on recitation of the Black Mass, and ritualistic satanic cantos composed by their leader.

For each ceremony Dupre would visit strip clubs in the North Beach District, an area near the waterfront known for its bawdy ambiance. His demeanor did not indicate that he would be interested in young women, but his close scrutiny of the dancers was not for personal tastes. He was hoping to procure another beautiful girl as an altar for his satanic ritual.

Members of his Temple included women, but they were generally not the kind who would draw admiring and lascivious interest when the Black Mass was performed on their nude bodies. Candy Knight's shift was ending and after some friendly prodding by Dupre—who had generously stuck twenty-dollar bills into her garter during her performance and his friendly persistence afterwards, along with a one-thousand dollar promise of payment—she agreed.

"Why me?" she asked as much out of curiosity as self-flattery, while they sat at a small table next to the stage with another dancer performing.

"Because you're natural," the procurer replied, looking over her well endowed, sinewy body barely dressed in her sequined dance costume. "We need a nubile natural look as you're lying on our altar. Implants are so tasteless," he said prissily.

She smiled and felt comfortable near this well-groomed, mature man with a smell of perfume all his own wafting in the dark, neon bordered show lounge. "Will you want a dance?"

"No, not really. All you need to do is be there," he assured. "You just relax on a covered table. We put some candles around you, and have our ceremony. The believers do everything. It's just a ceremony." He smiled. "Now, it's not kinky. We're very serious. We practice the Left Hand Path."

"What's that?"

"Just a ceremony," he replied and urged that they hurry along before the sun set.

As Candy Knight slipped out of her jeans and halter top near the altar, Dupre offered her a drink. "To get a little buzz," he said. The drink was laced with a benzodiazepine compound that soon rendered her semi-conscious and compliant. He helped her climb onto the altar and lay on her back, straightening and slightly spreading her legs and stretching her hands along the curvaceous sides of her body.

"How are you doing?" Dupre asked solicitously, as he draped his own robe over his shoulders with a practiced flourish.

She mumbled something unintelligible.

He knew from previous experience that now was the time to draw the ceremonial blood. He quickly retrieved a hypodermic needle from a credenza drawer behind him, pressed the plunger, and pricked her right breast. She winced a little, but seemed unaffected. The devil worshiper quickly drew the plunger back and filled the needle's chamber with several milliliters of blood.

Dupre smiled to himself. He was a good judge of natural tits. Too bad for her if she had lied and he pierced a saline implant. There'd be hell to pay, he remembered. For purification, the infernal powers would have demanded that the living altar be destroyed. He squirted the blood into a ceremonial decanter and placed it between Candy's slightly spread thighs. Then he pierced her left breast and drew another sample. She tried to lift her head to see what was pricking her, but felt too dizzy to move. When he reverently emptied the second draw into the decanter he retrieved a bottle of wine—deliberately altar wine—from the credenza and filled the rest of the decanter.

270

He opened the door to the adjoining room, where the sweet, heavy smell of marijuana dominated the air. "Enter the realm!" he summoned.

Members of the Temple of Satan filed in and surrounded the altar, gazing in laid back interest at the nude body on the conference table. Anton Dupre signaled to a member to distribute the goblets while he devoutly placed a cross, fixed upside down in its stand, at the head of Candy Knight.

He took the decanter and poured a measure of the liquid into a chalice of each of the faithful. Raising his own, he took a drink, followed by the others.

"Unholy spirit I invoke!" he intoned. "Come forth and manifest thyself within this body!"

The unholy congregation took two swallows of their drinks.

"Bard of Revelation, I invoke you! Bard of Revelation, I summon you! Bard of Revelation, I conjure you!" At each incantation the members took another mouthful of the wine mixed with the exotic dancer's blood.

Members were exhibiting varying degrees of euphoria, swaying in place, stroking the body on the table and taking sips on their own without waiting for the next salute. At some point Candy Knight moaned when someone stroked her between her legs and Anton Dupre called out with his glass in his outstretched hand: "Whore of Babylon, I invoke you! Whore of Babylon I summon you! Whore of Babylon, I conjure you!"

Members again swallowed the elixir at each phrase.

"Manifest yourself upon us as you do the Beast!" Anton Dupre chanted. He repeated the command three times and ceremoniously filled emptied goblets as members fell deeper into an hypnotic rapture. Some of the initiated began to stroke the nude dancer's body more vigorously while they rhythmically swayed back and forth.

Dupre then stood over Candy Knight with his chalice in hand and began to recite the Lord's Prayer backwards in conveniently broken pauses:"*Nema. Lihve morf su reviled tub noit at pemet otni ton su dael d-n-a... su tse naiga....*" Dupre looked around him.

"*Su tse naiga! Su tse naiga! Su tse naiga!*" his followers picked up the cadence.

"Against us! Against us! Against us! No other power can array against us!"

Frustration, rage, hate, despondency, cynicism, inferiority, lust, disappointment, loneliness, weakness, fantasy, even sociopathology of individual believers, whose singular human frailties had overcome their lives, fueled by intoxicants and released emotions, now intermingled and combined to give their Temple a palpable sensation of throbbing energy as they chanted.

Anton Dupre continued his blasphemous cadence: "*No e-htrea sa ti ni Lehh! No e-trea sa ti ni Lehh!*" he shouted loudly, perverting further the prayer by declaring hell instead of heaven as the realm of God's will.

* * *

While Anton Dupre and members of his Temple of Satan invoked infernal forces, Victor Sherwyck was hosting a dinner party at his mansion near Mount Vernon. Benefactors of the Hope Diamond Exhibit and Gem Hall improvements at the National Museum of Natural History, together with honored guests from government and society sat around a large, exquisitely set table in his dining hall.

Sherwyck had made some appropriately somber remarks about the most recent accident claiming the life of the Vice President and that it had been too late to cancel the dinner. He urged everyone bow their heads in his memory. "I expect, we'll pray together at the State Funeral," he said without emotion.

At a particular moment, Sherwyck's body began trembling and he leaned back in his chair in a swoon. He looked blankly with eyes rolled upward.

"Is he all right?" a socialite across from him asked with a worried look on her face.

"Is he having a seizure? Shall we call an ambulance?" a gentleman in a black tie near him inquired.

"It's all right! It's all right!" Mrs. Knowlton, who had been seated next to him, assured. "He just needs a little air." She loosened Sherwyck's tie and asked someone for a glass of water.

"He's just fine," she said.

Guests settled down, murmuring among themselves. How could Mrs. Knowlton presume about his health? Mr. Knowlton stood up with a wine glass in his hand. "Let's all drink to Mr. Sherwyck's good health."

"Hear, hear," resounded in the dining room amid the clinking of glasses.

Victor Sherwyck's face broke into a longing smile. He felt the enveloping aura of an unknown, but kindred spirit.

Chapter 40

Somewhere in the Egyptian Sahara south of Aswan a young American captain was standing in the turret of an M-1 tank at the head of an armored column. His company was part of regular joint U.S.-Egyptian military maneuvers in accordance with a treaty the two countries had signed in the wake of growing attacks on the Egyptian government by fundamentalists who were growing in numbers and increasingly well armed and organized in the perpetually volatile region.

The maneuvers were deliberately close to the southern border with Sudan as a pointed message to their government, which continued genocidal atrocities in its Darfur region despite international protestations. In the wake of resurgent fundamentalist terrorist attacks in unstable African countries, Sudan's role as a source of support for such activity was very evident.

The American officer was cursing the searing sun and looking for a likely spot to halt and wait out the mid-day heat.

"Captain, a message from one of the tanks," his radioman's unexpected voice crackled in his earphones. "They came across something off their right flank."

"What? A mirage?" the captain replied impatiently. "There's nothing out here."

"No, sir. Rotor blades. Broken helicopter blades sticking out of the sand. And part of a fuselage."

"Sounds like somebody's lost a chopper," the captain acknowledged with increased interest. "Is it one of ours?"

"They can't tell, sir," the radioman replied.

"Okay. We may as well stop right here," the captain decided. "Pass the word. We'll bivouac here. Advise the Egyptians."

The captain looked up at the broiling sun bearing down on them unobscured by a single cloud. "We'll get a digging party together as soon as this sun lets up."

Meanwhile radio communications between the column and military headquarters in Cairo became the focus of attention. The maneuvers had been tedious and routine, but the helicopter in the sand presented a genuine mystery—a focus of interest—something to shake the boredom of routine maneuvers, especially when the joint headquarters command radioed from Cairo: "No missing helicopters in area."

The American and Egyptian commanders were ordered to secure the site and not begin digging until a technical specialist team arrived.

Colonel Nicholas Vandergaard, commander of the U.S. force, pulled up to the lead tank in his sand encrusted Hummer command vehicle. "Captain Stallworth!" he called out. "Since your men found this thing, we'll have them dig out this chopper. If you need help, let me know."

"Yes, sir!" the captain replied.

"Since they're sending out an intelligence team, I don't need to tell you that you'll have to dig carefully," the commanding officer explained. "They must have some particular interest in this thing, because there's no reports of friendly losses. Not for some time. Especially not around this godforsaken area."

"Yes, sir," the captain acknowledged.

"Carry on, Captain!"

"Very well, sir!"

Two Air Force Intelligence officers had been dispatched to the scene and arrived at dusk. Colonel Vandergaard introduced them to his Egyptian counterpart and presented them to Captain Stallworth, who had prepared the area for digging. The spot was obvious from the huge canvas canopy that stretched above the scene, held up by three telescoping poles and the turret of one of the tanks. Another tank equipped as a bulldozer and a heavy crane for towing disabled tanks were parked near the exposed blades and section of exposed fuselage.

The scene was lit with a battery of lights mounted on several tanks. Since the maneuvers were meant to be as visible as possible, the intense lights illuminating the barren desert were a conspicuous calling card for the Sudanese and any Middle East governments that cared to get the message. The nighttime activity was a relief to the soldiers, who would not have to dig in the scorching sun.

"Let's see what we have," one of the intelligence officers said as a group of officers and soldiers approached the twisted blades protruding from the sand.

"From the looks of these rotors, I'd say it's a big one," said Major Michael Lee to his companion.

"A transportation helicopter or a troop carrier," suggested Major Thomas Billingsly.

The intelligence officers were speaking as much to the nearby soldiers of the armored company as to each other, good naturedly flaunting their knowledge of aircraft from barely identifiable pieces of metal.

"It's buried on its starboard side," Major Lee continued. All the soldiers around him could accurately surmise that much.

Major Lee knelt down near the exposed fuselage and brushed some sand away with his palm.

"Eastern bloc," he said matter of factly. "The rivet work is functional, but not aesthetic." He stood up and rubbed sand granules from his hands. "If it's not Egyptian, it could be one of the other client states of the old Soviet Union."

"Shall we start digging, sir?" Captain Stallworth prodded.

"Uhh, yes," replied Major Lee. "Dig toward the front here so we could find a hatch. This could be a big sucker and your men won't appreciate digging the whole thing out with shovels. Let's see if we can get inside. Then we'll know if we need to be careful or if we can just bulldoze the thing out."

Captain Stallworth motioned his men to dig where the Major was pointing.

After some strenuous digging the soldiers uncovered an air intake for turbine engines.

"Holy shit! This thing *is* big," Major Billingsly declared. "We're still near the main rotor shaft."

"If it's laying on its side, a hatch ought'a be over there somewhere," Major Lee said.

The soldiers dug farther away from the rotor shaft where the Major was pointing. Each shovel seemed to be thrust with eager anticipation until finally one soldier hit glass. "A porthole, sir!"

"All right! Let's concentrate over here! Right here!" Major Lee shouted enthusiastically. "The main hatch should be right here. This looks like one of the biggest choppers the Soviets ever built."

"A Mil," Major Billingsly offered.

"Bingo!" replied his intelligence companion.

"I'd hate to have to dig this out by hand," Major Lee told the captain in charge. "If it's an Mi 6 or 10, it's more than thirty meters long and nine meters tall."

"There were only about five hundred of these babies built," Major Billingsly told Captain Stallworth and the men around him. "It had the biggest rotor system of its time and set world records in speed and payload."

"NATO designation 'Hook'," Major Lee added. "The rotors and shafting were tremendous. Its gearbox alone weighed more than three tons, more than both its engines. It had little wings to help with lift."

"What would it be doing out here, sir," Captain Stallworth asked the obvious.

"Good question," the intelligence officer replied. "It depends on how long it's been here."

"It first flew around Nineteen fifty-seven," Major Billingsly said. "So, by the time it passed into client hands like the Bulgarians, North Vietnamese, or in this case, Syrians or Iraqis, I'd say it would have to be of pretty recent vintage."

"I'm still not convinced it can't be Egyptian," Major Billingsly added for good measure. "I'm not sure some of these local militaries keep such good inventory or know what's going on in their own forces..." He quickly caught himself to see if any Egyptian officers were within earshot.

"Well!" announced Colonel Vandergaard who had come with his Egyptian counterpart upon the brightly lit circle highlighting pieces of rotor and fuselage exposed in the sand and surrounded by a tight ring of curious soldiers. "The only way we'll know anything is if we dig. So, let's end this speculation and find out what we have here. A little muscle exercise trumps intellectual exercise in a case like this."

"Right on! Yo! and Yes, sir!" echoed anonymously among the soldiers in support of their commander's retort to the intelligence officers.

Soon the digging party had uncovered the forward hatch of the helicopter. When it was completely exposed they stepped back. The soldiers look warily at the hatch, wondering what was inside this flood-lit entrance made eerie by the darkness of the desert around it.

"Who wants to check it out?" asked Major Lee.

"Well, sir. They sent you gentlemen here especially..." Captain Stallworth began.

"You got some 'night eyes'?" Major Billingsly cut in. "Let's open the hatch and get to it."

Sounds of approval erupted from the troops, while several soldiers grappled with the hatch. They opened it without too much effort.

The floodlights were enough to illuminate the pilot still strapped in his seat, hanging downward toward the co-pilot's seat. The co-pilot was missing.

A hint of the stench of death emanated from within. The heat and dryness of the desert were kind to those it claimed and entombed in its shifting sands. So much so, that it was difficult to say how long the helicopter had been there.

"I see the pilot, poor soul," said Major Billingsly as he looked into the cockpit with his night vision goggles. "Can't make out his features, but he's pretty well preserved. Co-pilot's gone. If his harness broke on impact, maybe he's farther down."

The major looked towards the opposite hatch directly below him. He saw the crumpled form of a figure.

"The co-pilot's down there too. He's lying on the starboard bulkhead."

Major Billingsly sprawled onto the fuselage next to the open hatch, lowered his head and peered deep into the cargo area. "Looks empty back there. No troops. No equipment." He scanned back and forth with his goggles.

"Wait a minute! I think I can make out something—one, maybe two men! We'll need to go inside with more light. These goggles don't give me enough detail."

Minutes later he was gingerly stepping inside the cockpit of the huge helicopter lying on its side. Major Billingsly used the side of the pilot's seat as a step, then carefully placed his other foot on the side of the co-pilot's seat as another step. As he did so, he brushed against the shoulder and head of the pilot's remains. He heard a scurrying sound and quickly looked toward it. Two scorpions darted into openings of the shattered instrument panel.

A chill coursed through the major's spine. What if there were snakes here too?

"Let's get some more light down here!" he shouted. Meanwhile, he did not move. He stood on the side of the co-pilot's seat with the dead pilot's head and right shoulder resting against his calf. The major tried not to think about it.

Someone from above shined a beacon into the cockpit. The Major recognized by the windowed bomber-like nose that this was likely an Mi 6. He looked all around him to be sure there were no other living creatures nearby as he waited for more illumination and for someone to join him in this cavernous tomb to alleviate his sense of unease.

"We'll rig up a rope ladder!" Major Lee said. "We'll send down a party with pallets and body bags. How many do you need?"

"About three or four at this point!" his intelligence partner replied. "I don't know what's back in the payload area. This thing can carry about seventy troops."

A rope ladder dropped next to him and he felt his way onto it. Alongside it was a rope with a heavy duty flashlight attached. Billingsly undid the flashlight and aimed it downward as he climbed. After several more steps he was on the starboard bulkhead of the helicopter, where he now looked for footing. He fixed his light on the crumpled figure at his feet. The co-pilot was huddled with his face turned away from the Air Force intelligence officer, as if looking at the instrument panel. The major panned around the body, which was dressed in a khaki flight suit. It looked old fashioned.

"This craft could not have been here that long," he thought. "Everything looks so well-preserved." But he knew the desert climate could force inaccurate conclusions.

Meanwhile, Major Lee and Captain Stallworth were carefully negotiating the rope ladder.

Major Billingsly played his beam around the body and focused on a navigation map lying on a porthole near the co-pilot's head. Landmarks were in the Cyrillic alphabet. There were some handwritten notations near Aswan to the northwest, indicating the site of the Aswan Dam—a project still in progress. Another notation in the margin indicated some geographical coordinates and the date: 30.XI.58. The major bent down to get a closer look at the map and noticed the co-pilot's withered, but well-preserved face. The features did not appear Egyptian.

"This guy's not a local," he said to the other two officers who alighted in the tight space on the bulkhead next to him.

"Russian?" Major Lee ventured.

"Most probably."

Major Lee shone a flashlight upward and aimed it into the face of the pilot strapped and dangling like a rag doll in his seat several feet above him.

The beam created deep shadows in the hollows where his eyes used to be. The rest of his face was tight, dried, but clearly enough Caucasian.

"Both probably Russian," Major Billingsly said. He shone his light back on the porthole. "Look at that map. This chopper's been here a long time."

"How long?" Captain Stallworth interjected with rapt attention.

"Nineteen fifty-eight."

"Nineteen fifty-eight?" the captain and the other intelligence officer replied in unison.

"There's some coordinates in the margin. We'll see what our friends have been up to."

"What's in the back?" Major Lee asked.

"Let's check and let's get out of here," his companion replied. "This thing is starting to give me the creeps."

Major Billingsly worked his way carefully to the cargo area, playing his beam back and forth with slight movements of his neck. The huge payload area was empty, except for two other figures lying near one another in the dark. The beam of the flashlight could not take in the whole scene in one sweep, causing alternate light and shadow on portions of the flyers' remains.

"It looks like two more bodies," Major Billingsly said. He continued shining his light back and forth along the bulkhead of the helicopter. "Both in old flight suits." He worked his way closer. "One of them is wearing a shoulder holster."

Billingsly crept closer along the uncluttered bulkhead towards the figure with the shoulder holster, whose hand—now illuminated in the beam—was outstretched above his head, as if reaching for something. A knife lay loosely in his palm, released from a clenched grip of death. There seemed to be some words etched in Cyrillic on the bulkhead. The major leaned forward with his flashlight and stretched his hand toward the bulkhead to get a better view.

He could not have seen the sand viper coiled under the flyer's armpit. As he focused his light it struck him on the forearm with a lightning lunge.

"I'm bit! I'm bit!" he yelled more from surprise, than pain. He dropped his flashlight. "Snake! Snake!"

Major Lee and Captain Stallworth instinctively shuffled backwards in the dark to avoid a strike, pulling Major Billingsly with them.

"Where did it hit you?" Captain Stallworth asked urgently as he hurriedly pulled his belt from his pants. Major Lee had drawn his pistol and was shining his light back and forth in front of them.

"My arm! My arm!" Major Billingsly said breathlessly.

"Stay calm! Stay calm!" Captain Stallworth urged. He tied his belt around the intelligence officer's right arm as they groped for the rope ladder.

"Medic!" Captain Stallworth yelled up the hatch. "Snakebite! Get ready with antivenom!"

He guided Major Billingsly up the short stretch of rope ladder and followed him out of the helicopter's cockpit. Major Lee hurried up behind them.

Below, dimly backlit by the abandoned flashlight in the cargo area, the helicopter evoked the look of a temple-like tomb of the four mysterious flyers.

Chapter 41

"Something's come up," General William Bradley intoned over his secure telephone to Colonel Caine. "Report to Andrews. You and Arie are going back to the Middle East."

Caine hoped that his General was not fixated on Middle Eastern terrorists again. He had seemed reluctant to accept paranormal scenarios up to now, but he also had not categorically rejected them.

Caine had promised Laura again during his hospital visit with her uncle, that he would investigate the museum connection. His interest was no longer a favor to her, but self driven. Now in delaying it once more, he hoped her vigil at her uncle's bedside would prevent her from delving on her own. No more coincidences, he thought. There was something dangerous going on.

He would start with his friend, Al Carruthers, the assistant curator. Caine dismissed the thought that he might be involved with something. Carruthers was too trusting, God-fearing. He saw only the best in people. Al would more likely be oblivious to something sinister around him, than part of it, Caine thought with a private smile. Nevertheless, he would not share his suspicions.

"Our units found an old chopper in the sands," General Bradley said. "It's Soviet built. Looks like it's been there for some time. This is a good change of pace for you—being our expert on everything Soviet."

"What about Jeannie?"

"We're all working on it. You can come back with a fresh perspective on her case. In fact, while you're there, see if you can circle around other leads on terrorist connections. It's Egypt this time."

"Yes, sir," Caine replied perfunctorily. He felt diverted.

"You'll get your orders at Andrews." The General ended the call.

* * *

Soon Colonel Caine was back at George Washington University Hospital's Intensive Care Unit. When he walked into Jonas Mitchell's room again, Laura knew he was leaving for somewhere.

"Always the vagabond," she said bittersweetly from his bedside.

"Hopefully, not for long. Any change?"

"The same as when you left. It's been touch and go from the start."

Caine approached the other side of the bed and took Jonas Mitchell's hand. Mitchell squeezed it in response. "You're a spry old man," Caine said looking at him with a reassuring smile.

"He's been through a lot," Laura said. "His body knows hurt. It remembers physical assaults and years of abuse. That's why he's strong."

"We'll get to the bottom of this assault," Caine declared.

"It was no accident," Laura asserted looking probingly at the Colonel.

"No. It was no accident."

"How long will you be gone?"

Caine looked at her.

"I know. You don't know."

"As soon as I get back, I'll look into the museum."

"With Al?"

"With Al and whoever. Just don't try anything yourself."

She looked at him without responding.

"Promise me."

"Chances are, I'll be spending most of my time here."

Caine walked around the bed to Laura. He patted her uncle on the

284

shoulder, squeezed his hand, and then kissed her on the cheek.

"Promise me," he urged as he walked to the door. He turned and looked at her somberly.

"Come back safe!" she answered.

* * *

Colonel Caine was driving southeast along Pennsylvania Avenue towards Andrews Air Force Base when he noticed a blue sedan half a block behind him. It seemed familiar, like the tails he occasionally had shaken before. The sedan followed him until a highway interchange near the airbase, entered a cloverleaf and turned back towards Washington.

"Must think I'm going to Andrews," Caine thought dismissively. "What else?"

On arrival he was escorted to a C-130 cargo plane and entered through the extended rear ramp. Colonel Garrison Jones was already inside the empty cargo area near the cockpit. As Caine joined him on the bench seat, a black limousine drove up the ramp and into the cargo area, stopping opposite the two officers.

General Bradley climbed out of the back seat with a large brown envelope in his hand.

"Just in time, gentlemen. Here are your orders," he said extending the envelope to whichever officer would grasp it.

Colonel Jones took the envelope.

"And good luck," the General said. "It looks like that helicopter's been there more than fifty years. Depending on what's inside, we may get a better idea of their strategic thinking at the time. And if there's some link to now."

"Do we follow up on anything intriguing?" Colonel Caine wondered.

"That's what I like about you, Chris," General Bradley said with a smile.

"Always anticipating. That's part of our intent. Your assignment is good cover. You'll be near Ras Banas, Egypt's air base on the Red Sea."

Colonels Caine and Jones both recognized the drift of their general's plan.

They nodded their heads slightly in acknowledgment as General Bradley continued. "Our Joint Special Ops Command for tracking and killing terrorists is operating out of Yemen, just across the Red Sea. Yemeni leaders are still running scared from Al Quaida, so they're cooperating. I'm sure any intelligence scuttlebutt will spill over among your Egyptian counterparts stationed out of Ras Banas."

"So the terrorist angle on Jeannie is still in play?" Caine asked.

"I know what you're thinking, Chris, but we can't discount it. We have to continue to follow all plausible leads."

Caine cringed a little at the word "plausible," but said nothing.

"Yes, sir," Colonel Jones assured the General for both of them.

"Very well, gentlemen. Good luck. Keep me apprised."

General Bradley climbed back into the limousine. The driver made a full turn in the cargo area with a distinctive squeal of rubber on metal and drove down the ramp of the giant plane.

"Here we go, again," Colonel Jones said as the ramp started rising to become part of the fuselage. "Too bad, it's not Beirut," he added wistfully.

"The Old Man said we have some leeway," Colonel Caine replied.

"It doesn't say so in the orders."

"Orders are made to be interpreted," Caine said purposefully. "Who knows where that helicopter may lead us."

"I *would* like to see her again," Colonel Jones said.

"Maybe it can be arranged."

They sat thoughtfully for a moment, listening to the increased pitch of the engines as the C-130 made ready for takeoff.

"How come it's empty this time?" Colonel Caine asked idly.

"The pilot said it's a 'homecoming trip'. They're returning with caskets and an honor guard. Fallen comrades."

Caine nodded solemnly.

"What about Ramstein in Germany?"

"With the increase in casualties, the pilot says that gateway drew too many photographers."

"If they were as clever in solving the problems...," Caine started, then let his sentence trail away.

"You can't get too philosophical, my man. It's dangerous in our line of work. Causes hesitation."

"I'm not the one hesitating."

"You mean General Bradley?"

Caine did not answer."

"You have to admit, we've encountered some bizarre events," Jones observed. "The General's used to Standard Operating Procedures. And what can we prove?"

"We've got to see that Hammad fellow again," Caine answered. "We didn't get enough out of him on those cults in the desert. Where his men don't tread at night."

"As I remember, we were rudely interrupted," Jones replied sarcastically.

"More reason to let him finish what he was telling us."

"That was part of our original mission to Beirut," Colonel Jones noted.

"To get information from Mustafa Ali Hammad."

"Right."

"Some pieces are missing."

"I like your kind of thinking, my good brother," Colonel Jones said with a broad smile.

They drifted into silence and eventually sleep as the plane flew over the Atlantic, heading towards the Egyptian military airbase outside Cairo.

* * *

The early morning sun was already heating the tan fuselage of the Egyptian version of a Sea King helicopter on the tarmac when the two officers arrived. They climbed out a side hatch of the giant transport, wearing camouflage fatigues and their military issue Berettas. The two Colonels quickly transferred to the helicopter for a 450 mile flight along the Nile River to Aswan where they would refuel and rendezvous at the site of the discovery in the desert somewhere to the east of the famous dam.

"Welcome, sirs!" Colonel Mohamed Abdel Mahmoud shouted as Colonels Caine and Jones climbed out upon arrival with sand swirling around them from the decelerating rotors. Mahmoud was accompanied by Major Michael Lee, who had initially surveyed the helicopter.

The terrain around them was relatively flat from tread marks of the armored column, which had moved on, except for a few support vehicles. Behind Colonel Mahmoud the two officers glimpsed the broken helicopter resting on a plateau of sand with a large circular depression cleared around it. A makeshift pontoon footbridge spanned the depression. Several electrical wires extended from a generator nearby, spanned the depression and disappeared into the hatch. The helicopter looked like an isolated castle surrounded by a sand moat. Soldiers stood casual watch in the area.

"Looks like some serious work was done around here," Colonel Jones commented.

"The men were anxious to see what they found," Colonel Mahmoud responded in a distinct British accent. "It always amazes me what a stimulus curiosity can be."

The three officers smiled in agreement and introduced each other. "I am Colonel Mohamed Abdel Mahmoud, of the Egyptian Air Force, co-commander with your Colonel Vandergaard in Operation Bright Star. This is Major Michael Lee. Perhaps you know each other?"

"We have met, sir," Colonel Jones replied.

"Shall we see what we have?" Colonel Caine offered.

"Certainly," Colonel Mahmoud said. "We are just as anxious to know more, since this helicopter has no tie whatsoever with the Egyptian Air Force."

"What brought it down?" asked Colonel Jones.

"That is a mystery, gentlemen," Colonel Mahmoud replied. "All the systems are in working order. It could fly today, if not for the damage on impact."

"The helicopter's been cleared," Major Lee said as the officers approached the pontoon footbridge.

"My teammate, Major Billingsly, he was bit by a viper inside. He's doing all right, but we had to be sure the interior was clear. We found four bodies. They were removed for further examination."

The officers crossed single file across the narrow bridge and gathered next to the cargo door, which was open to the sky. A metal ladder was propped alongside. They climbed single file up the ladder and down another one inside, stepping onto the starboard bulkhead of the prone helicopter. The interior was lit by several lamps hung by the digging party, although the light of the bright day washed out their affect.

The officers looked forward and saw the cockpit at a ninety degree angle.

"Any documents?" Colonel Caine asked.

"Scant," Major Lee replied. "Some maps and a piece of paper with coordinates."

"Are they here?" Colonel Jones asked.

"Yes, sir. We left them as we found them. They're up there in the cockpit. There was also something scratched on the interior bulkhead, here."

"Scratched?"

"You can see it right here, sir," Major Lee said pointing in front of his feet. "It's in Cyrillic, though."

"Well, it proves, they're Russian," Colonel Caine asserted as he crouched in the direction the Major pointed.

"Yes, sir. It looks like one of the flyers—the one wearing a shoulder holster—was etching words before he died."

Caine peered closely at the crudely etched words, barely visible on the metal.

"Curse...on...Ame...," he read aloud slowly as he made out the words.

"Curse on America," Major Lee concluded. "Curse on America! That must have been some Cold War," he observed. "They swore at us even in their dying breath."

Colonel Caine straightened from his crouch.

"Maybe they weren't swearing, Major. Maybe they were warning us," Colonel Caine replied.

Colonel Jones exchanged a knowing glance with Caine.

Major Lee shrugged off the cryptic reply, while Colonel Mahmoud looked tellingly at Caine.

"Any idea so far who they were?" Colonel Jones asked.

"No," Colonel Mahmoud replied. "We have a joint team examining everything we found inside."

He paused then noted. "It's curious. We made inquiry with the Russian government, which is obsessed with information and received only shrugs from official sources."

"That's odd, isn't it?" Caine observed.

"Indeed. Our government had cordial relations with Moscow at the time—as it does now. After all, they were helping us build the Aswan Dam. Maybe there is some connection here."

The four officers nodded in agreement.

"There's a map up here in the cockpit," Major Lee said as he worked his way forward and retrieved it. "We found it lying on the bulkhead between the pilot and co-pilot. And this paper with coordinates on it."

He handed the items to Colonel Caine.

"It's obviously a navigation map," Caine said with the other officers huddling around him.

"Looks like the area around Aswan," Colonel Jones said. "With handwritten notations in the margins."

"Thirty, eleven, fifty-eight," Colonel Caine read in Cyrillic. "November thirtieth, nineteen-fifty eight."

The year suddenly gripped him. "Nineteen fifty-eight," he enunciated while trying to connect its significance. "Nineteen fifty-eight."

"Colonel?" the Egyptian officer spoke. "What about nineteen-fifty eight?"

"Nothing. Sorry. I was just thinking."

"The helicopter was probably involved with the Aswan Dam project," Colonel Mahmoud offered.

"Possibly," Colonel Caine replied. "But what's it doing here far from Aswan in the middle of nowhere?"

No one answered.

"And from what you describe"—he said to Major Lee—"project engineers don't dress with khaki flight suits and wear shoulder holsters."

"Did anyone check the location of these coordinates?" Caine continued.

"No, sir. Not specifically. But from the general location, it's likely they were flying to or from Aswan and Ras Banas- the airbase."

"With all due respect, Major," Caine said matter of factly. "Ras Banas was only built in the nineteen-sixties, almost ten years after the flight of this 'copter."

The officers standing in the sun baked, stifling cargo hold glanced curiously at the Egyptian.

"Colonel. What's out there, between here and the Red Sea?" Caine asked.

"Nothing."

Chapter 42

As they clambered out of the helicopter Colonel Caine requested Colonel Mohamed Abdel Mahmoud to fly them over the coordinates.

"Our orders from Bright Star Command were to transport you back and forth from this site to Cairo," replied Colonel Mahmoud.

The four officers alighted next to the overturned helicopter.

"You understand," Mahmoud said solicitously as he straightened his uniform, "foreign officers reconnoitering Egyptian land without specific permission would be...you understand. This is outside the scope of our joint maneuvers."

"We understand, Colonel," Caine replied politely. "But, it doesn't have to be outside the scope. I'm sure you can see, we were not sent all this way just to look at an old helicopter. We know every bolt in this machine. What we need to find out—and I'm sure you share that curiosity—is what the hell it's doing here in the middle of nowhere."

"Ahh, you see gentlemen," Mahmoud said with a smile. "It is a question of cultural perspective. We are people of the desert. Curiosity about 'nowhere' is not a major preoccupation with us."

Colonel Mahmoud, casually rubbed his hands together to shake off some sand. "The flyers got lost—perhaps in a sandstorm, the Soviet Union no longer exists, and the Mi 8, the successor to this craft"—he raised his hand and grasped a twisted leg of the landing gear for emphasis—"is the most widely produced helicopter in the world today. We have a large fleet in our Air Force, as we do other craft of older vintage," Mahmoud said emphasizing "older vintage."

Caine sensed the Egyptian officer would not let his request for a reconnaissance flight go unreciprocated. "We understand, Colonel, and we sympathize with the position of the Egyptian Air Force."

Colonel Mahmoud saw an opening. "As you know, Colonel. We have a longstanding order from your government for a fleet of F-15 Strike Eagles," he said off handedly. "Do you think, perhaps, you can do anything to help with our order? You know our deal has been blocked for some years now."

"So, I understand," Colonel Caine replied. "There were some protests from Israel, if I remember."

"Too effective, I'm afraid," Colonel Mahmoud said. "A pity. We are now having to deal with the former Soviets for some of their most sophisticated equipment."

"We are not politicians, Colonel, but I believe Egyptian war games with the F-15's targeted Israel as the enemy."

"Well…" Colonel Mahmoud left the thought unsaid.

"If that were changed," Colonel Caine said spontaneously. "If, for example, you targeted some other neighboring country theoretically taken over by Al Quaida in your war games, perhaps some obstacles could be overcome."

"Perhaps," Mahmoud replied thoughtfully. "Perhaps a word to your relevant superiors that we are addressing that issue?"

"We will certainly pass it along," Colonel Caine said as Colonel Jones and Major Lee nonchalantly looked on.

The Americans surmised that reporting this initiative to his superiors might mean a promotion or added prestige for the Egyptian Colonel.

"Besides"—Colonel Caine emphasized—"There could be some ancient tomb out there. That might be of supreme cultural interest to you. And you would be the discoverer."

Colonel Mahmoud responded with friendly, dismissive humor.

Within the hour they were flying in an Mi 8 turbo helicopter with Egyptian Air Force markings towards the coordinates.

The terrain below them was desolate and foreboding. Stretches of hilly sand were interrupted by craggy stone outcrops suggesting mountain ranges covered by the desert. As they flew in an easterly direction from Aswan in line with the discovered helicopter, the desert began to give way to a preponderance of gray mountainous terrain surrounded by vast islands of sand where the wall of mountains could not hold back the desert winds piling hills of sand at their feet.

The officers peered with keen interest through the windows of the cargo area when the pilot announced that they were nearing the location of the coordinates. They were somewhere north of the Administrative Zone claimed by both Egypt and Sudan.

"This is absolutely desolate," observed Major Lee. "Who could live around here?"

"No one," Colonel Mahmoud declared above the din of the turbo engines and whirling blades. "There are ancient caravan routes through some areas and nomadic herdsmen pass by. The only settlements are Berenice and Bir Shalatayn, both on the Red Sea farther east."

Among the irregular outcroppings below them, Colonel Jones glimpsed something at the end of a mountain canyon ahead. It looked man-made and jutted out of one of the mountain faces.

"Look there!" he exclaimed pointing.

The officers looked out the port side while the pilot turned the helicopter to starboard, so that the edifice could be seen clearly through the side windows.

"Exactly where the coordinates showed," Colonel Caine said.

"They knew exactly where they were going," Colonel Jones asserted.

"What is it?" Major Lee asked. "It's built right out of the mountain. Like some fortress."

"It is most likely a monastery," Colonel Mahmound said. "There were numbers of them through the centuries built on caravan routes.

294

For prayer and protection. Most are ruins now."

The pilot flew a wide circle high above the edifice.

"It looks pretty impressive. Way out here and all," Colonel Jones said.

"Isolated monasteries in the wilderness were not unusual," Colonel Mahmoud replied. "Members of the early Christian church, vying for ascendancy, valued hermits above all else. They claimed to be closest to God by discarding all things material—awaiting the imminent end of the world. The more ascetic, the more authority they claimed. Later—for obvious reasons—they disappeared."

"Obvious reasons?" wondered Major Lee.

"Of course," Colonel Mahmoud replied. "They renounced all carnal pleasures. So they left no heirs to carry on their beliefs."

Major Lee nodded with a grin.

"For someone who follows the Prophet, you seem versed in Christian history," Colonel Caine observed.

The Egyptian Colonel smiled. "I took my studies at Cambridge." He let the phrase linger with the Americans.

"You know, Muhammad was driven out of Mecca and spent several years in a desert cave. That is where he received his divine revelations. As you know his inspired teachings eventually prevailed. By the time of his death in the year Six hundred thirty-two, the entire Arabian Peninsula professed Islam," Colonel Mahmoud proudly declared.

The American officers kept looking at the awesome structure rising seamlessly out of the mountainous outcrop as the pilot slowly circled the site.

"So, we gather that isolated redoubts scattered in the desert are not extraordinary," Colonel Jones said.

"They have been here since antiquity," Colonel Mahmoud replied. "Most are abandoned. Remember these coordinates were written more than sixty years ago."

"I see," Colonel Caine said with ironic emphasis squinting towards a barricaded courtyard in the distance below. "Except for this one."

The officers suddenly strained to see where Caine was pointing. The structure was washed out by the sun and momentarily blended with its surroundings due to the angle of the circling helicopter. Seconds later, with sunlight behind them, the observers caught a glimpse of several figures scurrying from the courtyard into a doorway.

"Hermits?" asked Major Lee.

"Herders. Nomads. Possibly holy men on retreat. I daresay it is too isolated for permanent habitation." Colonel Mahmoud looked at the pilot who had turned towards him from the cockpit and motioned a falling dial with his finger.

"In any event, gentlemen, we must return if we don't want to test the desert by walking."

The Mi 8 veered westwardly toward the helicopter in the sand and Aswan beyond. Colonel Caine gazed at the jagged, sandy outcrops below them and soon lost sight of the edifice, which melted into the receding rugged mountaintops.

"We hear there are stories circulating in the desert," Colonel Caine said pensively. "Stories of devil cults in the wilderness."

Mohamed Abdel Mahmoud laughed. "We are not superstitious, are we, Colonel? Of course there are stories. All kinds of stories. That is the legacy of desolate places. Stories are told by the campfire. They grow with each telling."

Colonel Jones and Major Lee shifted their attention to the conversation.

"Most stories have some truth at the core."

"That may be," Colonel Mahmoud replied. "There is the Malektaus. It is much misunderstood. Many claim they are devil worshipers. Although believers—mainly a sect of Kurds in Iraq—say they worship a fallen angel who redeemed himself."

"Yes, so we've heard. I'm talking about real devil worshippers, invoking diabolical forces and acting on them."

Colonel Mahmoud laughed again. "As you know, Colonel, many people in this part of the world say that America is the 'Great Satan'."

Caine did not reply, but remembered the words etched in the bulkhead of the fallen helicopter—"Curse on Ame—." It had to be a warning, he thought. Final revenge for some betrayal that befell the unfortunate flyer.

"We need to visit the site," Caine wondered aloud.

"I'm afraid it would be complicated," Colonel Mahmoud replied.

"I am content to think that the flyers were simply looking for some strategic outpost in the height of the Cold War. As you know this area at the time was swept by warfare, revolution, military intervention and political posturing by both East and West," the Egyptian Colonel recited.

"Unfortunate fallout from World War Two," Colonel Caine agreed.

"It lingers to this day, I'm afraid."

"That's why we have to see that place," Colonel Caine pressed. "We've established that the flight was in November of Nineteen fifty-eight. As you know, Colonel," he flattered, "the Mi 6 was still in experimental stages at that time."

The Egyptian Colonel nodded as if he knew.

"It was more than a routine reconnaissance mission to have that craft shipped here all the way from Russia for such a flight."

"The proverbial camel's nose in the tent," Colonel Mahmoud replied laughingly.

"First an overflight, now a visit." The Egyptian Colonel heaved a deep breath. "Very well. Due to my commitments with our joint maneuvers, I cannot spare time or resources. I can requisition a helicopter, perhaps this helicopter. But you will be on your own. And for a short time only. As far as I know you are analyzing the Mi 6 found in the desert. Can you manage?"

"Certainly," Caine replied with questioning looks from Colonel Jones and Major Lee.

"Your persistence is persuasive," Colonel Mahmoud acknowledged grudgingly. "It's making me doubt the obvious."

The helicopter flew over the wreckage site and landed a short time later at a military airfield at Aswan.

"I am ordering the pilot and craft to be at your disposal for twenty-four hours," Colonel Mahmoud said when they alighted. "I am also dispatching several soldiers."

"Thanks, we could use the extra manpower."

"Only to guard the helicopter."

"I see," Caine replied. "In that case, can you arrange one more thing?"

"What is that?"

"Can you arrange a secure line to Washington?"

The Egyptian Colonel looked at Caine with a sense of relief. "Now, that is an easy one."

He pointed near a hangar where an American Humvee, modified as a communications vehicle, stood with a tall dish antenna dominating its cargo bed.

A short time later Colonel Caine was conferring with General William Bradley. He reported their progress and said there were possible new developments. He did not elaborate, but requested that General Bradley personally and secretly make arrangements with Mustafa Ali Hammad in Beirut to meet them at Aswan as soon as possible.

"So the terrorist connection on Jeannie is bearing some fruit?" General Bradley's voice sounded enthusiastic over the line. "Some new developments through Egypt?"

"There are some new developments, sir." Colonel Caine responded indirectly. He did not want to frustrate his General further by associating the etched words "Curse on Ame—" into the occultist scenarios he had propounded. He would save that for their return, hopefully with even more information. Persistence in that theory just now might risk curtailment of their mission.

To his relief, he heard General Bradley's voice assure: "I'll see what I can do."

Chapter 43

The sun was disappearing over desert ridges west of the Aswan airbase when a Gulfstream G500 landed near a control tower. Its fuselage was painted gray and a small insignia on the business jet's tail read "United States Air Force." Colonel Caine and his small entourage walked briskly towards it as the cabin door opened into a stepped ramp.

Mustafa Ali Hammad, dressed in a khaki safari shirt and matching pants hurried down the stairs followed by his cousin, Aida, who wore an olive colored campaign shirt and matching slacks. Both wore sidearms. Behind them came two armed men dressed in camouflage fatigues and carrying back packs.

"I would normally not have come," Hammad said with outstretched hand to Colonel Caine. "Let this be proof that women in our culture have much more influence than you give credit for." He glanced with a smirk towards Aida who threw back her head dismissively, as if dodging his words.

Colonel Garrison Jones smiled briefly in her direction as the group exchanged cursory introductions.

"Your General Bradley urged that I come. It's in your vain search here for your missing woman." Hammad looked skeptically at Colonel Caine and the officers next to him. "I, myself, first thought this was an elaborate matchmaking scheme. Especially when my cousin insisted I inquire if your bronze companion is with you."

He glanced playfully at Aida, as he continued, "When General Bradley said Colonel Jones is with you, I could not refuse his request." Hammad smiled broadly at his cousin who was giving him a stern return glare. "It was a short, uneventful trip, so we thought we would take some respite from our burdens in Beirut."

"I'm glad you can join us," Colonel Caine said and went straight to the point: "We came upon a remote structure in the mountains—a monastery or something." He refrained from giving details. "Our Egyptian contacts are preoccupied with joint maneuvers, but gave us some leeway in exploring it."

"This is more than archeological curiosity," Mustafa Ali Hammad declared and inquired in the same breath.

"We're following up on all angles," Colonel Jones interjected. "Including your own."

"My own?"

"What you told us last time we met in Beirut. Malevolent cults in the desert," Colonel Caine reminded.

"I am surprised," the shadowy militia leader replied. "These are not the kind of things that superpowers waste their time on." Hammad paused thoughtfully. "But then, perhaps I'm not surprised. We have heard about the tragedies falling upon a number of your government elite. Unexplained accidents. Technology fails to find answers."

"We came upon some information," Caine generalized. "We would appreciate your perspective. We have a helicopter at our disposal."

"You mean, now?" Hammad asked dubiously. "I told you during your last adventure here, I avoid going into the desert at night."

"We'll be flying, not trekking. Besides, Colonel Mahmoud gave us little time."

Hammad turned to Aida who had a determined look, while his two companions were expressionless. He could not lose face. "Your General Bradley is getting deeper into my debt," Hammad declared with resignation.

The American officers led them to the waiting Mi 8 where the pilot and three Egyptian soldiers were already inside. After silent nods of introduction the party settled into bench seats along the bulkhead of the cargo area. Soon the helicopter was heading towards the coordinates locating the monastery on the mountain.

A bright moon illuminated the desert with a bluish sheen that outlined the darker profiles of the mountains ahead.

"What are you proposing to do?" Hammad asked Colonel Caine who was sitting next to him.

"We fly in for a visit," Caine said tentatively, hoping the practiced militiaman would offer any concrete alternative.

Mustafa Ali Hammad nodded his head in thought. "And what do you take this place to be?" he finally asked.

"It's supposed to be a monastery or some hostel for traveling nomads," Caine responded, but not convinced himself. "That's what Colonel Mahmoud concluded."

"I see."

"He didn't seem too curious about the place," Major Michael Lee interspersed from a bench on the opposite bulkhead.

Colonel Garrison Jones next to him was looking with playful eyes across to Aida who sat next to her cousin with a reserved expression on her face. Her raven hair tied into a bun added to her determined demeanor.

"Live and let live," Hammad responded. "These desolate areas are ruled by clans and have their own boundaries. Maybe your Egyptian Colonel is looking the other way in an area where there is no central authority. To admit knowing about it means you have to care about it."

"That's precisely the kind of area that breeds trouble," Caine declared.

Hammad's expression indicated agreement.

Almost an hour later the helicopter arrived at the coordinates and flew just above the deep canyon leading to the edifice. The dark walls of the canyon were outlined starkly against the moon-bathed blue of the night and seemed like a pathway of approach.

As the helicopter neared the center of the fortress high above the courtyard a beam of amber light suddenly shot skyward.

"Veer off! Veer off!" shouted Hammad in Arabic.

The apprehensive Egyptian pilot eagerly complied, banking the large helicopter upward and sharply to his left. The momentum pressed the passengers on one side into the bulkhead behind them, and pulled those on the other onto their safety belts. Aida's belt was not fully secure and she tumbled directly across the cargo floor into a startled Colonel Jones' embrace. He held her tightly until the pilot leveled the craft while heading it around a crest behind the monastery.

Colonel Jones and Aida fixed their eyes on each other, then he gently eased her onto the bench next to him. She did not resist when he helped her latch into another safety harness.

"What was that?" Major Lee was exclaiming.

Colonel Caine looked knowingly at Mustafa Ali Hammad. "Yeah! What was it?"

"We have to land out of sight," Hammad declared.

"Tell the pilot!" Caine directed and Hammad repeated the command in Arabic.

With everyone straining to see, the pilot steered around the mountain behind the abbey. He saw a ridge outlined by the light of the moon on the blind side of the redoubt. Faintly visible pinpricks of light from several places along the ridge contrasted sharply with the night. A narrow flat outcrop extended from the ridge. On the other side, unseen, was the fortress. The outcrop seemed hewn by hand and was likely a material staging area during ancient construction of the monastery.

"Find somewhere behind the canyon!" Colonel Caine ordered. His words were simultaneously repeated by Hammad and Colonel Jones in Arabic.

"I speak English!" the pilot said huffily. "Don't confuse me at a time like this! Too many chiefs!"

He cleared the canyon and looked for level ground beyond. Several miles farther he spotted a sandy alcove and gingerly settled the helicopter down.

"Strange light piercing the sky!" Hammad said tensely "The stories speak of it, but no one could ever find it! People have disappeared here!"

"So, we can't knock on the door as weary travelers?" Colonel Jones said with grim humor.

"We have to see what's going on," Colonel Caine said, remembering the words etched in the bulkhead of the downed helicopter.

"I agree," Mustafa Ali Hammad declared to the surprise of the American officers.

They looked expectantly at the wiry militia leader.

"This is beyond mercenary services. This could be the source. The source of our troubles. We could end them."

"I take it you know how," Caine offered, looking at the bleak mountain canyon in the distance. "The place is a fortress."

"All of them were. The walls and buildings were above ground. But they had elaborate underground tunnels and caves. For protection, for escape—from the heat, as much as from enemies—and for secure water supplies from underground streams."

"That's helpful," Caine said sarcastically.

"Those points of light on the ridge—they are likely air holes," Hammad said. "There is activity in chambers underground."

"Accesible?" Colonel Jones wondered.

"They were excavated by hand, so there have to be footholds," Hammad continued. "The problem is they are too high and rugged for swift climbing and a helicopter drop would give us away."

Colonel Caine pondered awhile and looked to his partner. Colonel Jones knew what he was thinking. "This helicopter was requisitioned from the joint maneuvers," he said. "It should have contingency equipment."

"It should," Caine answered.

They retreated to the back of the cargo area. Minutes later they emerged with two parachute packs. "This might do it," Colonel Caine said. "We parachute to the outcrop—check out the air shafts—head down the ridge and meet you at the helicopter."

"That way there's minimal risk," Colonel Jones explained. "Everyone wait out of sight with the helicopter until we come back."

"I want to see what's there myself," Mustafa Ali Hammad declared. "I hope we didn't fly from Beirut on a moment's notice for nothing. Besides, gentlemen"—he looked to Caine and Jones—"who else gives credence to your unusual theories?"

"Did you ever use a parachute?" Caine replied.

"No. But I have seen tandem jumps with parachutes. It seems like a sport."

"You've been very helpful to us," Caine conceded. "I suppose we can't refuse."

"Besides, you know the architecture," Colonel Jones added. "That could come in handy."

"I will go with my cousin!" Aida declared defiantly.

"We *are* playing this by ear," Jones said with a smile to his fellow officer.

"All right, all right," Caine replied impatiently. Then with a drawl he murmured: "Now who would you want to be strapped to?"

At a signal from Major Michael Lee the pilot started the turbo engines and lifted the helicopter into the night sky. They flew high above the mountain ridges until they arrived at the proximity of the monastery. With attentive pointing from several of the passengers he spotted several pricks of light on the mountain ridge behind the fortress.

"Stay about here," Colonel Caine ordered as he fastened a harness around Mustafa Ali Hammad, then attached it to the front of his own harness and parachute pack. Major Lee then slipped one of the backpacks onto Hammad's outstretched arms like an accordion. Colonel Jones was strapping the harness onto Aida, who wasn't sure if the repetitive adjustments to the crisscross belts were necessary. But she said nothing, aware that her safety harness along the bench had let loose earlier.

One of the Egyptian soldiers pushed open a cargo door, assisted by one of Hammad's gunmen. They were flying at three-thousand feet, which gave Caine and Jones enough time to open the chutes and maneuver towards the dots of light, where they would land on the flat outcrop behind the mountain of the monastery.

"Land on the other side of the canyon!" Caine shouted above the wind rushing into the helicopter. "We'll rappel down and join you as soon as we can! Before daybreak!"

Several of the others nodded.

"Okay, let's walk in tandem," Caine said to Mustafa Ali Hammad as he clipped the release cord of his main parachute onto a hook. He took a few waddle-like steps with Hammad secured in front and jumped into the night.

Colonel Jones clipped his release cord onto the hook, then lifted a surprised Aida off the deck, carried her to the edge and jumped out holding her.

"Yell, Geronimo!" he shouted in her ear.

Seconds later he released his hold on Aida, who shivered as she dropped several inches to the limits of her tandem harness. Both Caine and Jones intently worked the cords of their parachutes to maneuver them towards the pinpricks of light below.

Meanwhile the helicopter dropped to the visible outlines of the mountainous crags around them and slowly worked its way to a landing spot on the outside of the horseshoe canyon which would block its view from the monastery and its sound from unwelcome ears.

Caine and Hammad landed first. They both tumbled forward and found themselves on the edge of the outcrop nearest the lights. As Caine was unstrapping them Jones and Aida landed almost on top of them, tumbling forward toward the craggy wall of the mountain.

"Normally, I land on my feet," Jones said breathlessly and began to undue the straps of their parachute rig. The four gathered the parachutes into bundles and shoved them behind some large rocks at the face of the crag.

The mountain had looked sheer from afar. As they studied its walls, they saw that the slope was craggy and rock strewn, but climbable. They carefully worked their way toward the source of the lights, here and there climbing along what seemed like ancient narrow footpaths winding erratically upward.

When they reached the nearest opening they lay prone around it and strained to see deep inside. The only thing visible was the angled shaft dimly lit from below. A characteristically musty smell emanated from beneath, mingled with a hint of smoke and a sulfurous odor. The four wordlessly looked at each other with curiosity and wonderment.

Caine rose, pointed to the backpack and Jones hurriedly pulled out a length of cord to which was attached a mechanized grappling hook. Caine tied the end of the cord into a bowline knot around his waist while Jones pushed a button on the metal shaft at the other end and four sharp hooks sprung out like spider legs.

"Just in case," Caine murmured.

Colonel Jones placed the grappling hook around a nearby rock. Caine groped around inside the edges of the shaft and found notches in the sides. He looked up at Hammad.

"Those are footholds," Hammad whispered. "When they were chiseling out the air shafts."

Caine nodded and lowered himself feet first into the shaft. He worked his way slowly down the steeply sloped shaft, feeling with each foot the next step down, while grasping each notch he passed.

Jones, Hammad and Aida huddled around the opening and followed Caine's every calculated move. Caine felt the notches at regular intervals, but he worked his way in slow motion to avoid disturbing loose gravel or dislodge stones that might betray his presence. Soon he was out of sight and the light from below was blocked by his downward progress.

Colonel Jones glanced next to him to see the line from the grappling hook continue to play out. He estimated Caine had descended more than fifty-feet and was still moving. Caine kept working his way down until he saw more light and the end of the airshaft, which curved into a short perpendicular at its terminus. Under it was a small ledge overlooking some vast cavernous interior. He figured the ledge was a starting point for construction of the airshaft out of the cavern's jagged and irregular wall.

Caine rotated his body so that he was on his back looking through the short perpendicular end of the shaft. The ledge was a few feet from the opening and seemed isolated. He inched forward, stuck his legs through, pushed himself out and landed crouching on the ledge. He pulled his Beretta from his holster and stealthily leaned forward to see what was below.

Past a jutting cavern wall to his right, centered in the vast underground chamber he gaped directly at the head of a gleaming, black, obsidian statue three times the size of an average person and chipped into the shape of a demon faced goat sitting on its haunches. Artfully carved ram horns, a goatee and curvature of the mouth gave the features a sinister, leering, Mephistophelean look.

The eye sockets were shaped into catlike ovals. In the left socket there burned an elaborate torch in place of an eye. In the right socket rested a large, iridescent blue diamond dimly back-lit by oil lamps.

The idol rested on a tiered square block carved from stone and surrounded by numerous votive candles. At the foot of the idol—reminiscent of Mayan sacrificial altars—was a slightly concave stone table inlaid with obsidian between carved grooves ending in a drainage vent.

On it lay a long obsidian dagger with a well-worn handle wrapped in the hide of some desert creature.

Torches embedded along the cavern walls lit the scene with restless flames.

The idol was attended by a number of black hooded monk-like figures.

Colonel Christopher Caine stared in shocked realization.

Chapter 44

Colonel Garrison Jones felt three tugs on the rope extending into the airshaft. He jerked it. The rope was slack. Jones hurriedly pulled in the line while Aida coiled it next to him. Near the end he spotted three large knots.

"He wants us to come down."

Hammad and Aida surmised the same.

The mercenary handed Jones the backpack and eased himself into the shaft like Caine had done. He started down followed by Aida and Colonel Jones.

When Hammad's feet were visible, Caine took hold and guided them out of the shaft, signaling him to crouch as he landed. He repeated the move with Aida and Jones who followed soon after.

Caine put his finger to his lips with a stern look on his face, lay on his stomach and snaked his way to the edge of the ledge, motioning with his hand for the others to follow.

Aida almost gasped aloud when she saw the idol, putting her hand over her mouth to be sure she made no involuntary sound.

They stared in amazed silence.

About two dozen hooded figures sat on crude benches made from stone slabs facing the idol. Behind them was a raised bench with armrests and a backrest also hewn from stone, but more elaborate. Woven black and red material lined its seat, armrests and back. It appeared to be a throne. Several hooded figures walked reverently around the idol and the throne, looking to be sure that surrounding candles were all lit and re-lighting any that expired.

"It's the Hope Diamond," Colonel Jones whispered, staring at the eye socket.

"It's his big brother," Caine whispered back.

"What the hell?" Jones replied in a hushed tone. "Looks like a gathering of little anti-Christs."

"Maybe not so little," Caine replied in the same tone.

"The stories are true," Mustafa Ali Hammad murmured. "They go into the world to sow their curse."

"For what?" Jones asked.

"To break the grip of moral belief. To foment chaos, confusion. To pave the way for their Master."

Colonel Caine looked sternly at him with a finger to his lips. Hammad didn't realize his voice was rising.

Colonel Jones groped behind him for the nearby backpack. "We'll have a hell of a time getting down there," he whispered as he quietly unzipped the pack.

"Do we want to?" Caine reflected.

"I like your thinking."

"We'll need an army for this."

"I'm glad you two aren't trigger-happy," Hammad whispered to Caine. "There is a force here beyond their numbers."

As they lingered in awe, staring at the gleaming, towering effigy they noticed commotion below. The monks looked to an arched opening into another, smaller antechamber. Two hooded men appeared with AK 47 assault rifles slung around their necks. Behind them shuffled and jostled the occupants of the helicopter with two more armed monks prodding them on.

"Holy Jesus!" Colonel Jones exclaimed half aloud.

Colonel Caine instantly grabbed for the backpack and pulled out a grenade. Jones turned and groped quickly for a sub-machine pistol.

He smiled grimly, thankful that Hammad had the presence of mind to bring along their gifts.

Aida had a stricken look on her face and turned to her cousin. Mustafa Ali Hammad raised his palm slightly, indicating caution. She turned again to see what was happening below.

The monks pushed the prisoners towards the center of the cave near the stone benches and sacrificial altar. A low murmur started among the monks on the benches, growing in cadence and volume. *"Elohim, Elohim, Eloah Va-Daath, Elohim el Adonai. Elohim, Elohim…"*

As the chant progressed two of the monks grabbed one of the prisoners at random and pulled him towards the altar. The other monks turned to the remaining restless captives and pointed their assault rifles in threatening gestures. They motioned them back against the cavern wall. Several other monks leapt from their benches to assist in subduing the frantically struggling man in camouflage fatigues as they dragged him towards the altar. One of them picked up the dagger from the sacrificial altar, as the others strained to lay him onto it.

Looking on with a permanent leer was the insidious idol.

In the midst of the pending impromptu sacrifice other monks kept up the humming chant. *"Elohim, Elohim, Eloah Va-Daath, Elohim el Adonai…"*

Suddenly, Aida pulled her pistol and let out a blood-curdling shriek that echoed through the chamber drowning out the chant. Everyone momentarily froze. She leaped over the ledge, landed on her feet and somersaulted with the momentum, rising again with her pistol pointed at the nearest monk. She fired a single shot and dropped him, then shot the monk holding the blade. The captive jerked violently and broke the hold of his tormentors who were still stunned by what had just happened. Aida shot another monk as she charged, grabbed the captive's hand and both ran towards the other prisoners along the wall.

"It's my cousin Amir! Her brother!" Hammad shouted.

The monks below, pointing their rifles at the captives along the wall, instinctively turned to see what was happening. Major Lee grabbed one of the monks from behind in a headlock and tightened his grip around the man's neck. The monk, desperate for air, dropped his AK 47, which one of the Egyptian soldiers quickly grabbed and shot the other monk guarding them before he could react. Hammad's other gunman grabbed the dead man's rifle and pointed it towards the commotion at the sacrificial altar. Aida and Amir, running toward them, were in the line of fire. He hesitated, then turned the weapon on the monks at the benches. They dived for the cavern floor as he pulled the trigger in a rage.

On the ledge at that same moment Colonel Jones looked expectantly at Caine. He let out a piercing rebel yell to the grim amusement of his partner and was ready to spring. Caine yelled in echo, pulled his Beretta, and leaped into the fray with the grenade in his other hand. He landed squarely on the shoulders of a monk below him who crumpled to the cavern floor and broke Caine's fall. Jones was next to him, landing on another man and sending him sprawling. Mustafa Ali Hammad leaped onto the prone figure Caine had prostrated to cushion his fall. They ran into four of the monks who had been holding Amir. Jones shot one of them at point blank range with his Uzi submachine pistol. The rapid fire noise startled everyone around. Hammad shot another one as they ran to the other prisoners. Caine aimed his pistol towards the throne, but it was empty.

The captives along the wall were already heading for the opening to the antechamber when Caine, Jones and Hammad reached them. Aida was already their excitedly pointing her pistol in the direction of the idol.

"Where to?" Caine yelled.

"This way!" shouted Major Lee.

They hurried through the arch into the dimly lit antechamber where tapestries of various scenes of sorcery, witchcraft and devil worship were hung along musty cavern walls.

"That stairway!" Major Lee shouted breathlessly.

At the far end of the antechamber, a narrow, stone stairway curved its way upward.

"Go! Go! Go!" Colonel Caine shouted motioning everyone along holding the grenade high in his other hand.

Everyone without hesitation scurried single file up the stairs. Caine followed, but stopped at a point where he could still see the archway. He pulled the pin of his grenade and waited. The only witness to his daring act was his pounding heart. He heard muffled sounds of gunshots above and a burst of Jones' submachine pistol. Before he could visualize the scene, he heard shouting and the shuffle of feet near the archway. He lobbed the grenade at the entrance to the chamber beyond and scrambled up the stone stairway, holding his Beretta at the ready.

Seconds later the grenade exploded. He heard screams of pain and sounds of perplexity.

Caine hurried to the top of the stairs, looking breathlessly behind him to see if anyone was chasing. No one appeared before he reached the top and stepped out of the opening onto a long, dark hallway. The opening had to be part of the mountain wall and the hallway seemed like a corridor of the abbey. Torches along the way provided just enough light to see. At the far end in front of a massive wooden door, he saw his companions beckoning. Caine ran toward them and noticed several rough hewn doors ajar on either side of the hall. Lying in the doorways or in the hall were several figures dressed in hooded cassocks in various poses of death, their assault rifles next to them.

As Colonel Caine ran for the entrance another door opened. Caine pointed his Beretta as he ran. As soon as he saw a black form appear, he shot several rounds at it. The form slumped inside the room with the door barely open. Another door began to open just as he ran by. He shot several rounds through the door, not sure if they penetrated, but the thud of the bullets seemed enough to keep the door from opening.

His companions had taken a large brace from its hinges and were ready to push open the main door of the abbey.

"The chopper's out there!" Major Lee announced. "It's guarded, but they won't be expecting us!"

"Let's make sure!" Colonel Caine said. "Grab a couple of those cassocks!"

Caine motioned to Colonel Jones for another grenade and ran back to the opening into the mountain. He watched as Hammad and one of his gunmen roughly pulled the hooded robes off four corpses along the hallway.

Caine leisurely pulled a pin and bounced the grenade down the circular stairway. He ran back to join the others and heard a muffled explosion followed by screams and excited voices.

Colonel Jones, Mustafa Ali Hammad and Aida had already put on the cassocks. Caine draped the fourth one over himself and the group pushed opened the abbey door onto the courtyard. Caine and Hammad were in front, herding the passengers of the helicopter, with Colonel Jones and Aida acting as if they were guarding them from behind.

Two guards were standing leisurely in front of the Mi 8, but unslung their Kalashnikovs when the group approached. Hammad shot both before they could react and the group rushed towards the hatch. Two other guards appeared from behind the helicopter, ready to fire, but Colonel Jones, shooting through his cassock, killed them both with a burst from his Uzi.

Everyone scrambled into the helicopter. The pilot started the turbo engines while the others crowded around the hatch aiming their weapons at the abbey door and the periphery of the walled courtyard. Amid a cloud of dust raised by the swirling blades, a group of black hooded armed men charged out of the abbey, blindly firing their AK 47's in the direction of the escaping helicopter.

Colonel Jones squeezed another burst from his Uzi through the open hatch, while the others shot wildly downward in the direction of the black stream running to the center of the courtyard. The dust obscured any effect.

An amber light from the courtyard suddenly pierced the sky, but the helicopter was beyond it, high above the monastery and heading westward toward Aswan. The occupants felt relieved in their metal cocoon, even though they were flying over desolate wilderness and unsure if gunfire from below had damaged any critical avionics. The group slowly took their places along the bulkheads.

Colonel Caine lingered at the cockpit. "Are we okay?"

"I think so, Colonel," the Egyptian pilot replied staring at his gauges.

"How about back there?"

"Everyone seems all right," Colonel Jones replied.

Caine returned to the cargo area and slumped onto a bench. He slowly buckled his safety harness.

"Some strange looking dogs..." Major Michael Lee began.

Colonel Caine nodded wearily. He looked to Colonel Jones, then to Mustafa Ali Hammad. They glanced back knowingly.

"Familiars," Caine declared.

No one offered a logical alternative.

"They came from nowhere," Major Lee continued. "We were well hidden. Then these hooded goons jumped us before we knew what happened. They forced us to fly to the abbey. You know the rest."

"We know the rest," Colonel Caine repeated, thinking of much more than the incident.

He looked across at Aida.

"What would you have done?" she declared defensively.

Colonel Caine smiled grimly. "Surprise can outwit even the devil."

He remembered Laura Mitchell explaining her imps at the Smithsonian reception. He was anxious to be by her side. Her uncle had been targeted. His theories were too close to something. Caine was afraid she had become a target too.

"What the hell is that place, anyway?" Major Lee insisted.

Mustafa Ali Hammad looked somberly across the bench. "It is an ancient monastery that gave in to evil. Stories of such a place have circulated for generations. Misfortunes of people and empires have been attributed to it. They had become legend. After a time, doubt set in. It had become a tale worthy of the Arabian Nights."

Hammad paused. "Especially, since no one could ever find such a place."

The flopping of the helicopter blades, together with the whine of the engines was having an hypnotic affect on the listeners.

"Now that they are discovered by others than their followers, who knows what will happen?"

"So, who are their followers?" the American intelligence officer asked. "This place is a barren, sand choked, wasteland."

"People who have fallen into the temptations of their emissaries," Hammad replied as if it should be a known conclusion. "Stories tell of supplicants going out into the world to ingratiate themselves into circles of power. To lure kings and conquerors into their evil embrace."

"Easier said than done," Colonel Jones reflected.

"Indeed," Hammad replied. "But they evoked demonic powers, just like we beseech an Almighty. One can be inspired to do fantastic things, if they feel a supernatural power behind them. That feeling is internal—it is *internal*—" he emphasized. "It does not matter if the force exists or not. Actions in its name are always real."

"I do believe it exists," Colonel Caine said slowly, fingering his Beretta and shoving a new clip of bullets into the grip.

He looked across to Colonel Jones who was sitting next to Aida. They were unconsciously leaning into each other. Her brother, Amir, at her other side, was holding her hand. Major Michael Lee, next to Jones was deep in thought, pondering how a derelict Soviet helicopter lying half a century in the sand, could lead to this. The three Egyptian soldiers murmured missives to Allah. Mustafa Ali Hammad turned to

Caine as the Colonel holstered his weapon. Their glance signaled recognition of a common deadly challenge that bridged their separate cultures.

Caine looked to the pilot, unbuckled his harness and moved forward to the cockpit. He eased himself into the co-pilot's seat. "How are we?"

"So far, so good," he replied.

As the steady thump of the rotors sliced the dawning sky, everyone fell silent, pondering their good fortune in escaping from the infernal mountain abbey.

Caine remained in the co-pilot's seat. His mind was racing. He had to get back to Laura before she followed her suspicions about the Museum of Natural History. The pentagram centered on the museum, sentinels along its points, goons around the museum perimeter, the woman's scream, the body with markings in the park, the freak accidents breaking the chain of nuclear command—suspicious animals—familiars.

One more victim before Victor Sherwyck's protégé—Philip Taylor—controls the nuclear codes: the President. One more ceremony. One more sacrifice. Just like in the cave. The same stories from disparate sources over the world and over time. Her uncle, the soviet secret policeman in the Gulag, Mustafa Ali Hammad. Laura's lectures—with historical threads around mysterious eminences whispering in the ears of doomed queens and emperors and—and a mysterious eminence holding sway over a current President.

It was too obvious, too storylike, too unbelievable.

Until they found the demonic monastery.

The pilot looked over to Caine who was leaning into the windshield and peering toward the far horizon.

"Is something on your mind, Colonel?"

"Can't this thing go any faster?"

The light of the sun was beginning to show over that same mountain when the helicopter landed at the military airbase at Aswan.

An Egyptian major drove to the tarmac in a military van painted in camouflage. As the group alighted he greeted them with a salute.

"Colonel Mahmoud regrets that he cannot meet you in person. He is with the joint command in the field." The Major gestured towards the van. As the group followed him, he asked Colonel Caine perfunctorily: "The Colonel asked me to inquire: was your visit satisfactory?"

"Yes, it was, thank you," Caine replied coldly. "Relay a question for us, will you, Major?"

"Yes, sir. Gladly."

"Ask the Colonel, what are your laws around here related to human sacrifice?"

Chapter 45

Most of Victor Sherwyck's dinner guests were leaving his estate north of Mount Vernon.

"We had a marvelous time," said Diane Shaw, news anchor for a national television network. "I hope you're feeling better."

"I'm fine, I'm fine," Sherwyck replied as he escorted her onto the veranda. "There's no need for you to worry—or hurry."

"Thanks, but it's late," she replied as he took her hand and kissed it.

"Good night, Victor. Thank you," said Malcolm Kirby of the State Department. "You're a real charmer. I could listen to your stories all night."

"Come now. Your repertoire is second to none," Sherwyck said shaking his hand.

He waved to two other guests who were already on the driveway.

Several guests were making ready to leave, but hesitated. Among them were the philanthropists Mr. and Mrs. Knowlton, Senator Everett Dunne, and Secretary of Defense designate Philip Taylor.

One more confidant arrived through a rear entrance when other guests had left: Stanley Brooks, union steward of the Labor and Maintenance Union, Local 1315 of Washington, D.C. He had parked his dark green van in the usual spot out of sight along the stables.

They drifted into an elegant drawing room where ornate sofas surrounded a large flagstone fireplace. They sat down in their usual places. They had done this before.

Victor Sherwyck walked in looking triumphant in his dinner jacket. "Let us toast to our impending success. The funeral of the Vice President is in two days. Tomorrow we offer our supreme sacrifice—something of outstanding sentiment to this country. Then the last impediment to our victory—the President—will fall. We shall prevail. All that I have promised you is here!"

His followers' eyes gleamed with anticipation of personal fulfillment, power and glory.

"Symbols of religious faith in this country are challenged. More and more they are challenged. The State is pulled away from its spiritual anchors. Scandal abounds in churches. The energy of our own rituals to the true Prince of the Underworld is filling the void. Witness our power by our tumbling enemies! We are ascendant!"

He glared at each of them in turn.

"Does anyone have any doubt?"

His supplicants stared attentively, saying nothing.

"Our colleagues in the hidden corridors of the Kremlin are poised to step forward. Their people still pine for strong leaders. They will have them!"

Sherwyck eyed Senator Dunne. "As you know, there is disarray in political office. Major issues go wanting and brilliant minds wallow in minutiae. That is why when the moment comes, they will follow a firm, resolute leader—a leader forged by crisis. You, my dear Taylor!"

Philip Taylor smirked in self-satisfaction.

"You, who will for a short, critical time—when the President falls—command the nuclear arsenal and—as a patriotic gesture to save your people—capitulate when threatened by our resurgent comrades and believers from my world!"

He eyed each of them individually to see from the wide looks in their eyes, whether questions remained.

"Fear of insecurity is far greater than love of democracy," Victor Sherwyck declared with finality.

Their looks were now rapt, firm in the belief that his every word was right.

"We will gather, like we do, several hours after the close of the museum," Sherwyck instructed.

"The delivery entrance will be manned. There'll be night crew vehicles in the lot," Stanley Brooks, the union steward, reported. "The van will not look out of place."

"Be sure the perimeters are protected," Sherwyck scolded.

"Our men have always scared away passersby."

Sherwyck looked at him sternly.

"Except for that last time. He was armed. It won't happen again. I assure you. We lost a couple of true believers."

"Fools!" Sherwyck declared. "True believers win, not lose!"

"It won't happen again, I assure you."

"How will you bring the offering?"

"She's already there. She's closely guarded in one of the exhibit rooms under construction." Brooks answered with a confident tone of efficiency.

Sherwyck raised his eyebrow. "What about Alvin Carruthers, the curator? He's been asking questions lately during rounds of the building."

"His domain is the daytime, sire. We plead 'union rules' after five in the evening. He has no access to those keys, especially the construction areas or the level beneath the gem exhibits. Our people rule after hours."

Sherwyck's eyes narrowed. He looked threateningly at Brooks. "Make sure the remains are hidden for good. We cannot have corpses turn up in parks with our symbols on them!"

"Yes. Yes, of course! It won't happen again."

The Sorcerer's face turned into a sarcastic smile. "You scared the devil out of Senator Dunne here when the last one was found." Sherwyck reveled in his psychological puppeteering. "But, no matter," he continued more convivially. "In several days the whole axis of power in this world will change. These details will be irrelevant."

He lifted his glass in a toast.

"I think I'll ask to see the President tomorrow. One last time, so to speak."

The others snickered expectantly.

"Someone from the memorial committee asked that Blaze be the riderless horse in the Vice President's funeral cortege into Arlington." His lips turned into a mordant grin.

"What about the investigation into General Starr's accident?" Mr. Knowlton cautioned. "The reports of a black horse involved?"

"Is my prized Arabian the only black stallion in Virginia?" Sherwyck replied with feigned indignity.

His cynical grin turned into a longing sigh. "My child of the desert. He reminds me so much of home."

Chapter 46

Laura Mitchell was quietly sobbing at her uncle's bedside. He had been pronounced dead more than a half hour earlier. She held his hand and looked at his peaceful face. All wrinkles of a lifetime of struggle were gone. He looked younger, just like in old, but treasured photos of a band of partisans in the forests of his beloved homeland.

She stroked his head. The body was still warm. "I know you can hear me, Uncle. You'll always be with me. I am what you taught me."

She took a deep breath of resolve. "I'll prove you right. Chris will help me. And I swear we'll destroy whoever killed you."

A woman in business dress came into the hospital room. "Are you all right? Do you want more time?"

Laura looked with red, but drying eyes at the solicitous face. "Thanks, I'm all right."

The lady shook her hand. "I'm with family and social services. I'm truly sorry for your loss. You know, he made arrangements some time ago. There's a connection through an Embassy."

"Yes, of course," Laura said with an emerging smile. "He wants to be buried with his brothers—the Brothers of the Forest."

"Oh?" The woman sounded intrigued. "It seems like there's some story there."

"A long one," Laura replied.

"You'll take good care of him?"

"Certainly," the woman assured and hugged her. "You go home and get some rest."

"Rest will have to come later," Laura said determinedly. "Right now I have some business at a museum."

"But, it's near closing time."

"So much, the better."

* * *

Outside the hospital, she phoned Alvin Carruthers and told him what happened to her uncle. Carruthers sounded distraught in expressing his sympathies.

"Meet me at the museum," she said resolutely.

"But, Laura," came over the phone. "It's closing time."

"There's a back entrance, isn't there?"

"Well, yes, for maintenance and security. It's not for visitors."

"I'm not going as a visitor."

* * *

Laura Mitchell hurried to her car and drove the short distance from George Washington University Hospital to the National Museum of Natural History. She turned from Constitution Avenue onto 12th Street, then turned left into the hedge enclosed service area of the museum. The stretch of 12th Street in late afternoon looked so different from that dark night, she thought with a determined look, that night when Christopher Caine had fought off their deadly accosters.

She parked her car next to some other vehicles and started for the service door. Several people had just entered before her. She wondered if the door was unlocked or if she would have to wait for Al Carruthers outside.

Just as she reached to try the door, two muscular men grabbed her from behind. One muffled her mouth and the other jabbed her arm with a muscle relaxant. She struggled violently, but briefly, before they dragged her out of sight.

Chapter 47

As soon as he landed at Andrews Air Force Base, Colonel Caine headed for Washington University Hospital to see Jonas Mitchell and hopefully find Laura with him.

The hospital was on the way to the Pentagon where he had orders to brief General William Bradley. Colonel Garrison Jones had stayed behind in Egypt to inform officials about the infernal monastery and see how they would react to it.

Caine had just passed the highway interchange from Andrews and was speeding northwest on the divided stretch of Pennsylvania Avenue when he saw a blue sedan in traffic behind him.

The tail so benign on other occasions, now took on menacing significance after the revelations in the desert. The sedan was close and kept pace with him in traffic. He slowed for a changing traffic light where the road merged near the Anacostia River in the southeast part of the city. Glancing in the rear view mirror he saw the sedan coming at him. He could see that it was not going to stop and braced himself for impact. Seconds later the dark sedan banged into the rear of his Viper.

Caine pulled to the curb and stopped in a lurch. The other driver had pulled up behind him and was climbing out of his own car. Caine stormed out to confront the man when he noticed the diplomatic license plate.

Other traffic was slowly maneuvering around them, drivers aware that getting involved in a fender bender with a diplomat's car was useless.

"What the hell?" Caine exclaimed just as the driver was raising his hood. "You had no intention of stopping!"

"I am sorry," Colonel. "Truly."

Caine stopped short when the man addressed him by rank.

"You are a difficult man to contact. I tried several times, but it is dangerous."

"What the hell are you talking about? And what the hell are you going to do about my car?"

"I am Oleg Alekseev of the Russian Embassy. This is the most innocent way we can meet."

"Why the hell should you want to contact me?" Caine demanded as he looked back to the rear of his roadster. "Do you realize what it costs to fix a car like this?"

"I envy your ability to be concerned about such things," the Russian diplomat and spymaster said. "It is a luxury most of my own people can only pine about."

"So, what the hell do you want to prove?"

"I always thought you to be more a reserved man," Alekseev said as he walked to the rear of Caine's Viper. "Not fazed by small irritants." He leaned over and looked at the buckled bumper and cracked trunk area.

Colonel Caine watched him. His anger turning to curiosity about this distinguished looking, slightly overweight stranger with gray hair, who seemed to express more than casual familiarity with him.

"There is not much time," Alekseev said as he straightened himself to face Caine. "This is the only way someone like me can meet someone like you without suspicion."

He bent down again and animatedly looked at the rear of the Viper. Caine slowly bent down next to him and ran his fingers along the damaged trunk area.

"Your people found a helicopter in the desert near Aswan," Alekseev said to allay any doubts of his credibility.

Caine straightened to look at Alekseev who slowly stood full length and strode to the front of the sedan to assess the damage. Caine followed. The raised hood covered them from oncoming traffic.

"Your inquiries are unsuccessful in identifying the flyers. The flight was a deep held secret among a cultist group in the secret police."

Colonel Caine stared at him with steely eyes.

"But, I know who they were."

Caine stared at him unflinchingly. He could not reveal who he was, even though it appeared Alekseev knew about him, nor could he seem interested in the story of the helicopter, let alone the names of the flyers. But he dare not dismiss the man either.

"Your discovery has helped me solve a lifelong puzzle." Alekseev looked around to see if the accident had not stopped traffic. Vehicles seemed to be moving by at a tolerable pace. He continued: "My loving wife is Natasha, formerly Rudenko."

Caine started rolling his eyes. He was familiar from Russian literature with obtuse storytelling.

"She had an older brother, Yuri Rudenko, who was sent on a secret mission more than fifty years ago from which he never returned."

Caine was interested.

"I suspected over the years that he was betrayed by his own comrades."

"So, what else is new?" Caine thought to himself.

"They were NKVD, but that's another story."

"Weren't they all," Caine kept thinking, his thoughts beginning to drift to the damage done to his roadster.

"Now, with your discovery of the helicopter, I know he was betrayed. My beloved wife has never forgotten, never forgiven. And she has never been the same."

Caine's look indicated some bewilderment.

"Let me quickly say that there are patriots among us who are struggling against great odds to avoid retrenchment to an evil system."

"From idealism or from revenge?" Caine said facetiously.

"The motive does not matter, Colonel. Do not be so patronizing. You are in danger of falling under such a system yourself!"

Colonel Caine could not let on that he understood what Alekseev was saying. "And just how is that?" he challenged.

Alekseev pulled a vest pocket calendar from his jacket and began scribbling something on a piece of notepaper. "We are exchanging insurance information," he said as an aside.

"The quest for answers to the fate of my wife's brother has led to our meeting, Colonel," Oleg Alekseev said somberly. "I—and some others not as fortunate, who met mysterious ends—have trailed rumors for years. Rumors of a worldwide cult of forces ascending through evil."

"And you expect me to believe this?" Caine asked to assure that he continue.

Alekseev took a deep breath in frustration. "That is a pillar of their success. Nobody believes it! That is why, I'm afraid, they will succeed in collapsing your government!"

"You *are* nuts! You know that!" Caine goaded.

"Let me assure you, that no matter what positive developments have come between our two countries, there is a powerful cabal within the former Soviet secret police that will never relent. This circle is exclusive and unknown even to high ranking progressive ranks within the former KGB itself—now the FSB."

"A lot of arm chair conspiracy buffs figure that. What else is new?"

"No, my friend. They are not nostalgic for Stalin. Their leader is not in the Kremlin. This cabal pays homage to the devil. And he may have followers in your own government!"

Caine was riveted, but could not let on. He feigned polite, but frustrated interest, staring at the damage to his roadster.

"The key, Colonel Caine, is the helicopter."

Caine glanced sideways when his name was mentioned, then returned his stare to his car.

"I appreciate and admire your discipline, Colonel. You don't have to acknowledge anything of who you are or what I say. But listen, please!"

"I'm listening," he replied by indirect means of acknowledgment and appreciation.

"I learned over a lifetime of secret and dangerous inquiry that three agents were sent to the Middle East in Nineteen-fifty-eight on an ultra-secret mission. They brought back someone from a secret place in the desert to Aswan. They never returned."

"And from Aswan to America," Caine thought. He was seeing a juncture between Alekseev's narrative and his own discoveries.

"Now that you have found the helicopter, I know Yuri Rudenko was betrayed. He was left behind at whatever secret place they were bound for."

Caine imagined the poor wretch on the sacrificial altar in the cavern. A bloody bond for some hideous plan.

"The flyers you are trying to identify are General Anatoli Lysenko and Colonel Nicholai Kuznetsov. Together with the two pilots, they were the only men found aboard. Yuri Rudenko should have been with them."

Colonel Caine's features froze at the name *Nicholai Kuznetsov*. *Warlock*! Dead in the desert for over half a century; dead in every instance that Senator Everett Dunne quoted him. Dunne the exclusive conduit for Warlock's information. Dunne the disinformer. Dunne the traitor!

Caine's mind raced over everything connected to Jeannie McConnell's disappearance while the Russian spoke. Everything was suddenly clear.

"My wife will rest easier, knowing what fate befell her brother. She can now pray for him in peace," Alekseev said. "Because, now she believes in God. She promised me."

He closed the hood and hurried to climb into his sedan. "I'm sorry about your car. I will make arrangements for repairs. Privately."

Alekseev started the engine. "You must know one thing, Colonel. You are dealing with forces beyond physical science."

Caine nodded slightly. He had heard that before.

"Do something…For all our sake."

Colonel Caine's curious look prompted Alekseev to add: "If you cannot. No one else can."

"Now, why would that be?" Caine probed.

"You *are* a member of an official secret group are you not? No holds barred? Omega?"

Oleg Alekseev backed up his car, made a quick maneuver around Caine's roadster and merged into the flow of traffic.

Chapter 48

Caine cursed under his breath as he climbed into his roadster. He groped behind the seat for his blue flasher, put it on the dashboard and peeled away. He watched the sedan turn onto the Anacostia Freeway as he sped by. Getting to the hospital seemed more urgent than ever.

He was perturbed that the Russian knew so much secret information, but his anger was mixed with grudging professional admiration. Oleg Alekseev's concern was about Yuri Rudenko. Colonel Caine's became the revelation about Nicholai Kuznetsov.

There was only one way Senator Dunne could know about Nicholai Kuznetsov. Someone had told him. Someone who had been on the helicopter. Someone—whoever he was—before he became Victor Sherwyck!

A chill ran down Colonel Caine's spine.

Senator Dunne for many years had filtered information through Warlock, the code name, he claimed, Kuznetsov insisted upon. "A sinister running joke," Caine thought. Certainly propounded by the mastermind. "Warlock—an in-your-face reference to a sorcerer. Warlock—someone in league with the devil," Caine thought with a sheepish smirk.

But, Nicholai Kuznetsov, betrayed, had the last macabre laugh, Caine mused. A warning etched on the bulkhead of his tomb.

Senator Everett Dunne betrayed the rendezvous in the Mediterranean, so that he and Colonel Jones would not meet Mustafa Ali Hammad, the mercenary contact arranged by the Omega Group. The entire mission was based on Warlock's lead as reported by Senator Dunne. Dunne knew that any response by Hammad—who flowed freely in lawless circles—would raise doubts about Middle East terrorists involved in Jeannie McConnell's disappearance.

"Wild goose chase!" thought Caine. Just as he had speculated to General Bradley earlier. While the Omega Group chased the usual terrorist suspects, critical links in the chain of nuclear command fell by the wayside. Freak, but innocent accidents. Coincidental events. But not so innocent with an overlay of the occult, which Colonel Caine and others had now witnessed with their own eyes.

All that the perpetrators needed was time. Time for the final and supreme accident, when their man took sudden control of the nuclear arsenal.

Another sacrifice was necessary to topple the President. A high value sacrifice for the ultimate target.

* * *

Weaving in traffic as his mind raced, he almost missed the left turn onto I Street. With tires squealing, he turned and sped ahead, then screeched right onto 23rd Street, stopping at the emergency entrance of George Washington University Hospital. He left the flasher on and hurried inside.

Caine bounded up stairs to the second floor and turned a corner into the Intensive Care Unit. No one said anything to the imposing, athletic man in the tan slacks and matching pleated shirt with epaulettes. He walked into a quiet, sterile room with an empty bed. He stood there reverently, staring at the taut sheet of linen over the bed. The woman from family counseling walked in.

"Where's Jonas Mitchell?" Caine demanded.

"I'm sorry, he's gone," replied the woman.

"Gone where?" he pressed, hoping not to hear expected words.

"I'm sorry, sir. He expired."

"You mean, he's dead," Caine declared with rage welling in his chest.

"I'm sorry."

"What about his niece, Laura?"

"She said she had an appointment?"

"Where."

"She said a museum," the woman replied with a quizzical tone.

Caine pulled out his cell phone. The woman gave him a stern look and pointed to a picture on the wall with a red stripe across a cell phone.

Ignoring her he dialed Alvin Carruthers. The curator answered on the first ring.

"Get to the Natural History Museum as fast as you can!"

"I'm already here," Carruthers answered. "I'm glad you called." His voice sounded concerned. "Laura said to meet her here. She's not here, but her car is."

"Stay where you are!"

"Is something wrong?"

"I'll be right there." Caine ended the call.

"Sorry," he said to the woman as he hurriedly brushed past her. "And thanks."

In the parking lot, he jerked open the damaged trunk of his Viper and reached unerringly for a slim, black, rectangular case holding his Beretta. He removed the pistol and a tubular cylinder, then quickly threaded the silencer onto the barrel.

Street lights around the periphery of the hospital were beginning to shine in the growing dusk.

He jumped into his roadster, placed his pistol on the passenger seat, looked around for entering ambulances, and sped out of the Emergency lot.

* * *

Within ten minutes Alvin Carruthers could hear his roadster ca-
reening onto 12ᵗʰ Street from Constitution Avenue and saw him turn
into the maintenance area of the museum.

"She said her uncle died and to meet her here!" Carruthers said
urgently as he ran up to the roadster.

"He was murdered!" Caine replied emphatically and climbed out
with his pistol in hand.

"Murdered?" Carruthers exclaimed staring at the elongated pistol.
"What's this?"

"Where's Laura?"

"Maybe someone let her in."

Caine looked around and saw several vehicles parked near
Laura's. One of them backed up near the door was a dark green van
that Caine was sure had his bullet hole in it.

"Her uncle? Murdered?" Carruthers repeated incredulously.

"Sorcery!"

"What?"

"She's in danger. And no one inside now is a friend."

"What do you mean?"

"What did you say at that reception about the unions and the
night crews and the contracts and Victor Sherwyck interceding to let
them supervise everything after hours. Job security, seniority and all
that crap!"

"Yes. It's frustrating. I'm a curator and blind to what goes on for
nine hours every night."

"Let's get inside before it's too dark."

Carruthers hesitated for a thoughtful moment. "I see what you're
saying, Chris. I don't have a key."

"The hoodlum guards will be showing up," Caine said and started
for the delivery door.

"Is that who you fought with that night?"

"I'm sure."

At the door, Colonel Caine motioned his friend to stand behind him. Carruthers stepped back and adjusted the jacket of his tailored blue suit. Caine put his pistol to the lock and pulled the trigger. A sharp sound of metal against metal was all that resounded from the suppressed barrel. Caine tried the door. It jiggled, but did not open. He pointed the pistol between the edge of the door and the frame and fired again. This time the latch gave and Caine pulled the door open.

They slinked past the kitchen of the cafeteria and hurried to a curved stairway leading to the main floor of the rotunda. They climbed the stairs, along the wall, looking upward for any guards or workers.

They reached the top and hid behind a marble support for one of the portals into the main hall. There they faced the bull elephant in its perpetual stately pose on the African savannah.

"Do you think they have Laura?" Carruthers whispered, surprised how his voice carried in the empty hall.

Caine nodded and indicated silence. But, too late. A uniformed guard, unseen on the opposite side of the raised diorama, looked towards them. A pistol was in his hand. The guard took aim in their direction.

Caine swung his Beretta upwards and holding it with both hands fired two muffled shots in quick succession under the elephant's belly. The guard fell behind the diorama.

Caine and Carruthers bent low and rushed around the diorama. The guard lay motionless.

"Behind that desk!" Carruthers urged. He grabbed the body by the jacket collar and started dragging him. Caine joined in. The information desk was at a portal entrance into an exhibit hall radiating from the circular rotunda.

"Normal guards don't shoot at visitors," Caine observed as they shoved the body into the desk well.

"This uniform 's not the museum's," Carruthers panted.

"Take his pistol."

Carruthers looked at this friend.

"You were in the Army, weren't you?" Caine said under his breath.

"I spent my time in intelligence."

"You had basic training, didn't you?"

"Well. Yes. Twice, actually."

Hurried footsteps echoed on the floor above. Someone leaned over the marble railing and peered below. Caine and Carruthers were huddled over the body behind the desk directly across from the man. Colonel Caine raised his eyes upward. He recognized him immediately — the ill-tempered overseer he met at Sherwyck's estate.

The man scanned the hall below, then hurried out of sight.

Carruthers grabbed the guard's pistol. A bullet was already chambered, ready to fire. He nodded knowingly. "They mean business," he whispered. "Whoever they are. We have to find Laura."

The curator pointed to the second floor where the man had just been. "She was interested in that gem area. Around the Hope Diamond."

Caine cursed himself for not investigating sooner the suspicions Laura had from the start.

Chapter 49

Victor Sherwyck, in fact, had been at the Smithsonian the night Colonel Caine wanted to meet him at the reception in the Old Castle. Except, he was across the Mall in the Museum of Natural History officiating at a demonic ritual.

On recurring occasions after the museum closed and the night crews took over the grounds, Victor Sherwyck and his fanatical followers would arrive unobtrusively through the service entrance. They would climb in solemn fashion individually, or by twos and threes up the marble stairs to a maintenance level below the gem exhibit.

There, at the end of a hall cordoned by a red velvet rope with a sign "Restricted Area Employees Only," they would file through a door with no handle—opened with two key cards held by Sherwyck and one of his attendants—into an empty area featuring a thick glass shaft—the secure repository for the Hope Diamond which would descend from the floor above if someone tampered with the display.

Farther beyond the column was a door into another maintenance and storage area where myriads of items not currently on display were neatly stored in large pull out drawers, on movable metal tables, in theatrical trunks and clothes racks. The trunks and racks held various costumes and donations of historical clothes that would, in time, be circulated into the exhibits. One rack, off to the side and mingled with period fashions, had a sign draped over it stating: "Not for Display."

The rack held black velvet robes for Sherwyck and his supplicants. High born and low who had fallen into his sway, would gather together and drape themselves in the robes. All would be equal, no fashion outstanding, no threadworn shirt too poor.

But active participation in the most infernal elements of the rite was reserved for influential members and those growing in influence through committed membership. Over time all could see the results of their evil devotion assisted by the aura of the Devil's Eye. The supplicants gathered in the large chamber where black candles were aligned in a circle around the glass shaft.

They were led in chant by Victor Sherwyck: *"Elohim, Elohim, Eloah Va-Daath. Elohim, El Adonai, el Trabaoth, Shaddai. Tetragrammaton, Iod. El Elohim, Shaddai. Elohim, Elohim…"*

At a given moment a large vault, triggered by member security guards upstairs, would descend from the floor above and come to rest in the middle of the circle of candles. Inside, rested the Hope Diamond, gleaming on its pedestal; its blue radiance thrilling hundreds of visitors on the floor above just hours previously. Now, with an ultra violet light positioned from a tripod over the supplicants' shoulders, it would begin to glow a phosphorescent red.

"Behold the Devil's Eye!" Victor Sherwyck would begin. "Behold its power! Now and into all Time!"

Supplicants would resume their chant as two members wheeled in a metal autopsy table from the storage room. On it was a dark red cloth covering the slotted surface. A struggling young woman, and rare occasions a man, would be handcuffed naked to the corner supports of the table.

Their screams, reaching only ears in the know, were a hopeful sign that Baal would respond.

Participation in ritual murder was reserved for those members demonstrating unwavering belief in the diabolical and submissiveness to their Master. Once involved they stepped outside the pale of normal society and their infernal bond was stronger. Discipline, silence and devotion were welded by latent fear of the Sorcerer.

Supplicants had witnessed Victor Sherwyck's prophesies and promises. They achieved fortune, power and prestige. They saw that his rituals evoked results—incidents bringing humiliation and ruin, destruction and death.

He seemed to be everywhere, staring through the eyes of birds, cats, horses, dogs, and other creatures known and unknown—triggering events in their presence. Soon they would witness the imminent takeover of a world power—the last obstacle in their quest for total domination: the last god-fearing democracy strong enough to ward off their age long quest.

It would happen swiftly, and without conflict, hardly noticed by a population mourning a departed President, Vice President and two vital government officials. Their man-in-waiting, Phillip Taylor, would suddenly inherit the ultra secret codes of the nuclear arsenal of the United States and hand over power to threatening members of a resurgent totalitarian state acting on behalf of the Prince of the Netherworld.

Taylor had already participated in the sacrifice. He was steeled for what was to come. His moment in the world was at hand. Several others would hold the sacrificial dagger for the first time.

Their evil actions would be protected by the bodyguard of faithful goons who patrolled the outside of the museum intimidating any passersby.

This night they had gathered as before. It would be a culminating ritual.

* * *

Colonel Caine and Alvin Carruthers crouched in the desk well over the body of the guard Caine had shot minutes earlier.

A two tone gong echoed through the sound system as if ending a concert intermission.

Several workers started filing up the stairs opposite them, as several more came from separate exhibit halls radiating from the main rotunda. Among the custodial crew ascending the stairs were three uniformed guards who would normally provide building security at night.

"There must be others," Caine whispered in Carruthers' ear.

"They're scattered throughout the building," Carruthers whispered in return.

The workers gathered solemnly at the hallway door, ready to listen to the ritual proceedings. They were not yet fully initiated to observe the deadly rites, but were fanatic enough to act as devoted sentinels at the door, called to protect the practitioners who had already filed inside.

"We could take 'em," Caine began to whisper.

"They might hurt Laura," Carruthers interrupted. "I'm the curator, remember?"

Caine glanced at him expectantly.

"I know places through here that don't need a key."

Chapter 50

"Behold the Devil's Eye!" Victor Sherwyck intoned with outstretched hands and resplendent in his black velvet robe. "Behold its power! Now and into all Time!"

The blue diamond started glowing red in the beam of the ultra violet lamp above them. Gathered in the darkened chamber, lit only by a circle of black candles, were a group of velvet robed believers who stood outside the circle of candles in shuddering anticipation.

Facing Victor Sherwyck was Senator Everett Dunne, whose round, cherubic face and wire-rimmed glasses looked incongruous in his velvet black robe. Next to him stood Philip Taylor, tall and gaunt and in the ceremonial robe, easily mistaken for Sherwyck, himself. Next to him were two veterans of the museum staff, both of whom Laura Mitchell had encountered days earlier in the elevator. Behind them hovered Stanley Brooks, the union steward. On Senator Dunne's right stood Mr. and Mrs. Knowlton, the philanthropists supporting museum innovations. They were dressed for a formal dinner under their oversized robes and would make excuses later that they were "unexpectedly delayed."

The fanatical believers began their incantation to summon their Master from the Underworld. "*Elohim, Elohim, Eloah Va-Daath. Elohim, El Adonai, el Trabaoth, Shaddai. Tetragrammaton, Iod. El Elohim, Shaddai. Elohim, Elohim…*"

The door to the storage area opened and two robed supplicants pushed an autopsy cart into the room. It was bedecked with a red velvet swathe covering the perforations for collecting blood. On the table, squirming in desperation was a voluptuous blonde woman, handcuffed naked on her back to the four posts of the cart. She was screaming loudly, cursing, pleading, and jerking at her shackles until her skin was raw and bloody.

Along each side of her body lay two obsidian daggers with handles bound in hide. Their cold edges touched her as she writhed, evoking greater terror of the inevitable.

The robed attendants wheeled the cart slowly to the middle of the chamber, ignoring the woman's screams and gazing with prurient pleasure at her undulating body.

Sherwyck stared at the black robed figures around him and commanded them to chant louder, enveloping the screams into their cadence. "*Elohim, Elohim. Eloah Va-Daath. Elohim, El Adonai...*" As they repeated the words in a tedious tempo, a trancelike euphoria began to overtake them.

Sherwyck looked to the Diamond illuminated red in the vault and incanted over the screams of the victim and the droning chant:

"Rise, invincible Eye and grant favor upon us! Grant that this body be worthy of Baal! Hear our plea!" he intoned. "Hear our command!" he added with resolve.

"Favor your vanguard as ever in time! We spill the sweet blood of your power before you! Red will it be as the red of your Eye! Take this body as bond of our pledge!"

"Rise, invincible Eye and grant favor upon us! Look down with consent for we herald your reign!"

The base on which the Diamond rested slowly began to rise in its thick glass shaft. The guards had reset the safety mechanism and the legendary jewel was returning to its showcase vault on the exhibit floor above. As it rose past the ultra violet lamp, it turned iridescent blue again and slowly continued to its place of prominence in the Gem Hall.

The two robed attendants then pushed the gurney with the writhing, screaming sacrificial offering next to the shaft in the center of the circle of candles.

Victor Sherwyck loomed over her, his hands outstretched over her body, glistening with sweat.

"Do not fear!" he intoned.

The woman fleetingly, desperately believed and fell silent. Her body heaved with her short and rapid breath.

"Do not fear! All will be over! All will soon be over!"

She stared at him and hung on every word.

"There will be no pain! There is no need to fear!" the Sorcerer assured.

"Mark the symbol of *Grimorium Verum* on this flesh—so our Prince will know through whom we speak."

At this point Mr. Knowlton approached the gurney and with his forefingers took a swab of blue grease paint held by one of the attendants and smeared a line on the woman between her clavicle bones.

She cringed in fear and yelled: "What are you doing? Are you crazy?" She let out a primeval scream and tried to turn over, tugging at her handcuffs, and squirming futilely.

Knowlton backed off slightly to get more grease paint. He then smeared a line from her left clavicle bone across her breast through the middle of her belly to her right hip as she squirmed and yelled.

The smear was crooked—evidence of her vigorous protests.

Next Mrs. Knowlton came up to the victim and dabbed grease paint on her forefinger from the container held by the silent attendant.

She looked menacingly at the woman and quickly smeared a line from her other clavicle bone, across her breast and through the middle of her belly to her left hip.

All the while the woman squirmed and screamed, but her movements were weary and her voice was getting hoarse and barely audible.

An X with a looped top was now displayed on her torso.

"You will rest soon in comfort, oblivious to everything," soothed Victor Sherwyck in mock consolation. "You will be our vessel into the Netherworld, where you will be welcomed with open arms! Are you not pleased that we have chosen a most valued treasure to bring about our most cherished wish?"

"You fucking mad man!" the woman spat while she writhed, hoping desperately to break her metal bindings. "I'll kill you! I swear! I'll kill you all!"

Sherwyck smirked. "Be pleased that we will partake of your blood to see the vision of our Master. Be honored that it is you we have chosen! You are the medium through which the Final Order comes to this world!"

He looked around at his suppliants who nodded eagerly as he spoke and awaited the warm elixir of power.

"You will be peaceful and serene when we partake of your passionate heart! Imagine yourself peaceful and serene as you suddenly enter our Master's domain."

The woman tried vainly to raise herself from the pallet, squirmed back and forth and fell back in a faint.

"Hurry! Before the moment is past!" Sherwyck commanded.

Senator Dunne stepped up to the gurney and took the container from the attendant. He gazed longingly at the naked body on the red velvet cloth, then dabbed two fingers deeply into the greasepaint.

The Senator smeared a line from one shoulder down her side, across her body just above the pubic area—sighing at how luscious she looked—and swirled it back up several inches along the outside of her opposite thigh.

He did the same—longingly—along the other side of her body and across to the other thigh.

Victor Sherwyck came up to Senator Dunne, who cringed slightly when he did, and took the container from him.

"Our time has come! May this night bear us fruit, so tomorrow we rule!"

Sherwyck dabbed his forefinger into the greasepaint with a flourish and smeared a V from between her legs several inches up her belly then crossed the tops like a T.

At this point she began stirring into consciousness.

"Behold the *Grimorium Verum*! Behold the vessel that will carry our plea!"

Victor Sherwyck nodded to Senator Dunne, who approached the gurney.

He then nodded to Mr. Knowlton, who stepped up next to him.

Sherwyck nodded again and Philip Taylor came to the other side of the autopsy cart with the woman looking back and forth in terror at the faces leering down at her.

He nodded one more time and Mrs. Knowlton approached the cart next to Taylor, looking with sneering envy at the beautiful body before her and eager to destroy it.

A small circle of other cultists loomed in the background, droning their infernal chant.

Victor Sherwyck gazed up along the shaft to the floor above. He stretched out his hands in a dark embrace formed by the long flowing sleeves of his black velvet robe.

"The aura of the Devil's Eye! Enfolding all around! Its ageless power moves the earth, to grant our deserved plea!"

"Raise your daggers!" he commanded.

The two attendants stepped back towards those gathered in the background. The closely bunched group blended with the darkness like a sinister, swaying velvet wall.

Those around the gurney grabbed at the handles of the sacrificial knives lined along the struggling woman's body. They raised them slowly over their heads.

The woman let out a piercing, elongated scream.

"Let nature act to hide our hand! In causing what's to be!" Sherwyck shouted above the shriek. "Strike at our foe, high placed and: 'Lo! Bring on our victory!'"

At that instant, Philip Taylor, tingling with expectation of world renown, and excitedly poised to strike at the breast of the woman, fell in a heap to the floor, hitting his face on the edge of the gurney and tumbling onto his back. The blade was still clutched in his limp outstretched hand.

A stream of blood was spurting between his death glazed open eyes.

All froze in shocked silence and peered in the darkness toward the light of the door that had opened from the storage area.

There stood Colonel Christopher Caine, slowly unscrewing the silencer from his Beretta.

"Sure enough," he said icily. "The center of the Star."

He looked to his right and left and strode toward the group.

"Unlock those shackles!" he snarled in a slow, commanding voice.

Senator Dunne, closest to him, immediately raised his hands in surrender, then clumsily placed his dagger behind him onto the gurney. It touched the woman's knee. She vigorously shook it aside.

Knowlton, still entranced, recognized Caine immediately as the quarrelsome Colonel at the reception and shouted: "How dare you?"

He flashed his dagger in defiance and shouted again: "How dare you?"

Knowlton slashed the blade downward toward the woman's torso amid a loud report from Caine's pistol. He dropped instantly on the opposite side of the gurney from Taylor; the dark blade catching the edge and flopping onto the ground next to him just as the echo of the shot subsided.

Mrs. Knowlton looked on in horror as her husband fell and scurried comically around the cart in her oversized robe. Pushing past Dunne, who jostled the obscene altar, she saw the velvet clad body alongside it and turned on Caine in a rage.

"You beast!" she hollered and charged him with her dagger poised to strike.

He wagged his pistol to ward her off, but to no avail. She was upon him in seconds. Caine squeezed the trigger and she fell at his feet; his shot resounding through the chamber.

Victor Sherwyck edged along the gurney and looked down in shocked disbelief at Philip Taylor—his instrument of glory—mouth agape in the same way Taylor's was locked in terminal surprise.

Caine saw one of the supplicants beyond the cart fumbling at his hip for something under his robe. Caine sensed it was a weapon and fired unerringly across the room. The bullet whizzed audibly past Senator Dunne's ear and instantly dropped a disciple who was one of the night shift guards.

Sherwyck kept edging around the autopsy cart—followed by the terror stricken eyes of the struggling woman upon it—until he was next to Senator Dunne. Dunne shuffled slightly, but perceptibly away from him.

Caine waved his pistol at them. "Get back! Away from her!"

Dunne quickly joined the others, while Sherwyck hesitated, staring, testing.

Caine aimed demonstratively at Sherwyck's head. Sherwyck was confident he would not fire. Caine squeezed another round, the noise of which reverberated once more through the chamber.

Sherwyck's face was pale. He felt the searing heat of a bullet passing next to his ear inside his hood. He was not sure if this arrogant interloper was a bad shot or deliberately provocative.

He looked back at shuffling noises behind him and saw the remainder of the robed group mumbling over the fallen body of the union steward.

For the first time since he was ensconced in America, Victor Sherwyck felt unsure. A fleeting thought of failure crossed his ancient mind. It could not be! Philip Taylor was dead. Still, he was but a temporary cog. Capitulation could still be had. Everything was still in place.

The sacrifice could yet be made. She lay before the group.

The President would fall. Sherwyck, through his force of will, could still impose on the next in nuclear command.

He will, he thought. He needed just a little time to outwit this despoiling intruder. He would salvage the triumphant moment.

Sherwyck raised his hands, as if in compliance, turned and walked slowly around the shackled woman to the group behind him. He looked intently at her, spread eagled on the red velvet cloth, then resignedly at Philip Taylor's body, spread eagled on the floor.

In the momentary silence, footfalls and shouts filled the hallway amid urgent banging on the door to the chamber. Then, gunfire.

Sherwyck smirked at his remaining followers. Their sentinels would save the night. He would have his victory. Sherwyck stared at his supplicants in cold calculation.

"Our people are at hand! The infidel has used all his bullets! Take him! Kill him!"

At this, Sherwyck's sycophantic butler shouted: "Take him! Kill him!"

His stupefied followers flayed their hands and charged at Caine on the other side of the gurney. Their robes flowed as one, covering Sherwyck's quick move to grab Philip Taylor's sacrificial dagger from his lifeless hand.

Only Dunne, the Senator, stood frozen in place.

Caine opened fire on the charging line, cursing the Sorcerer, and toppling his cultists in rapid succession. Two of the infernal worshippers pitched onto the gurney, pushing it towards him. He quickstepped back as he fired. Several realized too late that bullets were spewing from Caine's empty pistol. They fell in a line, deceived by their false Master.

The terrified woman looked helplessly on, but heartened by the bedlam around her that she might still survive.

Sherwyck stood still with his hands crossed, the obsidian blade deep in his sleeve.

Senator Dunne stood nearby staring in fear at Caine.

The other robed figures lay in various positions of death along the floor.

"Where's the other woman?" Caine demanded as he roughly unbuttoned his shirt, then deftly switched his Beretta from hand to hand as he pulled each arm from the sleeves.

A flash of perplexity in the Sorcerer's piercing eye betrayed to Caine that Sherwyck didn't know. His goons have her elsewhere, he thought. Alvin Carruthers knew every corner of the building. He'd find her. He had to.

Caine moved to the autopsy cart. She huddled to the limits of her shackles as he stretched the shirt over her torso, barely covering her. She winced seeing the prominent scar on his chest.

"Where's the key?" he commanded.

"One of these poor souls must have it," Sherwyck replied in a cynically innocent voice. "They provide. I merely preside."

"You have the smell of hell about you," Caine said dismissively.

"And how is it you presume to know?" Victor Sherwyck asked haughtily.

"I've been to your roost."

A look of rage came over Sherwyck. "You lie!" he shouted. "Only those who rise from there are witness to the place! An ageless legion of disciples preparing the way for our Prince!"

Senator Dunne listened quietly, hunched slightly in humiliation.

"Now, now," Caine said in deliberate belittlement, baiting the ever composed Presidential adviser. "You overreach!"

"You impudent fool!" Sherwyck raged. "The power of the Devil's Eye is seared in every page of history!"

"Now! Now! Now!" Caine goaded—keen to the shuffling outside the door and eager to get the woman off the gurney.

"The spell of our Prince captivates all! It pulsates through every fragment of the priceless Eye so purposely given in shares to the world!"

"And we're supposed to thank you for it?"

"You are supposed to worship it!" Sherwyck yelled, his veins bulging at his neck.

"I've seen it, Victor," Caine said derisively, using his first name. "I spit on it!"

"You lie!" Sherwyck shrieked again, his body throbbing with increasing rage. He had never been challenged before. "How dare you? You saw nothing!"

"Warlock told me."

"Warlock? Warlock?"

"Nikolai Kuznetsov. Remember him?"

"How? What?" Victor Sherwyck felt vulnerable beyond the Beretta pointed in his direction.

"So long ago. Smuggling you here. You shouldn't have killed him. He wouldn't have talked."

"Nonsense! You lie! Dead men don't talk!"

"Ahh, but what is this?" Caine said with a grand sweep of his pistol. "Human sacrifice. Necromancy. Seeking favor through the dead?"

"You insolent infidel!"

"Your vocabulary is diminishing," Caine scoffed with narrowing eyes.

Victor Sherwyck breathed heavily, sputtering with rage. No one alive had ever insulted him, much less dared flaunt authority over him.

Senator Everett Dunne unexpectedly lifted his round, boyish face and blurted: "He told me to say it! He told me to use 'Warlock' all these years! He told me it was Nikolai Kuznetsov! He gave me all the leads out of Moscow! He told me what to do!"

Victor Sherwyck's rage suddenly found an outlet.

He pulled the hidden dagger from his sleeve and drove it wildly into Dunne's chest

"You said you would never betray me!" he yelled and followed the collapsing Senator to the floor with his hand still on the handle of the blade. "Traitor!" He snarled into the Senator's fading face. "You're not worthy!"

Victor Sherwyck stood up, ignoring the Senator's dying gasps.

"An unaccustomed setback," he said serenely.

"A permanent setback."

"No one dares tell me that!"

Never since Soviet agents had planted him in the United States at the command of the Old One through arrangements with Commissar Vladimir Dekanazov—a principal in the cursed cult—was he ever challenged or confronted.

Never in his steady climb in financial, social, and political circles did he ever sense a hint of impediment or failure. Never did anyone dare direct him, much less command him to do anything. Never did anyone dare threaten him.

"You'll pay for this!"

"I'm sure, I will," Caine said, hovering over the woman, adjusting the shirt on her and rattling one of the handcuffs.

"I'm going to ask you one last time. Where's the key?"

Victor Sherwyck slowly approached the gurney.

"Keep your distance!" Caine hissed.

"The key is in hell!" Sherwyck shouted and reached for the abandoned blade at her knees.

"Back off!" Caine commanded as Sherwyck fumbled for the obsidian dagger.

"I am invincible!" he declared raising it above the sacrifice to be.

Caine fired.

Victor Sherwyck collapsed onto the woman who jostled in terror to get him away. Caine pushed gruffly and he sank slowly to the floor, holding onto the edge of his demonic altar.

"You'll... pay... for this!" he wheezed, kneeling next to it with head bowed from draining life.

"I'm sure, I will," Caine murmured.

"Legions...behind me...through ages...will avenge."

"I know," Caine replied. "They're next."

Sherwyck lifted his head in defiance, stared at Caine with profound hatred and collapsed on his back.

"Is he dead?" the woman asked fitfully.

"He's dead," Colonel Caine answered cryptically. "For now."

Chapter 51

Alvin Carruthers walked into the room from the storage area, followed by Colonel Garrison Jones. Both had pistols in their hands. They looked warily around, focusing on the velvet covered autopsy cart. They saw Colonel Caine comforting the woman, who was now wearing his tan campaign shirt and standing huddled next to him.

"Jeannie McConnell, I presume," Colonel Jones said perfunctorily.

"Jeannie! Meet my friend, Colonel Garrison Jones. We were all very worried about you."

Caine looked to the curator. "And that's my friend, Al Carruthers. Where's Laura? "

"She's not in the museum," Carruthers answered. "We'll find her."

Caine was disheartened.

"We'll find her, Chris!" Carruthers insisted. "We'll find her. Maybe someone picked her up. She does have her uncle's arrangements to make. We can't always think the worst."

"Do you believe that?"

"Well..." Carruthers began. He looked at Jeannie.

"Come here, sweetie," he soothed changing the subject. He could see she was still trembling. "Let's get some real clothes on you. We have a whole history back here to choose from. Then we'll get you some medical attention."

The curator put his arm consolingly around her and led her into the storage area.

"Who are all these people?" Colonel Jones asked pointing his pistol around.

"Some of the cream of Washington society."

"Gone sour?"

"Long ago."

"We'll find her, Chris. I'm sure."

The image of the woman lying in the street in Beirut flashed across his mind. He was reaching out to her—a haunting resemblance to Laura Mitchell—a face that destined him to meet the alluring professor—a professor who ignited his burning love for her. Was she now, too, beyond his reach?

"The General said I might find you here."

Caine looked at him.

"You were supposed to report."

"I was on my way."

"I can see," Jones said nodding at the bodies strewn around the room. "He called me back from Egypt as soon as I told him what we found. He figured you'd be takin' a detour to the Pentagon."

Colonel Jones stepped among the velvet robed bodies, reminiscent of the monks in the cavern. "My, my, my. Some fancy names. What do we have here—ten, twelve people? Not counting your guard downstairs and our few outside the door."

He looked back at his friend. "We thought you were in real trouble when we heard the gunshots in here. Al said you had a silencer on your piece."

"This deserved louder attention."

"I imagine," Jones agreed. "But how far can it carry?"

* * *

With their sidearms drawn, Colonel Caine and Colonel Jones escorted Al Carruthers and Jeannie McConnell to the service area.

Unmarked official looking sedans and several coroner's vans were parked in the lot. Forensic technicians were examining Laura Mitchell's car and the dark green van with Caine's bullet hole in the rear panel.

"We'll keep looking around here," Colonel Jones said. "Question some detained workers."

"I'm heading back to the hospital," Caine said. "Maybe there's something there."

"General Bradley's office tomorrow, Chris. That was his order."

Caine nodded, thanked Carruthers, hugged Jeannie McConnell, and hurried to his roadster.

* * *

Driving west on Constitution Avenue in the glow of evening lights, he noticed one pair of headlamps in his mirror that were immediately suspect. He saw the lights glow brighter and dimmer as they weaved in traffic and soon were right behind him. The gap between his Viper and the car behind him was closing. He was ready to accelerate, but evening traffic boxed all lanes.

Inside the trailing car, Oleg Alekseev looked to his driver. The driver looked back—anticipating. Alekseev nodded approval. The driver accelerated.

"Hold on!" Alekseev cautioned.

Caine saw in his mirror the beams switch to high. He braced himself and readied for another impact.

Seconds later Alekseev's sedan banged into the rear of Caine's Viper.

Alekseev was already at the side of the sedan when Caine jumped out and started for him.

"I'm sorry, Colonel! Truly sorry!" Alekseev said loudly above the din of traffic slowing and them moving around them amid the sound of several horns. "There has to be a better way for us to meet!"

Before Caine could react, Alekseev motioned towards the opening rear door of his sedan. Out bounded Laura Mitchell and ran towards him with open arms.

"Chris! Chris! Chris!" she said as he enfolded her in a crushing embrace.

Behind her two muscular men in dark suits, had climbed out the back seat and began guiding traffic around the vehicles.

"What the—!" He began in Alekseev's direction only to be cut off by Laura.

"It's okay, Chris! It's okay!" she assured breathlessly. "Alekseev explained everything! I was scared at first, then I was mad as a banshee, but he explained everything!"

The three of them walked across a lane of traffic to the sidewalk.

"I'm sorry, Colonel. I know we caused you distress. But it was to save her life."

"Why didn't you tell me sooner?" he challenged with a seething voice.

"We had to make sure you followed your suspicions—that she was kidnapped."

"She *was* kidnapped!" Caine snapped.

"A minor inconvenience, Colonel. In the face of profound threats. We had to make sure you went into the museum."

"I *was* going to the museum."

"We didn't know, Colonel. I regret. We have heard stories like your charming friend has. I must admit we had followed her now and then."

"Because of her uncle," Caine declared.

"Because of her uncle," the Russian diplomat and spymaster admitted. "I extend my condolences to both of you for his loss. We are very much attuned to telling events that do not seem to have a natural explanation."

Laura hugged Caine closely and shivered at the thought of her uncle alone in his office with a wayward cat creeping inside.

"When we realized the conjuncture of various legends and

events—including diabolical conspiracies in our former Soviet state, we knew someone had to act," Alekseev explained. He looked at Caine and said straightforwardly. "As you know, Colonel we are guests in your country. We cannot act on our own—even if we perceive it for our mutual good."

Caine said nothing, but grudgingly understood.

"And as you know, Colonel," Alekseev said with a wry smile. "Our reporting something like this to your government would cause immediate suspicion as an outrageous provocation."

Caine knew. His own implications were treated warily, even dismissively when he broached the occult in their investigation.

"You had to do this yourself, Colonel."

Laura Mitchell could only imagine what Caine had done, but she knew it would provide for the closing chapter of her uncle's quest. Tears of relieved emotions flowed down her cheeks as she quietly hugged the man she had grown to love.

"I'm truly sorry about your car, Colonel. I'll arrange for repairs. Privately, of course."

Caine looked at him in exasperation mixed with diminishing fury over Laura.

"We have not been formally introduced. And these repairs may get expensive," Alekseev added above the din of increasingly congested traffic around their vehicles.

"I must go," he continued. His companions were moving their sedan into traffic. "I expect we'll meet again."

Alekseev looked both ways and stepped into the street saying offhandedly: "I'm pursuing diplomatic channels."

Chapter 52

"I hear there was more gunplay at the Smithsonian last night," General Bradley said.

Colonel Caine and Colonel Jones, dressed in their blue service uniforms, had just settled into the leather sofa opposite his desk at the Pentagon.

The General was leaning back in his chair, elbows on the armrests and tapping his fingertips together in contemplation.

"Let's see—what with a ranking U.S. Senator, a Secretary of Defense designate, an esteemed presidential adviser, the manager of his Virginia estate, two multi-millionaire socialites—a husband and wife, no less—a couple of Smithsonian guards and employees."

He looked at the two officers.

"I'd say 'carnage' is the word."

"Yes, sir," Colonel Caine volunteered.

"You were going to just talk with Sherwyck. Do I understand that right?"

"Well, sir," Caine began. "In a word—all hell broke loose."

The General squinted at him past his tapping fingers.

"We're not practicing puns here, Colonel."

"No, sir. I'm quite serious."

"Chasing demons?"

"No, sir. Real people acting in their name."

"Well gentlemen," General Bradley declared leaning forward and stretching his hands on his desk, "All I know is that we have more than a dozen bodies strewn about a couple of floors of the Natural History Museum and how are we going to explain it?"

"We found Jeannie McConnell," Colonel Caine answered. "That's what it took."

"She was going to be ritually murdered inside the museum. They were making supplications to infernal spirits. They were evoking an aura associated with the Hope Diamond. That was real. They might have been demented, but that was their motive for murder," Colonel Caine declared. "The whole thing revolves around the Hope Diamond."

General Bradley took a deep breath in reflective frustration.

"We can't blame it on the Hope Diamond. You know that," he reiterated.

"What? An evil wizard leading our leaders around by the nose? Scions of high society throwing millions at altars of devil worship? The diamond pulsating calamities on our nation ever since it was donated here?"

General Bradley paused. "When was that again? Nineteen fifty-eight?"

"We can count back," Colonel Caine suggested. "See what's happened to us since."

General Bradley waved his hand in dismissal.

"Remember the gossip of a former President consulting astrologers? Most of the country went nuts about it. Wanted to drive him out of office."

Bradley shifted in his chair. "I'm not blind. But until we have complete, indisputable evidence, we're going to have to hold back certain information—especially on this paranormal business."

The two officers eyed their General.

"Ongoing investigation," Bradley explained by way of defense. "We need to follow up on what you saw in the desert."

The officers slowly nodded their understanding.

"You were right about Jeannie McConnell. She *was* here all the time," General Bradley acknowledged. "Who was holding her?"

"Terrorists," Caine instantly replied. "A different kind of terrorists. A cabal more insidious than any we've ever encountered—with cells all over the world."

"Sherwyck?" General Bradley offered.

"Sherwyck," Colonel Caine replied. "I venture we'll find a connection between his estate and the green van I shot at. His goons transported victims from his place to the museum, then disposed of the bodies after their rituals. Dressing them in jogging outfits was a diversion."

"That'll answer some questions about bodies found in the parks over the years," Colonel Jones added. "Especially that latest one with the blue symbols on it."

"Just like they were painting on Jeannie," Caine emphasized.

"Likely so," General Bradley rejoined.

He arose from his chair and began to slowly pace his office.

"Speaking of his estate," he said to no one in particular. "You know that one of Sherwyck's stallions was requested or offered as the riderless horse in the Vice President's funeral procession?"

Both officers expressed surprise.

General Bradley turned to them. "We're investigating a black stallion tied into General Starr's horse riding accident—and someone's trying to prance one in front of the President of the United States!"

"Probably, somebody up the line never knew about it," Colonel Jones offered.

"That's the problem with this 'need to know' philosophy."

The General returned to his desk with his slightly perceptible limp. He settled in and leaned back.

"Well, the stallion almost demolished his stall at the Old Guard stables near Arlington. They were going to pull him. The horse was too dangerous with the President walking in the procession."

"Then, last night, a funny thing happened," the General revealed.

He looked warily at his officers from behind his desk.

"The horse—Blaze—I guess his name is—turned docile as a lamb."

The General focused on Caine. "That's just about when your wizard left this earth."

"He was ready to stab Jeannie."

"I understand," General Bradley said. "I'm talking about the horse. Vets were able to check him out."

"Cloven hooves," Caine interposed.

"Let's say 'split'," the General replied. "It sounds a little less sinister for now. It's a condition—conformation, poor trimming, bacteria—not too common on all four legs, but treatable."

"Well, well, well," Colonel Jones exclaimed.

"Sherwyck's prized sacrifice—poor Jeannie—for the ultimate hex, a runaway horse with the President walking in a funeral procession," Colonel Caine posited.

"It makes sense," Colonel Jones said.

"Just like poor Ben Starr and his ride down the trail," Colonel Caine added.

"It makes sense if you're a devil worshipper," General Bradley snapped. "And if the occult is an accepted point of reference for public discourse."

"For us," he continued resignedly, "it's like pushing a long piece of thread in a straight line. The most we can declare is 'Coincidence'!"

"It doesn't matter, sir, we, still put an end to it," Caine asserted. "No matter who, how or what. Their target was control of the nuclear button!"

"Yes, indeed. So it was," Bradley answered. "The hard part is going to be the explanation."

The General stood up.

His officers followed suit.

"I'll need to brief the Omega Group. We have to find out how deeply Dunne betrayed us."

"There's a potential source, sir—a Russian diplomat," Caine began. "He helped unravel this. He may want to establish a clandestine contact."

"That remains to be seen," the General answered dismissively.

"You'll need to go back to the Middle East, gentlemen. We'll have to see how enthused the Egyptians are in cooperating on this. A lot of these ancient countries like to protect their mystical roots."

"Yes, sir," the officers agreed.

"Be ready for major investigations about this bloodbath," General Bradley said. "Desecration of our nation's attic."

"It needed some dusting, sir."

Chapter 53

"I wish you could come with me, Chris," Laura Mitchell said at Dulles International Airport. "It's an official ceremony for Uncle Jonas at the memorial for fallen partisans. The anti-Stalin resistance in Lithuania."

"I'll pay my respects as soon as I can," he replied.

"You know, Oleg Alekseev is giving me some hidden archives. He said it's to make amends for kidnapping me."

Caine lifted his eyebrow in smoldering memory.

"I think they'll fill some gaps in Uncle's research."

"I believe they just might," he assured her.

He put his arms around her waist and she put hers around his neck.

"I wish I could come with you, but I'm on assignment."

"I know, you're going to the Middle East somewhere."

"How do you know this?" he asked pulling her closer.

Passengers smiled as they passed them toward the gate.

"Al Carruthers told me."

"He's not supposed to know either."

"It's all right, I would have run into you anyway."

"What do you mean?" he asked slyly as he pulled her even closer.

"I've applied for a Sabbatical," she whispered intimately.

"Oh?" he replied with their lips almost touching.

"Research on Napoleon in Egypt," she continued in a whisper.

"The Cairo Archives seem more interested in some obscure aspects of their recent history."

"Interesting."

"I hope I get it."

"I know you will," he replied.

They kissed fervently in a warm embrace.

"I'll be late." She slowly, reluctantly pulled away.

"Napoleon and his soldiers found the Rosetta Stone, you know," she said handing her identification to the gate attendant.

"Yes, they did."

"Some researchers claim he had a familiar."

"Do they, now?" he said with a knowing smile.

"I'll bring you back a souvenir from the Devil's Museum in Kaunas."

He blew her a loving kiss and she hurried down the ramp.

He lingered at the empty gate, imagining her boarding the plane and settling in for a long trip. He wished her a silent prayer for a safe flight and eternal peace to her dear uncle.

Outside, Colonel Garrison Jones was waiting for him in the passenger pickup lane.

"Everything, okay?" he asked as Caine climbed into the sedan.

"Yeah. Everything's fine. How about you?"

"Okay," Jones replied as he pulled away into traffic.

"How about if we stop awhile at the National Cathedral?"

"Not a bad idea."

Epilogue

That same week General William Bradley dispatched a personal courier to Egypt where U.S.—Egyptian joint military maneuvers under Operation Bright Star were still underway. The courier sought out an Air Force general to whom he relayed an urgent personal request from General Bradley.

Phases of the operation were battalion level with close air support east of the High Dam at Aswan. A half dozen MIG 21 jets of the Egyptian Air Force were flying in coordinated formation with the same number of U.S. F-15's. Except for distinct fuselages, wings, and national insignia, the planes looked similar in their tan mottled camouflage paint.

The fighters made several low flying sweeps over the maneuvering troops, then two from the Egyptian formation and two from the U.S. wing suddenly veered off towards a line of mountains to the east. They flew for nearly one hundred miles and then, unerringly, into a narrow canyon between two mountain cliffs.

The jets flew in a single file over the ancient monastery jutting from the mountaintop. Every seam of the canyon resounded with the high pitched screams of the jets that loosed rocks from the canyon walls.

On a second pass each of the jets released two electronically guided bombs that tore into the walls and parapets of the fortress and leveled the main building of the monastery. The successive explosions sent tremors like an earthquake through the cavernous labyrinth inside the mountain beneath the crumbling fortress abbey.

Hearing muffled sounds above him, the Old One looked up from his stony throne with a knowing, defiant leer and motioned his hooded supplicants to bow and pay homage to Baal.

"*Elohim, Elohim Eloah Va-daath....*" the faithful began chanting as they gathered around the glistening obsidian idol of their Prince glaring over them. A faint variation in the flames dancing from the torch in the idol's left eye socket betrayed any effects of the violent explosions above. A large, blue iridescent diamond remained firmly set in the right socket.

A heavy mass of blinding dust ballooned upward from the ruins of the edifice above, enveloping the entire mountainside in a choking debris laden cloud. The fighter jets passed once more above the mushrooming cloud, then banked towards another dust cloud barely visible in the far distance where troops were maneuvering in mock battle on the desert sand.

* * *

Later that month in Washington, larger than usual crowds gathered outside the museum waiting for it to open—perhaps trying to picture the grisly scene inside the building described repeatedly on the news.

Stories still swirled of an ongoing investigation into an exclusive black tie fund raising event gone tragically wrong; the search for missing employee witnesses; the possibility that suspicious ruffians seen in the area eliminated witnesses while trying to steal priceless artifacts; that some guard or even attendee had gone berserk.

Most tantalizing was the fact that Victor Sherwyck, the legendary financier and adviser to presidents was among the dead. Was it to silence monumental corruption or investment failings? Curious was the fact that the Chairman of the Senate Intelligence Committee, Senator Everett Dunne, was stabbed by some ancient dagger that could not be identified as any artifact under display. Investigation included relationships the respected Senator may have had with unfriendly states. The specter of foreign espionage was widely rumored.

Darker suspicions circulated on radical blogs that thrived on conspiracy. Rumors spread that Victor Sherwyck had persuaded the President to appoint Philip Taylor as Secretary of Defense against his own better judgment. Was that decision rescinded in a most unspeakable way? Responders scoffed at such an abomination.

Or was it as pathetically simple as a society love triangle ending in a rampant jealous rage?

The sensational speculation swamped a celebrity item that the daughter of the Speaker of the House of Representatives, Jeannette McConnell, was found safe and aboard a yacht that had gone aground on a coral outcrop near one of the numerous out islands of the Bahamas. A family lawyer stated she was not aware anyone was looking for her and apologized to investigators for any inconvenience it may have caused.

Countless visitors filed through the Museum of Natural History, lingering conspicuously at various displays throughout the building, anticipating a chance to catch a glimpse of the gem exhibits that would soon re-open to the public.

There, on the second floor, the large iridescent blue diamond rested serenely, enigmatically on softly lit velvet in its glass enclosed vault.

A gift to the people of the United States.

About the Author

His award-winning non-fiction *Day of Shame* (David McKay Co.), written under Algis Ruksenas, is about the unsuccessful defection of a Lithuanian seaman from a Soviet ship onto a U.S. Coast Guard Cutter near Cape Cod in the height of the Cold War.

The book and attendant publicity helped free the seaman from a labor camp in the former Soviet Union.

His book *Is That You Laughing, Comrade?* (Citadel Press), prompted President Ronald Reagan to take up referencing underground Russian humor as a hobby, noted by his speech writers in letters to the author.

His satirical play *A Summit Meeting in Hell* won first prize at an international Theater Festival held annually in Chicago.

Devil's Eye is a reflection of his many years of interest in people's universal fascination with witchcraft and demonology.

Al Ruksenas is a former reporter for United Press International, government aide, and executive director of an NGO (non-government organization). He is a ghost writer, lecturer and author of numerous articles.

He lives with his wife, Nijole, in Northeast Ohio. They have three grown children.

Breinigsville, PA USA
20 December 2010
251816BV00002B/2/P